SPIDER ROBINSON
NIGHT OF POWER

BERKLEY BOOKS, NEW YORK

NIGHT OF POWER

A Berkley Book / published by arrangement with
Baen Enterprises

PRINTING HISTORY
Baen edition / May 1985
Berkley edition / January 1986

ISBN: 0-425-08475-2

A BERKLEY BOOK ® TM 757,375
The name "BERKLEY" and the stylized "B" with design
are trademarks belonging to Berkley Publishing Corporation.
PRINTED IN THE UNITED STATES OF AMERICA

ACKNOWLEDGMENTS

Night of Power was written with the assistance of the Canada Council for the Arts, and the Nova Scotia Department of Culture, Recreation & Fitness. Additional invaluable assistance, in the form of time, expertise, research, advice, and/or general support, was given to me by (among others): George Allanson, Susan Allison, Isaac Asimov, Stanley Asimov, Bob Atkinson, Jim Baen, John Bell, Bill and Sue Bittner, Ben Bova, Kathy and Tom Cullem, Patrick Doherty, Robert A. Heinlein, Don Hutter, Bill Jones, Jack MacRae, Kirby McCauley, Betsy Mitchell, Major H.K. O'Donnell, USMC, Fred Pohl, James V. Robinson, Charles Saunders, Richard Seaver, Fred Ward, and Eleanor Wood. My thanks go to all these individuals and institutions, as well as any I may have omitted. And of course Night of Power, like all my books, could never have existed in anything like its present form without the ongoing love, encouragement and support of my wife Jeanne and my daughter Luanna.

CHAPTER ONE

"The infant mortality rate in Central Harlem and the Fort Greene section of Brooklyn is almost double the city rate, and twice as high as the national rate, according to a recent report.

"The report . . . showed that of every 1,000 babies born in 1980, 27.8 in Central Harlem died and 26.6 in Fort Greene died. The citywide infant mortality rate was 16.1 per 1,000 births compared with 12.5 per 1,000 births nationwide. . . .

"The infant mortality rate for minorities here in 1979 was 68% greater than the rate among white New Yorkers, the report indicated.

"The infant mortality rate is an indicator used to measure the quality of life. . . ."

> —Esther Ross, *New York Amsterdam News*,
> August 21, 1982

"In the first years after the [First World] War, 70 black Americans were lynched, many of them still in uniform. Fourteen were burned publicly by white citizens; 11 of them were burned alive. During the 'Red Summer' of 1919, there were no fewer than 25 race riots across the country. A riot in the nation's capitol lasted 3 days; in Chicago, 38 people were killed and 537 injured during 13 days of mob rule."

> —C. Eric Lincoln,
> *The Black Muslims in America*

"The white man need expect no more Negro blood to be shed on his behalf . . . the dying to be done by the black man in the future will be done to make himself free."

> —Marcus Garvey, 1920

"There's a shitstorm coming."
                                    —Norman Mailer, *The White Negro*

                    *   *   *

It was, of course, just after they had passed the last exit
from the New England Thruway that the car cleared its
throat apologetically.

"Ahem. Excuse me," it said with its usual irritating
diffidence. "I will be needing fuel within the next fifty
klicks."

Russell Grant groaned silently; had traffic permitted,
he would have rolled his eyes skyward.

"Oh, *good*," thirteen-year-old Jennifer said from her niche
in the back seat, confirming his worst fear. "I've been
needing a bathroom for simply *klicks*."

"Me too," Dena agreed before he could speak, and
Russell's dismay increased.

"Sorry, ladies," he said to both of his passengers and
the car. "We just left the land of rest-stops behind. The
next toilet you see will be called New York." And we'll be
lucky to find proper fuel there, he thought to himself; I'll
probably have to reset the carburetor for gasoline.

"Dad-*ee*," Jennifer cried in horror. "Why didn't you *tell*
me before we passed the exit?"

"For the same reason you didn't ask me, princess," he
said as patiently as he could. Jennifer required him to
explain the obvious considerably less often than might
most thirteen-year-olds; consequently he tried to bear her
occasional lapses. "Because I didn't think of it. Sorry."

"Can't be helped," his wife said at once. "We'll survive,
Jennifer. Hang on to it—it's good exercise."

Russell almost glanced at Dena, wondering if she meant
what he thought she meant. But he preferred not to find
out. Besides, the road demanded his full attention. "Get
the map for me, would you, hon?"

Dena keyed it to display on her side of the windshield.
"We want the Bruckner Expressway, I think. It'll say
either that or 'Route 278.' "

"Got it." He liked the way his wife gave directions.

Short, clear, accurate. It was one of several thousand things about her that he liked.

"Ahem," the car said again. "Excuse me. Toll station in one klick. Two dollars U.S." Dena got out the coins, and he fed them to the toll booth when they reached it. "Welcome to the Empire State," Jennifer read aloud.

It was as though the invisible border between Connecticut and the State of New York had real, tangible existence; things changed. It began subliminally. The traffic seemed no heavier or more aggressive than it had been since Boston—but the individual cars were older, shabbier, more battle-scarred. Potholes became worse, then more frequent. The sky itself seemed to darken just perceptibly.

But the first change that Russell Grant consciously noticed was the sound. It grew from a hum to a distant rumble, audible even over the sound of traffic and the rush of air through his open window.

The realization of what he was hearing struck him all at once. It was the approach of New York City. The three days' drive from Halifax, Nova Scotia was nearly over.

Russell was more than ready for the trip to end: his whole body was one large cramp. Above and beyond the physical discomforts, he had for the last eight hundred klicks or so been an uneasy combination of bored silly and scared to death, with absolutely nothing to do except meditate, chat with his wife and daughter, listen to music, watch yellow and white lines whiz at him, and foil the occasional and unpredictable attempt of a homicidal psychopath to kill them all.

But as he realized now how eager he was for this journey to end, Russell realized simultaneously, and for the first time, how little prepared he was to reach his destination. A small voice in his head whispered, you have not thought this thing through. Somehow in the last umpty-hundred klicks of highway narcosis, of jumbled thoughts and boredom, he had neglected to get ready for New York.

It rumbled now on his horizon, approaching at over 100 kph, and heaven help him if he slowed down.

"Damn," he said, trying to sound cheerful. "I can actually hear the city coming."

"I can smell it," Jennifer said grumpily. She was not ready for New York either.

Russell raised the car windows and put the air conditioning on low. "Nonsense. That's the East River you're smelling. The smell of the city itself could never penetrate that."

But his attempt at light humour fell through, because by then they were barreling through the South Bronx, and what was visible to their right struck them all speechless.

"Re-*pulse*-o!" Jennifer was the first of the three to regain her powers of speech. She was a prodigiously bright and imaginative child; both her father and stepmother had laboured mightily—and successfully—to develop her faculty of empathy; nonetheless, she was thirteen years old. The horror of the South Bronx in the year of Our Lord 1996 was, to her, primarily an aesthetic offense.

"Fuck," Russell breathed finally. He ordinarily made a point of cussing creatively, but on this occasion invention failed him. "It's worse than I remember. It's worse than I read. It's worse than I imagined." Russell was forty-eight years old; he had been born in New York, but had not lived there since early adolescence; he had been living in Canada, in the pleasant seaport city of Halifax, for the last twenty-odd years. Aesthetic dismay was a strong component of his own reaction. He was a designer; this was obscenity. But human empathy for the pain implicit in what he was seeing shocked him just as badly.

There was a third component to his emotional turmoil, represented by the foreground past which he saw the South Bronx. In the background, the burned out cars were black; the burned out buildings were black; the glassless, curtainless windows opened onto a deeper black; the doomed faces seen in some of those windows were mostly black; the few doomed people visible on the streets were black. He saw all this past the hair, the nape and part of the left cheek of his wife, all of which were also black.

Dena's curly hair was the kind of black that is sometimes called blue black. Her complexion was the deep, glowing black of lightly burnished obsidian, and as she turned her face forward Russell saw that it might as well have been carved out of that volcanic glass.

What must it be like for her? he wondered. His designer's mind groped for an analogy. Perhaps an American Jew, driving past Dachau in a brand new Ford, while the ovens were still in operation? That made him the Nazi behind the wheel. Dena had been born and raised in Halifax—not in the North Preston ghetto outside Dartmouth, or in the tiny slum district around Gottingen Street, but in the South End of the city. Both of her parents full professors at Dalhousie University, she had been one of the comparative handful of Haligonian blacks who grew up in, and were fully accepted into, white society. Poor blacks were as despised and feared in Halifax as in any other city (although some met with great tolerance in rural Nova Scotia, where everyone was poor), but middle-class blacks fitted in well. Halifax was one of the few remaining cities in North America in which interracial couples—such as Russell and Dena—could walk together anywhere without the slightest paranoia. While no black grew up without an awareness of racism, Dena had throughout her life been subjected to about the absolute minimum of personal contact with it.

Now they were racing together toward the Big Apple.

Tell me again, he said to himself, why this is necessary. Remind me, please.

Okay, Dena is a dancer. Not, Dena dances sometimes, or Dena has done a lot of dancing, or even Dena dearly loves to dance. Dena *is a dancer*, a Modern dancer. Not a choreographer, a dance maker. Not a particularly good teacher. A *dancer*. Give her some choreography, put a dance on her, and she will go out there and dance it better than almost anyone on earth, make it live and sing. Dena is a gifted dancer, gifted by God. And God is an Indian giver.

Dena is a thirty-seven-year-old dancer.

The injuries have been coming more frequently, taking longer to heal, healing imperfectly. A normal human being would probably envy Dena her physical conditioning; nonetheless she has no more than one or two good years left. If that long: tomorrow an ankle or a knee could let go, just like that, or that fourth lumbar could decide to start chewing on her sciatic again—and not let up this time.

And her old friend Lisa Dann has offered her a chance—one last chance—to dance in New York, and not just in New York but at the Joyce Theatre, *the* showcase, the worldwide Mecca of Modern dance. The opportunity cannot be passed up ... and so the Grant family is entering the combat zone.

Only temporarily, Russell reminded himself. Only for three months. A quick smash-and-grab; hopefully we'll be in and out before the city notices we're there.

As if on cue, the skyline of Manhattan appeared on the port bow, shimmering in the heat.

"There it is," Russell said a little too jovially, glad to end the uneasy silence in the car. "La Grande Pomme."

"Froky." Jennifer was impressed. Child-geniuses were even harder to impress than normal thirteen-year-olds—but this was *New York*.

"Sure looks pretty," Dena said quietly. (Was there the slightest hint of emphasis on the second word?)

"Just look at the energy being thrown away," Russell said. "One day they're going to have to put a Fuller Dome over that town."

"Yuck," Dena said as politely as that syllable can be said. "New York is dark enough already."

"Transparent dome."

"And how long would it stay transparent over that smog?"

"Hmmm. Touché. But dammit, *look* at that thing. You couldn't design a more efficient energy waster—all those hot spires sticking out into ocean breeze, like the biggest radiator in the world. The only thing I can think of that has that much built-in waste is ..." His voice trailed off.

Dena waited, then said softly, "Something?"

"Huh. It just came to me. The two most energy-wasteful appliances in the world. Just as stupid, in their own way, as that skyline. Two of the most common appliances in the world—naturally."

"The stereo and the TV," Jennifer said at once.

Russell chuckled. "No, princess. The refrigerator and the stove. A fridge spills money on the floor every time you open it. And an oven spills money on the ceiling the same way. Now, if you designed a fridge to lay on its back, like a freezer, and moved the heat-sucker so it wouldn't be underneath ... or if you designed an oven door to *roll up* like a garage door ..."

"The fridge would take up too much room," Dena said argumentatively. "And it'd be too hard to get at stuff in it."

"Well, maybe, but suppose you combined the two, the fridge and the stove? Silly to have a heat-maker and a heat-loser side by side, unconnected."

"I don't see it. Connect them how?"

He did not answer. He went instead into something as near to a warm creative fog as is possible for a man driving on a New York highway. His women left him alone in it; he did not see the glance they exchanged. The fog lasted through several successive toll booths, all the way through the Bronx and across the Triboro Bridge.

And then he heard Dena's cry, and looked to his left. "Creeping Jesus!"

The overpass that led to the FDR Drive was down. Russell knew just enough about municipal construction to be certain that it had been dynamited, by a freelancer. That shocked him, but not as badly as the secondary realization that he was now committed to driving his family through Harlem, with a near-empty fuel tank.

Dena was already reading the map display. "Left on Second Avenue." Traffic was slowing drastically.

"No good. Look." Second Avenue was sealed off by police barricades. "I'll try Third."

"That's no good either—it's one-way uptown."

"Slithering mother of shitcakes and syrup." Traffic came to a halt, then began a spasmodic crawl.

Jennifer picked up on the sudden increase of tension. "What is it? What's wrong, Daddy?"

"Nothing, honey," Dena said. "Just a detour."

Russell glanced around: no other white motorists were visible anywhere. Belatedly he remembered that the prudent New York driver monitors the radio traffic bulletins. "What's the next entrance to the FDR south of here?" he asked.

"This map doesn't say."

"Great."

At the beginning of their trip, Russell had physically disabled the car phone, rather than simply switching it off. The symbolic gesture now seemed excessive—to reconnect the phone he would now have to park and open the hood . . .

They left the bridge, heading west at an average speed of perhaps twenty kph, stop and go. The squalor of East 125th Street was indescribable, on the verge of incomprehensible. Those buildings still standing should not have been. Garbage lined the street on both sides; Russell noted one abandoned building which seemed to be entirely filled with trash from sidewalk to rooftop. An incredible swarm of people surged on all sides, the summer sun boiling them in their pitiful clothes. Some were in uniform; Russell reminded himself that this country, unlike his own, was at war. (A jungle war—Africa. What must *that* be like for a black G.I.?) The sound, the chaos, defied belief, and the smell penetrated into the air-conditioned car. Russell had once spent a few days in Bombay, on the edge of a slum district: this was worse.

The same question kept occurring to him as he drove, searching feverishly for a way—any way—off 125th Street. The question was: Why aren't they killing me? What is preventing these people from opening my car like a can of deviled ham and pulling me out and killing me with their hands and teeth? If I had to live here, and I saw a man driving through who obviously did not have to live here, *I'd* kill him. And it can't help, having Dena in the car . . .

He kept recoiling from the last thought.

Traffic came to a complete halt as they reached Third Avenue. A tomato struck Russell's window, burst like a red blossom. He decided that his most pressing need was to remain in motion at all costs; he turned uptown, shutting down the air-conditioning. It was powered by a solar collector on the car's roof, and its energy could give him a few more blocks if his alcohol fuel tanks ran completely dry. He was up to 128th Street before he saw his chance, turned left and got the car up to forty kph. But when he turned south on Lexington, he learned what had been holding up traffic on 125th: the street was torn up from

Lexington to Park for sewer repair. He was forced to dogleg again, and again, which brought him up against Marcus Garvey Park—where his luck ran out.

A red light immobilized him at a T-intersection, near an entrance to the Park. Four youths saw him, grinned at each other, and left the Park to approach the car.

"Jennifer, are both your doors locked?" he asked, trying to sound calm.

"Daddy, I'm scared."

"Are both doors locked?"

"Yes."

"Then sit tight and shut up. We're okay, they can't get in."

Three of the youths were pragmatists. Ignoring the occupants of the car, they methodically began stripping it. The first got the antenna, the second the windshield wipers, the third popped off a front hubcap. Russell, blocked in front and in back, was helpless. The fourth and last to arrive looked over the Grant family and acquired a ferocious expression. He came around to Russell's side, banged on the window, and made an open-it gesture. Russell glared back at him. The young man produced a spray-can of what seemed to be orange paint, and aimed it theatrically at the windshield. Russell got the message and cracked his window a careful ten millimeters.

"You losin' more than your car now, motherfucker," the young man said. He might have been fifteen. "Be your ass for sure."

"Why?" Russell asked him.

"Shade come uptown for pussy, he gotta die," the boy said. He seemed to be enjoying himself immensely. "That's all it is to it." He looked Dena over and licked his lips. "You shoulda stuck wit' the teeny in the back."

"We're from Canada," Russell said, trying not to let the desperation show, trying to maintain some sense of sanity, of civilization. "These are my wife and daughter. We're just passing through."

"Wife?" boy said, astounded. "Then you die *twice*, fuckwipe: Your wife too . . . after a while." He shifted his gaze to Dena. "Don't worry, sugarlips, your little white daughter don't die. Ain't her fault." He glanced at Jennifer. "She can work for me."

Both license plates and all four hubcaps were gone; one of the busy boys was working on the nuts with a tirejack that had appeared from nowhere. He was cursing; his jack was not metric. Russell was prepared to run the light and force his way into traffic, but he did not expect to succeed, and even if he did, the traffic was moving too slowly to afford any real protection.

Time had stopped for him. He was conscious of everything happening around him, flooded with details. The young man threatening him had a scar on the left cheek and two missing front teeth. The trees in the Park ahead of him were mostly elm and ash. The smell of fried food was in the air, and somewhere a radio with excellent bass response was predicting continued sunshine through Thursday. A mosquito bite on Russell's left forearm itched unbearably. One of the cars passing by in front of him caught his attention. It was a blue and white police cruiser, heavily armored. Both officers were black. They saw the situation; the shotgun man met Russell's eye briefly.

"You comin' out?" the youth asked, shaking his paint can so that the ball inside rattled. "Or we comin' in?"

The police car went by without so much as pausing. Russell was numb. He heard a sound from the back seat which he absently identified as Jennifer hyperventilating. And Dena screamed past his ear.

"GET AWAY FROM THIS CAR," she screamed, with more volume and more rage than he had ever heard from her before. "You son of a bitch, *get away from us!*"

The boy grinned even wider.

Russell knew that he had a maximum of five seconds of paralysis left; then he would do something. Time to decide what. He took inventory of the car's contents: incredibly, among the several hundred items which had cramped them all so badly on their journey, there was nothing more deadly than a thermos of lukewarm Mr. Donut coffee. The man with the tirejack was trying to pry open the trunk now; he was seeking a metric jack, but would find the trunk packed to absolute capacity with pawnable objects. Let's see, Russell thought. I can panic, throw her in reverse, crush that guy back there, put her in drive, bounce off the passing traffic, reverse again, and keep that up until I smash something vital and the car stops. Or I can just get out and die right now. Is there a third alternative?

One came to him. He could turn right, gun the car onto the sidewalk and parallel all the traffic, cut back in when convenient. This would kill many pedestrians ... people who were either watching, or ignoring, his plight, the hell with them all. He began cutting the wheel—

—and saw three small children, about Jennifer's age or younger, directly in his planned path. Back to the first two choices. He had just decided on Plan A, since it would take out at least one of his opponents, when the situation changed again.

The young man with the paint-can now had a brick in his other hand. He pulled it back, plainly intending to smash in the window and gain access to the door-unlock system. He paused with his arm all the way back, picking his spot—and the brick was plucked from his hand just as he was whipping it forward. The sudden loss of weight cost him his balance, and he fell heavily against the car and went to his knees.

The hand which had snatched the brick was considerably blacker than the hand from which it was grabbed. Past the startled and angry face of his assailant, Russell saw his rescuer. The newcomer was well on the way to seven feet tall. He was barefoot, his only garment a vivid red robe that fell to his ankles. He was bald and clean-shaven. He might have been anywhere between thirty-five and sixty years old. Russell did not believe in auras, but this man had an aura. His face was magnificent sculpture, and at the moment it held an expression of deep, ancient sorrow. All at once Russell realized where he had last seen such an expression. As a child, he had been taken to the Lincoln Memorial in Washington ...

"Brothers," the man said, "I am disappointed." His voice was a splendid instrument, deep and resonant and edged, like a baritone sax. "Is this measured?"

The four thugs were wearing crestfallen, hangdog expressions. They looked as though they wanted to look sullen but did not dare. Russell was sure that countless parents, girlfriends, teachers, preachers, and policemen had tried hard to elicit just such expressions from them in the past—and that all had failed. "Shit, Michael," the spokesman protested feebly, "we measured the set from the jump. A shade with a sister, in this neighborhood—he was askin'. I mean shit, the raise clocked it an' just drove on by. They was hip, it's a righteous rip."

The man called Michael looked even sadder. "You measure better than me, brother? Lickety-Split, that's your name, right? You saying you measure better than me, right out here on the street, Lickety-Split?"

Many people were watching. Lickety-Split went one shade lighter in complexion, and his three companions flinched away from him. "Hey, Michael, listen," he said urgently, "I know who the egg man be. I know who be the lily o' the valley. Don't be hangin' no sign on me."

Michael held the boy's eyes a few seconds longer, and his terrible sorrow seemed to affect Lickety-Split like a heavy yoke. Then he nodded. "Nobody gonna hang a sign on you, son." A corner of his mouth twitched. "You're too fast on your feet, way I hear."

Absolved, Lickety-Split smiled sheepishly. "I ain't slow."

"Be digging you later, all right?"

"What about the loot, Michael?" asked the jack-wielder.

"Nothing wrong with a toll booth, son, long as the levy ain't too heavy. But give back those plates; they can't get Canada plates here."

The four went back to the park, bearing Russell's hubcaps and antenna, and the crowd began to disperse. Michael approached the car, and Russell powered his window down with a hand that felt like a paw.

He was as disoriented and traumatized as he had ever been in his life, and he wanted badly to babble. But there was something about Michael which held him in check. He felt somehow reluctant to waste this man's time with unnecessary words. "Thank you, father," he heard himself say, and was silent.

Michael smiled, and if his face in repose was sad, his smile was sorrow insupportable. "Son," he said, "you picked a bad time to visit the Apple. I'm sorry for your trouble." He bent his long frame without effort and glanced past Russell at Dena and Jennifer, who were embracing over the seat. He met each of their gazes in turn, and nodded. "You are all nice people, and I'm sorry. How long are you planning to be in the city?"

"Three months."

He winced. "Got to be? Yes, I see it does. I'm sorry," he said again. He straightened to his full height. "Now how am I going to get you downtown alive? Guess there ain't but the one way. Would you open your sunroof, please?" Russell obeyed without thinking—then stared as Michael placed one foot on the door handle and vaulted into the car. He stood up between Russell and Dena, the upper half of his long body sticking out the open sunroof. "Keep a constant speed," he directed.

The light had changed during all this—Russell was too numb to be surprised that no drivers behind had interrupted Michael by honking—and was already going red again. But the cross-traffic waited for him to pull out, and when he did the traffic before him melted magically away, as though his family sedan were an ambulance or a fire-engine. He took it gradually up to nearly 40 kph. Michael kept his balance easily. Occasional pedestrians called respectful greetings to Michael, and he acknowledged each, often by name.

Inside the car, the Grants were speechless.

After a time, Russell began to notice something. The people they drove past, the throngs of beaten people who lined the sidewalks, all stood straighter, walked prouder, held their heads higher if they caught sight of Michael. Where Russell had sensed hostility from pedestrians before, he now sensed curiosity. The reaction was not universal: one or two people glared at Michael, and one shook an angry fist—but these were a distinct minority. Russell drove with extreme care, following Michael's directions, and was soon heading downtown on Madison Avenue. They passed one side street which had been abandoned utterly: it was filled from side to side, from end to end, to about second- or third-story height, with garbage. Things grew in the garbage; things scuttled. Half a block later they passed a sidewalk knife-fight; it broke up under Michael's stare. Russell saw it resume in his rear-view mirror. Dena took his hand silently. Central Park came up on the right.

Russell's designer's eye was programmed to notice incongruities; storefront signs caught his eye. "Sister Venis. Palms red. We'll tell you're fate" was located next door to "East Harlem MENSA," and just beyond that was a restaurant called "Chez Swill." One especially ornate sign announced "The East Side Social Club and Massage Center: Home of Discount Around The World," while a few doors away a garish neon sign read simply, "PUSSY PARLOR." Several signs frankly advertised the services of unlicensed physicians ("Three years Bellevue E.R.—why pay more?"); others just as candidly offered unlicensed bodyguard service ("CYA Protection Bureau: not much to pay to C.Y.A."). Just as Russell was wondering if there were formal law enforcement of any sort in Harlem any more, he saw a commotion ahead on the right. Two black policemen had a large man down on the sidewalk; they were methodically kicking the piss out of him, while a small crowd watched. Michael gestured Russell to pull over and stop. The policemen paused in their work when a bystander drew their attention to Michael. The larger of the two touched his cap. "Good day, Michael."

"Good day, Brother Raise. What it is?"

The shorter officer was holding a black leather shoulderbag. He opened it. "Stud had this on him, Brother Michael." He took out a handful of nickel bags of white powder. "Marseille Grey, look like."

Michael nodded slowly. "Yeah."

The man on the sidewalk spasmed and mewed, a piteous sound.

"Yeah," Michael said again, "well, I can see he's continuing to resist arrest, so happen I'd best be goin' along while you two raise finish subduing him. I only hope you don't have to kill him to bring him under control. You know, it always seemed to me that they are the best example to the community when they are still on the street, ain't it?"

The first cop nodded. "I was just sayin' to my man Bobby here, Michael, that if this skell didn't stop resistin' arrest pretty soon, maybe we'd be best off if we just broke his elbows."

"Well, if that should prove necessary," Michael said, "I only hope that young man has someone in this world who loves him enough to put the food into his mouth for the rest of his days."

"That'd be a comfort, at that."

"You men are good raise, Brother."

Both policemen smiled for the first time, pride evident in their faces. "Thank you, Michael," they chorused.

Michael looked down at Russell. "Ready when you are, sir," he said politely, and Russell pulled away from the curb.

The rest of the trip downtown was comparatively uneventful. Eventually they reached 90th Street and Michael waved them over to the curb again. He vaulted from the car, landed easily on his feet.

Russell leaned out his open window. "Thank you, Michael—for all of us."

Michael smiled, and the smile made Russell want to burst into tears. "Don't say that. I don't know that I've done you any favor at all."

"*I* do!"

Michael surveyed the three of them. His gaze lingered longest on Jennifer. He reached in through the car window and she took his hand. His smile changed subtly, became less hurtful to see.

He stood back then. "Hear my words. You three have a strong connection going. Don't let it go, no matter what. Don't let it go, and happen you'll be okay." His eyes seemed to bore into Russell. "Don't you let it go."

"I won't," all three Grants said at once.

"Too bad you didn't get to see *West* Hundred-Twenty-Fifth. It's right pretty this time of year." And with that Michael turned on his bare heel and strode off back uptown, a Masai warrior somehow transported halfway round the world to a deadlier jungle.

Russell and Dena both began speaking at once, both to Jennifer.

"I'm all *right*, Daddy," she said solemnly. "Truly. I'm not a child any more, you know."

Russell opened his mouth and then closed it. He saw Jennifer's dead mother in her very plainly, the strength and courage, and his eyes stung. "I'm sorry, princess."

"Why? Because you didn't get out and get killed like some guy in the movies? It's all *right*, Daddy." Suddenly she was thirteen again. "Except I *really* have to pee now."

Russell and Dena laughed immoderately, and all three embraced tearily.

He drove another few blocks, until they were indisputably in safe territory, then he double-parked and reconnected the car phone modem while the ladies used a tavern toilet. While he was waiting, a police cruiser pulled up. Both cops were white. They listened with absolute indifference to his account, took down the numbers of the Nova Scotia plates he showed them, told him that he was lucky the big red nigger hadn't killed them all himself and eaten them, and gave him tickets for illegal parking and failure to display license plates. Russell felt he should be furious, but he accepted the tickets without argument and put them away. Welcome to New York, he thought to himself. If the right one don't get you . . .

Dena had managed to buy two fifths of vodka; they poured them into the fuel tank and were able to restart the car and get to a service station.

Dena snuggled close to him all the way down to 23rd Street, squeezing his upper arm tightly while he drove. Occasionally she would point out a landmark to Jennifer, or a place where she had lived or worked on previous visits to New York. She had been here three times before she married Russell, and she remembered the city better than he. Russell had not been back since his move to Canada over twenty years ago. He saw too few things he remembered; he was shocked to find the Scribner's building torn down, and Grand Central Station was all wrong. Nonetheless, nostalgia gripped him hard. There is a *smell* to New York, unlike that of any other city in the world.

Again he found himself noticing how many young men and women were in uniform, how many military vehicles

were on the streets. It is, he thought, *almost* exactly like a
re-run of Viet Nam. Once again the United States is heavily and hopelessly involved in an undeclared, unwinnable,
unpopular land war, complete with destruction, draft and
demonstrations, and once again it all seems unreal and
theatrical to a Canadian. Summer reruns—when the '50's
Revival craze came in the '80's, we should have realized
that it implied a *'60's* revival just around the corner. The
significant differences are, this war is in Africa rather
than Asia ... and Canada isn't accepting draft dodgers
this time. A pressure-vessel with no relief valve. . . .

While musing thus, Russell phoned ahead on the car
phone; the rental agent was waiting to meet them on the
corner of 23rd Street. A short thin fussy man with a phony
British accent, who had obviously had a few drinks recently,
he greeted them with a harassed air and directed them
back uptown to 31st between First and Second.

"Really, you're quite fortunate, Mr. Grant," he said.
"It's donkey's years since I've had an apartment as nice as
this one to let. I think you'll be pleased."

At twenty-two hundred U.S. a month, Russell thought,
I'd better be. "So my father tells me, Mr. Shaw. He refused to describe the flat, but he insisted that if I didn't
like it he'd refund my money. I must admit I'm intrigued."

When they reached 31st, Russell could not find a parking space anywhere near the address he wanted.

"Oh *good* luck," Shaw cried, adjusting an invisible
monocle. "Look there: a parking space."

"Where?"

"There. A good omen, what?"

"But that's a fire hydrant."

Shaw looked uncomprehending—then suddenly laughed,
just a bit too loudly to be polite. "Mr. Grant, you obviously have been away from New York for some time. This
city has not had the resources to chase down unpaid
tickets for decades. I use my own for bookmarks."

Russell involuntarily touched his jacket over the inside
pocket which held his own tickets. "But won't they tow
me away?"

"They haven't the trucks or drivers. Those they have
they tend to concentrate in business districts. I can't

guarantee you'll be safe—but I would park there. Of course, my nephew is a detective."

Russell parked there. "Why do they still give out tickets?"

"You know, there's been considerable speculation about that. My nephew's theory is that the police officials want to keep their men from more serious mischief. But the prevailing theory is that the Borough President's brother-in-law owns the company that prints the tickets."

The neighborhood seemed okay, Russell saw as he locked up the car. Pedestrians were well-dressed; the buildings were, for New York, in excellent shape—which was to say that they would probably have been tolerated in Halifax's worst slum areas. He adjusted his expectations for the new apartment accordingly—and was therefore pleasantly startled when Shaw led them inside.

In the first place, it was on the ground floor. Such treasures are rare in New York, and out-of-towners seldom get a crack at one. Second, he saw when Shaw unsnapped the third lock and let them in, it was enormous—fully the size of the living room-dining room of the Grants' Halifax home. So big, that is, that he began to believe that a family of three could really live there for three months without going insane. There were indeed two bedrooms, and the master bedroom actually had space for a bureau and a small night-table in addition to the bed. The apartment was furnished adequately if tastelessly, in a style which Russell immediately dubbed Space-Age Public Washroom.

The location and size were enough to persuade him that twenty-two hundred U.S. was a good deal—with the dollar conversion it was only twice the amount of his monthly mortgage bite back home. But then Shaw, with the air of a runty pseudo-British Santa Claus, unlocked and opened a door at the far end of the room which served as living room, dining room, kitchen and study, and Russell's jaw dropped. Dena and Jennifer both cried out.

There was a garden out there.

All three Grants clustered round while Shaw unlocked the security-gate and slid it back, then hurried outside together. "By the chamber-pot of the Buddha," Russell breathed.

"Jennifer," Dena said, "tell me what you see."

"Like a garden."

"Thank God. If you see it too, it must be there. I thought my software had dropped a byte."

"As you can see," Shaw said smugly, "it wants tending. But I think you'll find it agreeable on hot nights."

Anywhere else in the world, the garden—*qua* garden—would have been a bad joke. It comprised three brick-lined islands of earth defining a T-shaped path which led from the concrete patio on which they stood. The soil was sandy and miserable; it supported assorted knee-high weeds and three twisted, forlorn and self-conscious looking trees of a species that Russell, an experienced woodsman, could not identify.

But it existed. It contained as much square footage as the apartment itself, and the sun shone on it, and cool breezes blew through it, and green things lived in it. It was well fenced off from similar courtyards on all three sides, and better than half of it could not be observed from the balconies of the apartments stacked above this one.

Russell murmured, "Dena, remind me to tell Dad the apartment is adequate." He turned to the agent. "Mr. Shaw, remind me not to play poker with you. I never saw this coming." Shaw preened. "What immortal *fool* gave this place up?"

The little neat man coughed discreetly. "The previous tenant was a gentleman of Peruvian extraction. He, uh, paid the first six months' rent in advance, in cash, if you follow my drift. That was the last I ever saw of him. When the rent had gone two weeks unpaid and my letters and calls elicited no response, I entered the place. He had been gone for at least a month by then, I estimate. I have no idea how to locate him. I had to leave it for two more weeks before listing it—applying his security deposit against the rent, you see, in case he should return—but that was used up three days ago. I happen to owe a friend of your father's a number of favours, and when he mentioned your situation to me . . ."

Russell smiled and shook his head. Given the rent asked,

Shaw must owe Russell's father's friend some large favours indeed.

"You'll be requiring the place for three months, am I right? Mrs. Grant, I understand you'll be dancing here in New York?"

"Dena. Yes, at the Joyce, with Lisa Dann's company."

His right eyebrow rose, and his manner became subtly more respectful. "With Lisa *Dann?* Oh, I say! Really." He squinted suddenly. "By God! May I ask, Mrs.—Dena—do you by any chance perform under the name 'Dena St. Claire'?"

"Why yes, Mr. Shaw. My maiden name."

"Oh do please call me David. Why then, I've heard of you. You worked with Miss Dann in the past, did you not?"

"A long time ago, yes," Dena said, plainly tickled to death. "We studied together at Julliard."

"I look forward to the opportunity to see you perform," Shaw told her, and she thanked him.

Russell noticed that Jennifer looked just as proud as he was.

"Well," Shaw said, "I expect that the first priority is to remove Mr. Figueroa's belongings and have them put into storage." The doorbell rang. "Oh good, that will be José. I told him to meet us. He's your super—a very competent man."

José turned out to be a short dark handsome seventeen-year-old Puerto Rican with long unruly curls and an air of cynical amusement. He measured Russell as they shook hands, and plainly decided to reserve judgement. His eyes went from Dena to Jennifer and back to Russell. "Please' to make your acquaintance, Mist' Grant."

"Russell, José. Good to know you. Do you live in the building?"

"Up the street, I'll give you the number. During the day I work in a discount place around the corner."

They began packing up the previous occupant's gear, while Shaw looked on and made helpful noises. Dena tackled the worst part, a fridge full of fungal cultures which had once been Peruvian foodstuffs. Jennifer attacked the bathroom, while José and Russell took the bedrooms.

"Nice clothes this bastid had," José said, opening a closet and shaking out a large garbage sack. Russell glanced over; everything in the closet looked hideous to him. José seemed to be waiting for something. Suddenly Russell twigged. "Looks like he was about your size."

"Yah."

"The place where you're going to store all this—"

"The basement."

"—yeah. Junkies ever break in there, steal things?"

José grinned broadly. "All the time, man."

"I can dig it." Fascinating, Russell thought, the street talk, the inflections, all come back effortlessly. I sound like I never left the city. "I'll decoy Shaw when you leave with the stuff."

"Solid, man. You all right."

"No sweat." He began boxing up small items, radios and books and such. "You could maybe help me unload my ride?"

"You got it."

Russell opened the top dresser drawer, and froze. José sensed it and came over. In the drawer, amid the expected items, was a Smith & Wesson 9 mm semiautomatic pistol, complete with a hundred rounds of ammunition.

"Mother*fucker*," José whispered.

"Peruvian, you say he was."

"Bet your fuckin' A, man!" José was so excited he could barely keep his voice down. "Hey, that's the steel-frame 559! That's a good fuckin' piece, man! Look here, he's loadin' hunner'twenny-fi' grain hollow points in this bastid."

"Heavy ammo?"

"Hey man, like it's only nine millimeter, you know, but wit' that hollow point you hit a stud and the slug blows up to about 70 fucking caliber, dig? Look, he had this fucker customized, see here? Hey, wit' this piece you could kill a Buick down on the corner, no shit."

"My." Russell was not sure what to do.

"You found it, man, it's your piece as far as I'm concerned. You want to sell it? I'll give you five hundred cash, tonight."

Russell owned no gun, had never expected to want to.

But his drive through Harlem was on his mind. "No, José. I think I'll hang on to it awhile."

"That's what I'd do, man." José paused, undecided. Then: "Hey man, can I say something to you?"

Russell braced himself. "Go ahead."

"Look, your wife, she's black. I'm part black, all right? What I'm trying to say, there's black people and there's niggers, you understand me?"

"I understand."

"I can see that little girl of yours is offa some other lady. But niggers see you walk by wit' a black lady and a white kid, an' it don't look like she's your housekeeper or somethin', you gonna *need* that cannon, fuckin' A."

"Is it really that bad now, José? Last time I lived in New York, it was okay downtown anyway."

"Some places, fine. Right on this block, no problem. A couple blocks in either direction, maybe. But you wanna see a play, maybe you better go there in a cab, all right? You wanna walk careful. This is a town full of angry niggers. They didn't bust *all* of them Mau Maus, you know what I mean?"

"I'm hip." Russell briefly narrated the story of events in Harlem.

"Woo-*eee*," José said when he finished. "That Michael, he's somethin' else, you know?"

"You've heard of him."

"Man, everybody that ain't white is heard of that stud. You don't see him on TV, he ain't in the papers, but since he showed up, niggers don't take no shit no more. Even black people don't. You must be okay if Michael passed you. Man, you got shit-lucky, an' that's fuckin' A." He shook his head. "You better hide that piece before Shaw Nuff comes in."

Russell barely had time to comply when Shaw did open the door. "Find anything interesting?"

"Yes," Russell said, sifting through the rest of the top drawer. "Two passports in different names. Each with the same picture. A confirmation for a flight to Lima in a third name, two months ago." He palmed the ammo box while Shaw was examining these. "Business cards for three different massage parlors." He opened a bottom drawer. "Bingo."

An attaché case, strong enough to withstand sledge or ax or even airport baggage handler, triple-locked.

José's eyes lit up. Shaw blinked rapidly.

"José," Shaw said, "that case had better not be missing from storage the next time I look for it."

José tried to look wounded, and sensibly gave it up. "Mist' Shaw—that guy prob'ly got himself shot down there. You know them Peruvians."

Shaw looked tempted, but Russell's presence inhibited him. "No. What if he comes back?"

"Ah, *shit*. All right," he added hastily. "You the boss."

"Perhaps I'd better take charge of it personally. Junkies sometimes steal things from that cellar, don't they?"

José shot Russell a disgusted look which Shaw did not see. "Yeah, well, you know, it been known to happen."

"Yes. I'd better . . ." He held out his hand, and reluctantly José gave him the case. He left the room with it.

José was angry. "Motherfucker gonna rip off what's in there," he whispered. "Then if the stud *does* come back he'll lay it on me, you watch. I know him, man."

Russell reached a decision. "José, look," he murmured. "You've treated me right, and I'm driving Shaw home when we're done here. In ten or fifteen minutes, could you come up with a case *just* like that one?"

José looked puzzled, and then his face split in a broad grin. "I told you, I work in a discount place. Lemme see, I gotta put something inside it for weight . . ."

"Epsom salts," Russell said, and José's grin got even bigger. "Maybe he'll try and sell it," he added, and the youth laughed out loud.

"You're my man, Russell. You need anything, you got trouble, you come see me. I got a lot of friends."

"You've got three more than you thought you had."

After José had left, Russell examined his decision with mild astonishment. What in hell had possessed him to enter into a conspiracy to steal something of great value, perhaps drugs, with a Puerto Rican boy he had known for less than an hour? Russell was a law-abiding citizen of a law-abiding country. He did not so much as smoke pot.

He filed honest tax returns. The most significant item he had stolen since adolescence was a kiss. It was not as though he had any reason to dislike Shaw. The man was a phony and a closet lush, but those were not grounds to steal what looked like being a sizable sum of money from the man. Why, Shaw had been particularly gracious to Dena, made her smile. And God knew that Russell, eight years retired at age forty-eight, did not need or especially want the money.

It was exactly the sort of puzzle which should have fascinated Russell; the inexplicable was, for him, one of life's greatest delights. Whenever he caught himself behaving inexplicably, it was his custom to sit down and play with the mystery until he had it solved, like a child with a new Rubik's Cube.

Got to get moving if I'm going to have a bed to sleep in tonight, he thought, and had forgotten his puzzle within ten seconds.

CHAPTER TWO

Between 1900-1930, two and a quarter million Blackamericans left the farms and plantations of the South. Most of them emigrated to selected urban areas of the north—New York, Philadelphia, Chicago and Detroit being among the most popular destinations . . . [from 1910 to 1920], the black population in the North increased from a mere 75,000 to 300,000, an increase of 400% . . .

"One hundred Blackamericans were lynched during the first year of the Twentieth Century. By the outbreak of the First World War in 1914, the figure stood at 1,100 . . .

"Many industries sent agents into the South to lure the blacks north with promises of good jobs . . . it was a common practice for the agents to purchase tickets for whole families and to move them en masse for resettlement in the great industrial cities. The war had drained away the white manpower needed to build the ships, work the steel, pack the meat, and man the machines; and it had also cut off the normal supply of immigrant labor from Europe.

"After the war was over, the black man's welcome wore thin . . ."

—C. Eric Lincoln,
The Black Muslims in America

"New York City's population shifted as dramatically during the decade of the 1970's as at any time in the history of the city.

"That is the conclusion of demographers . . . who have now had several months to study the first reports from the 1980 census.

"The figures provide a profile of a shrinking populace that nevertheless includes more old people and young adults, but markedly fewer children and teenagers.

"The figures show what may have been the largest exodus of New Yorkers in the city's history . . .

"And they show a city where the traditional 'minority groups' are now close to being—if they have not already become—a majority of the population."

—Michael Oreskes,
New York Times, Sept. 20, 1982

*   *   *

Dena turned out the light and sat on the edge of the bed.

"Jennifer, honey, I think it's time that you and I had a little talk." I always knew we'd have to have this talk someday, she thought. Why didn't I prepare?

"Mother," the girl said, wrinkling her nose and pulling the blankets up to her chin, "we *had* that talk. *Ages* ago."

"Not that talk. This one we've never had. Time we did."

"Oh. That talk. About race, you mean."

"Yes. After what happened uptown this afternoon, something has to be said." Dena shifted uneasily. "I just don't know what."

"Me either."

"Do you understand why those four boys were mad at us?"

"Because you're married to a white man."

"And because you're white, and they thought you were my daughter."

"I don't understand that part."

"I'm not sure I do either, honey. But . . . See, one of the reasons that many black people hate to see a black marry a white is the question of what color the children would be. In North America the whites so badly outnumber us, some of us are afraid that if we interbreed with whites, one day we'll disappear entirely. You look to them like their greatest fear come true, as long as they think you're my daughter."

"I *am* your daughter, Dena."

"My biological daughter, I mean, and you know it, girl. But that gets you a hug anyway."

The two embraced, and held on. Jennifer's hands were strong on Dena's shoulder blades. The child smelled sweet. "Jennifer," Dena murmured into her ear. "Oh Jennifer, I feel as though I ought to apologize for those boys, apologize to you."

"Okay," Jennifer whispered back. "Then I'll apologize for all the generations of white people that made them so crazy; then we'll be even. Is that good?"

Dena giggled. "Sweetheart, when I grow up I hope I turn out as wise as you." She brushed hair back from her daughter's face.

"Well, I'd say you've got a shot. You married well."

"Goodnight, Jennifer. Dream pretty dreams."

"G'night, Mom." She started to roll over. "Do you know why I love you so much?"

Dena nodded. "Sure. Because I never call you 'Jen' or 'Jenny' but always Jennifer."

"Almost. Because nobody ever had to tell you that."

Dena closed the bedroom door and stood awhile, smiling. I don't *need* to have one of my own, she thought. I couldn't love a child more than Jennifer no matter whose belly it came out of. I thought child-geniuses were supposed to be insufferable.

She looked around her own bedroom, at the heaps and stacks of things that would have to be unpacked sometime soon. If she started now, she'd be going at it at five AM—and she was already tired. The bed was made, there was room to reach it; sufficient unto the day was the evil thereof.

She left the room, went into the main room. The shade was up; through the heavily-barred window she could see her husband out in the garden. He was sitting in a white canvas-and-magnesium director's chair, facing the back fence, looking up at the sky. She noted that his glass was almost empty. She made two of the same and brought them outside. The night was warm and humid; she smelled curry and burnt pasta. "Any stars up there?"

"A few. They look sick."

"City air. Here's a fresh drink."

"Thanks, love. As far as I'm concerned, the brightest star in this garden just walked in, carrying two drinks. Oh—let me get you a chair."

"What would I do with a chair?" she said, sitting on his lap. "Russell, about this afternoon—" She felt him tense.

"Yeah."

Thought so, she congratulated herself. "I just wanted to say I think you handled it well."

"Sure. Sat there and watched it happen. Brilliant strategy."

"Yes, it was."

"Perhaps it might have been, if I'd had the slightest alternative."

"But you *did*. Two at least that I can think of. You might have gone all macho, charged out of the car and made me a widow. Or you might have gibbered and wept with fear and terrified Jennifer."

"I wanted to."

"But you didn't. I *did*."

"And what did *I* do? Nothing whatsoever. I sat there and waited for a miracle."

"And just by coincidence, that turned out to be the best thing you could have done, didn't it? If you'd been trying to fight them when Michael came, it might have turned out differently."

He thought about that, searching her face. "So I'm just being a jerk," he asked softly, "feeling bad about my performance?"

"I didn't say that. What you're feeling, my true love, is what is sometimes called The Sorrow of the Survivor. And it is a *wonderful* feeling—compared to the alternative. So be miserable and enjoy it."

He set his drink down, hugged her close, and ran a hand through her hair. But Dena could feel tension still in him. "How's Jen?" he asked after a while.

"Fine, fine." She sat up straight in his lap. "No, that's a little glib. She's shook up, of course. I *think* that was the first real-life violent confrontation she's ever seen. But she's tough, Russ. She checked out the bars on her bedroom window really carefully—and then never glanced at them again. We talked a little. She's okay. Am I too heavy on your lap!"

She always asked; he always said no. "Yeah, a little." She got up, and he did too. "Sit down, darling, I want to show you something."

She did as he asked, and looked around her new back-yard while he went back inside. Five-story apartment build-ings on all sides cut off all but an overhead square of night sky. The head-high board fence that enclosed the garden was festooned with wires for phone, power, and TV hookup, running every which way. She heard two stereos going, different songs that coincidentally happened to be in the same key. The music harmonized most of the time, occasionally diverging in a weirdly interesting way. She saw glimmerings of a dance set to such music. Dena saw such half-formed images frequently—and had wasted many hours of her life proving to herself that glimmerings were all she was ever going to see, that the gift of choreography would never be hers. Sometimes it pleases the gods to visit itches on a person with no arms.

She shifted position in the chair, and a sudden clutch of pain in her lower back reminded her that soon she would not even be able to dance other people's dances . . . she shied away as always from that thought, and sat up straighter. The pain receded.

Russell came back outside with a second chair and sat beside her. "Listen," he said, "this afternoon while José and I were cleaning out the bedrooms, I found something. I don't want Jen to know about it—but I *do* want you to know." He produced the gun.

"Russell, Jesus!"

"I'm going to keep it under our mattress, on my side. There's a box of a hundred slugs with it. The firing pin will be in the top dresser drawer. There'll be a note with the gun, telling Jen that it's not a toy in case she finds it somehow."

"Wow. That Figueroa must have been a drug-runner, huh?"

"Well, he wasn't an evangelist."

"Russell, I don't know if I want that thing around."

"I'm sure I do. And I want you to know how to use it if the need ever arises while I'm not around."

"But—"

"Use your head, Dena! What are the odds that Michael will happen along the next time the animals come?"

She thought about that. "What do I do?"

He showed her how to remove or replace the firing pin, how to load or unload, how to remove a burst shell-casing, how to aim and what to aim for, how to fire and when not to fire. "Get your first shot off *quick*, then take time to aim the second one. It rattles them, spoils their aim." He stripped the gun down again, had her practice loading and arming it as fast as she could, then had her dry-fire to get the feel of the action.

"Russell, how do you know about this stuff? You were never in the Army."

"I grew up in New York."

"Oh, bullshit. When you grew up in New York, hand-guns weren't part of a kid's wardrobe."

He reddened slightly. "Well, you can learn a lot by reading John D. MacDonald novels."

She wished she had let it ride. Her husband was suffering from machismo leakage—and she had reopened the leak. "All right, dear. If you don't want to tell me the truth, you must have a good reason. I'm just glad you do know about guns. I like a husband with romantic secrets in his past." She saw him buy it; his spine straightened almost imperceptibly. "Should I take this with me when I go downtown to work?"

"Let's talk about that. You'll have to go through some rough territory. You can have it if you want it."

"But you don't think I should?"

He made a face. "I'm not sure. Twenty-five years ago I'd have been sure. This morning I'd have been sure. Now I don't know."

"Why would you have said no this morning?"

"Two reasons. First, if you get caught carrying this thing around town, you could be doing your dancing on Riker's Island. Second, when you have to go through rough turf, you're usually better off unarmed. It keeps you alert and cautious and scared. A gun gives you the entirely false impression that you're invulnerable. What I just taught you was how to operate a gun, not how to use one."

"I follow your logic. So why aren't you sure now?"

"As to the first reason, it doesn't seem like they're enforcing a whole lot of laws here. Possession of a gun may be good for a twenty-dollar ticket these days. As for the second reason . . . I think that after what happened this afternoon, you'd be alert and cautious and scared if you had a bulletproof leotard and a machine gun. I know you pretty well. You wouldn't shoot if you didn't have to—and you would shoot if you did have to."

"Thanks."

"But I'm not sure you'd hit what you aimed at—and as a rule it's better not to show a gun than to pull it and miss."

Dena finished her drink and thought about it. The gun lay on her lap, its teeth pulled. She picked it up and sighted at a broken flower pot near the back fence. "Here's the way I see it. If some guy hits on me in the street, there's three things he could be: an entrepreneur, a rapist or a maniac, what they call here a mucker. If he wants money, I give it to him, *including* what I've got hidden in my sock, because there's more where that came from. If he wants my ass, I show him the best time I can, 'cause there's more where that came from too."

"As long as you stay alive, there is," Russell agreed. "Be careful there. Some kinds of rapist, cooperating is *more* likely to get you killed."

"Whatever the customer wants, I can deliver. There's no such thing as a fate worse than death."

"How about category three, the mucker? A gun could be useful there. There's nothing on earth that will placate a mucker, you know. He's in a berserk frame of reference."

"Baby, from what I read about these muckers, it'd take a lot of bullets to even slow him down."

"Good argument for having a lot of bullets. And that's a lot of gun there. But a mucker isn't the only kind of maniac you could run into."

"Eh?"

"Look, this afternoon racism almost bit me on the face on

East 125th Street. Black racism. But things always balance, there's always a backlash. If I was a target uptown—"

"—I could be one downtown, I get you." She twirled the pistol in the manner of a TV gunslinger. "Well, I'm glad you said that; I'll be alert for that sort of thing when I start going to work. But I think the gun should stay here, where it can protect Jennifer." She held it out to him.

He did not reach to take it. "I'm inclined to agree. But I'd feel awfully stupid if you happened to get killed some way that a gun could have gotten you out of. You'll be the one out there on the streets, the bad streets—"

"Honey, the city is a giant kid's playground of corners and alleys and hidey-holes. Run and hide is an easy game to play out there. Where are you going to run and hide in this concrete box here? When they're coming in the window and it takes thirty seconds to unlock the damn door? You know the statistics: an apartment is much more likely to get robbed than a pedestrian. You handle that gun the best; you keep it here." She looked down at the weapon, still on her outstretched palm. "In fact, I'm wondering if we shouldn't tell Jennifer about it instead of hiding it."

"Hell no!"

"Russell—"

"Dena, for God's sake, you don't tell a child where the family gun is. She's liable to start fiddling with it and—"

She began to get annoyed. "Russell Grant—does that girl or does she not use the chainsaw back home? Are you trying to say she's stupid?"

"Of course not. She's too bright for her own good."

"I think you should teach her to use it, just the way you've taught me."

He stared at her. "Are you out of your mind? Teach a child to use a gun?"

"That's the second time you've used that word. Russell, watch my lips: Jennifer. Is. Not. A. Child."

"She is thirteen fucking years old. Genius or not, she's a child *emotionally*—she hasn't reached menarche yet—"

"How did she come through this afternoon? Weeping? Hysterics? Panic?"

He sprang up from his chair and began pacing around the garden, speaking in that peculiar strangled voice of one who wishes to argue over distance without being overheard by the neighbors. "Dammit, I don't *know* how much this afternoon traumatized her—but I'm not going to add to it by telling her that she might need to use a gun at any time."

"Even if it's true? She's never going to be alone in this apartment for five minutes?"

"I've got that covered, I think." He came back close to her and sat down, lowered his voice. "That gun wasn't all I found today. A black attaché case, triple locked, heavy to the heft. Shaw tried to take it aside for himself—so José and I switched cases on him. José got it open. Somewhat disappointing: only five thousand in cash inside."

"Jesus." Something was becoming clear to Dena. She kept her features neutral.

"It made a pretty problem. I didn't feel good about taking drug money—but if I gave over my share to José, it placed him under too much obligation to me. It could have spoiled our relationship, an imbalance like that, and I like that kid. So I hired him as a part-time guard for Jen, in exchange for my half of the money."

Dena thought about José. The boy had impressed her as efficient, courteous, and intelligent. She'd liked him, and had sensed that Jennifer liked him too. "I think that's brilliant, honey. I like José. He seems trustworthy."

"And streetsmart."

"Has he got weapons of his own?"

Russell mimicked José. "Bet you fuckin' A."

Dena giggled. She handed him back the gun, and this time he took it. "Under the mattress, you say?"

"And the firing pin in the top drawer, right hand side, near the front, with the box of ammo. I'll keep the gun loaded for quick use—just slap in the pin, take off the safety and squeeze the trigger."

"Okay." Dena realized that they had wandered from the subject of Jennifer's maturity, and was tempted to return to it. But she knew that topic would take years of patient work, and she had a more pressing problem that she could do something effective about. Nor were her motives entirely unselfish, she thought with a smile. "Now will you do me a favor?"

"Sure."

She brandished her drink. "Now that you've got *me* loaded, for quick use ..." She set the drink down and began unbuttoning his shirt. "Why don't you, uh, slap me across the pins—" She tugged the shirt out of his trousers. "—take off my safeties—" She licked his neck. "—and squee-eeze *my* trigger?" She looked into his eyes from a distance measured in millimeters. "I might just go off."

"Well," he said, reaching out his tongue to lick her lips with infinite gentleness, "I don't often meet a woman of your caliber ..."

Her hand touched his left thigh, quite high up on the inside. Russell's tailor would have said that he "dressed on the left." "Talk about high caliber," she murmured, "I think I just found a .44 Magnum." His own fingers were brushing against the base of her throat, and she preened exactly as a cat would have done. "Now, a man with a special gun like that needs a special holster—and I've got just the thing."

"My darling," Russell said, bringing his hands along her shoulders and down her arms, so that his palms brushed the sides of her breasts, "I have always maintained that you have *much* more than just the thing."

"My place or yours?" Maintaining her grip on the bulge in his trousers, she led him back indoors.

One happy and energetic hour later, Dena lay back in the darkness and listened to Russell's breathing returning to normal and congratulated herself on her intuition.

She had been very surprised when her husband casually mentioned that he had helped José defraud Shaw of drug money. It was absolutely atypical behaviour for him. The Russell she knew would have stood back and had as little as possible to do with anything so unsavoury and dangerous. Dena had sampled cocaine a few times in her younger days, as had most of her contemporaries in the dance world; she had stopped because she simply did not like it very much. But Russell, she knew, had never tried it. He still would not share a joint with her. And given his personality and lifestyle and social class, one would have expected his sympathies to lie more with Shaw than with

José. Though she knew Russell had been born in the Bronx, he had moved to Long Island at age eight, when his father's ship had come in, and had lived in what used to be called "gentler circumstances" ever since. . . .

That had been the point in her thought-train at which she had seen the answer. Close contact with violence can make a man revert, in some ways, to his childhood. Russell had made of himself a cultured, civilized man—but somewhere down in there were the remnants of a New York street kid. Badly frightened, and shamed by his helplessness, he was subconsciously seeking powerful allies—and José must look much more like the eight-year-old Russell's image of manhood than Shaw. . . .

In short, his masculinity was threatened even more than he had admitted to her in his opening words. And there is one good way to deal with shaky masculinity—or rather, she corrected herself, hundreds of lovely ways that all come under the same general heading. And there, she thought, is a pretty good impromptu pun.

The vigour and intensity of his response had convinced her that her insight was correct, and that her cure was effective; she felt contentment in more than just the physical sense.

Then suddenly she remembered something that had happened earlier this afternoon, before the trouble started. Perhaps there was one more task she might work on tonight. A long-term project, like the one about making him see that Jennifer was growing up under his nose. If she could just do this deftly enough to not get caught at it—

"I think I'm going to like this apartment," she said aloud.

"Me too," Russell said lazily. "Much nicer'n I expected."

"Of course, it's still a New York apartment. Those damned roaches. I've got to do something about them."

"Have you figured out where they're coming from?" Russell asked, falling into the trap.

"Yeah," she said sleepily, faking a yawn. "Got it pinned down. Whole city of 'em back there. All interconnected, between the stove and the fridge. . . ." And although she wanted to hold her breath, she made it deepen as if toward sleep, to cut the conversation off there.

"The stove and the fridge—" he repeated, as she had hoped he would, and trailed off as she had hoped he would, remembering as she had prayed he would his own words from this afternoon about redesigning those two appliances. Dena girl, she told herself, you are such a clever bitch that you ought to be ugly, just to make things fair. She could almost *hear* him thinking about his idea, and when, ten minutes later, he slipped carefully out of bed and left the room in search of pencil and paper, she had to roll over to hide the smile.

She and Russell had been married for five years. Extreme success with some of his early designs—including the solar-powered air conditioner which had kept their car cool over two thousand kilometers of summer driving, functioning only when it was needed—had allowed him to retire almost ten years before; he need never work again unless it suited him. Dena and Jennifer were quietly determined between them that before long it would suit him. It was one of the strongest bonds cementing stepmother and daughter: a shared conspiracy to bring joy to the man they both loved. And just as Dena had hoped, the sight of his childhood home on the horizon had woken old instincts, started the long-unused creative engine in his mind.

Perhaps, she thought, the engine would cough fitfully a few times and die. It had before. But she was going to keep jump starting it, and if necessary she would push the damned thing up to speed and pop the clutch.

Feeling so pleased with herself that she completely failed to notice the turmoil in her own subconscious, Dena snuggled more comfortably into her pillow, clenched her thighs around the memory of their lovemaking, and drifted into sleep.

She dreamed. Since the dream was not recorded anywhere in her conscious or unconscious memory banks, it had no more—and no less—existence than the sound of a falling tree which nobody hears.

She was back home in Halifax, on Gottingen Street, the shabby half-kilometer strip on and around which the city's black population had tended to center, since the forcible relocation of Africville in the early '60's. It was a street which had attracted and repelled Dena all her childhood, an alternate world in which she did not thoroughly understand the rules, a world whose rules her parents did not want her to learn. She walked past the Casino Theatre, saw the posters for the usual porn double feature and felt the familiar tingle of disgusted intrigue; ahead a group of black boys stood outside a tavern, laughing and strutting, and she hoped they would hit on her and was prepared to draw blood if they dared try. But as she approached the tavern, Gottingen Street melted and ran and flowed like a time-lapse film of entropic decay, became East 125th Street, and she was no longer walking but sitting in a stationary car, and the boys were surrounding the car, menacing and gleeful. Her child was crying, and her lower back hurt.

She became a tigress, burst from the car, confronted the attackers, brandishing an enormous straight-edged razor. "Come on, *chumps*," she snarled, the black Amazon in her wrath.

They burst out laughing.

"Woo-ee!" the middle one said mockingly, pantomiming great fear, "danger on the set!" His face flowed like the street had, became the face of Jerome Turner, her old lover and dance partner. "Look here, Dena-mite," he said, using his old pet name for her, "You come on bad-ass nigger like that, maybe you gonna fool white people or pakis. But a *real* bad-ass nigger see through you from jump-street." Suddenly he dropped the jive accents and spoke in his natural voice. "All I see is a shade with a tan, and a razor in her han'."

The razor wilted and drooped; she flung it away. "I'm blacker than you are, Jerome!"

"No you aren't. Your skin, maybe, but not you."

She remembered this conversation, knew how she would convince him. She would dance. She would strut, shuffle, shake, snap her body around in those funky steps that white dancers could imitate but never master, and then he would have to admit that in her bones and sinews where it counted she was black. "Watch this."

And as she began her lower back spasmed. Pain shot down her right leg clear to the ankle. She tried to adapt her dance to the injury, and the left knee went; she nearly fell. She managed to complete the series, but it was a stiff, feeble parody—the way a white person would have danced it.

Jerome laughed. "About as black as pharmaceutical cocaine. Just look at yourself."

She looked down, and it was true. Her skin was changing colour, getting lighter. It was still Negroid, but barely so; as she watched, it reached sun-tanned Caucasian, then bleached further until she was as pale as Jennifer. She whirled toward Jennifer, and her daughter was not in the car any more, was just disappearing around the distant corner in Russell's arms, waving and smiling back at Dena.

She turned back to Jerome, angry and afraid. "Give me back my black," she said, voice dangerously soft.

He rolled his eyes and grinned. "Give *back?*"

"You took my black. Now give it back," she screamed.

The surrounding youths became a rap-group, chanting her words like Grandmaster Flash and the Furious Five. Someone improvised a fingerpop bass line, another played conga with a pair of trash cans; a call-and-answer chorus developed:

$$\quad 1 \qquad 2 \qquad\quad 3 \qquad\quad 4 \qquad\qquad\quad 2$$
*"You **took** my **black** now* ___ *give it* **back** *You* **took** *my* **black** *now*
___ *my* **black** ___ ___ **gimme***backmy* **black** ___

Over this foundation Jerome improvised, strutting and leering:

"You want your black back that's too bad
 Can't give back what you never really had
 It isn't where you been or the color of your skin
 Or even how you like to sin—it's just a feelin' from within
 You never been used you never been warned
 You never been abused and you never been scorned
 Never been cheated and you never been afflicted
 Never been mistreated and you never been addicted
 Never gone hungry and you never been cold
 Never been rented let alone been sold
 Never been shabby let alone been naked
 Never needed anything so bad you hadda take it

Never hated anything so bad you hadda break it
Never had a child that you knew could never make it
If you see that you're whiter than you think you oughta be
Complain to your Mama and your Daddy, not me!"

He repeated the last line several times. Dena turned and
saw without surprise that her mother and father were
now sitting in the car, regarding the horde of dancing,
chanting youths with distaste and another emotion she
could not identify. She approached the car, melted through
the door, knelt on the back seat leaning forward between
them. Her back still hurt.

"Mama? Daddy?"

"Yes, dear."

"What color am I?"

"Dena, a person's color is the least important thing
about them."

"Yes, but what color am I?"

"Child, I'm color-blind—I just can't tell."

"Mama, tell me!"

"I just couldn't say."

Her back hurt too much to hold her position. Angrily
she lay back on the seat and closed her eyes. *"Tell me!"*

Outside, the boys were still rapping; the volume of their
chanting increased and drowned out any answer her mother
might have made. Dena screwed her eyes tighter, and
when she opened them again she was on stage somewhere,
a hall she didn't recognize, and she *didn't know what piece
this was*, her partner was waiting for her, improvising
frantically as he waited for her to snap out of it and get
back into the dance but *she didn't know what piece this
was*, the costume was no clue and her fourth lumbar was
pinching the sciatic again sending terrifying pain down
the outside of her right leg and the left knee still felt
wobbly, she couldn't dance this even if she could remember what it was. She was a pro, she kept moving, improvising like her partner, you *never* freeze up on stage, but it
was no good, her improv clashed with his and as he came
closer she misinterpreted and then couldn't get out of the
way in time and his elbow caught her full in the face. It
did not hurt at all, but the impact spun her offstage and

into the water. The last thing she saw, in mid-air, was the angry face of her partner, and he was Russell. But Russell can't dance, she thought, and then the water crashed over her and she sank like a stone, noting as she sank that her pale skin was visible even in the black, black water . . .

When she woke, Russell was beside her, in deep sleep. She slipped out of bed without waking him, shrugged on a robe and donned slippers, and went out into the main room which served as living room, dining room, and kitchen. Her back hurt from three days on the road.

"Morning, Jennifer."

"Hi, Mom. Was he good?"

The question was rhetorical, facetious, and familiar. Dena gave the ritual answer: a wiggle of the hips, and a "He was dyno-mite!" Then she took in what she was seeing and hearing and smelling. "Jennifer, you angel, you have been *busy*."

Jennifer had located the carton which held kitchen gear, and cleared several heavy items off the table. It was set with paper plates, silverware, cups and condiments. English muffin halves were in the toaster waiting to be popped down into heat; eggs were sitting out on the counter, by the stove, which held the egg-poacher and the Melitta pot, into which Jennifer was just pouring the last slug of boiling water. She set the water-pot back on the burner, turned off the gas, and got orange juice from the fridge. "That supermarket where we got the food really sucks," she said cheerfully.

"You know I don't like that kind of language," Dena said automatically.

"Aw, we're in New York now."

"All the more reason to preserve the amenities."

"You're right," Jennifer decided. "But it really does suck."

Dena sighed. "I'll tell you what. Every time you make breakfast like this you can talk as crudely as you like. Until your father gets up. And don't you say it, girl, I've heard that pun." Caffeine tropism drew her toward the coffee. "In what particular respect does the store suck?"

"Two eggs were cracked, the English muffins are stale,

and the milk's bad—the coffee cream's okay, though. Why do they call them 'English' muffins, anyway?"

Dena picked up a half-muffin; it was, as advertised, going stale. "Because if you throw them like a frisbee, with enough English on them, they'll always come back to you."

"And they call it French toast because it's so sweet to the tongue," Jennifer finished with a giggle.

Dena arched an eyebrow. "What do *you* know about French stuff, girl?"

Jennifer crossed her eyes and grimaced wistfully. "A girl can dream."

Dena grinned. "You lie. You were French-kissing boys before I met you, I bet."

"I'm not the kind that tells. Shall I put the eggs on for all three of us?"

"Just us two." The coffee was finished dripping; Dena poured gratefully and spooned up the first sips. Then she leaned close to Jennifer and whispered, just in case the smell of coffee had Russell stirring: "He worked last night."

Jennifer froze, then whipped around eagerly. "That fridge-stove thing?" An expert would probably have ruled that her voice was, technically speaking, a whisper, but it carried better than normal speech might have.

"Shush. Yes, I think so. I planted the hook and 'went to sleep,' and after a while he got up and came out here. My," she went on in conversational volume, "you make good coffee."

"Now if I could only stand to drink the stuff," Jennifer replied in equally loud tones, and dropped again into a whisper. "Evidence. There should be evidence around here somewhere—and I don't see it. Notes, sketches, something."

"For sure?"

"Hell yes—Daddy leaves paper behind like worm-tracks. Let's look!"

Dena found the sketchpad and pencil on the floor in front of the couch, but there was nothing written on the pad. "Damn, he must have pulled a blank."

Jennifer took the pad, sighted along it at an angle. "No! Look, there are impressions on the top sheet, and some pages are missing. Now let's see—" She sat on the couch, pantomimed her father sketching. She shook her head, scowled ferociously, tore off the top sheet, crumpled it with her left hand—and automatically tossed it behind her and to the left. The couch was near the corner of the room, offset from the lefthand wall by perhaps half a meter where one of Figueroa's end tables had formerly stood. The crumpled piece of paper richocheted in the corner and dropped quite naturally into the hidden space between couch and wall. Jennifer and Dena exchanged a glance. The girl got up and pulled the couch sideways. "Jackpot," she cried, snatching up nearly a dozen balls of paper. "Oh Mother, you did it."

"Maybe." Dena unrolled one of the balls and studied it dubiously: three square boxes interconnected by a spaghetti of arrows, surrounded by copious notes in an absolutely illegible hand. "Let's not celebrate until he produces some sketches worth keeping."

"The only sketches he saves are the ones he sends to the patent attorneys. Believe me, he's working again."

"Are you sure? You were only six the last time he turned anything out."

"I remember. I remember good. I mean, 'well.'" She tossed a couple of the balls up to the ceiling and caught them happily. "Come on, let's cover our tracks."

"Oh—yes. Breakfast is getting cold."

By the time Russell awoke, Dena and Jennifer were well into the task of unpacking and distributing their possessions, Jennifer doing all the bending and heavy lifting without having been asked.

Russell was always useless when he first woke up. But both women knew how to deal with him: they ignored him and stayed out of his way while he botched his own eggs and toast, firmly suppressing their natural urge to giggle. As always, breakfast recapitulated phylogeny. He reached the vertebrate stage halfway through his meal, and was nearly human by the time he finished. A second cup of coffee completed the resurrection. He cleaned up after himself and joined them at their work, throwing Jennifer a smile the first time their paths crossed.

Dena enjoyed the morning that followed. Spending time

with her family always gave her a warm happy glow, a deep pleasure in having not only a family, but such a nice one. Her husband was a special man, who gave her what she needed, and needed what she had to give; her daughter was a special young woman whom she had always loved, and who had always loved her—at first because Russell did, and then because Dena loved Russell, and at last for her own sake. Dena appreciated what she had in her family—and only hoped that it would be enough to fill her life when she could no longer dance. Because she had no idea what else to do with herself . . .

José came by with a bootleg TV converter which he connected to a bootleg dish hookup that apparently came with the apartment. The 50 cm dish on the building's roof provided them with exactly the same channels they got at home, from the same STI satellite. He told them where to go to get Figueroa's phone disconnected and their own installed (literally around the corner, thank God). He explained about mail, and where the nearest laundromat and deli and supermarket were, and where the best laundromat and deli and supermarket were, and a number of other basic New York survival tips. "You keep one hand in your pocket all the time. It never comes out. The mugger is a businessman. What do you got in that pocket? He don't know. It ain't worth the risk to find out, because somebody stupider is gonna come along in a minute, catch?"

Dena took him aside discreetly. "José, my husband told me about his arrangement with you, regarding Jennifer."

"Yes, ma'am."

"I just want to say that I think it's one of his better ideas." She looked him square in the eye and held his gaze. "I trust you with my daughter—I just wanted you to know that."

"Thanks, Miz Grant."

"Dena."

"Thanks, Dena. You want your daughter to know?"

Dena thought quickly. No—it could not be kept secret, not even clumsily. "Yes. Look, one tip: her name is Jennifer. Not Jen, not Jenny—Jennifer, got it? Catch?"

He smiled. "I figured that out."

She felt even better. "This is going to work out okay, I think. *Jennifer?*"

Jennifer came at once. "Yes, Mama?"

"Jennifer, you've met José, I believe?"

The girl looked at José, inclined her head. "Yes. Hello, José."

"Hi, Jennifer."

"Darling, José is going to look after you whenever your father is busy."

Jennifer was expressionless. "Like a babysitter?"

"No, dear," Dena said hastily. "More like a bodyguard."

"Oh." Jennifer seemed to field the novel concept well. "I see." She turned back to José. "Are you dangerous?"

He did not crack a smile, though Dena believed it cost him some effort. "Yes, Jennifer. I am very dangerous."

She looked him up and down, making no attempt to be polite about it. "Show me."

He blinked, then slowly nodded.

The three went outside to the garden, collecting Russell on the way. José had them stand just outside the door, then walked across the broad patio to the edge of the garden proper. It was marked by a border made of small half-bricks set diagonally in the earth. He loosened a half-brick with a kick and tugged it free, tossed it to Jennifer. It was an excellent toss, slow and high enough to let her see it coming, not so slow as to give her time to panic. She caught it easily, then looked surprised and pleased with herself. It was the size of a cigarette pack.

"Wait a few seconds," he told her. "Take your time, walk around a little, talk to your mother. When you're ready—" He turned his back to her, folded his arms across his chest. "—throw that sucker at my head as hard as you can. Try to surprise me."

All three Grants frowned.

"It's okay," José insisted. "Try to knock my head off. I'm close enough, ain't I?"

"Mother," Jennifer said, "he *can't* be serious."

Dena opened her mouth to reply—and Jennifer let fly. She put her shoulder into it, and as Dena drew breath to cry out, she saw that the girl had apparently misjudged her trajectory—the brick was going to catch José square in the ass. And then José moved.

Even Dena's dancer's eye could not unravel exactly what he did. She *thought* she saw him separate his body into three components and move them in impossibly different directions. The others could have seen only a blur. Then José was facing them, his arms—again, or still—folded across his chest. "You're a sneaky person," he told Jennifer approvingly.

Russell was looking around. "Where is the brick?"

"In his shirt pocket," Jennifer said smugly.

José looked impressed. "You're gonna be a *handful*." He produced the brick from the pocket. Dena laughed and applauded, and Russell joined in. "But if you got such a good eye, tell me something."

"What?"

"Which hand did I throw the knife with?"

Jennifer frowned. "What knife?"

"That one." José pointed—and there was indeed a knife growing out of the furthest of the two trees, at chest-height. The trunk at that height was about the thickness of a man's arm.

Jennifer's eyes grew round, and she looked crestfallen. "I don't know. I was watching the brick."

"Let me tell you something about New York," José said seriously. "You can't stop lookin' around you just because there's a brick comin' at your head or somethin'."

"José," Russell said, "that was impressive. Can you teach me any of that?"

The boy looked politely dubious. "I could teach you to throw a knife good—anyway better'n you probably can now. The rest I can't teach. You just gotta spend enough time afraid. Look, I gotta get back to work. Are you people squared away here?"

"Yes, José," Dena said. "Thank you very much for everything. I won't worry about my daughter now when I'm at work."

José recovered his knife, replaced the half-brick carefully in its socket, tamped earth around it, and left, nodding to Jennifer on his way out. She hesitated, then nodded back.

*   *   *

After lunch Russell looked around and smiled. "By Thor's thundermug," he said, "I do believe we are unpacked."

"Oh boy," Jennifer cried. "Let's go see Grandpa!"

"Well," Russell said, looking at Dena, "that is next on the list."

"I'm sorry, hon," she said, doing her best to look sorry. "I have to get downtown and get plugged into rehearsals."

"So soon?"

"The show opens in less than seven *weeks*, darling. Everybody else has been rehearsing for three days already. I really should have gone in this morning and finished unpacking tonight."

"Well—I guess we could wait for the weekend to drive out to Dad's."

Dena cast about frantically for an objection.

"No," Jennifer said, and Dena could have hugged her. "I want to see Grandpa *today*. I've never *seen* his new house, and Sophie says her mother says Orient Point is almost as pretty as the Fundy Shore."

"And it *would* be sensible to get the car stashed safe outside the city," Dena added. The Grants had agreed that it was insane to keep a car on Manhattan, and intended to leave it parked at Russell's father's home out on Long Island for the duration of their stay. "You two go on ahead. I'll see your folks later—at the very least they'll be coming in for the show, and there'll be plenty of time when it's over. Give your father a hug for me." She saw that he was trying to frame an objection, so she kept talking. "I'll call the Long Island Railroad and find out what's the last train you can take back from Orient Point. You and Jennifer plot your course out there."

Map-reading and navigation were tasks Russell enjoyed; as she had expected, he got so involved in planning the journey that he shelved—for good—the question of whether he wished to make it. He and Jennifer huddled together over the computer, folding out the liquid-crystal monitor display and plugging in the tiny card which held the best Greater New York transportion data they had been able to buy (information no more than a year out of date), while Dena used the previous tenant's still-active phone line to call Lisa Dann.

"Hello, you have reached Dann'space, home of the DannCers Company, and no one is available to take your call. For a complete schedule of our classes and performances, you may call D-A-N-N-C-E-R; or the same information can be accessed from Dataworks, NYIN, or The Net. When you hear the beep, you will be able to leave a message of 60 seconds, and we'll return your call as soon as possible. Thank you."

"Lisa, it's Dena St. Claire. Pick up if you're there, honey— I'll wait."

Four seconds. Then—"Dena? Dena, is that you?"

"In the flesh."

"In the flush, if you're really in New York. And you'd better be, you miserable bitch—you're late for rehearsal!"

Dena grinned, feeling truly at ease for the first time since she had passed through the South Bronx. "I love you too, Lisa."

"God, it's good to hear your voice. Listen, Chocolate Eclair, I'm serious, if your ass isn't down here in twenty minutes, I'm gonna break in a new pair of character shoes on it. There's a Dena-sized hole in this dance, and about fifty-sixty hugs and kisses here with your name on 'em cluttering up the place."

"I'll be there as quick as I can, hon, but there's a few—"

"Woman, if you ain't coming, get going!"

"All right, I'll grab a cab—"

"No! Brush the hay out of your hair, cousin."

"What's wrong with a cab?"

"Anyone comes into this neighbourhood in a cab, it's like wearing a sign says 'I have interesting amounts of cash money on my person.' Where are you, the East Side in the 30s, right?" She gave Dena subway directions. "It's a ten minute ride, I'll give you five minutes." The phone went dead.

On her way downtown, Dena kept her eyes open for signs of racial tension. She saw them everywhere she looked. Whites, singly and in groups, seemed to make an effort to avoid the gaze of blacks, tended to give way to them in any pedestrian encounter. Black youths seemed to go out of their way to hassle whites. Interracial groupings were rare, and almost never seemed truly friendly or relaxed. Police officers of either colour seemed harassed and alert.

Something not-right nagged at Dena's subconscious; at last she puzzled it out. The racial mix was wrong for the time of day. When Dena had first come to New York, in 1982, the population of Manhattan had been seventy-five percent white—*by day*. At night, when the commuters had all fled their offices for the suburbs, the island had been forty-five percent black, with another twenty-odd percent composed of Puerto Ricans, Cubans, Chinese and other non-whites, leaving Caucasians a minority group.

The population mix that Dena encountered on the streets and in the subway now would have been about right for 1982 Manhattan—if it had been late evening. But it was early afternoon on a weekday.

She began paying attention to the whites she saw. The division which had been visible in 1982 was now marked and unmistakable. There were, with few exceptions, two kinds of white people on Manhattan these days: the wealthy, and the poor. The middle-class were gone to the outer boroughs and the suburbs, and even in these hard economic times apparently did not want work badly enough to venture into the inner-city for it in great numbers.

Which explained Dena's other observation: that there were more middle-class blacks visible than she had expected. To be sure, they were distinctly *lower*-middle-class, hanging on grimly to an economic rung which these days grew slipperier by the hour. But there were more black men and women in business attire than Dena had ever seen in her life before, walking with the hurried stride of those with appointments to keep and clients to meet and deals to cut. To her mild surprise they—and she—did not seem to arouse disdain or disgust in the lower-class blacks among whom they moved. She saw a balding black man in a pearl grey suit splitting a joint with a black messenger-boy in a doorway—which in 1982 would have been implausible. She noted that both men had their heads shaved. A new fad?

Like all dance studios, Dann's was up several flights of stairs. Dena took them slowly, mindful of lower back and knee. At the top she knocked on a frosted glass door and smiled at the security camera above it. Almost at once the door buzzed open, and as she went through it she just had time to brace herself. Lisa Dann came at her in a dead run and hugged her like a linebacker sacking the quarterback. "Dena!"

"Lisa!"

"You're late, you shit. Christ, it's good to see you! Get changed!" She kissed Dena, smacked her buttock, and stood back. "You're going to like this group, I've got some good people this time. One of 'em you know, I think—Jerry Turner, weren't you and he in Janine's pickup company together in the old days? Oh, and Phyllis and Sue Ann say hello. Come on, get it in gear, girl, we'll talk later." Squeezing Dena's arm, she turned and raced down the short poster-and-flyer-bedecked corridor which led to the studio proper—

—leaving Dena with her mouth hanging open.

Jerome?

She walked down the hall after Lisa, stopped where she could see the whole studio. Lisa had already reached the far end of the room where the big mirrors were. All seven dancers were facing her, their backs to Dena. She recognized Jerome at once. He was dressed in red shorts and a black t-shirt with the sleeves raggedly ripped off, brown leg warmers pooled around his ankles. The dreadlocks she remembered were gone, he was shaving his head now, but there was no mistaking his characteristic stance: legs spread a little too wide, weight on the balls of his feet, hands on hips, jaw thrust out challengingly.

I'll be damned, she thought weakly, it's him all right.

The convergence of his thighs and forearms drew the eye automatically to his ass, and it was as splendid as she remembered. She had a sudden vivid sense-memory of nibbling on it—followed by one just as vivid of kicking it so hard that she wondered if the footprint still showed.

Dena had perhaps as few scars on her soul as a North American black female can have, but Jerome represented one of the largest that she did have. Seven years before,

Jerome had been her lover, her first black lover. The relationship had been stormy and passionate and had ended explosively; she had felt the hurt of it so deeply and for so long that the thought of working with him again shook her.

But only intellectually. Five years of a very good marriage had intervened. Dena examined her own reactions very carefully, to determine whether any threat to her marriage existed, and decided there was none. True, her pulse was up and her cheeks hot—but she felt neither a lifting of the heart nor a tingling of the crotch. Her mind ran an instant comprehensive comparison of Russell and Jerome, and she knew that she had a better deal going than she could ever have had with Jerome. It might or might not be unpleasant to work with him again, but it would not be dangerous.

With that realization, her pulse already returning to normal, she turned and retraced her steps to the changing room, already planning how to tell Russell about this so that he would not worry.

CHAPTER THREE

"Children's programming on commercial U.S. television is so one-sided in its depiction of white, male characters that 'it can only be seen as a major barrier in the battle for recognition and respect for minorities in this country,' a public-interest group study says.

"In fact, children's programs have fallen behind adult shows in the frequency with which they feature minority as well as female characters, 'and both groups are portrayed in a more stereotyped manner in children's programming than in prime-time programming,' the study found . . .

"Of the 1,145 TV characters that appeared during the 38 hours [of the survey], only 42 were black . . . stated another way, 3.7% of the characters in the sample were black . . ."

—AP dispatch, summer 1982

"There was an old woman who lived in a slum,
Upscale-demographics-wise, strictly ho-hum.
But she had lots of kids, and they all wanted toys,
Plastic dolls for the girls, plastic guns for the boys.
And they watched our commercials, and begged her to buy
Lazer Death, Hunny Buns, Killer Zap, Kuty-Pie,
Spyshooter and KupKake and Elmo the Elf
(WELFARE MOTHER GOES SANE, MURDERS TODDLERS
    AND SELF)."

—Sean Kelly and Rick Meyerowitz,
National Lampoon

*   *   *

Jennifer preferred riding in the back seat. More privacy, better visibility, above all more room—for she had not yet quite reached the age at which it is possible to sit still for any length of time (although she had reached the age at which she tried). Fortunately her father had designed the family car for comfort many years earlier. Both front and rear seat belts were gimbaled on sliding tracks, which allowed passengers to be securely restrained in any position they chose. A front-seat passenger, for instance, could snuggle as close as she liked to the driver without unbuckling—and Jennifer could lie full-length on the back seat if she chose, then sit up and slide from side to side at will.

At the moment she was lying down, feet up on the righthand window, dress pooled around her lap, hands folded across her belly. Her eyes were closed; she was trying to deduce, from the accelerations she experienced, what the traffic around them was doing, measuring her success by how well she could anticipate new vectors. It was a game for avoiding thinking.

"Better put those legs down, princess," her father said. "Or cover 'em up."

"Why, Daddy!" she said, opening her eyes and grinning. "Incestuous feelings already! What's going to happen when I reach puberty?"

Her father sighed. "In the first place, *I* know you're my daughter Jenniflower—but my subconscious doesn't, and if it keeps making me sneak peeks in the rear-view mirror, we're going to have one of those Oedipus Wrecks you keep hearing about."

Jennifer groaned theatrically, secretly tickled.

"And in the second place that sixteen-wheeler in the right lane is *not* pacing us to annoy the people behind him."

She opened her eyes, shrieked, and was instantly vertical, dress covering her legs.

"Daddy! Do something!"

"For instance?"

She gave the truck driver her very best Withering Glare,

the one Dena had coached her with, and to her immense satisfaction it worked perfectly. The driver blushed, looked away hastily, and accelerated. She watched his truck pull ahead until it was out of sight. The driver had looked young, and Puerto Rican—

"Men are animals."

"What are women? Plants? Birds? Fish?"

"You could have growled at him, Daddy. Shaken your fist."

"Why? Because he had the nerve to obey a reflex?"

"So if a man peeks at me, it's my fault?"

"No, honey. It's nature's fault. But it's your responsibility."

She thought that over. Being a woman was complicated, and she wasn't sure she liked it. Women had all the responsibility, had to do the choosing, and Russell had once said that making choices was the hardest thing people did.

On the other hand, as Dena had once said, you seldom had much trouble getting your snow shoveled or your car started.

This was getting too close to what she had been avoiding thinking about. "Could I have the map back here, please?"

Her father fed the map display to the screen on the back of the front seat. She lay down again—with her legs out flat and covered—and fiddled with the controls. Long Island, she learned, looks startlingly like a miniature version of Nova Scotia. Both land masses resemble a fish swimming west, with forking tail to the east; both lie to the south and east of their respective mainland; the chief difference is that Nova Scotia is physically connected to mainland New Brunswick (about where the fish would keep its wallet if it had one) while Long Island is a true island.

"Chief difference," that is, to an observer in orbit. At ground level, the resemblance is almost nonexistent—for Nova Scotia has fifteen times the land area of Long Island, and about a tenth the population. Although Jennifer confirmed that they had already passed through Brooklyn and Queens (the two innermost Long Island counties which are formally considered boroughs of New York City) and were well into Nassau County, she had so far seen little out her window which suggested that they had left the city behind them yet. New York was eating the Long Island fish, and had swallowed the western half already. "When do the suburbs start?" she asked.

"About six AM," her father answered. "And they're usually on the Long Island Railroad or the Distressway by seven-thirty."

"Daddy, your jokes are awful. I mean: how soon does it stop being city around here?"

"I'm not sure, honey. *This* used to be suburbs back when I lived here. Hang on, Suffolk County should get a little more rustic. And by the time we get to Grandpa's you'll think you're in Nova Scotia."

She switched off the map and thought about Grandpa. She loved him dearly and, since she saw him about once every three years, looked forward eagerly to this visit. But his wife had divorced him five years ago; Jennifer had met his second wife a few years back, on their honeymoon in Nova Scotia, and had taken an instant dislike to the woman. Regina had not seemed to Jennifer to treat Wilson Grant with sufficient respect, and furthermore had displayed to Dena that breed of overpoliteness which one uses with social inferiors to whom one must be gracious. Worst of all, she was one of those adults who think that they can relate to children as equals, and are mistaken. Jennifer hoped that Grandpa was happy—and did not see how he could be. She wished passionately that his first wife Anna would give up journalism, come back from Germany, and throw the upstart Regina out; Jennifer thoroughly approved of Anna as a grandmother. But Russell had assured her that this was highly unlikely.

She understood Dena's reluctance to come along on this visit, was glad her stepmother had found a way to duck out—but she was going to miss Dena. She was not at all sure she would be able to enjoy this without help.

As Russell had predicted, the surrounding territory gradually became less urban as they penetrated deeper into Long Island's easternmost county, Suffolk. Buildings shortened, trees grew taller, and the murderous traffic began to ease up slightly. They sped on in silence, having exhausted most topics of conversation and all the songs to which they both knew the words on the long drive from Halifax. Jennifer passed the time by proving theorems of Euclidean geometry with jabberwocky logic on the computer screen; Russell pulled his headphones down from the ceiling and listened to music.

Jennifer was just deciding that if you didn't look *too* hard through the trees and notice the suburban tracts beyond and the utter absence of mountains in any direction, you might indeed pretend you were on Nova Scotia's Bicentennial Highway, when her father disengaged his headphones and let the ceiling reel them back up. "Jenniflower?"

"Yes, Daddy?"

"About our drive through Harlem yesterday . . ."

She sat up slowly. "I'm straight on that. Momma and I talked about it. It's history, Daddy."

"Then let's rewrite history."

"Huh?"

"I'm very proud of the way you conducted yourself: you were brave. Nonetheless I don't plan to mention it to your grandparents."

"Oh. You're right. No sense scaring Grandpa."

"It's Mrs. Grandpa I'm worried about." "Mrs. Grandpa" was their private name for Regina; Russell knew how Jennifer felt about her.

"Her? I don't care if *she's* worried."

"You should," he said darkly.

"Why?"

"Never mind. Just go along with me, all right? We had a nice uneventful drive to New York."

"Okay."

Orient Point was one of the Last Outposts of Gracious Living on the island, and intended to remain so forever. Here a handful of Long Island's wealthiest citizens, driven eastward by the inexorable tide of middle-class humanity spilling out of the city, had made their last stand with the sea at their backs. They protected themselves with a wall of money, which expressed itself in tough zoning laws, incredible property values and tax structure, and a physical wall of patrolled fence; the community had been enclosed for several years. The Grants had to identify themselves to a hard-eyed private cop, who checked them carefully against his Expected Visitors roster before opening the gate and giving them directions. Three more cops were visible; all four were armed. Jennifer guessed that they would have checked twice as thoroughly if Dena had been in the car.

She looked around as they drove down the blacktop road through Orient Point. If you looked out to sea, you might indeed think you were somewhere along the Fundy Shore. The houses were no closer together than they would have been there, gardens were just as frequent, Connecticut on the horizon could just as easily have been New Brunswick. But the houses were much too new and well kept, the lawns too neatly manicured, the gardens too small and impractical, the cars too new and expensive. Farmers and fishermen did not live here. And of course, if you looked over your shoulder the illusion was gone, for there was nothing resembling a mountain from one end of Long Island to the other, and its own sand dunes and wild rose hips were rarely to be found in Nova Scotia.

Nonetheless Jennifer began to enjoy herself; she was a sea-and-sky fan, however they might be decorated. And Long Island beaches were sand, not rock—that would be fun. A shame it was too late in the day for a swim. But perhaps just as well—the only bathing suit Jennifer had brought with her was the one she had bought just before leaving Halifax, and although Dena had overseen and approved the purchase, Russell had not yet seen it and would certainly hit the roof when he did. Jennifer herself was not certain she was ready to wear it outside a dressing room.

Wilson Grant's house stood on three acres of land overlooking Long Island Sound. Trees to east and west gave privacy from neighbours, and privacy from passersby was assured by a long series of two-meter-high pineboard and steel baffles set back from the road by about fifty meters. They were staggered so that they allowed maximum passage of wind and sunlight, yet allowed a view of the interior only to a man clearly and unmistakably trespassing. This not-quite-fence was bisected by the house, a wide one-story with built-on garage and boat shed and a large U-shaped driveway. Wilson Grant knelt in the driveway, tinkering with the carburetor of a Moped. He looked up at once when he heard the car slow, smiled when he recognized it, wiped his hands on a towel, and came to meet them.

He was just as Jennifer remembered him, short, slim, slightly pot-bellied, with a full head of snow white hair and a pepper-and-salt Van Dyke beard, and his eyes still held that mischievous twinkle she recalled so well. Her first impulse was to cry, *"Grandpa!"*, leap from the car before it stopped rolling, and hurl herself up into his arms for their usual greeting, The Battle of the Kisses—a ritual in which each attempted to kiss the other into unconsciousness, and which Jennifer always won. Barely in time she remembered that she was thirteen years old now. With an enormous effort she sat still, and when her father had shut off the car she got out the way she imagined a princess would leave a coach and waited demurely for her grandfather to approach her.

He had clearly been expecting a Battle of the Kisses, but he took in the situation at once and shifted gears smoothly. He came near, bowed lower than she had thought possible for a man of his age, straightened, and said, "Hello, Jennifer. It's wonderful to see you again. You look simply ravishing," with his face perfectly straight.

Immensely pleased, she curtsied in return. "Thank you, Grandfather," she said formally. "It's wonderful to see you too. Your new home is quite lovely."

"Thank you, my dear, but I'm afraid it is nowhere near so beautiful as it seemed before you arrived." He took her hand and kissed it. She felt a tingle of pleasure begin in her scalp and race to her toes. Oh God, she thought, I bet I'm blushing, oh shit. "Excuse me, won't you, while I say hello to your driver?"

He turned to Russell then and the two men hugged long and hard.

"Hi, Pop. You're looking great."

"And you look like a man who's driven the length of Long Island. You're just in time to help me out with a desperate problem."

"Name it."

"I've just learned there's too much gin in the house. It's an ugly situation, but it has to be dealt with. Can I count on you?"

"Isn't there something in the Bible about the gins of the fathers who are visited by their sons?"

Wilson Grant winced and turned back to Jennifer. "And perhaps a split of vermouth for you, my dear?"

She was fiercely proud that he was asking her and not her father. She wanted to peek at Russell to see what he thought of the idea, but refused to let herself. "That would be nice," she replied, and at once worried that the wine would make her lose her poise. She resolved to take tiny sips.

"Let's go in then."

"Shouldn't we get this heap stored before we get comfortable?" Russell said, indicating the car.

The elder Grant frowned. "I did my best. But you turned out practical just the same."

They parked the car out behind the boat shed; it would not mind exposure in the least and sunlight would keep its battery at full charge. It was not necessary to put it up on blocks; Russell simply extruded the built-in front and rear jacks.

"You still can't get Detroit interested in this car?"

"I gave up years ago, Pop."

"Cretins."

"No, they're reasonably intelligent. Look at her. I designed and built her the year after Jennifer was born. I might need to replace her in fifteen or twenty years, and I might not."

Wilson Grant frowned. "To quote a writer I worked with once, 'If the question begins, "Why don't they—?" the answer is, "money." ' "

"That's part of it," Russell agreed. "But look there where I've switched the pedals. In my car it's easier to get from the accelerator to the brake than the other way 'round—and that little feature has saved my life twice so far. It wouldn't cost a red cent to make all cars that way. But the average driver could never unlearn the habit of doing it the stupid way, and he'd kill himself *quicker*."

"So once a stupid mistake is institutionalized it's too late to change it."

"Well, you used to work in publishing."

Regina Parkhill was waiting for them in the living room, a petite slender platinum blonde in her mid-sixties who could quite easily have passed for thirty-five. Her tan was astonishing. She greeted Russell effusively, then turned to Jennifer and regarded her as though she had just materialized amid thunderclaps and fire. "*Jenny*," she cried, "my dear *God* how you've grown! Such a *big* little girl, I can hardly believe my eyes!"

You're such a *little* big girl, I *know* I can't believe mine, Jennifer thought cattily. "Hello, Grandmother."

Regina winced. "Call me 'Regina,' please, darling."

"If you'll call me Jennifer." *Same deal I offered you last time.*

The older woman blinked and smiled. "Of course, dear. Wilson, shall we take martinis out on the terrace—and a cola for little Jenny?"

"Good idea, darling—but I've already offered Jennifer a split of vermouth, and she's accepted."

"What? Nonsense, Wilson, she's just a child. I'm sure she'd prefer a soft drink—wouldn't you, honey?"

Jennifer opened her mouth—and caught her father's look. It was a private code between them, and it meant, "I know you have a perfect right to make a scene—but please don't, and I'll make it up to you later." She closed her mouth.

And Grandpa opened his. "Regina, don't be rude. Our guest has already expressed a preference; it's not our place to change her mind."

"Darling, she is thirteen years old."

"Which makes her husband-high by the standards of most of the civilized cultures in history. Her father has some rights in this regard, but he raises no objection—so please fetch along the vermouth and a pony glass." He turned and led his descendants to the terrace. Jennifer smiled to herself, loving him.

The view was stunning. A vast expanse of rolling green dotted with truly lovely trees and a Japanese rock garden ended in a cliff, beyond which lay the Sound. Three or four miles out an immense oil supertanker made its stately way east. The weather was perfect, the sky seemed clean and clear, Connecticut was a greasy smudge on the horizon. When the conversation of her elders turned to the war in Africa, Jennifer excused herself and wandered the grounds. She took mental notes, for Sophie would want to hear all about this when she got back home to Halifax—best friends were useful for helping you to remember things. The rock garden held her attention for some time. She tried to watch the rocks grow, and failed as always, but did not mind failing in such a beautiful place. There was a superb bonsai in the garden, and she devoted some time to trying to understand the nature of the gentle suggestion Grandpa was making to it with a guy wire. Again she failed; the proposed alteration would, it seemed to her, decrease the tree's *wa* rather than enhance it. She decided it was Regina's idea.

She felt a little like a botched bonsai herself: overdeveloped in some aspects and retarded in others. Intellectually she was genius-plus—but physiologically she was thirteen and a half years old and her goddamned period was *never* going to come. *All* her friends had gotten theirs ages ago. Grandpa had just said that she was "husband-high"—but she *wasn't!* She decided that if nothing happened by her fourteenth birthday she would try to prime the pump by cutting her throat.

She drifted over to the cliff edge. A wooden staircase led down the face of the bluff to the beach far below. Of course Regina had enjoined her to "be careful if you go down that staircase, dear"; of course the stairway would have been perfectly safe for a retarded five-year-old with Parkinson's Disease. The beach was indeed sandy and free of driftwood, absolutely unoccupied, and Jennifer yearned to climb down to it and get sand in her shoes. A year or two ago she would have—but it was late in the day, and the stairs were long and steep, and she did not feel that her father should have to handle all the socializing alone. She returned to the terrace and endured a ghastly hour of conversation with Regina, during which she was twice forced to literally bite her tongue.

Dinner was served on the terrace, and it was exquisite; it was not until after coffee and dessert that the argument began.

Jennifer started it, quite innocently, by wondering aloud why Wilson and Regina had sold their previous home and moved here. "I mean, this place is lovely—but so was the other one, and you had more land."

"I meant to ask that too," Russell agreed. "I thought you were settled in Southampton for keeps."

"They closed the golf course," his father said, smiling.

"No, seriously, Pop. I remember you telling me about trying to get a zoning exception so that you could be buried on that property."

Grandfather's smile remained fixed; he said nothing.

His wife broke the awkward silence. "Oh, for Heaven's sake, Wilson!"

"My dear—"

"I *know* he's married to one. But that's Canada—he knows things are different here. *Tell* him, for God's sake, it's not as if you've anything to be ashamed of."

Russell and Jennifer both set their glasses down and sat up straighter. They exchanged a brief glance.

"I hope you're right," Grandfather said, and looked his son in the eye. "Russ, it's like this: a black family moved in next door."

His son was visibly shaken. "Pop, you're not serious. It's a rib."

"Oh God," Regina said, rolling her eyes insolently. "I hear a knee jerking."

"Russ—"

"I thought I cured you of racism back in the '60's—"

"Mind your tongue, young man, and let me finish! You've been in New York, you must know that the world has changed since the last time you were around here straightening out your elders. You must have noticed how high racial tension is running—"

"I'm beginning to see why."

"It's a reality that has to be lived with, whether I like it or not. There's a difference between racism and simple self-preservation. This all happened back when the news was full of Mau Mau bombings and murders."

"Let me get this straight. Angry street blacks from Harlem moved in and started sneering at you and leering at Regina? Welfare cheaters with drug habits and ghetto-blaster radios bought a half-million-dollar house in the Hamptons?"

"They had more money than we did, actually. University professors." Just like Dena's parents, Jennifer thought. "I watched them move in—their furniture was beautiful."

"Then *why*—?"

"Simple economics," Regina said blandly. "Your father didn't want to sell—men are *so* impractical—but I insisted. And events proved me right. We were the first to unload, and we got back ninety-five percent of our investment. Within two weeks a dozen other families had sold their homes too, and the longer they hesitated, the more of a beating they took. We weren't being racist, we were protecting our investment—and we still took a small loss. If I hadn't put my foot down, we could have lost everything. I still don't see why we can't sue that realtor—the property values in the neighbourhood went down fifty percent thanks to him. It has nothing to do with race itself."

Russell opened and closed his mouth several times. At last he managed to say, "You know why there are so many cattle stampedes? Because every smart cow knows that the *first* cow to bolt has the best chance of not getting trampled in the stampede she starts."

"Russ—" his father began.

He turned to Jennifer. "It seems to me we passed the train station on the way in. About a klick or so back?"

She remembered it, the cleanest-looking train station she had ever seen. "On the left."

He nodded and stood up. "Thanks for the food and drink—it was wonderful," he said to his father and stepmother, and turned back to Jennifer. "Let's go, princess." He turned on his heel and strode off across the terrace, headed around the house to the road.

"What's the hurry?" Regina said, trying to persuade herself that the situation was salvageable. "The last train isn't for *hours* yet."

"It's the *next* train that interests me," he called without stopping or looking back.

"Russell, God damn it," his father began, and gave it up.

"Well of all the . . . *nerve*," Regina sputtered. "I, I *never* in all—"

Jennifer stood up, faced her grandfather until he was forced to meet her eyes. "Grampa," she said softly then, "I'm very disappointed." He looked away.

"—such a *rude* and unforgivable—" Regina was still raving.

"SHUT UP," Jennifer bellowed. Near the corner of the house, Russell stopped in his tracks. "Grandfather has you for an excuse. What's *your* excuse?"

Regina's mouth worked, but the sounds that spilled out were not words.

"I'll bet you cheat at solitaire," Jennifer said, and saw that one strike home, and went to join her father.

They walked in silence in the gathering dusk, listening to crickets and the occasional distant backyard stereo. They were obliged to walk along the roadside, as the community did not have sidewalks. There was no traffic. Most of the houses they passed were lit, but they saw no people. A very fat man passed them on a snarling Moped; he looked them over carefully. Less than a minute later a prowl car arrived to question them. Jennifer was impressed by the response-time.

The ritual that ensued impressed her as well. Russell was well-dressed, well-spoken, patently respectable, and traveling in company with a thirteen-year-old girl; none-theless he was questioned most carefully. He produced ID for himself and Jennifer produced her own. He gave the name and address of the resident he had been visiting and the time of his entry. He explained why he had left his car behind, and when asked why the Grants had not driven him to the station stated that the night was so pleasant he and his daughter had preferred to walk. There was a pause then, while the officer gave all this information to his partner. The latter had never left the car, and Jennifer noticed that his hands had never come into view. He radioed back to the main gate man, who not only verified their entry, but called the Grants to confirm that these pedestrians were indeed their guests. Only then did the first officer relax to the extent of a smile.

Even then he was not done with them. "Please let us offer you folks a lift the rest of the way."

"Thank you, officer, but we really would prefer to walk." Her father had remained quietly polite throughout the interrogation; only Jennifer could tell how impatient he was for these nosies to go away.

"Please let us offer you folks a lift," the officer repeated.

"No thank you," he said firmly.

"*Please*," the officer said.

"Constable," Russell said, deliberately using the Canadian honorific, "I am a stranger here. Is it really against the law to walk the streets in this country now?"

"No sir, not exactly."

"Good evening, then." He made as if to resume walking.

The officer looked pained. "Mr. Grant, *please* wait." Russell paused. "Look: every time one of our people looks out their window and sees you folks, they're gonna call it in. And every time they call in they gotta see a car respond, so they know they're gettin' good coverage. Look, roll down all the windows and move your feet back and forth, and we'll drive real slow and you can *pretend* you're walking, okay?"

Russell smiled and relented. "Is it really that bad here?" he asked as they got into the car.

"Not if we can help it."

When they were underway, Jennifer spoke up suddenly. "Do you have much trouble with niggers here?"

Her father flinched.

"Nah," the driver replied. "Not since we blew away a few last year."

"Really?" she said, making her voice sound approving and fascinated. "What were they doing?"

"Snuck over the electric fence on foot, stuck up a dinner party a mile from here. Sorry, for you folks that'd be a couple of kilometers, wouldn't it? Three of 'em, two draft dodgers and a woman, maybe twenty people at the party.

They pistol-whipped a few for laughs, took all the money and jewelry in the place, then they—"

"Harve," the officer who had interrogated them cut in, "she's a kid for Chrissake."

"Oh shit. I mean, sorry."

Russell spoke up. "Officer, my daughter is old enough to be allowed to read newspapers. Finish the story."

Harve shrugged. "They made everybody get undressed and play sex games, with them and each other. I guess they had a pretty crude sense of humour. They didn't kill anybody outright, but six hadda go to the hospital, and one committed suicide the next morning, and ten of 'em are still goin' to a shrink. Then the sc—excuse me—then the perpetrators stole a Jensen Interceptor and split. I guess they figured to shoot their way through the gate."

"And?"

"They ripped out the phones and tied everybody together in a big bundle, too big to get out the door. But they didn't notice the CB base unit the resident had in with his stereo gear. We were waiting for 'em with machine guns. Blew the block out of the Jensen, blew all four wheels off, blew up the niggers, cut to commercial."

Jennifer was not enjoying this as much as she had expected. It had been her vague intention to draw the cops out about racism, then tell them as she was getting out of the car that her mother was a nigger. She had since changed her mind. Had it only been yesterday that she herself had been in a nightmare much like the one he was describing? "Did the man mind about his car?"

"Not when he seen what was in it. I never saw a man smile like that in my whole life, and I hope I never see another one like it." Harve's own savage grin was visible in the rear-view mirror. "He traded us a signed waiver on the car for—" He caught himself suddenly. "For a couple of souvenirs, like. He's still got 'em, in a jar."

Russell shuddered. "What an incredible story!"

Harve shrugged. "I first heard a story like that one, almost exactly like it, back in '82, west of here, in Nassau County. Only difference was the silly bastards happened to pick a big fancy restaurant to have fun in, and the owner was a heavyweight in the Greek Mafia. Last mistake *they* ever made. But there's been a dozen incidents like that in the last ten-fifteen years, different places—this was just the first one we ever had *here*. Be the last, too."

"Niggers been turning animal the last ten years," his partner said glumly. "I dunno what the hell it is. Those Mau Maus ... I remember a time when I had nigger friends."

"I still got a couple," Harve said, surprising them all. "Couple o' guys I grew up with in Brooklyn. But I ain't seen either of 'em in a few years—and I wouldn't go to Brooklyn to do it."

"Fuckin' A," his partner agreed. "Sorry, miss. Well, here we are."

They had reached the Long Island Railroad station. Russell thanked the officers for the ride, and he and Jennifer got out. The prowl car drove off.

There were one or two occupied cars in the vast parking lot, but the ticket office and waiting room were locked and the platform was deserted. The next train west was already in place, idling noisily. They boarded and took seats in an empty non-smoking car which smelled faintly of urine and old vomit. Nearly every seat in the car contained a copy of that evening's *New York Post*, a tabloid whose front page shrieked about a draft riot in Harlem. The car did not seem to have been more than cursorily cleaned or maintained for at least a decade; some of its windows were opaque with grime, and most were translucent at best. This, Jennifer thought, is the train the rich people get. What do the poor neighbourhoods get?

At last Russell broke the silence. "I heard what you said to Mrs. Grandpa. What did you say to Grandpa?"

"I just said I was disappointed."

"Fair enough."

"I thought so. Dad?"

"Yes?"

"Why did he marry her?"

Russell was silent a moment. "Honey," he said finally, "Pop is a fighter. Some people just like conflict, something to sharpen their claws on all the time. He was never so happy, when I was a kid, as when I tried to buck him on something—and the older I got and the better I got at it, the better he seemed to like it. Back when he was an editor, his greatest joy was the acquisition of a new, worthy enemy. Now that he's retired, I guess he needs to have his conflict at home."

"And it cost him a home he really loved."

"A bully is someone who only picks fights with weaker opponents. Pop was never a bully. Sometimes he loses his fights. Hell, he lost Mom. It's the fighting itself he enjoys, not the winning."

"Is that why you walked out?"

Russell grinned ruefully. "You're sharp, peanut. I think you're right. Mean bastard, ain't I?"

She giggled, and that broke Russell up. "He's probably been looking forward to this fight for *months*," she said, and the two of them laughed harder. Russell mimed turning his back on an opponent and said, "Take *that*," and Jennifer howled, and it became one of those extended cathartic laugh-sessions where each punchline suggests another and breath becomes a rare commodity, and halfway through Jennifer wondered if making love would turn out to be this much fun one day.

The conductor appeared as they were tapering off and sold them tickets to Penn Station. "Change at Jamaica," he chanted ritualistically, and started to leave.

"God," Russell said, still grinning, "I haven't heard that in a long time."

The conductor gave him a half-curious glance.

"I used to live on the Island," Russell explained, "but I moved away twenty-five years ago."

The conductor grimaced. "You picked a helluva time to come back, Jack." He left.

"What's this about Jamaica?" Jennifer asked.

"It's a station in Queens, where just about everybody has to change trains to get in or out of the city. I must have spent half my adolescence there waiting for a connection."

The train got under weigh with extreme reluctance. Jennifer had ridden on very few trains in her life, and none that were not old and in poor condition, but this was easily the worst of the lot.

"Dad? Tell me something?"

"If I can."

"I don't really know how this stuff works, but . . . suppose Grandpa hadn't sold his house. So his property values go down—but he didn't want to sell it in the first place. So doesn't he end up with the same house, in the same location—with lower property taxes?"

Russell gaped, thunderstruck.

"—and with a guarantee that none of his new neighbours are stupid enough to be bigots?"

"I'll be damned," he said. "What Regina 'saved' him from was the chance to have the place he loved at half the cost. Jen, you're right! Great blithering mother of shit, I never thought it through . . . do you suppose I could rent your brain, times when you're not using it?"

"As long as you return it in good condition," she said smugly.

"I've been hearing that 'property values' argument for forty years, and you just put your finger on the hole in it. Oh, this is rich!" Suddenly his joy sprang a leak. "Poor Pop," he said, and was silent.

Clever me, she thought; *we almost overlooked the saddest part.*

After a few miles, her father spoke up again. "They leaned on me, while you were walking around the grounds."

"Grandpa and . . . *her?*"

"Yes."

"Leaned how?"

"Well, there was a long build-up about the growing climate of violence in the city, and the increasing racial tension. I kept my mouth shut about yesterday, but I had to agree. The punchline was, why doesn't little Jennifer stay with us?"

"Oh my *God.*"

"Yeah." He poked at a copy of the *Post*; it was open to a photo of the County Executive of Suffolk in her new topless bathing suit. "May I confess something?"

She blinked. "Oh, *Daddy.* Oh, don't say it."

"Before the matter of the black family next door came up, I was thinking the idea over halfway seriously."

"Stand up!"

"Jenn—"

"In two seconds I'm gonna kick you under the belt. If I were you I'd get up and turn around first."

"Dammit, I gave the idea up."

"Not fast enough. Daddy, I'd have been *miserable* there—how could you even *think*—"

"Button it."

She began an angry retort—then shut up.

"Put yourself in my place. You're Daddy. For the next three months your daughter Jenniflower the Beauteous, the most precious creature on Earth, *has* to be one of two things: in the dumps or in danger. Whichever one you pick . . . don't you think it over carefully?"

"You know when you are the *most* annoying?" Jennifer shouted.

Russell started at her volume. "When?"

"When you're right, you big jerk."

He grinned at her. "Princess, I intend to annoy the hell out of you until you're old enough to move out and make your own mistakes."

"When'll that be?"

"How should I know? *You*'ll tell *me*, when the time comes. Uh—I'd be nervous if you were younger than eighteen. Very damned nervous. No, I'd be outright afraid. But it's not my decision, sweetheart."

Jennifer tried to imagine herself independent, living apart from her parents. Nobody to tell you what to do, stay up as late as you want, leave your room a mess if it suits you. All the junk food and desserts you want. Access the adult channels on your TV without having to bribe the damned babysitter. Experiment with boys in the comfort and privacy of your own home.

Hmmmm.

Alone with a boy in a private place with a bed in it, no parents in the next room. That could be scary. And I'd have to *pay* for the private place—there goes staying up all night. In fact, there go over half my waking hours. And I'd have to keep the place clean to invite boys over. And if I eat too much junk eventually I get jelly-belly and pizza-face and the next thing you know, there I am alone in my private place, watching more fortunate souls humping away on TV . . .

And I'd be so homesick for Mom and Dad!

Jennifer decided that although the law allowed her to move out on her own at age thirteen, she'd be crazy to do so. Compared to the alternative, living with your parents was a good deal.

It kept things simple. You only had two people to outwit . . .

CHAPTER FOUR

"Suspicion used to be on an individual basis. Now each one of us, black or white, is a symbol. The war is out in the open and the skin color is a uniform. All the deep and basic similarities of the human condition are forgotten so that we can exaggerate the few differences that exist . . .

"Whitey wants law and order, meaning a head-knocker like Alabama George. No black is going to grieve about some nice sweet dedicated unprejudiced liberal being yanked out of his Buick and beaten to death, because there have been a great many nice humble ingratiating hardworking blacks beaten to death too. In all such cases the unforgivable sin was to be born black or white, just as in some ancient cultures if you were foolish enough to be born female, they took you by your baby heels, whapped your fuzzy head on a tree, and tossed the newborn to the crocs . . .

". . . no solutions for me or thee, not from your leaders be they passive or militant, nor from the politicians or the liberals or the head-knockers or the educators. No answer but time. And if the law and the courts can be induced to become color-blind, we'll have a good answer, after both of us are dead. And a bloody answer otherwise."

—John D. MacDonald, THE GIRL IN THE PLAIN BROWN WRAPPER

"Bobby Seale, the radical, the famous Black Panther, the firebrand whose blazing rhetoric helped shape the Sixties—Bobby Seale is writing a cookbook. He'll call it Barbecuing With Bobby.

". . . 'When I hear Rap Brown is running a health-food store in Georgia, that Stokely gave a lecture and only 22 people showed up . . . Hey, I'm the last of the Sixties. The rest of them are still living in the Sixties.'

"Nearby, his daughter J'Aime, 4, plays quietly across from the fireplace, absorbed by her twin blonde Barbie dolls . . .

" 'Look, I've got to send my kids to college. Not only that, people don't donate money the way they used to. If I have the ability to alter my standard of living, I want to do it. When I went into the struggle, I didn't go in to keep the ghettos the way they were.' "

—AP dispatch, July 19, 1982
(Seale's cookbook drew a $100,000 advance.)

* * *

It was a week and a half later before Russell got a chance to spend a free afternoon strolling around town by himself—and then only because José's day-job discount store shut down for inventory.

Russell enjoyed the trip uptown. The subway was just as he remembered it—except, of course, that a token cost nine times what it had in his youth, and vagrants were now tacitly permitted to sleep by the dozens in certain stations—and the sounds and smells were almost unbearably nostalgic. They acted directly on his subconscious, simultaneously soothing and exhilarating. This amused him—he remembered his childhood as one long scrabbling attempt to get out of New York City for good, and now he saw that he was forever doomed to think of this stinking town as "home." In recent years it had usually taken Russell upwards of half an hour to get to sleep—but for the past week and a half the sound of city traffic outside the window had knocked him out like a sleeping pill each night.

The ancient train reached Grand Central at last and shuddered to a halt. Solving the mouse's maze of stairways and corridors that led to the upper world, Russell emerged onto 42nd Street and stood a moment blinking in the sunshine. The day was splendid, unseasonably cool for Manhattan summer, and the air was electric with music.

It had been his intention to walk to the Public Library at Fifth Avenue and do some research. He had not yet told Dena and Jennifer that he was working again, because he knew that Jennifer in particular would make a big deal out of it and he was not yet ready to be committed publicly—the design might not fly, his motivation might leak—but he had at least admitted privately to himself that he was no longer a retired person. His preliminary work had progressed to the point at which he needed more data; six years was a long time in molecular electronics alone and he was out of touch.

But there was a deeper problem that he was suppressing. Russell had long ago learned that the best designs of which he was capable invariably went straight to hell in the manufacturing and marketing stages, became unacceptably diluted or perverted by the greed of the money men. The only way he was ever going to get a product from his mind to the consumers' hands unspoiled was to do the manufacture and marketing himself, with his own money. By the time he had reached age forty, brilliant work had brought him enough capital to begin doing so—whereupon, disgusted by the human race, he had retired. The intervening years had taught him that people did not *want* their lives improved, and manufacture and marketing were heathen arts he loathed. He had decided that his money was better spent on amusing himself than on bringing the world miracles it was too ignorant and lazy to deserve. What little philanthropic instinct he retained was satisfied by underwriting Dena's career.

So if this new design project came together, it would put him right back on the horns of his dilemma. He would find himself locked in a death struggle with the people who made and sold conventional refrigerators and stoves. Russell did not *like* death struggles with entrenched interests; he had learned that when he had tried to introduce a sensible bathtub and a comfortable toilet to the world. He had come out of that fiasco not only utterly defeated, but humiliatingly richer by his failure.

And so as his feet touched sidewalk Russell changed his

mind about doing research today. He had not walked
42nd Street in decades, and the sight of it triggered even
more déjà vu than the subway had. The first erection he
could remember having had occurred within a few blocks
of here. On a whim, he walked right past the Library—
noting that one of its magnificent lions had been spray-
painted and the other smashed entirely—and past Bryant
Park toward Times Square.

Except for the proliferation of video arcades, the district was much as he remembered it. A milling sea of
multicolored humanity filled it to overflowing as always,
shucking and jiving and hustling and rapping and break-
dancing and just hanging out. Every fourth person tried
to sell Russell something. Drugs, girls, boys, whatever
they thought he might find irresistible. Handbills were
forced on him every twenty meters; donations to a dozen
obscure causes were solicited. He knew he could avoid
most of this by walking twice as fast and staring fixedly
ahead. But he did not want to traverse the area, he wanted
to travel it, and accepted the aggressive solicitation as the
price required. Snatches of dialogue drifted to him:

"*Konichi-wa* yourself, motherfucker."

"—just don't think it's a Spring List book, Fred. It feels
like Fall to me."

"I wouldn't dream of arguing, Sal. You want me to
cross my feet? I see you only brought the three nails—"

"—mothafuck be talkin' shit about 'donatin',' and I'm
here: 'Mothafucka, I don' give away nothin' but bubblegum an' hard times, an' I'm fresh out o' fuckin' bubblegum.'
So he's here: 'Yeah?' An' I'm here: 'Man, get out of my
face or I—' "

"*Joa san, ah bok*—"

"What are you, stunadz? You got some pair of balls on
you, you know that?"

"Cop some of this good Mayflower, my man—all the
Puritan maidens come across on it—"

"*Chinga tu madre, pendejo*—"

"—the hell are we gonna meet a margin call at twenty-
two-five, for Chrissake? I'm telling you, Morris, it's Chapter
Eleven again, that's four times in six years, I just don't—"

"I ain't the baddest man in the world, but I'm in the top two, an' my daddy's gettin' older—"

"Macho like a *gabacho*, uh? Your mama says I do it to her better than you, *ioto*, so what's that make you?"

Russell's designer's mind could not help classifying the bits of conversation he overheard. There were numerous exceptions, but in general blacks boasted, hispanics insulted each other, and whites complained about money. He began classifying the people he saw as well. He noticed that while a few whites handed out religious or advertising circulars, the overwhelming majority of the vendors and barkers and sidewalk entrepreneurs who sold drugs and stolen goods were black or hispanic. That was a change from the 42nd Street that Russell remembered.

And where were the white teenagers? In Russell's day this strip had been jammed with boys and girls from out of town, all in pursuit of adventure and illicit thrills that could not be had in Levittown or Patterson, in search of improbable pornography or a case of venereal disease or a bag of oregano to smoke with their friends. He had been one of those daring white kids himself. Young whites were plentiful on the street even now—but half wore military uniforms, and most of the rest were whores of one sex or another. These clumped together in silent groups of three or four, and did not mingle with the black or chicano whores. Virtually all other whites on the street were prosperous-looking adults. Men in business suits or in short-sleeve shirts with sportscoats slung over their shoulders; women well-dressed and walking quickly on their way to somewhere else.

"Come on over here, sugar, we'll go back to my crib and fuck ourselves unconscious."

"—Right this way, ge'men, they han'cuffed, earmuffed, an' mouth stuffed, get 'em 'fore they sold to Japan—"

Russell was surprised by the boldness of the prostitutes, by the variety of explicit costuming, and the aggressively frank sales pitches. In his day whores had waited to be approached, or at most murmured something suggestive to passersby. Only a few of these people held back and sold by eye contact alone, and Russell decided that they did so only because a certain percentage of the market demanded it. The next time he was hit on, he stopped. "Look, I know you're working, one fast question, okay?"

"Sure. Maybe I'll even answer it."

"How could you make an explicit offer like that, sex for money, right out here on the street? What if I were a cop?"

She snorted. "*You*, the raise? Right." She wrinkled her ten-year-old brow. "Anyway, what the fuck would I care what you do for a living?"

"Never mind." He walked on, bemused.

Within a block he noted another odd pattern. Whores of all races and colors were doing firesale business with the G.I.s, which was not at all surprising—but Russell noticed gradually that no black prostitute, male or female, would have anything to do with a black serviceman. This puzzled him until he overheard an explicit statement of the policy—"You can fight for The Man, you can fuck y'own hand"—and then the logic dawned on him. A black man who would go to Africa to kill black men at the behest of white men was persona non grata here. But surely, Russell thought, most if not all of them were drafted. What were they supposed to have done, gone to prison? That or gone underground, apparently. It made him wonder how many of the hustlers on this street were draft evaders, gone off the books, living on cash transactions and thus invisible to The Man.

He came to a pornshop that seemed to meet his standards and went inside. Russell cherished a mild taste for quality pornography, although he had not bought any in years because the stuff offered for sale in Halifax was so lame and tame. The store was crowded and smelled of cigar and marijuana smoke.

Time, he soon found, had again changed pornshops. It had been in Russell's adolescence that all the shops had begun installing peepshow booths, within which a man could see two minutes of grainy eight millimeter porn for a quarter. Thanks to maxiplexing, which had brought *all* TV channels to *everyone*, there were only two of the booths left now, each accessing satellite porn channels for that dedicated contingent of New Yorkers so genuinely homeless that they did not have access to a TV set. Similarly, the long shelves of eight and super-eight millimeter movies were gone, replaced by small racks of videotapes and floppies and chips.

On the other hand, the live sex encounter modules, which had first appeared during Russell's early adulthood, were more popular than ever. There were four such structures, circular clusters of booths in the unseen centers of which people were performing sexual acts for those strangers willing to pay a dollar a minute to unlock the booths' window-screens. (It had been half a dollar in Russell's time.) The four booth clusters were labeled: "Sweet"; "Raunchy"; "Nasty"; and "Twisted." From the interior of "Nasty" could be heard the unmistakable sound of someone trying to endure a spanking in silence (whether male or female was indeterminate); from "Raunchy" there came driving flash music with heavy flanging, by the group called The Pulp; from "Twisted" came silence broken only by a muffled voice from within one of the booths, saying softly and reverently, "Holy Christ almighty." As Russell browsed past "Sweet," he clearly heard the high sweet sound of a young girl coming, and every customer in the store stopped what he or she was doing to appreciate it for a moment. It sounded (although Russell would have bet cash against it) as though it were her first orgasm, fearful and joyous. It should have brought all of them together, if only in a way and for a moment, to share the hearing of it, but it did nothing of the sort—an instant after the cry had ended each customer was back inside his or her own private skull again. That saddened Russell slightly; nonetheless he was glad he had heard her questing call.

Studying the feeling, he identified it as the same warm glow he got from a brand-new baby or a bunch of struggling kittens, a sense of being reconciled to being alive after all. The accompanying sadness was the same one that occurs when, looking up from a new baby, one smiles at one's neighbour and gets no smile in return. Russell had once studied Zen for a time, and remembered a quote he had read somewhere: "Enlightenment can be a lonely country." The magazines he browsed past enlightened him further— magazine porn too had changed with the years. For one thing, competition from TV had made the quality of the photography enormously better. But there were subtler changes. At the time Russell had left New York, a curious convention had prevailed: straight-erotic magazines (whether hetero or gay) could graphically depict genuine sex acts of any description, but bondage magazines contained no sex at all, and the rare sadomasochism magazine, while depicting discomfort, humiliation, and clumsily-faked torture, restricted sexual activity to very occasional cunnilingus (the vast majority of the victims being men). In neither of the latter categories was an erect penis ever seen.

Now these eccentric taboos were dissolved. The magazines were organized into the same four categories as the booths, with each category broken down into straight, bi, gay male, gay female, transvestite, and transsexual (a category which had not existed in Russell's youth), and each of these further subdivided. As Russell's meandering took him past "Nasty," he discovered that graphic sex could now be found conjoined with either bondage or violence; even gang rape was now vendable, and females had finally achieved parity with males as victims. Then he drifted past "Twisted," and after a few moments of horrified fascination he left that section.

The *least* disturbing things he had seen were three magazines featuring a surgically-created creature called Enigma. Enigma had wide brown eyes, webbed fingers and toes, no genitalia or hair of any kind, no ears, nose or thumbs, and exactly three bodily orifices: a single nostril and small tubelike protrusions where the mouth and urethra belonged. He/she/it was a featureless, sexless doll with whom no imaginable sex act could be performed, restricted to a liquid diet, and assured of a limited—but apparently lucrative—lifespan. Everything else in the "Twisted" section was much worse than Enigma; Russell decided that the recent breakthroughs in simplified surgery were not an unmixed blessing.

One thing had not changed. Russell had never in his life seen any genuine child pornography offered for sale in New York, and there was none now—just the same two or three sad magazines featuring eighteen-year-olds done up in pigtails, bobby socks, and saddle shoes. You could rent a live ten-year-old outside on the street, but you could not take her picture home with you. It appeared to be the only taboo of any kind still in effect, and as the father of a thirteen-year-old Russell was rather pleased by that.

As he came to a halt where he had ultimately planned to, midway between "Sweet" and "Raunchy," another change struck him. There was almost no written porn in the store. At first he wondered if the U.S.'s illiteracy problem could be even worse than he had heard—but soon he figured out the true reason. Erotic writing, as hardcore as could be asked, and much more competently written than the old stroke-books Russell remembered, could now be had in any bookstore. Pornographic literature at least had finally escaped the pornshop. It cheered Russell to think that somewhere Marco Vassi was earning a living at his trade.

In any visit to a pornshop, there comes a threshold point, at which the intrinsic interest of the merchandise reaches saturation level, and one begins to notice, and perhaps to covertly study, one's fellow consumers. For Russell that point came just as he was making his second selection. First he chose a magazine for himself, in which a man who vaguely resembled Russell was relieved of a great deal of tension by a redhead, a blonde, and a dark black girl who had apparently devoted a lot of thought to the creative uses of the feather. Then he looked for a present for Dena. He knew that her tastes ran along the same general lines as his own: someone who looked enough like herself to identify with, having fun with someone who did not resemble her spouse. Tasting variety in their fantasies, they were able to eschew it in real life. After some searching, he found a magazine on whose cover was depicted a woman who not only resembled Dena in face and hairstyle, but even had something like a dancer's body. She was smiling seductively at the camera, sitting on someone's lap. As Russell was reaching for the magazine to inspect the contents (another reason he seldom bought porn back home: it was offered for sale sealed in plastic), it suddenly struck home to him just *how much* searching he had had to do to find both these magazines, and he froze with it in his hand. The worst thing that Russell knew how to say to himself was, "You have not thought this thing through," and he said it to himself now.

There was plenty of white-on-white porn in this shop. There was plenty of black-on-black. There was very little interracial porn. Most of what there was had been back in the "Nasty" and "Twisted" sections, and Russell could remember no single instance in which a white of either sex had been dominant. He glanced around and his heart sank. He was the only white customer in the store standing anywhere near a magazine featuring blacks. He had two such in his hand. Three black youths standing nearby visibly disapproved of his taste.

Whites were in a slight majority in the clientele. He wondered how much difference that made. Bad tactics would be to put the magazine back and leave, inviting attack. Forcing himself to move slowly, he paid for his purchases, tucked them away in his briefcase full of scribbled designs. As he reached the door he turned back and stared squarely at the trio. They were motionless where he had left them, staring back at him. He tried to convey the impression that he carried at least four lethal weapons and was eager to be followed and challenged. There was no telling whether he was successful; the faces of all three were unreadable. He turned his back on them and left.

He was not followed.

He decided to keep heading west. He had heard about the complete rebuilding of the Port Authority complex, and was curious to know how they had solved several design problems. He walked that way, glancing over his shoulder from time to time to see if the three youths had followed. And so he cannoned directly into the Black Muslim.

"Excuse me. My fault."

Correctly identifying Russell by these words as an out-of-towner, the white-robed and turbaned Muslim said, "*Allah akram*," and thrust a pamphlet into his hand. It was covered with Arabic script, a series of pictures of the phases of the moon, and the words, "Fast of Ramadaan."

Even discounting the turban, the heavily-bearded Muslim had a good four inches on Russell; he chose his words with care. "Thank you for your gift," he said, trying to return it, "but I cannot give you a donation for it now."

The man made no move to accept the booklet back. He smiled a predatory smile. "Better change your mind, paleman," he said. "It's the month of Ramadaan, and the Night of Power is at hand. There's still time to heed the words of the Prophet." Russell tried to interrupt. "It could save your paleman life."

Was this a public shakedown, or just the usual aggressive Muslim hardsell? All Russell was sure of was that the longer he stood still on this street, the more attention he drew. "What is the minimum donation?"

"Couple dollar be sufficient."

To produce money was to show any nearby pickpockets where it was kept. As Russell weighed the situation, measuring risks, a distraction occurred.

"What you mean, 'no'?" a man shouted just behind him. Russell turned; a black G.I. was confronting a shaven-headed black hooker. He was hurt and trying to cover it with anger. "Tomorrow I get on the boat and go get my ass shot off, and today I can't rent a piece of yours?"

"That's right, come-drop," she told him coolly.

"Listen, sister, back home in Montgomery women pay *me*. Come on now, *tipe tizwe*."

She lost her temper. "I ain't your sister, fuckwipe, and you hear me good: if you get into some napalm over there, and your body be on fire from head to toe, why then that'll be the only day of your life when I wouldn't piss on you. Get gone from my face!"

He was stunned silent for a moment, and then his mouth twisted and he slapped her hard. At once Russell saw her bring her fist upward fast, as if she were serving a volleyball; it connected with the soldier's lower belly with a smacking sound, and it was only as it came away with a twisting motion that Russell saw the wicked little knife in it.

The Muslim beside Russell exclaimed something approving with "Allah" in it. The soldier glanced down in surprise, then looked back up into the flashing eyes of the whore. His face changed, as though he were about to say, "Aw now, let's not fight, sugar—I'm sorry I slapped you," but the first syllable was all he could manage. He loudly soiled his pants, and his knees hit the sidewalk with a sharp cracking sound. Blood dripped from the crotch of his khaki trousers.

Pandemonium broke out. Russell was chilled to realize that at least half the shouting was laughter and cheers. Soldiers and civilians began fighting one another. Something smashed Russell in the lower back, propelling him out of the center of the melee, and he kept on running without looking back, the Muslim pamphlet still clutched in his fist. He found that he was heading back toward Grand Central, and that it suited him. He had seen enough of New York for one day.

Within a block he was clear of the disturbance. Instinct yelled a warning; he stopped running, settled into a slow, measured walk. Just as he did so, pairs of cops began appearing as if by magic and racing past him to the ruckus. He was glad he had stopped running. As spiders instinctively go after anything that behaves like a fly, cops tend to be interested in anyone running away from a murder. He briefly tried to imagine himself explaining to a typical New York cop why he had a Muslim pamphlet in one hand and a briefcase full of interracial porn and circuit-drawings in the other. He slipped the pamphlet into the case and kept walking. He could not feel the ground with his feet. His back did not hurt at all.

Music beat at him from all sides as he walked. It had been everywhere since he had first emerged from Grand Central—personal headphones were not big on 42nd Street; they were more snatchable than necklaces—but he had not paid much attention, preoccupied by people and sights. Now it seemed that the whole world was music, that every fourth person had a ghetto blaster on his wrist or belt, each playing a different tape. First ten seconds of King Sunny Ade's ju-ju music, then Mingus's *Jazz Fusion*, then a flank attack by some anonymous processor group, then Carmen Lundy, then a cello solo by Abdul Wadud, then early Beatles—it was like being trapped inside the speaker of some monstrous radio programmed for constant-

search. Russell's head spun; when he reached Bryant Park
he had to sit down. He found an unoccupied bench and
put his head between his legs, holding his hands against
his ears to shut out the music, managing only to mute the
treble. Distantly he realized he was in shock.

Will that soldier die? If other people die in that riot,
will they ever know what started it, what they died for?
Do any of these people around me know or care that
people may be dying a few blocks away right now? He
was being shipped out to die in a far land, and he wanted
a nice sendoff and was willing to pay for it. Now he has a
hole in him. Pooh Bear, I think this is the wrong *kind* of
gash. Oh God.

A fresh-orange-juice vendor was pushing his cart by.
Russell had the vague idea that fluids were good for shock;
he bought a large cup and gulped it down. Suddenly the
temperature seemed to rise ten Celsius degrees. He turned
and put his head over the back of the bench; his stomach
twisted and gave up its contents. Dogs came running to
see the fun.

When it was over he felt a little better and his head was
clear, but he was not ready to get up and go home. His
back hurt now where he had been hit, and his legs felt
wobbly. He wanted to read something—anything. He took
the Muslim pamphlet from his case and began to read
that.

He got hopelessly confused until he realized that the
pages were numbered back to front. Even then a good
deal of the text was incomprehensible, heavily interspersed
with blocks of Arabic script with accompanying translation.
This was, apparently, the month of Ramadaan in the
Muslim year 1416, a time of great significance requiring
much fasting and prayer. Russell learned that "Ramadaan"
came from the root "Ramda," meaning "burning." He ran
across the phrase "The Night of Power," and remembered
the words of the Muslim who had given him the pamphlet.
The Night of Power, it seemed, had been the night, in the
month of Ramadaan twelve years before the Great Hegira,
on which the first suwrah of the Qur'aan had been revealed to the prophet Mustafa Muhammad Al Amin. The
term was also used in reference to something called the

Battle of Badr. Two years after the Hegira from Makkah to Medina which marked the beginning of the Muslim calendar, a group of three hundred Muslims had made a stand at Badr, and with the assistance of "Angels" sent down by ALLAHU SUBHAANAHU WA TA'ALA had held off a charge by three thousand "idol worshippers."

Characteristically, Russell noticed the numbers. The Muslims at the Battle of Badr had been outnumbered by a ratio of ten to one. There were roughly 250 million people in the United States, and 25 million black people. You couldn't ask for a Badr Battle than that, Russell thought, with a momentary vision of avenging black Angels stooping down from the skies on the idol worshippers.

Reading on he found more numbers. Apparently there was something mystically significant about the conjunction of the numbers 19 and 96. The first suwrah revealed to the Prophet on the Night of Power had ended up as Chapter 96 of the revised Qur'aan. Further, the first five verses of Suwrah 96 contained 19 words each, and Chapter 96 consisted of 19 verses, and Suwrah 96 was the 19th chapter from the end of the Qur'aan, and so forth. "This chapter," the pamphlet stated, "holds the key to the identification of the 19th night of the month of Ramadaan as the Night of Power. . . ."

It was therefore suggested that this year's Night of Power would be an especially holy and portentous one. Russell did not get the connection, since by Muslim calendar this was not 1996 A.D. but 1416 A.H.—but he thumbed idly to the calendar-translation section and worked out the Gregorian date for the Night of Power.

It was tonight.

He snorted and read on. The balance of the booklet's English text was fasting rules and regulations, with occasional photos of groups of small black children practicing karate and such. Russell decided he was strong enough to go home now, and stuffed the pamphlet back into his briefcase. He rinsed his mouth at a leaking fountain, dodged a junkie who wanted spare change, and went back to Grand Central Station. There was still a long list of places he wanted to visit while he was in New York, but they would still be there tomorrow.

Yes, he heard himself saying to a friend when he got back to Halifax, I was in New York for almost two weeks before I saw my first knifing. . . .

It was after five when he got back to the apartment. As he unlocked the second Medeco lock he saw José eyeballing him through the fisheye, and by the time he had the door open Jennifer was exploding out at him. "Daddy, you're late, we were just going to send the bloodhounds out for you but we couldn't find anything of yours they'd agree to sniff, when is supper I'm starving, Mom called she'll be home late, I beat José four straight games of Glory Road and I called Sophie but I didn't talk too long, let's eat!"

He disentangled himself from the hug and they went inside. Jennifer had the TV turned to ASN, which made Russell grin to himself. (Back home she made a fetish of ignoring Canadian TV and watching only the American channels. Now that she was in New York, she faithfully watched Halifax programming, made José sit through shows that she would not have been caught dead watching at home. NAMSAT East had made it possible for one to travel thousands of miles without changing one's viewing habits—and Jennifer changed them anyway!) "I know I am, soon, that's too bad, congratulations, that's good, let's." He went to the big crockpot and checked his Perpetual Stew. It was maturing nicely. "Another week and this'll be fit to serve company. José, you're not company, you're family—will you stay for dinner? To make up for your humiliating defeat at Glory Road?"

José flashed his quick grin. "Thanks, Russell. A man's gotta keep up his strength to run with this one here. I'll set the table."

"Cripes," Jennifer exclaimed. "Daddy won't let me cook, you won't let me set table—how am I supposed to learn the skills necessary to nail boys?"

"You can do the dishes," Russell said at once.

She tried to frown ferociously, but could not suppress the grin. "Walked into that one. I'll never learn to keep my mouth shut."

"That's another good one," José agreed solemnly, and

she threw a plate at him. Naturally he caught it. She had formed the habit of throwing objects at him without warning, and he always caught them. Two days before he had genuinely annoyed her, and she had let fly with an uncooked egg; when he caught it without breaking it, admiration had overcome her anger and she had given up her grudge. Dena wasn't crazy about the game, but it tickled Russell.

Over dinner Jennifer asked him why he was late. "Breakdown on the subway. Power was out for almost an hour and a half."

"Daddy, really? You were down there in the dark for that long?"

"There wasn't much choice. No real trouble—a couple of Guardian Angels and a transit cop took care of the claustrophobes, kind of kept order. Nobody seemed especially surprised."

"Nah, man," José said. "You'll be in one of those every couple weeks, wait an' see. Those Guardian Angels are really something, hah? I got to hand it to them. This town was a com*plete* shithole 'til they got started, my father told me."

"They were good. They talked down one old fellow who was mad as hell, wanted to leave the train and wander through the tunnel looking for a manhole, big appointment he had to keep."

"How'd they talk him out of it?" Jennifer asked.

"Opened a window and let him listen to the rats scurrying outside. They showed him one with a flashlight. He reconsidered."

"Yuck," Jennifer said in a complaining tone of voice. "Big rats. Like the ones Oscar meets in the Tower of the Egg in Glory Road."

"You and your Glory Road," José mocked. "Honest to God, Russell—pass the pepper, please—I thought I was pretty good at video games, but she's a demon."

"That she is. You know, I'm astonished at the number of video arcades in this town. There seems to be one on every block, and they all have the new programmable games with full keyboard. There was one in the Grand

Central complex, the biggest I ever saw, with *incredible* graphics."

"Yeah, they're everywhere. Especially popular with black people. The game ain't rigged, you know? Don't you people have arcades up there in Halifax?"

"Sure, a dozen or so, but nothing like this. Another funny thing: I just noticed today that half, better than half of the customers are adults."

"They have more quarters," Jennifer said.

"Yeah, it's funny," José agreed. "You'll see, like, a dude in a three-piece, and a kid in mylar with his face tattooed, and a big spade in shades, all side by side, paying no attention to each other at all. You know another funny thing? Once in a while I'll be watchin' a game, you know, and it'll seem like I saw the same exact game a week ago, the same moves and score and everything. Weird, huh?"

Russell chuckled and poured more apple juice. "I know what you mean. It's the ones wearing those red sunglasses I can't understand. Are the new screens supposed to be dangerous to your eyes, or what?"

"It wouldn't surprise me none, but I ain't heard it said yet. Some people just never take off their shades, I guess. Them red ones look sharp. I want to get a pair, but I can't seem to find any. This is good stew."

" 'Things are in a Perpetual Stew at the Grant household,' " Jennifer and Russell chorused. "If you think this is good," he went on, "come back in a week or so when it's ripe."

"Daddy?"

From the tone of voice alone, Russell knew he was about to be taken to the cleaners. But of course, foreknowledge was no help. "Yes, kitten?"

"I told you I beat José four games?"

"That's right."

"So you know I did double homework?"

Russell and Jennifer had both figured out early on that she was a genius, and decided it was best kept their secret. Since that time her education had had very little connection with her schooling. She carefully maintained a respectable B-plus average and a recorded I.Q. of 117, because Russell did not want her to be singled out and skipped ahead the way he had been as a boy—but she was doing college-level work in math and history, and he had privately measured her true I.Q. at 141. They still debated when to drop the masquerade; Jennifer wanted to do so on her College Boards, but Russell argued that she should get her teenage years over before taking on freak celebrity status. As one of his self-designed teaching aids, he had programmed the family computer console not to unlock the game mode for Jennifer until she had done an hour of skullsweat, most recently in math; even then it would only play two games before locking up again. There was a bypass code for himself and Dena, of course, and Russell privately suspected that Jennifer had somehow managed to either learn or deduce it. But he preferred not to find out, since an affirmative answer would have placed him in the position of being forced to punish ingenuity. "Yes," he lied.

"Well you're wrong, I did *triple*, and I still only played four games, so you owe me, right?"

"I concede no such thing. Assuming the situation is as you describe—"

"Daddy! You can check the—"

"—I said I assumed it. That being so, *you* owe you two games of Glory Road or agreed equivalent reward. All *I* owe you is your allowance—which, I admit, you have more than earned lately."

Jennifer pounced. "All right then, I'll make you a deal: I'll waive my allowance for this week, and throw in two games' worth of credit, for a favour."

"Mmmm." From the price offered, this would be a largish favour. And he didn't like that part about waiving her allowance—it suggested that she had alternate sources of income he knew nothing about. "Name the favour."

"I want to go to Madison Square Garden and see The Juice."

Even Russell, who hated flash music, knew about The Juice. They were a popular processor group—in the same sense that the Beatles had been a not-unsuccessful rock band. There was no chance that The Juice would ever play Halifax; there was no venue big enough. The favour was so enormous that he could not *not* grant it. But he did not much like the idea of Jennifer at Madison Square Garden late at night. "What night is the concert?"

"Tonight."

Reprieve. "Oh hell, princess, you'll never get tickets, they must have sold out before we left Hal—"

"I've got two."

He blinked. José was earnestly studying his stew.

"I wrote Grandpa before we left home, and he came into the city to get them for me."

"Sweetheart, I'm tired, and your mother won't be home until late—"

"Mama said it's okay with her if it's okay with you," Jennifer said at once, springing the trap.

"She did," José confirmed. "I'll take her if you don't want to go, Russell."

Russell thought of some of the drug-crazed defectives who went to flash concerts. Then he thought of José's knife, quivering in the center of the tree.

"*Please*, Daddy. The TV said Mark and H are going to be using the new Spangler Fives."

"You're sure you don't mind, José? You've been stuck with her all day."

"Well . . . I have a favour of my own I was gonna ask."

"Why do I get the feeling I'm going to leave this table dressed in a barrel? Let's hear it."

"See, I can't stay at my spot tonight. I'm havin' the roaches steamcleaned, so they'll be more presentable. It looks like a nice night, I thought maybe I could put a cot in the garden or something, if you don't mind."

"The living room couch folds out. Dena and I will probably be asleep when you get in—what, around midnight?"

Suddenly his lap was full of Jennifer. "Oh Daddy thank you thank you thank you!"

He hugged her back, reflecting that gratitude took years off her apparent age, and pushed her off his lap. "Finish your dinner. And you stick close to José tonight, you hear me?"

"Thanks a lot, Russell," José said, and threw a buttered roll at Jennifer's face. She caught it at almost arm's length— and gaped at it, surprised at herself. Then she smiled.

"I been workin' out with her a little," José said. "She'll be okay."

After they had left, Russell took a thermos of chilled Bushmill's out to the garden and set up a recliner so that he could watch the square of sky overhead. The day had been comparatively mild for New York summer, with some cloud cover and every third breeze a cool one. Perversely, the evening was becoming a hot one, muggy and oppressive. The few stars bright enough to be seen seemed to dance liquidly in the air.

Russell had long maintained that alcoholism was what happened when good booze got into the hands of amateurs; he drank seldom but well. He had never understood, for instance, how others could drink without looking at their watch—how could you measure dosage by wholly subjective parameters, when the point was to distort your subjective parameters? And why did they always add ice? Ice cubes diluted the taste, further confused the dosage—and were in addition about the least energy-efficient way to chill a drink he could think of. (One of the reasons he did not smoke grass was the impossibility of accurately quantifying strength, dosage or flavour. Old Bushmill's, on the other hand, had been a known quantity for almost four centuries. He kept a bottle in the fridge.) Russell could reliably achieve and maintain any of the five plateaus of intoxication, could change from one level to the next in as little as seven minutes or as much as an hour, and never had hangovers.

So he had no trouble staying at Level One, Buzzed, for the first hour, and when that proved unsatisfactory he modulated easily to Elevated. This is the stage at which one notices a small but marked increase in one's powers, a slight augmentation of everything from intelligence to peripheral vision. The problems of man in the universe are clarified; their solutions are just within sight and just out of reach. One feels kinship with all things living, and one's tongue has not yet begun to thicken appreciably.

But even this level failed to soothe him. Even from halfway up Olympus he could not integrate a universe in which a young man could be goaded to his death for the crime of having submitted to the draft. On all sides Russell heard babies crying, spouses bellowing, teenagers mocking each other, TVs and stereos adding subliminal undercurrents to the general uproar.

Dimly he knew that what he really wanted was to discuss the incident with Dena. She paid no more attention to politics than he did, American politics least of all, and their combined knowledge of the African war and its rights and wrongs was negligible—you could never judge a war until the data came in, fifteen years after it ended. But she was a black person that he lived with, and he wanted to know what she thought.

But she was still not home. There was no telling when she would be home, and he was not allowed to call the studio for anything less than a full-bore emergency. And so, secretly beginning to resent her for not being there, he gave the mental equivalent of a shrug and went to Level Three. If that did not work, he would taper off again, take two aspirin and go to sleep.

At Level Three, Inebriated, intelligence begins to decrease (while seeming to the subject to continue increasing) and the tongue starts to grow fur. Coordination and motor-skill impairment first appear, and the subject is prone to become restless and/or argumentative. Russell replayed the afternoon's events through a fantasy filter, tried out alternate versions in which he came off better. He stepped hastily between the soldier and the whore, caught her wrist with catlike grace, berated them both sternly for their mutual intransigence, browbeat them by sheer force of personality into seeing reason when reason itself had failed, then sent them on their separate ways with the grudging respect of both. The metropolis is safe as long as Spiderman is on patrol; if only he could be everywhere at once! The part he liked best was when one or the other of them tried to deflect his arguments by saying that he was just a racist honky, and he silenced them both with the stunning revelation that he was a Canadian with a black wife. Russell knew perfectly well that Canada's treatment of blacks, indeed of all non-whites, was far short of exemplary, so much so that the nation's shame was mitigated only by the presence of even greater horrors to the south. Canada was no longer accepting draft dodgers because the draft dodgers were no longer overwhelmingly white. But the whole point of Level Three is that reality becomes plastic.

He could not entirely override the true memories. They were too vivid. He remembered the last glimpse he had gotten of the prostitute. She had been standing over the kneeling soldier, grinning down at him, and in her eyes Russell had read exactly what she was thinking. She was thinking that the *next* time a black soldier was fool enough to approach her, she would accept him. And take him somewhere where they could be alone and naked, so that when the little knife came out there would be no hurry, no impeding clothing, and she could slash as well as stab. . . .

He actually flinched when he heard a sharp sound behind him in the apartment. It was the first of the front door locks snapping back. Dena was home. Nine o'clock. Bloody well 'bout time.

He wanted to get up and go in to greet her. But he also wanted to stay where he was in the garden, lick his wounds, and have her notice that he was miserable and come to him. At Level Two the former impulse would have won. He uncapped the thermos and replenished his cup of whiskey, kept his back to the apartment and tried with the exaggerated intensity of a first-year acting student to register Angst.

Of course there was a long pause, while she relocked the door, put down her bag and purse, drank apple juice, went to the bathroom, straightened this and that. With each second of delay, Russell became more irritated. Doesn't she know I'm in misery out here? Can't she *tell* somehow? Is she even going to come out at all? Has it even come to her attention yet that I'm not in the fucking house?

Finally the door behind him opened. "Hi, honey. José took Jennifer to the concert, I see."

Ah, that was better. From the tone of her voice he could tell that she knew something was wrong. "Hi, darling. I'm glad you're home."

"Bad day?"

"Medium bad. I saw a boy knifed."

"Jesus. Where?"

"In the guts."

"I meant where geographically."

"Times Square. I was sightseeing."

"Russell, how awful for you! Did he die?"

"I don't know. I listened to the news after supper to try and find out. Somehow I had the idea a thing like that would make the news in this town." He snorted and sipped whiskey, eyes on the stars. "I guess if they reported every stabbing in New York, they'd need a separate channel for the purpose." And I need you to come hold me, Dena, I need to hold you and smell you and run my fingers through your hair and tell you the whole story, and for some reason I don't understand I can't just come out and tell you that, so figure it out my darling, please. A little of that woman's intuition—come and touch me with your healing hands.

He heard her shut the door behind her and lean back against it. "How did he get stabbed?"

"A hooker turned him down, and he slapped her."

"And her pimp got him."

"No. She did. Low and fast."

"Ouch." Pause. "Well, he asked for it."

"I'm not sure that he did."

"He had no business slapping her. She has the right to choose her customers. Of course, a knife is excessive—"

"Isn't that the same logic that Alabama restaurant owners used to use when a nigra came to the door?"

"*Oh*. It was a race thing. That's different. But he still shouldn't have slapped her."

"She didn't *just* turn him down, Dena. She *put* him down, publicly humiliated him so badly I wanted to slap her myself."

"Because he was black?"

"Yes."

"Then I take it back. She didn't leave him much choice."

"No, she didn't."

"I'm surprised. You wouldn't think that a shade girl could get away with that kind of racism in this town any more."

"What makes you think she was white?"

"Huh?" He heard her shift her weight. "Oh, I see: she was hispanic."

"No. She was as black as you are."

"But you said she refused him because he was black!"

"That's right. Oh, I can't prove it—but I'm convinced she would have fucked a white soldier. Or at least have turned him down without castrating him."

"A *soldier*. That's different too."

His irritation boiled over. "Will you *listen* to yourself? One person stabbed another person today, maybe killed him. First you're on her side, because she's a woman slapped by a man. Then you find out he's black, and you're on his side because a white woman threatened his masculinity. But it turns out she's black too, so the situation gets fuzzy. But he happens to be in uniform, so it resolves again: he deserved to be knifed because of his politics. Would the moral situation change again if I said he were a *Swiss* soldier?" He began to get up and turn to face her, decided to take another sip of his drink instead. Let her talk to his back.

"What are you *doing?*" she said, anger beginning to enter her own voice. "*You* fed me the situation in bits and pieces—so I responded that way. Now that I've got all the pieces—if I do—I don't say that he *deserved* to be knifed. But I do say it's understandable, that he should have known better. If you and I went to a Ku Klux Klan meeting together and got assaulted, wouldn't it be at least partly our own damned fault?"

"He wasn't at any kind of meeting. On a public street he went up to a prostitute of his own race and said something like 'tippy tizzy' and she opened up on him."

"Ah." He heard her dress rustle as she changed position again.

"What does 'ah' mean?"

"What he said explains a lot. *'Tipe tizwe.'* It means 'give me a taste,' and the connotation is such that if a stranger says it to a respectable woman, it's grounds for yelling 'rape!' "

"How is that relevant?"

"It's *African*. Shona, from Rhodesia."

Russell was distracted from the argument by a sudden monstrous suspicion. "How do you know?"

"Eh?"

The trees before him rustled darkly. "You don't know any more about Africa than I do. Where did you learn Shona?"

"Russell, in this country at this time, black people talk about Africa a *lot*."

"—and aside from Odet, whom you can't stand, the only other black in the company is Jerome, right?"

"That's right."

The tone of her voice made 'danger' alarms go off in his head, but he ignored them. "So he's your Shona tutor."

"Listen to me. I told you about Jerome. I didn't have to, but I told you. And I told you there was nothing to worry about, that he didn't threaten us."

"That's right, you did."

Her voice rose slightly in pitch. "Are you telling me I have to have your permission to talk with an old boyfriend, to be civil to someone I work with?"

"Not at all. I'm just curious to know how the civil conversation veered onto the etymology of the expression, 'give me a taste,' which is grounds for crying 'rape!' "

"Damn it, Russell, he said it to Odet and she slapped him hard—so I asked him why. Do you really think—"

He believed her at once, was ashamed of his suspicion—and even more ashamed of having spoken it. To doubt a spouse's fidelity, out loud, is to challenge it. "I'm sorry, baby," he began, "I *know* better—" and got up to face her so that his expression could attest to the sincerity of his apology, and cried out in shock.

"Christ!"

Her head was shaven bald.

His expression must have been ludicrous; Dena burst out laughing. He was so stunned and horrified that he could not help joining her. They roared together for a few moments, and then both began speaking very quickly through their laughter.

"Oh shit, Russell—"

"—the fuck did you *do* it for?"

"—Lisa insisted, for the piece—"

"—your beautiful hair—"

"—it'll grow back—"

"—why didn't you tell me first—"

"I couldn't—"

"—oh, *Dena*—"

The laughter was gone now. "Oh Russell, do you really hate it?"

He went to her and took her in his arms.

As a dancer, Dena had often changed her hairstyle to fit a dance, had worn it curly, ultracurly, waved, straightened, braided, natural, and in corn rows. Although the gentle curls with which she had left the house this morning were Russell's personal favorite—it was the hairstyle she had worn when he met her—he had never minded a change before. There was a certain subconscious erotic charge in taking to bed a woman who looked and vaguely smelled like a stranger, yet knew intimately the topography of his desire. As he hugged Dena now, he had to admit that a completely shaven skull added yet another fillip, a touch of androgeny that he found appealing.

He held her from him so that he could see her, and looked closely.

"No," he said finally, "I don't hate it. It's startling, Odin only knows, but I like it."

His tone of voice was quite convincing; a stranger would have been fooled. But he and Dena were five years married. She knew that he hated it, and he knew that she knew, and it was agreed that neither would admit the knowledge. The only thing Russell did not understand was *why* he hated it, and he would certainly give that some thought in the near future, but right now he was busy reassuring his wife that she was still beautiful.

"It makes me wonder what *else* you've got shaved."

She grinned. "I *knew* you'd think of that."

"Does that mean—"

"Come on in the house and find out."

She was indeed hairless from head to toe, and he did indeed find it exciting, and if it took him a little longer than usual to reach orgasm Dena did not seem to notice, or mind if she did. When it was over he marinated in pleasure for a time, thinking, this is contentment, now are the demons of the day exorcized, my tension soothed, my fear eased. Catharsis. "Night of power," He murmured happily to himself.

Dena opened one eye. "Where did you hear about that stuff?"

Russell started to answer, then opened both eyes. "Where did you hear about it?"

"A streetcorner Muslim," she said, and something he could not define caused him to wonder if she was lying. "Me too," he said, hearing himself chuckle just a bit too loudly at this cute coincidence. Had there been the faintest hesitation before she spoke? No, perhaps not. "Well," he went on, "We've blown our chances of having a new Qur'aan revealed to us. As I get the story, you're supposed to abstain from food and sex."

"No, they only fast from sex during daylight hours."

Pause. "I see you got the whole rap."

Pause. "Yeah. He got me at a red light in Chinatown and I couldn't get away from him."

"Did you buy a pamphlet?"

"No. I'm not really into encouraging religious fanatics."

"I didn't either, but I've got one. He stuffed it into my hand, and then the riot started while I was trying to give it back."

Russell was hyperalert by this time, and when she said indifferently, "Mmm. I'd like to look through it sometime," he felt that there was a hair too much indifference. So:

"It's right in my briefcase in the living room."

"Mmm," she said again, and now he had the feeling that she wanted to go get it now but didn't want to seem that interested. So, in a growingly dangerous mood, he decided to see how far it would go if he pushed it, and gave her an additional reason to get up. "That reminds me—while I was in Times Square I picked us both up some new porn. Also in the briefcase."

"Really? I'd like to see it." She got out of bed, reached back, and gave him an intimate tweak. "You thoughtful husband, you."

He made himself smile. "You don't mind if I just lay here in the dark awhile and sort of bask, do you?"

"Of course not. I'll look through it in there. Then maybe

in a while I'll tiptoe back in and turn my basking ace into a basket case." She grinned and was gone.

He lay back and stared at the ceiling.

Admit it, Russell. You think she lied. You think she learned about that Night of Power crap from Jerome. He can't be a Muslim or he wouldn't be in a modern dance company, but he might know about that stuff. Interesting conversation it must have been. Found time to touch on the sexual conventions of Muslims. Apparently didn't get to that part you remember about "flirtatious behaviour" during the day. Or did the conversation take place after the sun went down? All right, let's review the record. Christ, do we really want to do that? Yes, of course we do.

Aw, shit.

The second and third nights back. Late rehearsal the first time. Costume fitting the second time. Both nights she said she went out for coffee with Lisa afterwards. An hour the first night, the second "we just talked and talked" and she got in just before midnight.

All right, back up, Sherlock. You have been married to Dena for five years. Long enough to know someone if the trick can be done at all. You trust her. You love her. You know damned well she loves you. Even when she's in rehearsal frenzy like this and can't take the time to show you always, you know she loves you. You've never had reason to doubt her, and Zeus knows she's had opportunities enough if she'd wanted them, it's not true that all male dancers are gay, and there's got to be something erotic about getting sweaty with a superb physical specimen in scanty attire all day, letting him put his hands on you—remember the time she had to do that pas de deux with that big guy from Montreal and she came straight home and told you right out that it was making her horny enough to bark and would you kindly fuck her brains out right *now*, and you were genuinely sorry four weeks later when the last show was over and he went back west? Come on, Russell old man, long ago you worked this out, with her help and thanks to her you came to terms with your perfectly understandable fear of losing her to another dancer.

Yeah, but what about a black dancer?

The door opened and she came into the room fast. Before he could adjust to the sudden flood of light something hit him hard on the nose.

"You son of a bitch," she said, her voice low and quavering and dangerous.

"What the *fuck*—"

"Of all the cheap, cowardly ways to bring a subject up." She grabbed a pillow and blanket. "Sometime you must tell me whether that was an accusation . . . or a suggestion." She stormed back out to the living room with her bedclothes before he could frame a coherent question.

"Christ in *crinoline*," he yelled after her, "what the fuck is *wrong* with you?" but there was no response.

He went up on one elbow, turned on the bedside lamp, and discovered that his nose was bleeding. He grabbed Kleenex and dealt with that, then saw the missile that had caused it. The magazine he had bought for Dena.

Oh for Christ's sake, he thought, is *that* all it is? What a silly misunderstanding. There's something objectionable in the magazine, she doesn't know I didn't have a chance to examine it before buying it, I'll just explain how it was and boy will she be apologetic. I guess I really should have looked it over before telling her about it.

I guess I really should look it over before I go out and explain.

He picked it up.

Title: *Afternoon Surprise*. Layout utterly simple: one photo per page, no text at all. Lefthand photo: black woman who looks like Dena and white man younger, broader and fairer than Russell, both getting dressed together in the morning. Righthand photo: the two in business attire getting into separate cabs, blowing each other a kiss. *Flip.* Left: woman entering her expensively appointed office, followed by black male secretary. Right: woman grinning over her shoulder as she lifts skirt to display bare ass to grinning secretary. *Flip*. Left and right: woman continuing to undress. *Flip*. She kneels before secretary; unzips his trousers and fellates him. *Flip*. She leans back against the desk while he returns the favour. *Flip*. White man (her husband?) sits at own desk with visible erection; takes cab. *Flip*. Couple are now fucking on desktop, vigorously.

Flip. Same scene, two more camera angles, they're having a wonderful time. *Flip*. White man is leaving elevator; black man is standing bolt upright, arms at sides, muscles bulging, apparently holding her clear of the floor by penis alone. *Flip*. White man reaches for office doorknob; couple are now down on the carpet. *Flip*. White man in office, openmouthed with shock, black couple looking at him in surprise; white man in identical position, black couple ignoring him and resuming copulation. *Flip*. Both shots: black couple in foreground achieving orgasm; white man in background staring. *Flip*. Left: black man gestures menacingly at white man. Right: white man is half undressed, black man is taking cigarettes from pocket of white man's jacket, woman is smiling. *Flip*. White man is naked, eyes downcast, penis at maximum erection, being questioned by black man, who holds in his hand a penis which is dripping wet, limp, and nonetheless noticeably larger in every dimension; woman is watching with a smile. Opposite page: white man on all fours between woman's legs; she is kissing and fondling black man.

There were ten or twenty pages left, but Russell carefully closed the magazine and stared at it edge on.

His first thought was: this was misfiled. It didn't belong in "Raunchy," it should have been in "Nasty." At *least*.

His second thought was: my, this bed is lumpy.

The third thought was: how *dare* she? How could she not guess, how could she possibly not *know* that this was a mistake, that I didn't get a chance to look this over? How dare she believe for a *moment* that I intended to give this to her, just because I gave it to her?

His fourth thought was again: god *damn*, this bed is lumpy.

The next one really twisted the knife, echoing over and over; it was: *the guilty flee when no man pursueth.*

Then, in an adrenalin-charged rush:

Wait a minute, you don't really *believe* this/maybe I do and maybe I don't/Dena *loves* you/"Was that an accusation . . . or a suggestion?"/you *can't* believe it/who told her about tippy tizzy and Muslim sex law/you have a good marriage, she *wouldn't*/I'll bet it *is* bigger/she has too much honesty/she's human/if she did, *don't find out about it,* one slip isn't worth a good marriage/*I* never slipped, in this marriage or the last one, and let me tell you sometimes it wasn't easy, and no the fucking bed is *not* lumpy, it's just got a Smith & Wesson tucked . . .

And then he stopped thinking altogether. He got up, joints popping, and cleaned the last of the blood from his nose and upper lip. He dressed carefully and quietly, in different clothes than he had worn earlier. He took the gun from under the mattress and the firing pin from the dresser drawer. He put them both in the righthand pocket of his windbreaker. He took wallet, money, and keys from the clothes he had worn that afternoon and redistributed them. He left the bedroom, went straight to the front door and left the apartment as quickly as the complicated locks allowed. If Dena was awake, she made no sound.

He walked east on 31st. It was necessary to get rid of the gun; a gun was no longer a good thing to have in the house. The East River was only a few blocks away, and there were so many handguns lying beneath it that the Smith & Wesson would not be lonely. When he got back home he would settle once and for all, one way or another, whether his beloved wife had betrayed him—but not with a gun around.

His head was aching dully as he reached Second Avenue. Thirty-first ended there, and if he had been thinking clearly he would have gone left up to 33rd or right to 30th and continued east to the river. But he was busy trying to rearrange his universe, and decided to cut straight through the Kips Bay complex. He and José had taken Jennifer for a walk through there a few days ago. It was only as he was entering the walkway between a pharmacy and a supermarket which led to the giant apartment tower complex that Russell realized this might be a dangerous place at night. He reached into the pocket of his windbreaker, put the firing pin into the gun, and kept his hand in that pocket.

Sure enough, the plaza between the three massive towers was a splendid place for a mugging. It was 10 PM; all the residents were indoors. The lighting was inadequate, and trees and shrubs and park benches and stone sculptures provided many shadowy places of concealment.

Actually, he realized, he was probably more likely to be mistaken for a mugger himself than to be mugged. He had, without thinking consciously about it, dressed for New York night streets. He wore cheap old clothes, so he wouldn't look temptingly prosperous. His shoes were noiseless. His wallet was in his left rear pocket, where it might escape a cursory search. His right front pocket held a measured fifty dollars, just enough to appease a mugger, while the balance of his cash was strapped to his left forearm with an elastic band (José had warned him that stuffing it down your sock no longer worked.) Between these things and the gun in his windbreaker, a cop might hesitate for some time before classifying him as either criminal or potential victim.

But there were no cops here, and no honest citizens to frighten. He followed the path left past the playground area, and would have turned right onto the great walk that bisected the plaza, but the throbbing in his head had escalated to jackhammer proportions now. He found a bench and sat down for a moment.

The night was oppressive, muggy. Leaves chattered desultorily, but the warm breeze brought no relief. It carried the usual New York symphony of bad smells. Russell dimly came to realize that there was an odd scent layered in there among the rest, a smell that was familiar but did not belong here. What the hell was it? A metallic smell . . .

Copper, that was it. Freshly sheared copper. Who does metalwork in Kips Bay Plaza at ten o'clock at night, without making a sound? No, wait, there was a sound. Behind him, in the playground. Now it made sense. Someone was repairing something in the playground, in the dark, making a little rhythmic bubbling sound as he worked. . . .

Russell sat perfectly still, his right thumb disengaging the safety catch. Then suddenly he was a meter to the right of the bench, on his stomach, gun pointing into the darkness of the playground.

The bubbler whimpered.

Whatever was there in the shadows was bad medicine.

Perhaps a trap. The prudent move was to back away with gun at the ready. Russell got up slowly and moved forward.

The bubbler lay on his back at the bottom of a child's tall slide. Jennifer's backside had passed over his resting place three days ago. He was black, in his forties, bald, and thickly bearded. He wore jeans, a leather vest, and snakeskin boots; his thin torso was powerfully muscled. The coppery smell came from the astonishing amount of blood he had lost—was still losing. It flowed freely from every orifice he had been born with, and several he had just acquired. Bellevue Hospital was a block away, on the far side of Kips Bay; it might as well have been on the far side of the moon.

"Why, it's you," the man said in horrifically conversational tones. The bubbling sound came from his chest.

Russell shook his head. "You don't know me."

"Seen . . . seen you yesterweek . . . drivin' Michael 'round on your ride . . . hand of God, you comin' along now." He tried to smile. "Hand of God." His voice was thick, wet.

Russell could not think of anything to say or do. He knelt beside the bleeding man.

"I got . . . got no time for no ID routine . . . you're with us, right?"

Russell did not understand the question, but he could tell that the dying man urgently wanted an affirmative answer. "Sure."

"Had to be," the other agreed. "Chaufferin' Michael around like that . . . you hip to the Night of Power."

"Yes. Fast of Ramadaan."

"An' all that other good shit. Well, the fuckin' Muslims ain't gonna play along after all . . . deal or no deal . . . you gotta tell Michael, brother: it's a cross . . . motherfuckin' Mustapha Khan gonna cross him tonight . . . let us do the work, then whack Michael while it's goin' down . . . fuck, my ches' hurts—"

"I'll go for help."

"Fuck help, man, get the message to Michael . . . they lookin' to whack him just before it goes down . . . after midnight . . . shit, I was really lookin' forward, you know? . . . now I ain't ever gonna see the day . . . go on now, you tell Michael . . . it was Willie Ray Brown died for him first tonight."

Russell was undecided what to do.

"Whassa matter? Oh, you ain't got your glasses on you . . . here—" With an effort, Willie Ray dragged a pair of sunglasses from his vest pocket and waved them at Russell, who took them with barely concealed confusion. "There's a place uptown on First . . . open all night . . . some quarters in my pants if you need 'em, I sure don't . . . go *on!*" Unexpectedly, he moved, with unexpected strength. Before Russell could react, the gun was snatched from his hand. He froze, totally confused, waiting to die. "God bless you," Willie Ray said, his voice deeper and louder. "You a black shade . . . you a white spade . . . everything up to you now, brother . . . thanks." And Willie Ray put the gun barrel into his mouth, closed his bloody lips around it, and pulled the trigger.

It all happened at once, but afterward Russell would remember clearly the sequence of sounds. The actual gunshot, muffled by Willie Ray's head. The louder sound of the slug whanging off the slide and up into the night, followed almost instantly by the wet sound of brains, bone, and blood spraying eight feet up the slide. Air bubbling out of the chest wound and nostrils. The gun hitting the ground. A shattered branch from overhead hitting the ground behind the slide. Finally the soft trickling sound of the ruins of Willie Ray's head sliding back down again . . .

And then silence.

I was in New York for almost two weeks before I saw my first knifing. But it picked up after that . . .

CHAPTER FIVE

". . . she had that slightly forced elegance of the educated
Negro woman, the continuing understated challenge to you to
accept her on her own terms or, by not doing so, betray the
prejudice she expected you to have. I cannot blame them for a
quality of humorlessness. They carry the dead weight of all their
deprived people, and though they know intellectually that the
field hand mentality is a product of environment, they have an
aesthetic reserve, which they will not admit to themselves,
about the demanding of racial equality for those with whom,
except for the Struggle, they would not willingly associate."

—John D. MacDonald, *Darker Than Amber*

"America is in trouble. [audience agreement] President
Reagan is in *deep* trouble. [loud audience agreement] The
country is so economically weak that the President in his efforts
to balance the budget and prepare for the War of Armageddon,
does not care how many black people he offends in getting
ready . . . His priority is that America survive. And if America's
survival means black folk out of work: let it be. If America's
survival means the death of you: let it be. Because this country
was not made for you, it was made for them and their progeny,
and you happened to come along to help them build what they
stole. [ovation]"

—Minister Louis Farrakhan, addressing a large group of black
   Muslims, Christians, Jews, Nationalists, Moorish Science
   Templars, and members of the Vice Lords, War Lords, Disci-
   ples and other street gangs—on the topic, "In Christ, All

Things Are Possible," Chicago, Oct. 3, 1981. (This meeting constituted a major rapprochement between black Muslim and Christian groups, and other power blocs.)

"At the level of individuals, violence is a cleaning force. It frees the native from his inferiority complex and from his despair and inaction; it makes him fearless and restores his self respect."

—Frantz Fanon

*   *   *

Roughly simultaneously, Dena was reaching the end of a thorough cry, and feeling no better than when she had started. Her eyes were sore, her head ached, she was too tired to think and too wired to sleep. She remembered a palliative for these symptoms, thought of the grass in her purse and wanted some. It was New York grass, legal and strong. She got up from the fold-out couch, got a joint and lighter, and hesitated. She usually did not smoke in the house, because both Russell and Jennifer disliked the smell. She was in a defiant mood now—but then again the apartment *was* already stuffy, and it might be a little cooler outside. She wrapped the sheet around her sari-style and went out to the garden.

How, she wondered as she lit up, had everything gotten so fucking *complicated?*

Only a week ago her world had been stable. Oh, the future had been uncertain, full of the looming question, what will I do when I can't dance any more? But at least she had known who she was *now*. She would have described herself as satisfied with what she had achieved, proud of what she had accomplished, and grateful for all that had been given to her.

Now it seemed that everything she had was shit, and furthermore that she might lose it all.

She took another toke and knew that somehow, somewhere along the line, she had been a fool. That triggered a line from one of her favorite childhood books, *The Princess Bride*: "Fool, fool, back to the beginning is the rule."

Okay, then, she decided, let's review the sequence. Where did it start to go sour? Where *is* the beginning?

Was it the assault in Harlem, on that first day in town?

Up until then, Dena realized, she had built herself a world in which her blackness effectively did not exist, did not matter one way or another to anyone she came in contact with. She could remember having been pleased when the dance press had stopped referring to her as a "black dancer" and started calling her simply "dancer." She had enjoyed living in a world in which skin color was irrelevant. And then she had reminded, forcibly and suddenly, that in the *real* world, skin color could still be a matter of life and death.

And Russell and I never really *talked* about it afterward, she thought. We talked about how it affected Jennifer, and how to deal with violence in general in the future. But we never discussed the racial aspect. Neither of us has spoken Michael's name since that day. We've swept the whole incident under the rug, by unspoken mutual consent.

But after all, she asked herself, what was there—what *is* there—to say?

Nevertheless, she assured herself, something should have been said and was not, and now the chance is gone.

Okay, what was the next sour note?

Jerome, of course.

Was there any way she could have handled that better, anything she should have done differently? No, the basic mistake had been made back in Halifax, when she had not asked Lisa who else would be in the company before accepting the job over long-distance phone. It had never occurred to her to ask. And from the moment she *had* learned that she would be working with Jerome, she believed she had behaved correctly in all ways. She had carefully examined her subconscious, honestly prepared to quit the job at the first hint of hidden yearning, of secret temptation, and had determined that it was not necessary. That established, she had devoted careful attention to convincing Russell. There was no way *not* to tell him—if nothing else, he would one day be reading Jerome's name in the concert programme. And would recognize it: she and Russell by now knew most of the details of each other's past. She had planned it well, had told him in the best possible way at a good time, had looked into his eyes and let the truth show through hers while she promised him that he had nothing to fear. And she had read in his eyes that he believed her.

Admit it, Dena, she thought now, that's not all you read. Oh, he believed you, all right. He accepted your sincerity. And still he was afraid. Not that you were lying—just that you were wrong. And again there was unspoken agreement not to talk about it. Again, what was there to say?

Like the business of Russell's visit with his father and stepmother. Jennifer had told Dena the whole story the next day, but Russell had still never mentioned it. So Dena had never raised the subject either. What was there to say?

Let's see, Dena thought. On account of me, he came to New York, a place he hates and fears. On account of me, he and his daughter were nearly killed. Out of loyalty to me, he estranged himself from his father and Jennifer from her Grandpa, and then he came home to find that for the next six weeks I'll be spending more time with an old lover than with him. No, nothing in there worth discussing with him.

But there hadn't been *time* for long talks, there hadn't been energy for complicated subjects. The rehearsal schedule was heavy, and the work was hard. Setting up housekeeping routine in a strange city was time-consuming. Just walking the streets, being battered by all the *people*, was draining for a Haligonian.

Even so, she had tried hard to ensure that her husband had no reason to feel threatened or unwanted. Over five years of a good marriage, she and Russell had worked out their sexual pattern: whenever she was in rehearsal, she became the passive partner, the one who is done to, and Russell ministered to her attentively. In between, they reversed roles. But for this past week she had made an effort to meet him halfway, not overdoing it but letting him know that he turned her on. She had really thought it was working. And then tonight he had reacted so strongly to her shaven head, and it had taken him so long to come, and then, and then that vile magazine . . .

Damn it, when had there been *time* to talk?

Ah, but there had been plenty of time to talk with Jerome, hadn't there? During breaks at lunch and after work? They had settled it between them on the very first day, baldly and in so many words—that he wouldn't mind fucking her again and that there was no way in hell she was going to let him—and had dropped the subject. But still he kept *talking* to her all the time. And if she and Russell couldn't talk about race, Jerome couldn't seem to talk about anything else. Race and politics.

And that was where it had really begun to go sour. . . .

Jerome had always been a powerful personality, a fast talker and a gifted manipulator. But he had never been political. He had been too self-involved to be political, too cynical to be militant, too intelligent to buy anybody's cheap rhetoric. Now he was a walking encyclopedia of black political awareness. He appeared to know the entire history of worldwide racial struggle backwards and forwards. He quoted Fanon, Farrakhan, Wright, Cleaver, King, Garvey, he talked about the Rastas and the Muslims and the BLA and the American Mau Mau, he talked about Toussaint L'Ouverture and Chaka Zulu and Bobby Seale and Nat Turner. He talked at great length about the situation in Africa and how it affected American blacks—why they were asked to die to assure America's access to chromium and other rare metals necessary to the high technology which, he claimed, put more blacks out of work every day. He talked and talked and talked, and at first she thought it was just a smokescreen for trying to make her, but it was not. He was genuinely trying to educate her, to politicize her. He had heroes now, and he had not had heroes when she knew him before, and she had to admit he was a better person for them—however foolish his heroes seemed to her. He was not a True Believer, he did not proselytize for any particular organization or leader; rather he argued for a united front of all organizations and leaders.

And for the last couple of days he had been talking vaguely of the necessity of armed struggle, in the near future. . . .

Dena had tried to argue with him, but it was hopeless. Jerome had always been able to argue circles around her.

And he had devoted a good deal of time and study to this argument, while she—

—had put it out of her mind years ago.

"Jerome," she had said this afternoon, "every black person in America has thought about armed struggle at some time. The only ones that keep thinking about it are the ones that can't do arithmetic. To try it would be suicide for all of us."

"Not to try it is sure suicide."

"We've come a long way since slavery. Not far enough by a *damn* sight, agreed—but a long way. It's gotten better just since I was born, in '59—we're *getting* there, slowly but surely. It'd be stupid to throw it all away now."

"You're wrong, Dena-mite. We've gone as far as they're going to let us go, and they take a little more back every year. We'll never be any stronger: it's now or never."

"Oh for Christ's sake—how far did the Panthers or the Black Liberation Army get? The Mau Mau fiasco was only a few years ago; have you forgotten it already?" The Mau Mau, essentially a re-run of the Black Panther Party, had first appeared in 1990. By 1991 they were involved in pitched battles with police in New York, Washington, D.C., and Miami. By 1992 the last of them were dead, in prison, or fled overseas.

"The Panthers were visible. The B.L.A. thought small, and the Mau Mau were a special case."

"What the hell does that mean?"

"I mean *real* revolutionary leaders don't wear uniforms and get their pictures in the paper."

So there it was, an open hint. There was some kind of black revolutionary underground. Was Jerome a member, or just an admirer? One more conversation that there didn't seem to be any sense in having.

Dena sighed, threw her roach deep into the garden, and tugged the sheet closer around her in spite of the heat. God damn it, how were black people ever supposed to get anywhere—when every black who did succeed at all, who got as much as one foot out of the trap, was immediately belaboured with guilt for all those still in chains? She wanted to live in a sane world, in which skin color meant nothing, and had managed to build herself such a world. Was it her fault that it was not yet big enough for everybody? Jerome tried to make her feel that every oppressed black person in the world was *her* problem, just because she had a similar complexion, that for her to have anything somehow hurt them, that to throw away everything she had would somehow help them. He made her feel guilty about everything of which she was most proud.

Was he getting to her? Was all his talk reaching her, was she communicating confusion and doubt to Russell in small unconscious ways and subliminal hints? Had Jerome seduced her mind, and was that why Russell had brought her home that damned magazine?

And was that why it had upset her as badly as it had?

With rigid self-honesty Dena admitted to herself that the magazine would not have produced such a violent reaction two weeks ago. Given to her then, by a husband with whom she had a secure relationship, it might have been enjoyable in a raunchy sort of way. The adultery theme would have seemed—as fantasy—pleasantly titillating, and she would have told herself that the skin colour of the participants was irrelevant. But now she was hypersensitized to race, and uncomfortable with it, and no longer absolutely certain that her husband trusted her, and no longer absolutely certain that she trusted herself. . . .

Behind her in the apartment, the phone rang.

It was awkward running in a sheet; it got snarled in the sliding-track of the security-gate, so she left it in the doorway and kept going. Jennifer was at the concert, it wouldn't be Lisa, it had to be Russell. She got it on the start of the fourth ring and said, "Russell?" Silence. "Russell, I'm sorry." More silence. "Come on home, baby, we've got to talk." Silence. "Russell, is that you?" Click.

Shit. Was that him, or wasn't it? Wrong number, heavy breather who chickened out, spurious signal from New York's overloaded phone system? Or was her husband about to come home? Or—oh God—could he have gotten mugged, and just made it to a phone booth before losing consciousness?

Stop that, she told herself. Even if that were true, there was no advantage to anticipating it, nothing she could do about it except go mad. She had to assume that he simply didn't feel like talking on the phone, that he was on his way home right now. *There* was a prospect that needed preparing for. When he did come in that door, what was she going to say?

Dena girl, it is time to take stock. Time to identify your priorities and cut your losses. What have you got?

Item: you've got one hell of a husband. Even from a totally cold-blooded and selfish perspective, he's a dancer's dream. He is retired, wealthy, mature, undemanding, intelligent, sexually sophisticated, and he's your biggest fan. He doesn't begrudge the time your career takes away from him, and he's free to travel wherever your career takes you, he doesn't care that your career makes beans, he supports you in a style to which you've always wanted to become accustomed, he already has a child so he doesn't mind that you don't want to have any now . . . and he's the best friend you ever had.

Item: you've got a hell of a daughter. Not only do you love her, you like her—and the feeling is mutual. You even have high hopes that the two of you might live through her adolescence without becoming mortal enemies. You've got all the good side of motherhood, without the pregnancy and dirty diapers and day-care and chicken pox.

No question about it, girl. Tell that man as soon as he comes in the door. You're going to quit Lisa's gig and pack your family and get your black ass out of New York just as fast as is humanly possible. It's survival time, honey—don't wait another day, and pray to God you haven't waited too long already. It's a shame to lose what is probably your last big Swan Song performance at the Joyce, and Lisa will be madder than a wet cat, but fuck her. She has five weeks to replace you, and she'll either understand or she won't, but don't you dare screw up a good marriage for the ego-thrill of showing your stuff on the stage of the Joyce Theatre. End up all alone again, with a great last line on your resumé? Hell, no—get back home to Halifax, where there'll be all the time in the world to figure out just what went wrong here in New York and what has to be done about it. Step one: Remove hand from flame.

Now why is he buzzing? Oh, of course, he was upset when he left, he forgot his keys. That was quick; he must have phoned from just around the corner.

She buzzed back to unlock the foyer door, immensely relieved that he was all right, and glad that she had used her time to reach a decision instead of wasting it on worrying. She wished this building were modern enough to have security cameras—it would have been useful to study Russell's expression as he approached. She opened all the locks, and strained to see him coming in the fish-eye viewer.

It was Jerome.

Dena had a dancer's atrophied sense of body modesty, but all at once she was acutely aware that she was naked. In a panic she snapped one of the locks shut again.

He knocked. "Dena? I know you're in there. We've got to talk."

"*Shit*." The clothes she had worn this evening were filthy and complicated to get into. She sprang across the room to the garden door and retrieved the sheet, tearing it slightly as she yanked it free. She slid the security-gate shut and locked it, closed the door, turned on a lamp, and arrayed the sheet so that she was totally covered. Then she returned to the hall door and said loudly, "Jerome, you can't come in. Go away."

"We've got to talk *now*."

"My husband is not home. I cannot let you in."

"*I* know he's not home, I'm the one that just called. I bet I even know why he's not home."

"Go away."

"It can't wait. You were supposed to come back to the studio for late rehearsal after you got your head shaved, I was going to tell you then. But you didn't come back."

"I called Lisa and told her I was cutting."

"Dena, I have something of life or death importance to tell you, and I'm not leaving until I do, and I am *not* going to yell it through a door!" He was shouting by now.

"Tell me tomorrow," she shouted back.

"*I expect to be dead by this time tomorrow.*" He stopped, and went on in a quieter voice. "And if we don't talk, right now, you might be too. Your husband and his child too, maybe."

The words were preposterously melodramatic, but Dena knew what Jerome sounded like when he was bullshitting and this wasn't it. With a premonitory thrill of fear, she opened the door—and stood blocking the way. "Is that some kind of threat?"

He was genuinely wound up about something, but still he smiled when he saw her. "God damn, you look fine. You look like an African *princess*. No wonder your husband got upset—".

"Say what you've got to say and go."

"I mean, with that shiny head and that African robe, there's no way in the world he can keep telling himself you're a whte woman with a deep tan—"

She started to close the door.

She expected him to try and stop her, was braced to repel him. Instead he stepped back and said quickly, "I am very sorry." He glanced toward the foyer. "Please let me in."

She stopped with the door half-closed. "No way in hell. You can talk from there, I hear you fine."

He glanced to the foyer again. "I am trying to save your life," he said in a low voice, "and I'm a target standing out here. *Let me in*. Five minutes and I'm gone, I swear by whatever we used to have."

She hesitated, furious at the situation; turned and walked away from the door. When he had closed it behind him, she whirled and snapped, "Jerome, look at me. Watch my lips. Russell could get back any minute. If you are still here when he gets back, I will personally kick your crotch up into your lungs. Subject to that, you have two minutes. Go."

So he sat down and was silent for a while, eyes closed. Just as she was about to throw something at him, he opened his eyes and started talking.

"I've been rehearsing this for a week, and I still don't know how to say it. I don't know how much to say. I have to tell you enough to convince you that I'm serious and sane—but I can't trust you not to drop a dime on me, now you've married white. I shouldn't say anything at all—but once upon a time you cared for me and did me good and I owe you."

"Jerome, will you just—"

"It's the Night of Power, Dena. Not that Muslim crap I told you about: the *real* Night of Power."

"Oh, for—"

"Listen to me. I am a member of a revolutionary underground—"

"I know that, you've been hinting for a week. I must admit I'm surprised. I thought you had more brains than—"

"You may be surprised again if you don't listen!"

She was beginning to be more afraid of what he was saying than she was afraid of Russell coming home while he was saying it. "Go on."

"An operation is going to take place tonight. I can't tell you how big, I don't have the whole picture myself, but the specific task I'm involved in is *big*. There will be a shitstorm. Riots, backlash. A black person in a white neighbourhood will be at extreme risk. If you were smart you'd get on the A Train right now, and be north of 96th Street by midnight, but you're not smart so the next best thing is to fortify this place and hole up for a siege. At least a week, maybe longer. . . ."

There are black people who have no hope at all, and there are black people who have some hope. In North America since well before the Civil War, many of the latter group have lived in more or less constant fear that the former will one day rise up as one in rage and despair and precipitate the pogrom that will exterminate them all. Nat Turner's doomed fiasco was only one of hundreds of slave revolts, and each brought savage and indiscriminate retribution. The fear is often admixed with guilt, especially in those who have achieved any measure of success in the existing society. An enemy could say, now that you've got yours, you don't want anybody rocking the boat. Dena was terrified—Jerome was not talking about a garden-variety riot, blacks tearing up black neighbourhoods, he was hinting at military insurrection in white territory. But she was reluctant not only to show her fear, but to feel it in the first place. She remembered the wretched people she had seen in Harlem, and knew she had no right to tell those people not to despair.

Oh God, it's finally come!

"I couldn't tell you before, Dena, can you see that? For the last week I walked around it, trying to decide whether I could get you to leave town altogether, whether I should try. But I couldn't take the chance. This is bigger than you and me."

"Oh, yeah," she said weakly. "So the revolution is at hand, huh? What's the name of your organization?"

"We don't have a name."

"Come on," she said, hearing her voice get louder with each word, "you can tell me. AfroAmerican People's Front? Sons of the Panthers? The New Mau Mau? What do you call yourselves?"

"We don't. No need to. I told you once, a real revolution doesn't issue press releases. It doesn't have any image at all."

"How about The Detonators? You know, the little tiny part down at the end of the dynamite that destroys the whole—"

"In my mind think of us as Michael's Brothers."

"—*Michael?*"

"Yeah, you know, I told you about him, big cat lives up in Harlem, The Man With No Spot—"

"I know Michael. I met him."

"You *did?* I didn't know that, why didn't you—"

"Never mind. *He's* behind this revolution?"

"Let's say it won't come as a shock to him."

Dena was stunned. In her mind "revolutionary" was defined as someone whose common sense had been exceeded by either his anger or his ego. There had been no anger in Michael. Even when he had suggested the breaking of the heroin merchant's elbows he had not been angry, he had been . . . sad, sad and resigned. Dena had once seen a policeman who liked dogs shoot a rabid dog; his face had held that same grim acceptance. Was Michael an ego-freak, then, one of those who yearned so badly for a place in history that he had forgotten blood is the ink of history? He had seemed to her to be as egoless as a man could be and still be strong. To be so universally respected in Harlem, he had to genuinely care about people: those people had seen every kind of con there was. And he was not a bigot—he had gone to considerable trouble to protect Russell and Jennifer. There was no way Dena could reconcile her vivid memories of Michael with the news that he was a revolutionary leader.

"Michael *knows* about this?"

"He has counted the cost. We all have."

"*What time* tonight?"

"I can't give you the exact hour. You won't be in danger here before sun-up—but long before that, you won't be able to leave Manhattan."

"What do you mean?"

"What I said—it won't be possible to leave the island."

"You mean physically possible? *When?* How soon?"

"I can't nail it down, I shouldn't have said that much."

"I see." Dena got up. "Stay there." She took great care to keep her face impassive and move slowly, but as she entered the bedroom her mind was on computer time, running dozens of alternate solutions for a problem with too many variables.

How long have I got?

Say we have three hours and Russell gets back in a half hour and Jennifer and José get back an an hour, say we just leave everything and *go.* Can we get clear of New York City in two hours by train? Not dependably at this time of night. By bus? Ditto. Cab? Not without more cash than we've got on hand. Steal a cab, maybe with José's help—but which way do we go? Two hours east is halfway to Russell's father's place, two hours west is deep Jersey, two hours north is Kingston or Bridgeport, which is better? Or can we try for the airport and hope for a red-eye flight to anywhere? Suppose José doesn't get Jennifer back for several hours—can Russell and I steal a car and get it ready? And suppose Russell decides to stay out there all night and sulk? Are he and Jennifer safe if just *I* leave? We've been out together a few times, some people in the neighbourhood—in the building—know he's married to a black woman. But if I leave him a note and just cut and run now, maybe he and Jennifer could check into a hotel and follow me whenever it becomes "physically possible" to leave Manhattan again? How much time have I got, and how far away is safe, and for that matter where is safe?

This whole thought train took her only the time needed to close the bedroom door behind her and walk to Russell's side of the bed. She had to have more data, and she could see only one faint hope of getting them from Jerome; it probably wouldn't work, but it had to be tried. Planning how, she felt under the mattress, and by the time she had a plan she liked it seemed that she had been fumbling around under the mattress for a long time, so she got a grip and lifted and the gun just *wasn't there*, she could see the imprint of where it had been on the mattress-pad, and in the busily humming computer that was her mind the system crashed, the cursor vanished, the screen went dark. She stood there, holding the corner of the mattress in the air, for a full ten seconds.

And then she heard the apartment door open.

"Dena—" Russell's voice began, and cut off.

She danced across the bed and burst out of the bedroom. Russell and Jerome were staring at each other. Russell was spattered with dried blood; for a heart-stopping second she thought it was his own. Both men turned to look at her, both absolutely expressionless. She realized suddenly that one of her breasts was exposed and yanked the torn sheet closed over it.

Tableau.

Her husband's eyes had the wild glitter of a wounded man in shock. But there were no holes visible in his clothing, and he simply could not have lost that much blood and lived. Had he killed someone? Had the God damned revolution started early?

"Russell—" she began.

"Shut up."

Shocked, she obeyed. He fixed his gaze on Jerome. She saw that Russell's right hand was in his windbreaker pocket. He usually kept his keys in his pants. Oh Jesus, she thought, he's going to shoot the only man who can tell us what we need to know. But before she could cry out, he spoke to Jerome.

"Can you get me up to see Michael right away?"

The pause seemed to last forever, and then Jerome burst out laughing. Dena very nearly joined him, but caught herself in time.

Russell frowned, and said over the laughter, "There is a plot against his life, and I only have a few hours to warn him."

Jerome only laughed harder, waving his hands to indicate that he could not help himself and would stop as soon as possible.

Russell sighed and took his hand from his pocket. Again Dena began to cry out, and again lost her voice. Russell's hand held, not the gun, but a pair of red sunglasses. The effect on Jerome was as dramatic as if they had been a gun. His laughter chopped off at once, and his face grew tight and dangerous.

"You've got a pair in your breast pocket," Russell stated. "I can see the shape."

A quizzical note crept into Jerome's expression. "If you've got those, what do you need me for? Call Michael yourself."

"I tried. I don't have the right passwords."

"You won't get them from me."

Russell put the glasses away, and when his hand re-emerged it held the gun. "Then you make the call. But if I don't see Michael in an hour, you and he are both going to die."

"Russell—" Dena tried.

"I told you to shut up." He spared her a glance. "We'll talk when there's time. Jerome?"

Jerome went into Street Nigger, the persona he generally used on whites. "Yeah, baby, I can straighten you. Try, anyroad—Michael be lookin' at a busy night this evenin'. Who's tryin' to whack him?"

Russell shook his head. "For all I know you're on *their* side." He put the gun back in his pocket. "Let's go."

"I'm going with you," Dena said.

He glanced at her, and she knew from his face that he was going to ask a terrible question, and he did. "Can I trust you?"

There was no time to be hurt or angry. He had cause to ask. "Yes. Always and forever."

He nodded. "Get dressed and leave a note for José

—we'll be back late." She started to turn away, and he added, "Give him Dad's address and phone code in case we don't get back at all."

She opened her mouth, then saw his expression, bit her lip and did as she was told.

Russell led them all in silence to an all-night video arcade on Third Avenue. As they approached it he called a halt and turned to Jerome. "I tried my call in a place over on First. I had to lay a man out and show my gun to get out in one piece. If anybody in here figures out that I'm holding a gun on you, you will die and then I will die and then Michael will die. Be measured."

"I hear you."

At this hour the arcade was almost empty. The few patrons were all black, and two wore red sunglasses. Dena would have bet serious money that a bloodstained man walking into a video arcade in the middle of the night in New York would go completely unnoticed, but the three of them drew stares. Seeing this, Russell stopped, looked around, and ostentatiously put on his sunglasses. Jerome put on his own. The starers looked away.

"You take first licks," Russell said to Jerome, who picked a machine at random and dropped in two quarters.

And for five minutes, to Dena's astonishment, they played games.

After a time a subtle observation came to her. Both Jerome and Russell punched the keys too fast for her to tell what they were programming—but she became convinced that it was not related to what appeared on the screen. A plausible game played itself out there, but they were not directing it.

Of course. The sunglasses. They were not seeing what she saw. Infrared lenses, perhaps? Or some other filter system . . .

She glanced around the arcade. The three of them were still being surreptitiously observed, and her subconscious alarms began ringing. She reached up to tug at her hair, in a nervous mannerism she had not known she had, and became aware of it when her fingers failed to find hair there. That's it, she thought, let them all know that you've only just shaved your head, they'll be more convinced than ever that you're some kind of double agent. She tried to look like a militant, and realized she did not know how.

Well, the first step was to stop being timid. She picked out the nearest man with sunglasses on and looked him square in the eye, projecting the message: look elsewhere, fool, you're compromising security. Dancers are actresses who don't use words; he bought it and looked away hastily.

Russell and Jerome finished their game. "Let's hit the street, my sweet," Jerome said, still being Street Nigger. She knew he was speaking for the benefit of their audience, and knew that Russell knew it too—to be plausibly in character, she had to be with Jerome, not with Russell— but she also knew that it got to Russell, and that Jerome had intended it to. They were in Jerome's world now, in which everything they had taken for granted for five years was unthinkable. He took Dena's arm and led them from the arcade, strutting it with dancer's grace.

"What happens now?" she asked as soon as they were outside.

"We wait for wheels," Jerome said. "Won't be long."

"We're going uptown?"

"That's right."

She turned to her husband. "Who is it that's trying to—"

He put his hand back into his windbreaker pocket and spoke to Jerome. "What do you think of the Black Muslims?"

Jerome looked at the pocket. "You wanna take yo' hand out from there, Jim. Brothers behind you got their orders by now."

She glanced over her shoulder; people were watching them from the door of the arcade, hands in their own pockets.

"I see them," Russell said. "They'll have been told not to shoot unless we try to go before the car gets here. Answer my question."

Puzzled by the question, Jerome dropped Street Nigger, spoke in his normal voice for the first time since Russell had come. "Black Muslims? The reconsolidated, post-Farrakhan one true Nation of Islam? Overall they've been good for the community, a positive force. Their theology is as whacky as anybody else's, and they hate a little too hard for my taste. But they make themselves clean and strong and pure, they keep their word, they help others. The last fifteen years they've been making a special effort to get along with Christians and other groups. Personally I'm not a big fan of their present leader, Mustapha Khan, but he's only one man. I wouldn't *be* a Muslim, submission to Allah's will is not my style—but overall they're okay, I guess. Why?"

"You told Dena a lot about Muslim lore."

"Sure. I told her about the Maroons, too, and the Rastas and the African National Congress. So what?"

Russell turned to Dena. "This is true? He's not affiliated with the Muslims?"

"Yes."

He took his hand back out of his pocket slowly and carefully, empty. "I don't know what you people are planning for tonight. Some kind of guerilla activity, that's clear. Well, the Muslims are planning a doublecross—or at least, Mustapha is. He plans to assassinate Michael tonight."

Jerome was startled, but recovered quickly. "What's that to you?"

"When my family and I first got to New York, we were forced to drive through Harlem. Michael saved our lives. I owe him."

Jerome's eyes widened. "You know what's going down tonight and you want to save Michael's life? You're telling me that your personal gratitude to him outweighs your loyalty to your race?"

"I have no race!" Russell snapped. "My body does, maybe, but my brain is a member of the *human* race. It hasn't got many members. I've met Michael and whatever the fuck is going on tonight I know that he too is a member of my race. I will not see him betrayed."

Dena was suddenly very proud of her husband, and wanted to say so, but just then the car arrived. In the front seat were two men in what she was coming to recognize as an inconspicuous uniform, shaved head and red sunglasses. Both men looked professionally inscrutable.

The passenger-side man got out and opened the back door for them; he was enormous and heavily muscled. Dena automatically moved forward to get in first, and then a second car pulled up even with the first and came to a stop in the middle of the street. She had time to see that it was full of white-robed and -turbaned Muslims before Jerome hit her from the side and carried her down onto the sidewalk. The big door-opener moved at the same instant, intercepted a hail of machine gun bullets meant for Russell; his shoulder burst and the arm was blown entirely off. His scream coincided with the sound of the shots, curiously light for machine gun fire, and as he dropped, Russell went down too—she could not tell if he had been hit. Suddenly the air was full of thundering gunfire: their driver, people in the arcade doorway, Muslims, all blasting away. The car windows exploded above Dena and showered her with glass; the arcade windows shattered and collapsed; someone called someone a cocksucker and someone else was weeping like a baby. Jerome rolled off her to a prone position and with methodical care and a gun she had not known he possessed he began blowing the tires off the Muslim vehicle. With six shots he got all four, and at once the Muslim car began to move forward noisily, rolling on the rims. All the shooting was from the sidewalk now, and it was all missing the driver, the car was up to thirty kph, it was going to get away, and Russell stood up straight and tall, assumed combat stance, and fired carefully. The rear window starred at the right, the front window exploded outward at the left, and the car slowed to a spasmodic crawl, like a crippled insect. Nothing moved within it.

The man who had saved Russell was thrashing on the sidewalk, convulsing in silent agony. The whole incident had taken less than ten seconds. Jerome went to the wounded man and examined his ruined shoulder. "You might live," he said. "Bellevue's not far away."

The man shook his head. "No . . . I might . . . start talkin' shit . . . in Emergency . . . lotta shade raise there . . . don't lemme fuck up, brother."

Jerome nodded heavily, stood and slipped a new clip into his gun. Russell stopped him. "My responsibility," he said. To the wounded man he said, "Thank you for my life," and shot the man through the forehead. The force of the shot burst the skull; the corpse's legs spasmed a ghastly few times and were still. "Get in the car, Dena."

She could not get up. He and Jerome simultaneously move to help her, then stopped and exchanged a glance. Jerome said, "Yours again," turned away and set about dragging the dead driver out of their car and cleaning the seat. Russell hoisted Dena to her feet. Trembling violently, she got into the back, making spastic attempts to sweep broken glass from the seat. Russell got in next to her. Jerome slid behind the wheel. The car was still running in Park. After some difficulty getting his door to close, Jerome pulled away from the curb, laying rubber, and roared away past the Muslim vehicle, which was still limping forward with its cargo of corpses, tires flapping wearily.

"Lucky only the side windows are fucked," he called back over his shoulder. "Roll them down, this car'll look no worse than a thousand other wrecks. Those guys were amateurs, they shot high."

"We got good covering fire from the arcade," Russell called back.

Jerome came to a red light and obeyed it. "Car full of blood, two pieces on us, this is no time to get stopped." He glanced back over the seat. "Russell . . . I don't hate you as much as I did an hour ago."

"Back when I was working," Russell said conversationally, "people used to ask me where I got my crazy ideas. I always told them, 'Right between the eyes,' and they always thought I was kidding. That's what that poor son of a bitch back there got. A shiny bright idea, right between the eyes. Ten days I've been here in New York. I think things are truly starting to pick up now—" Without warning or transition he was crying, explosively and silently, at the same cyclic rate as the idling engine. Jerome didn't seem to hear.

Dena was recovered enough now to realize that her husband was in shock. She called his name, pulled him to her, and they rocked together while the car pulled away from the light and sped uptown.

*   *   *

Marcus Garvey Park looked different by night. The parking space Jerome found was no more than thirty meters from where Dena and her family had first met Michael. The night was windless and muggy, the trees still. Car and foot traffic were light. Music was playing somewhere—music was always playing somewhere in New York—but it was distant and muffled. Dena felt unseen eyes on her as she got out of the car behind Russell.

So did he. "You wait here."

"No way in hell," she said, and slammed the door.

He gave up, took her hand with his left and followed Jerome across the intersection to the park. When they reached the far side he slowed, allowing the gap between them and Jerome to widen. "We haven't had a chance to talk," he murmured.

"No." On the way uptown, after Russell had finished shaking, he had told her the story of his walk through Kips Bay Towers. But there had been no time to talk of the quarrel that had sent him walking, and the presence of Jerome had inhibited them both. "Russell—"

"Dena—"

There was too much to say, and not enough time. Neither knew where to begin.

"If this goes sour—" he tried, and Jerome interrupted. "Come on," he whispered sharply. "We're targets out here."

They hurried on into the park. Did Jerome know what he had interrupted? She refined what she needed to say down to a few words, and started to say them, and Jerome and Russell both shushed her at the first syllable.

So she concentrated on squinting into the darkness for lurking assailants. The park appeared to be deserted, and either there were no lights or they had all been smashed. Dena thought of Point Pleasant Park in Halifax, through which she had walked in safety many a night—in which she had met Russell!—and wished mightily that she were there with him now.

They came to a bench which looked like any other, and Jerome sat. "Now we wait," he said softly. "You understand I've got to have your gun?"

Russell handed it over carefully. "I don't like it, but I understand. Does Michael live in this park?"

"No. Michael's a Spotless man."

"I don't understand."

"Street talk. Your spot is where you live. *Your* spot is on East 31st, mine's on the Lower East Side. Everybody has a spot, even if it's just an alley or a piece of sewer pipe. But Michael has no spot. He sleeps in a different place every time. There aren't many black people in this town that'd turn him away—or hispanics or asiatics either. Aside from sleeping, your spot is where you keep your shit—your belongings—but Michael doesn't *own* anything." Jerome had apparently abandoned Street Nigger for good. "But he hangs out here regularly. Tuesdays and Thursdays, anybody with a bad need to talk to him knows they can probably find him here. In return, they mostly leave him alone the rest of the week, unless they're really hurting too bad to wait."

"What do they talk to him about?"

"Where they hurt and how bad. Usually how it goes is, they come up with a problem it takes about a thousand words to tell, and they get out the first sentence or so, and he says five or six words and they go home straightened. Once I was thinking seriously about suicide. Too long a story to tell now, and I didn't get to tell it to Michael either. As soon as he knew where I was going, he reached out and grabbed me by the damn throat, started strangling me. I fought like crazy and couldn't break his grip; somehow the way he was looking at me I just couldn't hit him. Then he let go, just before I blacked out. 'You want to die,' he said, 'all you had to do was stand still.'

"So I figured out that the easiest thing to do was to go put my life back together, and I did that instead."

"Was that when Michael recruited you?" Russell asked.

"He didn't. He and I have never exchanged a subversive word."

"How do you know, for sure, that you're in *his* army, then?"

"Because a man I trust told me so, and because Michael has a special way of looking at you if he sees red sunglasses on you."

Dena suspected that Jerome was being so loquacious to keep her and Russell from having a chance to talk. She decided to wedge her way into the conversation. "I hope he gets here soon."

And from less than a meter behind her, the deep voice she remembered so well said, "I've been here a while, child."

They whirled around. He stood behind the bench, both hands lightly gripping the back of it, one of them centimeters from her shoulder. He seemed even taller than she remembered. The man at his right was nearly as tall, and even broader; at his other side was a shorter and slighter man who held himself with military erectness. In the darkness she could tell nothing more about them, but she had the distinct impression that if she did anything that Michael's broader companion did not like, he would crush her skull in his hands.

Michael addressed Russell. "Did I talk with you about half an hour ago?"

"I said I was the white Canadian who gave you a lift downtown two weeks ago."

"And you said you . . . knew how especially busy I was tonight, but that you had a message that wouldn't wait. Even on the Night of Power."

"I do."

"You said it was worth your life to deliver."

"It is."

"I'm here."

"You trust these two men with your life, Michael?"

"With much more than that, son."

"I don't know exactly what it is that you are doing tonight. But a man named Mustapha Khan is planning to betray you. He'll try to kill you tonight."

Michael's shorter companion visibly flinched and made a small exclamation, but Michael and the broad man did not react physically at all. After a short pause, Michael asked, "How do I know what you say is true?"

"You don't. *I* don't. All I know is that a man named Willie Ray Brown died telling me it was. I found him dying. If the light were better here you could see his blood on my clothes."

The shorter man made a sound in his throat. Although Dena could not make out any of their faces in the dark, she knew from the sound of Michael's voice that his face held that same deep sorrow she recalled so clearly. "Willie Ray is down. That's bad. He was a good man."

The shorter man spoke for the first time. "Why would Lieutenant Brown give his message to you? Even if he was dying, you're white."

"He thought I was one of you. He saw Michael ride downtown in my car a few weeks ago. He gave me his sunglasses, and enough hint to figure out how to use them."

The questioner pounded himself on the hip with clenched fist. "Damn. Michael, I think he's telling the truth."

Michael glanced at his other companion before he spoke. "He is, Tom."

"That treacherous *bastard*—" Tom began savagely.

"Now, Tom, we knew he was a treacherous bastard from the jump. We just mistook him for a smart one."

"Maybe he's not smart, but the son of a whore is *cunning*. I never had a sniff of this, I wasn't expecting it for at least two or three days yet."

Jerome spoke up. "Michael? I am Private Jerome Turner. My cell leader is Anthony Latimer. Our objective is the 59th Street Bridge, but I'm not essential to the operation. Kind of a utility infielder. I'd be honoured to kill Mustapha Khan for you."

"Thank you, son, but he's my personal responsibility. My bad judgement has already killed Willie Ray. I'll fix it."

"Yes, sir."

"Michael, no," Tom protested. "Motormouth and I can—"

"—see that I'm not interrupted," Michael finished. "We're getting ahead of ourselves." He turned back to Russell. "I don't know your name, son."

"Russell Grant. This is Dena St. Claire."

To Dena's surprise, Michael bowed to her and said, "I'm sorry I won't get to see you dance, Dena."

"So am I," was the only reply she could manage.

"Russell, Dena, I am very sorry, but I cannot let you go home now."

"For how long?" Dena asked at once. "Our daughter is

going to be getting home from a concert any time now, and—"

"There's someone with her?"

"A very good bodyguard," Russell said.

"Does he really care about her?"

"Yes."

"I'm glad to hear it. I won't be able to let you go for a week or more. And it might be a day or two before I can spare a car and manpower to have your daughter picked up. I'm sorry, but that's the way it is."

The broad silent man had moved nothing but his head since his arrival, but all at once he swiveled to their right and half-crouched. A few moments later the rest of them heard approaching footsteps. By that time the broad man had relaxed. A shape loomed up in the darkness, and a voice said softly, "The objective has been secured, General. Ready for you and Michael any time."

There was immense satisfaction—or was it relief?—in the voice of the man Michael called Tom. "Excellent, Lieutenant! We'll be right along. Any uproar?"

"No sir. They took it quick and quiet—we're the only people outside the building who know." He went away.

Slowly, Michael nodded. "So it begins," he said softly. "After all the—"

"Michael!"

"Eh? Yes, Russell?"

"I'm very sorry, but you have not thought this thing through."

The broad man did not react, but the general stiffened in anger. Michael put a hand on his arm. "What did I miss?" he asked Russell.

"Have I repaid you tonight for saving our lives?"

"That you have. With interest you cannot imagine."

"Then hear me. I don't know where you plan to take Dena and me, or how long you will keep us there. But I am *not* going to leave my daughter Jennifer with a hired gun, even a good one, on this night of nights. Sometime between now and dawn I will either escape you or die trying. Probably the latter. Now won't that be a hell of an omen for the Night of Power?"

"It surely will," Michael said thoughtfully.

"No way," Tom snapped. "Michael, I'll buck you on this if I have to—I'm grateful to the man too, but *he stays on ice*—"

"Please, Tom," Michael said softly, and the general shut up. "Russell, have you a suggestion I can live with? Tom is right, you can't go free."

"I think I have. Jerome just said he was not essential to his operation. Send him to bring Jennifer and her bodyguard to us."

Dena gasped. "Would you—"

"—trust Jerome? I trust him to obey Michael, and I trust him not to make you sad."

Jerome said nothing.

Dena knew somehow that Michael was sensing and interpreting the undercurrents here, weighing and measuring, and a part of her marveled at how much attention he was sparing to what must be a comparatively trivial situation at this moment in history. "Jerome, are you willing to do this thing for Russell and Dena?"

Jerome only hesitated for a second. "If it's what you want, Michael."

"Thank you, son. Bring the child and her guard to the Metropolitan Museum of Art, main entrance. You'll receive further instructions there."

"Yes, sir." He turned to Russell. "What's the bodyguard's name?"

"José Johnson. He's tough and smart and suspicious and more dangerous than he looks. How you convince him you really come from us is, you tell him three things. You tell him the Smith & Wesson was in the top drawer, and you tell him that Shaw has a nose full of Epsom salts, and you tell him that *I* said you're a black person and not a nigger."

Dena was horrified by the last clause, but all Jerome said was, "What's the difference?"

"We talked about it once. José is half black himself. A nigger, by his lights, is someone who would hate Jennifer because her mother is black."

Jerome was slow in answering. "I take your point," he said at last. "I don't hate her."

Was there extra emphasis on the last word?

"If I thought there was the slightest chance you did," Russell told him, "I'd leave her with José and hope for the best. But I want José to know that—so tell him what I said."

Jerome repeated back all three clauses, and got up from the bench. He stood directly in front of Dena. "I'll bring your little girl safely to you," he said, and strode away into the night.

"Please come with us now," Michael said.

CHAPTER SIX

"Our young brothers and sisters that are in what you call the gangs, they're a very strange breed. Parents, you never *seen* anything like your children before. They're a different breed, and you know why they're different? Because they represent the Age of Fulfillment—and you represent the Age of Hope. You've always *hoped for* freedom, hoped that one day you'd be delivered. Your children are born to bring into reality what you hoped for. [cheers.] And as fulfillment don't look nothin' like hope, your children are *from* you, but they don't really spiritually resemble anything *like* you. You can't get them to school, because they know white man's school is a failure. You can't drag 'em to church, because they had enough of that. They out in the street, waitin' for The Call! They are *warriors*. [cheers.] Just look at the name they call themself: the 'War Lords'! What do the War Lords know that you don't know, that Reagan knows? Reagan knows it's the time *for* war; the War Lords know it got to *be* war in order to get what rightfully belong to you . . . [ovation.]

"They're young and they're tough, because they're born to fight. They just don't have the general. The general to show them *who* to fight, and then *when* to fight, and when to train the right hand and keep it cocked—and when it's time to throw it, knock the hell out of the enemy in the name of God! [sustained ovation.]"

—Minister Louis Farrakhan,
Chicago, Oct. 3, 1981

"Men do not revolt merely because they are poor and oppressed. They revolt because they are aware of a gulf between their expectations and their present condition, and of a possibility of crossing that gulf in a single bound."

—de Tocqueville

* * *

"This," Jennifer thought as she left the apartment with José, "is the happiest night of my life." And it was just starting! Ecstasy too great to be borne—

Jennifer was an extraordinary child, and not only intellectually. She knew about the roller coaster of joy. She recognized the increasing acceleration and upward slope of her emotions, and she could discern that the peak ahead was a higher one than she had yet dared. She knew, from both her parents' counsel and her own experiments, that there was a scary downslope on the other side, that emotional binges are a fly-now pay-later deal which usually turns out to cost just a little more than one can afford. But she didn't give a damn. This was her second week in New York, and for the past week she had been an uneasy combination of tickled pink and bored stiff. A restless, reckless mood had been growing on her for days—if she had been an adult, she might have gone out and gotten gloriously drunk or stoned.

And then suddenly everything in the universe that could possibly go right had begun to do so, all at once. She heard the little warning voice in the back of her mind that whispered, this will be expensive, and she replied, stuff it, little voice. It's on the plate and I am going to *eat* it—as the Juice would say.

It had begun this afternoon, when José had produced the pair of tickets to the Juice concert.

A big part of it, of course, was simply the tickets themselves. Naturally Jennifer had known about the concert. Everyone in North America between the ages of six and sixteen knew that the Juice were on tour; she had known before she left Halifax that they would be in New York the same time she was—and that she was not going to see them. She had lied to her father this evening. Grandpa had tried valiantly for her, had stood on line for seven hours and failed to secure tickets; it was said that no one who had waited less than twenty-four hours had even got close to the window. (Russell heard nothing of this: knowing that her father hated flash groups in general, she had thought it best not to consult him before phoning Grandpa.)

So she had resigned herself. She had made José take her on only three pilgrimages to Madison Square Garden to contemplate the shrine-to-be, and had firmly resolved *not* to join the ticketless thousands who would surely surge around the Garden on The Night in the futile hope of getting a glimpse of the Fan' Five. She had planned to spend the night sensibly, maturely, bravely crying her eyes out at home—and now she was actually *going to see them* after all. Live! In person!

An equally large part of her exhilaration lay in the fact that the tickets had come from José.

For the last ten days she had been, as she put it in her diary, "discovering her sensuality," by practicing it on José. She was aware that he probably called it something else, but she intended to be fair—the last night before she went home to Halifax she was going to let him kiss her, perhaps even let him put his hands on her for a moment while her parents were out loading the car. Meanwhile he was an older man, he was gorgeous, he was virile and—unlike Bobby Amatullo back home—he was absolutely safe. She knew that honour was everything to José, and he was honour-bound not to notice her as a sexual being no matter what the provocation. Her parents had confirmed this by hiring him. So it was okay to make it tough for him, and she never overdid it, always slacked off as soon as the sweat began to actually pour off him. The whole idea was to keep it low-key, to keep him as bothered as possible without ever making an openly seductive move. At the Statue of Liberty, for instance, he had had to let her go first up the narrow helical stairs, which placed her shorts-covered rump in his face for several hundred steps; then on the way down she had gone first again, frequently stopping and turning to talk to him, so that her face was inches from his crotch, and he could not help but see down her neckline. She had caught him sneaking peeks—and he had *not* caught *her* sneaking peeks. It was a delightful, mysterious, fascinating game, the prize was a tented trouser front, and José had at least as much chance as any other fish in a barrel . . . she had just been starting, the last few days, to feel slight stirrings of guilt for the suffering she was putting him through. And now he had brought her the best present she could imagine.

On a sheerly financial level, the gift was impressive. She reckoned that the tickets had to have set him back at least a hundred dollars apiece, not to mention inconvenience. No man but her father had ever spent so much on her before. On a personal level, the gift was thoughtful, insightful. She had never mentioned the Juice aloud to him, had not explained why she wanted to walk past the Garden three times—she believed that truly mature people suffered silently, privately. He had guessed her need without a word being spoken. And on a subconscious level, the tickets said that he did not hate her for toying with him—a possibility which had begun to genuinely trouble her. Could it be that, despite everything that Bobby Amatullo and her parents had told her, boys actually enjoyed being tortured? Jennifer felt that she was at the verge of one of the great adult mysteries.

The whole thing had gone perfectly. José had produced the tickets early enough in the day for her to make plans. He had let her pay him for her ticket, but refused to accept more than twice its face value, a figure both absurdly low and within her budget. He had helped her work the old "Dad/Mom says it's all right with him/her if it's okay with you" gag on both parents in succession. Dena had been in a hurry to get off the phone, something about having her hair done, and Russell had obligingly come home too tired to escort her himself. Best of all, he had been distracted enough from a traumatic day to see nothing wrong with her choice of outfit when she left.

There had been nothing wrong with it when she left. A sensible, modest jacket-and-long-skirt affair, heel-less shoes, blouse buttoned to collarbone—the outfit could have been worn by a nun. But two blocks from her apartment, she made José wait while she went into a restaurant washroom.

When she emerged, he sucked a satisfying amount of air through his teeth.

She held the jacket slung across her shoulder. The blouse was entirely unbuttoned, tied together beneath her newly-developed breasts in a knot that was secure but looked flimsy. The snap-on heels were in place. The skirt had lost its side panels all the way up to the waistband, was in effect a long loincloth, which not only revealed green fishnet stockings, but made it seem that the garter belt supporting them was the only underwear she wore—the little front-to-back loinstrap did not show at the sides. Her hair was styled differently and her make-up was much bolder. The overall effect would have made Dena distinctly uneasy and sent Russell into cardiac arrest. She looked, in short, like most girls her age in New York.

Save, she thought smugly, that she looked better than most girls her age. Let her period take as long to show up as it wanted—in all other respects she was doing just fine, thanks.

"Jesus Christ, Jennifer!"

"What's wrong?" Blink. Blink.

"You look like a sex crime lookin' for the spot marked X, that's what's wrong."

"José, don't be *junior*. It's hotter now than it was this afternoon, and I wore shorts this afternoon—and it's going to be even hotter at the concert. You don't want to get me all sweaty, do you?" The last line was delivered with no English at all—a listening maiden aunt would have heard no double-entendre—but she saw it strike home and kept her face innocent with great effort.

"Jennifer, listen to me. I gotta explain somethin' to you. Suppose I come walkin' down this street with five hundred dollars in my hand, just wavin' it around, and some guy that hasn't eaten in a week drags me in a alley and takes the money. Who could blame him, right? It's my fault for bein' so stupid, right?"

"So?"

"It's up to me to protect my treasure. But you young fems, you got the treasure of them all, every one of you, and it's the only treasure in the world the owner don't have no obligation to hide. You can just leave it out on the windowsill and nobody's supposed to take it."

"But José, I have *you* to protect me."

He got mad. *"So how come you gotta make it hard for me?"*

She dropped her eyes. "José, you know the last thing I want to do is make it hard for you." Again, no emphasis on the words, and again she could almost *hear* the harpoon thud home. "Everyone else there is going to be dressed just like this . . . but if you don't think I'll be safe with you, I'll go change back and—"

"Don't bullshit me. We're gonna have to hurry if we want to get our seats—"

She rewarded him with her best smile, and came closer, until he was within the striking range of her (mother's) perfume. "Well? Aren't you going to offer me your arm?"

He glanced away. "I gotta keep my hands free."

"Of course. Shall we go, then?"

It kept getting better. She drew a few stares as they walked up 31st, and José had to glare fiercely at one middle-aged businessman in a pearl-grey suit. But when they reached the immense crowd around the Penn Station-Garden-Felt Forum complex, she saw that she was by no means exotically dressed for the occasion. She had heard about kids going topless in public, but had never actually seen it before, in Halifax or New York. Not for the first time she suspected that José was not taking her to the fun neighbourhoods. She noticed that all the topless fems were with a powerful-looking male or a gang. She saw only a few close to her age, with gangs—it must be hard for thirteen-year-olds to get a ferocious enough escort. She had total faith in José herself—and was wishing she had settled for unbuttoning a few buttons of the blouse. The crowd was vast and noisy and exciting and terrifying, the largest crowd that she had ever seen.

And the Juice were in there somewhere, getting ready to perform!

The next hour was a general chaos amid which the excitement of the crowd slowly built to something like frenzy. A ticketholders' line had been marked off with barricades. The lane was choked eight and ten deep with bodies, and the barriers were thronged along the outside with hucksters, hustlers, hecklers, vendors, dealers, pushers and scalpers. Everyone was shouting, laughing, dancing, smoking, drinking, eating. Those who had wristwatch video watched chips of the Juice, holding up their wrists so that their immediate neighbours could share and sing along; or else they tuned to a news channel and tried to spot themselves in the crowd. Every time a news chopper went by overhead, kids whose parents did not know they were here ducked frantically away from the cameras; the rest mugged. The air was full of pot and hash and more exotic smoke. The police looked harassed, and had evidently been ordered to ignore anything below a Class A felony; Jennifer saw one freebase dealer ask a cop for a light, and get it.

She did observe some incidents which disturbed her. As the hour approached, and the scalpers began quoting more and more unbelievable prices, she heard a boy blackmailing his date, making no effort to keep his voice down—"all three holes, right after the show, or I sell your ticket right now"—and when the girl tearfully agreed, a few bystanders laughed and cheered. Jennifer tried to exchange a glance of horrified disgust with José, and found him utterly expressionless. There was one small fight ahead of them, fists only.

But the general mood of the crowd was benign, benevolent; for its size and location it was an astonishingly well-behaved mob. She could tell that the police were pleasantly surprised, warily relieved. She was not at all surprised. The Juice were an *up* band: their work was happy, life-affirming; their magic was white magic. (Their dark clone, the Pulp, were another matter; they dealt in dark imagery and violent symbols. When *they* had played the Garden the previous Fall, there had been trouble: six deaths, over a hundred hospitalized, autos flung bodily into the lobby of the Statler Hilton and set ablaze. Her father said it had been much the same in his day, with the Beatles and the Skipping Stones or whatever they were. But the Juice had made it plain that they wanted no part of their quasi-imitators, and notoriously would not perform for a violent crowd.) This was the kind of joyous gathering that got to even hardened cops—the happy excitement was infectious.

"What pieces do you think they'll do?" she asked José excitedly. " 'Mental Floss'? 'Totality'? Or even—"

"I dunno, I guess they'll do whatever's their latest ones."

She stared in disbelief. "José! Do you mean to say *you don't follow the Juice?*"

He became defensive. "Well, I *know* about 'em, I seen a couple of their tapes. They're just not my brand, you know? Like maybe I'm too old for them or something."

"I don't believe you. You've got to know 'Eat It' at least."

"Yeah, sure. Everybody knows it. I dunno, though—if it's on the plate and I don't like it, I don't eat it. I go get another plate of somethin' better an' eat that."

"Oh, that's junior and bogus." Secretly she was delighted. He had gone to all this expense and trouble and *he didn't even like the Juice himself.* Power!

A collective scream broke loose as the doors were opened somewhere up ahead, and the vast serpent of ticketholders began to writhe forward spasmodically. The rest of the crowd simply writhed. She and José were swept forward as though by a terrible riptide, and he held her wrist with a grip like iron. He maintained it through all the madness that followed, but despite his best efforts she had been intimately groped at least half a dozen times by the time they reached their seats—once by a cop. It was not fun, being handled, but it was not not-fun either.

It was even hotter in here, and a cloud of smoke was already forming below the high roof, where immense fans struggled to chop it up. She began to perspire freely, and thought about losing the blouse now that she was safely in her seat. But there were several single males in her row, and anyway she did not dare. She could feel her face tingling from a combination of excitement and the hallucinogens in the air, and an even stronger tingling in her belly. She was beginning to wonder how much more joy she could tolerate.

Just studying the equipment waiting for them on the stage was exciting. It was *their* equipment, set up the way she remembered from their recordings. The high bubble-domed tower on which Tamila would dance the drums dominated the stage; clustered around its base were the twin synthesizer consoles (rumour was right: they were Spangler Fives) and the U-shaped array of visuals controls; mammoth columns of speakers and lasers at either side defined the area within which Travis would sing, speak, and dance.

A crescendo of shrieks. Tamila, proudly, chastely nude, strode out from the wings, entered the door in the base of her tower and was raised up into the transparent bubble. She was the Spiritual One, the perc-dancer: wireless EMG leads implanted in most of her major muscle groups would control the synthesized percussion while she trance-danced. She was nude because clothing would have masked or distorted the signals; it did not hurt that she was stunningly beautiful. The moment she appeared on her platform, the bubble's sensors picked up the tension in her thighs and set up a bass rumbling which was audible even over the swelling white noise of the crowd.

At once Mark and Iyechi ran out from either wing and took their places at the twin Spanglers. "H" was the Technician, who understood electronics and designed the Juice's equipment hookups; Mark was the Sexy One, achingly beautiful, and the composer who had earned the respect of the grownups. It was an open secret that the boys were lovers, but it did not affect their popularity: they were both bisexual and known to appreciate fem groupies. They wore matching Mylar tunics and boots. Jennifer noted that Mark, who usually wore his hair Mandinka-style, was shaven completely bald tonight, and it made him look even sexier. She had seen the bald-head fad in New York, but until now she'd thought it was strictly for grownup blacks.

Last came Maria and Travis, entering together hand in hand. The crowd's frenzy peaked and held. She was the Witty One, the visualist, who could make dreams real with her lights, lasers, smoke generators, and holograms. He was the Poet—the collaborative creation of all Juice pieces began with his words—and at nineteen was the oldest member of the group. The two were legendary lovers.

Their shorthand appelations were really a matter of convenience for reviewers and commentators—each of the five was a witty, sexy, spiritual poet, and technician, in varying degrees. Together they were what most kids dreamed of—a family so loving and self-sufficient that it did not need parents. And even grownups had to admit they were competent musicians; most of their tapes, CDs, and chips contained at least a few tracks that were faithful recreations of antique musical forms like rock, swing jazz, punk, or even classical.

All around, Jennifer saw and heard girls her age freaking out, shrieking and babbling mindlessly, flopping spastically in their seats. She felt amused and faintly superior—she understood how they felt, but one after all had one's dignity to preserve. She hoped they would ease off once the show started, so that she could hear the music.

The moment the Fan' Five were in place, Tamila raised up on the balls of her feet and began to dance. Thundering drums filled the great hall, cymbals hissed, counterpoint crickets rasped. On this "floor," H wove a carpet of sound, over which Mark's twin Spangler walked in eight-league boots. The stage shimmered and sparkled, lasers swept the air above it, giant holographic images flitted among the beams and out over the crowd. And Travis began to raise his arms slowly over his head. By the time his hands met, the cacophony sounded like all the cymbals in the world being destroyed by heavy caliber automatic weapons fire while God played the electric violin. Travis held it for an aching three seconds—then whipped his arms down and the whole band slammed as one into "Let's Do It Tonight," their first megahit.

The Garden dissolved in pandemonium.

And Jennifer's dignity went south without saying goodbye. This was precisely what she had been anticipating all day—and the reality was unendurable. She lost all control, lost the power of rational thought, lost her identity. It was not a choice she would have made—to let go utterly in the presence of José risked destroying the psychological edge she had established—but it was not a matter of choice.

Her mind melted; she became only one of thousands of capacitors in the huge circuit the Juice was building.

She had been masturbating for years—though *never* in the presence of a male—and while once or twice she had achieved a kind of release very like a sneeze, she had never had what she was prepared to call an orgasm, until now. She did not recognize it for what it was, for she was not touching herself at all—could not; her arms did not work—but she did vaguely understand that her life had changed in some major way. Only later would she work out that the origin of the sensation had been genital. It went on for years. Fortunately José was strong enough to keep her from hurting herself or destroying her clothing.

By the fourth number she lay limply in his arms, utterly unaware of him or the chair-arm that dug into her ribs, too exhausted even to weep any more. The music and spectacle still reached her, but she was too spent to react.

> *Eat it . . . if they put it on the plate you better*
> *Eat it . . . it won't help to hesitate, they'll just*
> *Repeat it . . . for all you know it might be great, go on and*
> *Eat it! Eat it! Eat it!*
> > *Don't be queasy*
> > *It goes down easy*
> > *Fill the hollow*
> > *Go on and swallow*
> > *Eat it now or heed my warning*
> > *You'll have it cold tomorrow morning*
> > *Close your eyes and hold your nose*
> > *Now open wide and down it goes, just*
> *Eat it! Eat it! Eat it!*

By the end of the song a large portion of the crowd shared her stupor, and the Juice sensed it and shifted gears, played the piece called "Hardon You." It was a slow, gentle piece—one of those in an antique mode which Russell had told her was called the jazz ballad. Its sweet melody and blues-tinged harmonies contrasted ironically with its diction. Although the sentiment it expressed could have been—had been—expressed in the songs of Grandpa's youth, it could never have been so explicitly stated then. Travis sang it directly to Maria:

> *I know my constant horniness gets hardon you*
> *Sometimes it seems I'm always in the mood*
> *If that is so I truly beg your pardon too*
> *It wasn't my intention to be rude . . .*
>> *My love is like my horniness*
>> *in that it never quits*
>> *But I'd love you if you didn't have those tits . . .*

The crowd's—and Jennifer's energy level valleyed out and began to climb again, slowly but irresistibly. Maria put her board on automatic and sang the second verse, playing it for laughs and getting them:

> *Well, men have only got the one thing on their minds*
> *It gets so repetitious it's a crime*
> *I've always said a hard man is good to find*
> *—long as you don't find him every goddam time*
>> *It may have been what caught my eye*
>> *But it isn't why I stick*
>> *I would love you if you didn't have a dick . . .*

Travis started the bridge:

> *I'm neurotically erotic—with a taste for the exotic*
> *But your body is hypnotic when it's next to me*

—and Maria finished it—

> *You're relentlessly attentive*
> *—I admit at my incentive—*
> *But you know you represent much more than sex to me*

—and Tamila and the Syn Twins poured it on hard as Travis, bathed in warm colours by his lover, took the final verse:

> *You know that I was horny for you from the start (ah, baby)*

And that's the way it's always gonna be (just wait and see)
But you ought to know your sexiness is just a part
Of the value you will always have for me
  You are not only something
  That I lust for, that I hunt
  I would love you if you didn't have a cunt . . .

—and as the final C major seventh washed away and
the lights went to black and the last cymbal-shimmer
whispered to silence, Jennifer discovered that she was
alive again. The palms of her hands hurt. Gradually she
worked out that this was because she was beating them
together; the sound was quite inaudible in the roar of the
revitalized crowd. She made herself stop, grabbed José's
arm with both hands without looking at him.

The Juice had their house back now and knew it. They
picked the energy up a notch—but only one—with a fast
funny number, a verbally, musically, and visually pun-
strewn piece called "Current Events." Then they held it
there with an extended trance piece called "Totality," a
Maria showcase based on the solar eclipse she had once
made them all fly halfway around the world to see. The
sun she built in the air above Tamila's bubble was *not*
bright enough to damage retinas—there were strict laws—
but it seemed to be, when at last the Moon had turned it
loose.

Then the four on the floor sat out while Tamila did her
solo, "Heritage," a hypnotic tour-de-force which mixed
and brilliantly blended the rhythmical traditions of her
Tamil and Tagalog ancestors. New York held sizable com-
munities of both Southern Indians and Filipinos; enough
were present that when Tamila's fingers made the last
tabla roll and hit the tonic the Garden seemed to go mad
with joy. The instant the applause began to diminish,
Tamila's comrades, who had been so still as to be invisible,
suddenly whipped into the opening bars of one of their
most driving numbers, "Older Than I Look," and the fans
screamed even louder. The entire throng clapped and
stomped along with the beat, the vast hall shuddered,
cops and Garden personnel went white with fear and
began edging toward the exits, and Jennifer, who in her

heart loved this song more than any other in the Juice's repertoire, turned shrieking to share her joy with José—

—and as she saw his broad white grin, the Indescribable Thing happened to her for the second time.

She could tell this time where it was originating from, and knew it for what it was. Her ears roared louder than the surrounding din. Her vision began to grey out from hyperventilation. She felt her legs turn into water and knew she must be going down. And faintly—but oh, unmistakably—she heard José bellow in her ear: *"You're all right! I got you!"*

She let go. She never knew how long she clung to him, did not know that she was beating her crotch urgently against him, was not conscious of the responsive hardening in his own. By the time she returned to sentience, she was sitting in her seat again, head buried in the hollow of his neck. Her face and his collar were soaking wet, and a different song was already in its closing bars. She had never felt so wonderful and terrible. The music and lights were something far away and unimportant—beautiful, fitting in their beauty, but not truly necessary—and the screaming thousands had ceased to exist. She marinated in bliss.

What made her mind switch on again was Travis's amplified voice saying, *"This will be our last one tonight."* That reached her even in her languor. The Juice *never* did encores. This was it—the last morsel to be savoured. *"It's a new piece we've just composed, especially for this concert."* That reached her too. She looked at José, and found that she could not bear to look him in the eyes—there was so much to be said that eyes might burn out under the traffic-load—so she kissed him hard and quick on the cheek, and turned her eyes to the stage. *"Mark wrote the words for this, it's called 'The Night of Power'—"*

The piece was just what she wanted it to be, an attention-holder. It was hard to grasp. The musical underpinning was more like the Pulp than the Juice, dark and simplistic, full of ominous power chords and evil vamps. But the accompanying visuals were pure Juice, happy and positive and good; the lasers tended toward golds and blues and the hologram images were something like erotic angels with dark skin. The lyrics seemed opaque, ambiguous. Something about changes, something about sad but necessary, something about desperate times calling for desperate measures, desperate crimes and desperate pleasures, precious junk and useless treasures . . . Jennifer concentrated, but the words slipped away from her grasp; she retained only the chorus, which kept repeating:

> It is the Night of Power
> The appointed hour
> They're tearing down the tower
> The shit is gonna shower

She watched Mark, who had composed this, and he was absolutely unreadable—was actually wearing sunglasses. Red sunglasses.

There was an extended instrumental coda, plainly improvised, and it turned into an event, one of those once-in-a-career moments when each member of a group transcends herself and achieves telepathic rapport with her partners. The beat was infectious; most of Tamila's body was only a blur. Mark and H were working with four limbs apiece, grinning furiously at each other across the stage. Maria made shades and shapes that hovered on the very edge of recognition, and Travis sang with his eyes closed, throbbing with the power. Their combined energy whipped the crowd into its ultimate excitement; again stomping feet threatened to shatter the great hall. People swayed and wept and babbled, until finally the sound swept up into one final ear-splitting, teeth-grinding explosion, a thunderous final chord, a nova-blast of pure white light in all directions, and—total darkness, total silence. And in the split second before the audience went mad, a hundred Travises shouted *"NIGHT OF POWER!"* from the bottom of a great cavern.

Thousands of voices echoed the shout in the dark hall. For an endless few seconds, the only illumination came from the exit signs and a few hundred smouldering cigarette- and joint-tips. When the house lights went up, the stage was empty. A few reporters, half-blinded by the sudden glare, were nonetheless astute enough to activate their stopwatches at that instant, and the *New York Times* would have quoted the final ovation at fourteen minutes and forty seconds if the *Times* had published an edition the next morning. It set a new all-time decibel record for the Garden, and may have killed a janitor with a bad heart.

Jennifer took part in it, of course, screamed off what remained of her throat-lining, but somewhere below the conscious level she knew this moment was *not* the emotional high point of the evening, and it made her feel a little strange. Vaguely she noticed a few people in the audience and staff removing and putting away pairs of red sunglasses like the ones Mark had just worn; they all seemed to be black people. She decided it was some New York thing she didn't understand and dismissed it. She would have to write every detail of the concert to Sophie *tonight*, before it blurred in her mind. What had that last song been about, anyway? My, it was hot in here; her whole body felt clammy and her feet squished in her shoes.

The ovation officially ended at the moment when the decibel level dropped below 90 db, but it was some time after that before the mass stampede for the exits really got under weigh. José did not need to restrain Jennifer; she was far too intelligent to join a line that was not going anywhere. Russell had taught her that the last passenger to stand up in the airplane left the airport in the best mood. They sat together, silent in the din, and waited while thousands of stupider people dissipated a great deal of their good spirits trying to achieve the impossible among the incompossible. Jennifer passed the time by scrutinizing every person within her field of vision except José, cataloguing their peculiarities to herself. She was done long before the herd showed any significant movement toward the doors, so she decided to look herself over, straighten her seams, repair her face and get ready to meet the public again. She was certain the butterflies on her cheeks were smudged, and the eyes were sure to be a total loss. She reached down to get her compact from the pouch at her hip, and felt dampness as her hand brushed her lap. God, she thought, I'm dripping with sweat, how gross—thundering shit! She froze, afraid to look down.

That's not sweat, that's—I must be *lubricating*. I didn't
know there could be *that* much, really making love must
be *sloppy*. Shit, I hope I didn't stain my dress—

She looked down, and her first thought was that José
had had to stab somebody while she wasn't paying
attention, and here was the blood. But almost at once she
knew what it was.

Oh my God—

Oh, my *God*—

Oh my dancing lefthanded baby-pink God, *I've got my
period*. It came down, Mom will flip and Dad will freak
and what in the hell am I going to do now?

No more fuzzy thinking. Time to act like a grownup.
She folded her hands across her lap, sat perfectly still,
and began soto zen breathing, using the silent chant to
measure her respiration into four slow equal parts, con-
centrating her attention on the air that entered and left
her. Gradually the adrenalin was absorbed, the buzzing in
her brain diminished, even the noise of the crowd went
away. Once she had reached tranquility and her thoughts
had stopped altogether, she restarted her mind and considered her dilemma dispassionately. "José?"

He was staring at the high ceiling, frowning slightly.
"Yeah?"

"I hate to tell you this, but I just laid an egg."

"What are you—oh wow!"

"My very first."

"No shit?" He smiled warmly. "Hey, that's fantastic!
God damn, what do you know, that's really somethin'.
Congratulations, Jennifer, no shit—that's terrific."

She loved him for that reaction. "Yes it is. I think. And
thank you for not saying 'Fuckin A.' But it presents a
problem. This spot in front is nothing to the one I'm
sitting on, and I can't do anything with the side panels of
the dress—it's going to be dripping down my legs. Any
ideas?"

"*Ai, chinga.*" He frowned in thought and looked around.
"Wait a minute."

They waited until there was no one left forward of their
row. "Look," José said then, "the dress is shot anyway.
Okay if I cut it up some?"

"Sure, I guess." The blood would not wash out. She arranged the jacket across her lap, unsnapped the waistband at either side and worked the skirt out from under her as discreetly as possible, wiping herself dry with Kleenex. He produced his knife—she still did not know where he kept it, it always seemed to simply occur in his hand—and picked at stitches with it until there was nothing left but waistband. She caught on at once, put the waistband back on and rotated it ninety degrees so that the snaps were now at her navel and spine. When she reattached the skirt's side panels to their velcro fasteners, they would be front and back panels, and she would be acceptably covered.

"José, you're a genius. But there's still a problem. Pads are the only thing I'm going to find in the ladies' room, and I've got nothing to hold one *on* now."

"First off, forget the ladies' room. All the pads'll be ripped off, and you don't wanna meet the kinda fems that hang out in the bathroom after a concert. I got a big hunk of Kleenex—"

"But what's going to *hold* it there? Uplifting thoughts?"

He took the discarded former front panel of her dress, folded it below the small stain, slid his knife into the fold and ripped upward, cutting the swatch in half. He folded the unstained half lengthwise and handed it to her. "You put this under you, pull it up through the garter belt in front and back, then fold the ends over and tuck 'em under the skirt. Presto—one Kleenex holder."

She was impressed. "You're as good a designer as Da—Father." He looked away while she assembled things. The scheme worked on the first try, and she felt infinitely more secure with the thick wad of Kleenex held up against her. She realized that she was losing her zen detachment, and that the three dominant feelings seeping back into her were relief, fatigue, and elation. "How's that?"

He looked her over as carefully as she had been wishing he would for weeks. "That's gonna work fine."

She was slightly annoyed. He was not seeing her, he was seeing his design. She struck a pose that exposed much thigh and to the tune of the American national anthem sang, "José, can you see . . . ?" She regretted it at once: he looked away and she wished she could borrow his knife and cut her tongue out. Computers were better than people in only one way: they let you unsay things.

A rentacop was shouting at them. "Hey! Come on, God dammit, take her home and fuck her, we're closed."

José went rigid, and for a second Jennifer thought there was going to be a fight—over her!—but he relaxed, and the knife the guard had not seen magically vanished from his hand. "Come on, let's go, your parents'll be getting worried."

She followed him up the aisle. The Madison Square Garden, nearly empty, will make anyone feel small.

He insisted they take a cab home, and she was glad to give in. It felt strange to walk with something so thick between her legs; her whole lower belly felt subtly, disturbingly *rearranged*; her upper thighs were sticky; and her legs were much too tired for a long walk. The passenger compartment of the taxi was, of course, essentially an air-conditioned bulletproof cell from which one had to pay to gain exit. The windows, of course, would not open. The air-conditioning was, of course, not working. Within a minute Jennifer understood José's logic for not walking her down 31st Street in the middle of a hot night. She smelled like an invitation to gang rape. It made for tension in the confined space, so she chattered all the way across town.

"What did you think of that last number?"

"Be honest with you, I didn't understand it."

"Neither did I. Mixed metaphors, ambiguous signals— symbols, I mean—murky imagery, it was all scary somehow. Sort of sad and scary and . . . resigned."

"I thought it sounded like those other guys, what is it, the Pulp?"

"Yes! Or even that stupid new nihilist band that call themselves the Rind."

"Hah! Long career *those* guys are gonna have, with a member suiciding every third or fourth concert. I mean, they're huge in a lot of cities, but fuckin' A, how long can it go on?"

"I hear they're down from twelve to five. They're not allowed into Canada, you know."

"In this country we got a law that a person can pick the time and manner of his own death, as long as he don't freak nobody out or leave a mess. I think that's a good law. You can't freak nobody out if they paid to see you do it. And they pay plenty. There's people in the world—fuckin' A, there's people in this town—that'd do themselves up with a blowtorch for a hundred bucks cash to give to their kids. I think it's gonna catch on."

"You use up a lot of musicians that way."

"There's some shortage?"

"And of course they *won't* record . . ."

"Why have your big farewell scene in some recording studio? Who'd believe it wasn't faked?"

"I suppose. I just thought of the word for that 'Night of Power' song. My da—father taught it to me. *'Weltschmertz.'* "

"Jewish?"

"German. It means homesickness for a place you've never seen."

"Sounds Jewish to me."

"Are you prejudiced against Jews, José?"

"Me? Nah. I almost got married to a Jewish girl once."

"Really? What happened?" She imagined some romantic tragedy.

He grinned. "The same thing that just happened to you. Her period came. So it wasn't necessary. She dumped me."

"Oh. Are you prejudiced against anybody?"

"Hey, look, you live in New York you gotta prejudge people. Only I don't do it by colour or ethnic. I'm prejudiced about size and money. Like, if a guy is bigger than me, seven chances out of ten sooner or later he's gonna push on me some way, and I gotta push back. If a guy is real skinny and his sleeves is rolled down, eight chances out of ten he's a junkie and you gotta watch him. If he's dressed rich, eight chances out of ten he's a cocksucker, excuse me."

"You don't like gays?"

"Hey, my brother down in Miami is gay. That word is just like a expression. I mean, like, most rich guys in this town, they don't think that nobody else is a human being that isn't rich. They don't like Puerto Ricans and black people and Chinees and Pakis 'cause they're scared we might be hungry enough to do them up. And most of them, even if they're heterosexual, they don't think *any* women are human beings, no matter what color they are or how much money they got."

"What about rich women?"

"They're the worst. They don't even believe theirselves is human beings."

Jennifer thought about that. By José's standards, she was rich.

"But the people I'm prejudiced about the most you can't tell from appearance. They could be white or black or Puerto Rican, rich or poor or middle-class. I can tell 'em when I see 'em lookin' at me, and I keep my hand near my knife. People that are prejudiced about *me*— because I'm half black, or because I'm half Puerto Rican, or because I'm half black and half Puerto Rican. Some white people look at me like if my old man was *gonna* marry outside his race he should have married white. Some black people look at me like my old man shoulda been castrated. Funny thing, Spanish people don't give me too much shit. But people like Shaw Nuff, the guy that rented you your spot—some times—I want to kill that bastid."

Traffic was slow. Jennifer saw a man staring at her from the curb. He was her father's age, black, heavily bearded, and totally bald. He looked sad. Somehow she felt as if it were her fault. "José?"

"Yah."

"About tonight—"

"You don't hafta—"

"Let me get this said, okay, we're going to be home in a minute. A lot of girls, when they get their first period, it's like a major trauma. I always wondered what mine was going to be like. That wasn't the time or place I would have picked. It could have been a disaster." She reached across the seat and took his hand. "You were *wonderful*. You helped me a lot. Not just what you did, but the way you did it. You didn't freak out or anything. You made it good. This has been the best night of my life, and I owe you for it."

"Nah, you don't—"

"Shut up, please. I have been cockteasing you for almost two weeks now. I'm not going to do it any more."

"Oh."

They were passing Third Avenue; a few blocks uptown she absently noted a great number of police cars and ambulances with attendant crowd. "Not just because you were nice to me, understand. Not even just because it's mean. It's—it's like before it was okay, because I was just kind of practicing. Now it's for real. You can't fool around with a gun any more once it's loaded. Pay the man, we're here."

He secured their release from the mobile sauna, tipping as he thought appropriate, and insisted on getting out first and checking the street in both directions before letting her out. She bought a box of Maxithins in the drugstore on the corner. He stopped her when they were safely inside the apartment building.

"Two things. Your parents aren't gonna be too crazy about what happened, me bein' there and cuttin' up your dress and stuff. They wouldn't understand. So why don't we make it that you got your period in the can, and a nice lady with a pair of scissors helped you out?"

"Sound. What's the second thing?"

"What you said in the cab, what you been doin', it's okay."

"I've been a bitch."

"I'm not bogus, it's really okay." He hesitated. "But I'm really glad you're not gonna be doin' it no more."

She felt a warm glow. "Was I terrible?"

"Hell no, you were *great*. A regular Cruise missile. You're gonna break some hearts, no shit. Come on, your parents'll be waiting up for you."

But they were not. The light was on in the main room, and the door to her parents' bedroom was open, but no one was in sight. "We're back," she called, and got no answer. She checked the garden and they were not there either. A small alarm bell was ringing somewhere in the back of her head, and she didn't know why. Perhaps it was the air-conditioning cooling the sweat on her body, giving her goosebumps?

"They left us notes," José said, taking two envelopes from the top of the refrigerator. He opened the one with his name on it in large block letters, and handed her the other.

Hers was in Dena's sprawling hand, and covered two sheets of note paper: "Jennifer, hon, your father and I got the crazy impulse to go out for a walk and talk a bit. We might be late, so don't wait up for us. I know I have to be up early for rehearsal, and I guess it does seem like an awfully hot night to leave a perfectly nice air-conditioned apartment—but you know dancers love to sweat, and your father and I just don't seem to get a chance to spend a lot of time together lately, and we're tired of spending it in a little stone box, no matter how comfortable. Now, it must be way past your bedtime, so pop right in, okay? I understand José is sleeping over tonight, so help him fold out the couch and then get a good night's sleep. See you tomorrow. I hope your concert was wonderful. Love, Mom."

Mom must have smoked some grass, Jennifer thought, this rambles all over the place. She looked up; José was just slipping his own note into his pants pocket. "What did yours say?"

"Oh, just says they went out for a walk, and she told me where to find the sheets and stuff."

Suddenly she realized why the little alarm bell was ringing. "José, the TV's off."

"And it stays off—time you were asleep."

"You don't understand. You taught us that we should leave it on whenever we were leaving the apartment empty, to fool the junkies. *Once*, I forgot, and Daddy gave me a lecture. He doesn't forget things like that."

He took her note and glanced through it. "Okay, let's say he didn't forget. How about this: some junkies came in through the locked door and held them up, marched 'em out of here with machine guns, and waited real polite while your ma wrote us both long chatty letters. The part *I* don't understand is how come the TV is still there at all. Of course, it weighs about eight ounces, and those junkies ain't strong—"

She glared him into silence. "All right, dammit, lay off. Menstrual women are *supposed* to be paranoid."

"And they're supposed to be asleep by this time of night."

"All *right*. Dibs on the john." She got pajamas and clean underwear from her room, noticing on the way that her parents' bed was unmade—really unmade, the mattress visible on Russell's side. Once in the bathroom she opened her first box of Maxithins and studied the instructions, then stripped down and cleaned herself up. She studied the soiled kleenex for a long time. Somewhere in there, she told herself, is what was nearly another human being. Fantastic. How sad to waste it. Briefly she fantasized having a baby with José, and giggled. Its first words would be, "Fuckin' A." She put the minipad in place, the way she and Sophie had practiced in secret months ago, put her pajamas on, and went through the ritual of washing and brushing and flushing. When she emerged from the bathroom she could see into her parents' bedroom. José was standing on tiptoe, looking for sheets on the closet shelf. "In the box on the floor," she called.

"Oh yeah, how stupid, I just read that five minutes ago." He found the sheets, brought them out and began making up the unfolded couch-bed.

"Won't my parents wake you up when they come in?"

"I never have no trouble getting back to sleep. Goodnight, Jennifer."

"Goodnight, José. Thanks again for everything." She gave him a chaste peck on the cheek and went to bed. Where she lay and stared at the ceiling and tried to put all the chaotic events of the evening into some kind of perspective and integrate them. But she got sidetracked.

She was exquisitely tired, her brain spinning with a thousand randomly skittering thoughts, which would soon melt into the white noise of sleep. But before they could, a few of them bumped together—and became more than the sum of their parts.

The first thought was: boy, Mom sure went on and on in her note. Half of one of those little notepad sheets is all she usually ever uses—and in the whole two pages she really had nothing to say except goodnight.

Which led to: why a separate note for José? And why sealed up in envelopes, for heaven's sake? And why leave them on top of the fridge instead of the usual place on the table?

And: why didn't José know where the sheets were, after Mom wrote him a special note just to *tell* him, when *I* could have told him and in fact did?

Suddenly she was not tired at all.

She heard the bathroom door shut and water begin running. She was out of bed at once, and silent as a ghost she made for the living room. As she had hoped, with her "safely in bed" José had stripped down—even with air-conditioning, it was warm in the apartment. His trousers were folded on the arm of the couch. She knelt beside it, rifled his pockets and slipped out the folded note.

The only point she could see to all the rigamarole with the notes was to make sure she didn't get to them before José did, and to keep her distracted long enough for him to absorb his own. She actually hesitated with the note in her hands, knowing there was something in it that she wouldn't like. But José might shut off the sink at any minute, and she needed the noise to cover the sound of unfolding the paper. Now or never!

"José: Jennifer's note says we've gone out for a walk. Act like this one does too. We're in big trouble and a big hurry. Some time before dawn a major race riot is going to happen. Protect Jennifer. We hope to be back before then, but if we don't get back by [there were four successive crossouts here] noon, she's in your hands. There's a yoghurt container full of cash in the fridge. Try to get her to Russell's father's place. Wilson Grant, 3 Seaside, Orient Point, phone 516-555-1858. We're depending on you. —Dena."

It was only on the third and slowest reading that she grasped all the words. She closed her eyes tight, and then tighter, until she saw purple novae in a paisley universe. The floor began to shift under her, and she dug her knees into it savagely until it held still.

I am not, she told herself, a normal child. I know the difference between TV and reality. Clearly this is TV.

Therefore I am only a character, an actress, and my motivation in this scene is *I can't deal with this now* and that means it must be about time for the commercial—

It was actually then that she fell asleep, and not ten seconds later when her head hit the pillow; her automatic pilot got her to bed.

Sleep can be an interval of unconsciousness, blessed escape from pressing problems—or it can be a kind of superconsciousness. Without the distraction of a conscious mind colouring everything with emotion and editing everything for memory, the underbrain can run multiple high-speed evaluations of a problem with cold ruthless honesty. A sleeping person can think the unthinkable, can work with and plan for it. It is often wrongly said that this part of the mind is totally selfish, loyal only to itself. That is not true; it can encompass as many others as that mind loves. But it *is* totally devoid of any trace of hypocrisy, polite or otherwise.

Some kind of race riot and they're out in it *together?* Bad, bad, they're a walking focus of trouble, have to assume they're not coming back. Sit out a race riot at Mrs. Grandma's? Bogus program. Sooner hole up here. How long can it last? Worst case, say three or four days, we've plenty of food for two people even if power fails. Fill the tub and all the pots with water, heavier curtains. This apartment is a fortress. Might use up José, staying here, but that's an acceptable risk and he could just as easily be hurt getting me out to Long Island where I am *not* going to go. Resist being moved; fuck him if you have to but stay here. And if you have to move, anyplace is better than Orient. If I can make it back home to Halifax somehow maybe Uncle Fred will take me on, real uncle or not. I'm running out of guardians too fast. Maybe go underground with José—would he take that much risk for me? Work on him . . . for a start tell him to God damn it

"—stop *shaking* me, José!"

He was leaning over her in the darkened bedroom, hand on her shoulder, face close. Behind him, the door was closed. Her dream mind had time to think, well that was easier than I thought it would be, before her conscious mind woke up with a jolt of fear. *Now? No!* She twisted violently away.

José stepped back at once. "Jennifer, I'm sorry to wake you, you only slept an hour. But we got bad trouble and you gotta wake up."

"I'm *not* going to Grandpa's, I don't care."

"Yeah, I figured you read the note, you forgot to put it away. You ain't going to your Grandpa's, not now anyway. But we gotta talk, and fast. You sure you're awake?"

She sat up. "Sure."

"Did your mother ever mention a dancer named Jerome?"

"Yes. Jerome Turner. Why?"

"What did she say about him?"

"Why?"

"Because there's a guy out in the living room right now says he's Jerome, and he's got a message from your parents, and I gotta know how much to believe him. Okay?"

"She used to work with him once before. I think he's black, and she said something about not recognizing him with his head shaved. What's the message?"

"What else?"

"Noth—uh . . . I think, I'm not sure, but I think he and Mom were close once. Daddy acted funny. *What is the message?"*

"Okay, that fits. Look, this guy says your parents sent him to get us, you and me, and bring us to them. He don't say where and he don't say why, he just says he ain't leavin' without us. I asked him about the race riot and he says he don't know about no riot, but I don't believe him. He told me some stuff only your father would know about, but he could have made your father tell him that stuff, you understand? He's black and bald and he moves like a dancer and he doesn't seem to like your father worth a shit and he's got funny vibes like he doesn't want to do this and does at the same time. So from what you say it fits."

"Do you think we should go with him?"

"It could still be a setup."

"It doesn't make much sense that way. In the middle of a race riot, why go through all this trouble for a thirteen-year-old hostage?"

"Maybe to put some kind of pressure on your folks."

"They could do that just by threatening to firebomb this apartment. Okay, suppose we *don't* go?"

"For a start, I'll have to fight that guy out there. He's pretty determined."

"So if Mom and Dad really did send him to get us out of danger, maybe they know what they're talking about and we should go. You say he knows things only Dad could have told him."

"But they could have made him tell them that stuff."

"I don't think so."

"Jennifer, the world ain't like the movies. Anybody can be tortured into telling anything."

"If so, I want to get closer to the people who did it. Give me one of your knives. The small one."

"No way! I may need it."

"José, if this is some kind of a trap, they're going to take your weapons. But they won't search where I'm going to put it."

"Oh." He thought for a second. "You promise you'll give it back when I tell you?"

"Give me the fucking knife and turn your back."

She had fetched a second panty-shield in case it turned out that one was not enough to get a person through a night—how did she know, who could she ask? She checked, and the first one wasn't bad. The knife was a flick knife; folded it was not much bigger than a tube of mascara. She made a knife sandwich of the two pads, adjusted it for comfort, and turned her attention to dressing. Jeans would make the knife inaccessible, but a dress would slow her down if she had to run. She settled on a shortie, a currently fashionable item whose nearest relative was the miniskirts of her father's youth. She did not like to wear one without pantyhose, but it fit her needs, and it made her look little and undangerous. Red sneakers supported the image. "Did Father leave us the gun?"

"No. I checked."

Daddy and Mom *were* in trouble then. She wanted a weapon easier to get at than the knife. She got a hatpin from her dresser, a vicious little thing ninety millimeters long, and slid it down the inside of the flap that covered the zipper in the back of the shortie, so that only the head showed, looking like a button. She could think of nothing else. "Okay. We don't go anywhere until I've talked to this guy. If I decide it's not Jerome, or he's bogus some other way, I'll mention how hot it is. If I do, take him out."

"You want me to ice him?" José asked, and she completely missed the irony in his tone.

"No. We can use him for a counterhostage. Maybe *we* can torture information out of *him*."

"We," he said, with no irony at all. "Jesus Christ. Hey, we're taking too long, he's gonna be paranoid. Let's go."

"José?"

"What?"

"Have you ever killed anybody?"

"Have you ever let a boy touch you between the legs?"

"*That's none of*—oh. I get you. Let's go."

He stopped her at the door. Mostly José looked old for his age; now he looked as old as Russell. "I killed two guys but one don't count. I went to punch this guy and he moved and I got him in the throat. The other guy, I was trying to stay alive and that's what it took. I didn't get tagged for either one."

His face held an expression of deep sadness that seemed vaguely familiar; she had seen one much like it not too long ago, somewhere. She could see that both deaths bothered him, but that he had learned to live with both. "I let two boys touch me, but one didn't count. I had jeans on and he couldn't find it. The other was fun." He grinned, and the sadness was gone. "So come on, killer."

They left the bedroom.

Her first sight of the man on the couch made her ears hot. She kept her face impassive with a conscious effort. José was handsome by anyone's standards, and in her eyes strikingly so. But this man was . . . the current buzzword was *lickable*. After the briefest of glances, he ignored her, so she let herself look him over carefully. There was no visible part of him that was not ideally formed: he was even better looking than his contemporary, Gene Anthony Ray. He wore cords and a jean jacket, and was barechested. She decided he could not have been more than adequate as a dancer, to have evaded fame into his thirties. He rose to his feet with lithe quickness, his gaze fixed on José's hands.

I hope, she thought, that we don't have to kill him. It would be a terrible waste. No wonder Daddy gets all crinkly when his name comes up. And he's the exact same colour as Mom. Maybe I *should* kill him . . .

"It took you long enough," he said. To José. "I told you that minutes counted. I called for a cab, it's probably waiting now so let's get her—"

Jennifer stood tall, and with just enough volume to override him, said, *"Hold it, chump!"*

He stopped talking and stared at her, for the first time. She imagined that he would have had that same expression if a tree had suddenly addressed him, or a fire hydrant.

Maybe I *will* kill him. "Do an arabesque turn on a tilt, arched spine, into an inside turn with a contraction."

"What?"

"Do it."

"Now? Why?"

"You claim to be a colleague of my mother. I do not identify you." She pressed José's arm to keep him where he was and crossed the room to move a chair out of the way. "If you expect me to go anywhere with you, do the combination I said."

He frowned ferociously at his watch. "Damn it, little girl, there is no *time* for this nonsense—"

"Any minute now it is going to dawn on you that what you are talking to is a human person, who happens to be shorter than you and smarter than you and, oh yes, younger than you, and once that happens we'll be out the door in no time, wait and see."

She gave him credit; he wasted no more seconds, but rolled his eyes and did as she had requested. He did it fairly well. His contraction wasn't quite deep enough, but he was unmistakably a professional. "Can we go now?" he said as he finished. José was looking at him reappraisingly.

"First tell me the three things my father told you to tell José."

He started to protest—then gritted his teeth and did as she told him. José explained the significance of all three briefly, and she nodded, satisfied. If her father had been *made* to supply recognition codes, she was sure that he would have built in some innocent sounding tipoff that would ring false, at least to her ears. Provisionally, this was a trusted emissary of her father. But was he trust*worthy?*

"Where are you going to take us?"

"To your parents."

"Where geographically?"

"I can't tell you that, because I don't know. The first stop is the Metropolitan Museum of Art. They are in a place of safety, waiting anxiously for you to join them."

"Safety from the race riot?"

If she had hoped to knock him off balance she was disappointed. "Your bodyguard mentioned that too. I know of no race riot planned for tonight." She could tell that he was telling the truth—but not all of it.

"What about after tonight?"

"I am not a party to any race riot at any time."

"Safety from what, then?"

"I've answered all the questions there is time for. We have blown that cab by now, we'll have to pick one up on . . . damn. I am leaving now, Miss Grant. If you're staying, that's up to you."

She decided to bluff a little—she could always run after him—and stood quite still. He got halfway out the door before whirling in his tracks and hollering, big, "You've got to come! *I promised Michael.*"

"Michael? You mean—"

"The man that saved you and your parents when you first got to town."

She blinked. "Well, why didn't you say so in the first place?" She scooped up her pouch on the way to the door. "Maybe the cab will still be there."

But of course it was not. Jerome turned left and started for Second Avenue.

"Second is one-way downtown," Jennifer said. "We're going uptown." Her father had taken her to the Met the week before. She pointed right toward Third Avenue.

"We want Second," Jerome called back, continuing to walk east.

She turned right and headed west to Third. José followed her. They heard muffled swearing behind them and Jerome caught up nearly at once. "When we get to the corner," he said in a clenched-teeth voice, "we are going to turn left."

"That's still downt—"

"God damn it, stop jerking my chain. I've got my reasons, and I am not about to explain them to a thirteen-year-old with a smart mouth."

José stopped. "Then why don't you explain them to me, motherfucker?"

Jerome bristled. "Look—" he began. Then he closed his eyes, took a deep slow breath, opened them again. "I am here because Michael wants you two protected, for reasons I am finding increasingly hard to understand. José, Russell said you define a 'nigger' as someone who would hate Jennifer just because of her colour. I am getting the idea that you two are niggers."

"No, we're n—"

"Then *why are you giving me such a hard time?*"

She thought it over. "Left at the corner it is." She resumed walking, and José took up the rear.

Mollified, Jerome unbent enough to explain. "There was a small altercation a couple of blocks up on Third, not that long ago. It'll still be crawling with the raise—the police—"

"I know the word." She remembered seeing something like that on the way home from the Garden.

"—and if they see a spade, a spic and a little shade teeny with no pants on flagging a cab at two in the morning, we're going to lose time we can't spare."

"I'm sorry, Jerome. I—"

"It's all right. Forget it."

"I didn't mean to—"

"I said 'forget it.'" His voice was flat. He did not want her for a friend. He wanted a cooperative parcel.

She wondered about his attitude as she walked. She had the confident, unsmug awareness that she was not easy for a man of mature years to dislike, even one as handsome as Jerome, but he was managing. It was more than the usual disdain some adults had for all children. She wondered if somewhere in there Jerome was, by José's definition, a little bit nigger. What else could account for the chip on his shoulder?

As they turned the corner she glanced uptown. She noticed that neither of the others did, so she did not look long, but she could see that while the crowd and the ambulances and many of the blue-and-whites had gone, the police crime scene barricades were still up and there were plenty of people, in and out of uniform, still on the street. She wondered what the event had been. A robbery? A gangland hit? Another draft riot?

The third cab they signalled opted to pick them up. Jennifer made sure the air-conditioning was working before getting in—the night was even hotter and muggier than it had been earlier. She sat carefully, but the hidden knife caused no great discomfort. Jerome got in last.

"Look," he said when their destination was named and the privacy curtain drawn, "let's get something settled right now. When we get to the Museum, your weapons will be taken from you." He was, she noted smugly, speaking only to José.

"Nobody takes my weapon," José said, and the total lack of expression in his voice made him seem more sincere than any amount of macho posturing could have done.

Jerome rolled his eyes heavenward again; Jennifer was beginning to recognize it as a characteristic expression. "There is no argument," he said patiently. "You can not see Michael or Dena or Russell holding. If you won't give up your gun, settle with the driver and get out right now."

Jennifer and José exchanged a long look. At last she said aloud, "We put ourselves in his hands the moment we left our building. There could have been an ambush waiting. We have no choice now."

José turned back to Jerome. "Look at me. Will she be safe?"

"As safe as anyone in New York. Safer than most."

"You want it now?"

"Whatever."

José had not moved, but somehow the knife was in his hand. "Here." He passed it over quite slowly, hilt-first.

"You don't carry a gun?"

"I prefer wet work. Guns are too noisy, I don't like them."

"Uh huh. And you only carry this one knife? Balanced for throwing?"

"Well—" José added another knife.

"Doesn't really matter," Jerome said. "They'll search you thoroughly anyroad."

José frowned. "Shit. Well, in that case—" He produced a third knife and a small automatic. At Jerome's look he shrugged and looked bland. "I said I didn't like them; I never said I don't carry them sometimes."

"Jesus. T-shirt, vest, and tight jeans on you, and you have all this tucked away. Hell, I have more pockets than you, and *I* haven't got room to put all this shit. Take this fucking piece back until we get to—" Suddenly, incongruously, he smiled broadly. It was a dancer's professional smile, and it was one of the most beautiful things Jennifer had ever seen. He was *so* glad to be here tonight, so proud that God had given him this opportunity to express the magic of dance, his whole career led to this night and his legs didn't hurt a bit. And smiling that brilliant smile, he slowly said, "Oh, my, *God*."

He was looking past them out the lefthand window. They were stopped at a red light. "Raise?" José asked without turning around.

"Yes," Jerome agreed happily.

"Can he see the iron?"

"No. But he can see our colour mix, and he doesn't like it. Oh, Christ."

A shrill police whistle split the night. Jennifer looked then, saw a beefy old Irish cop who was gesturing the cabbie to stay where he was with one hand and waving for backup with the other. She smiled at him.

"Nowhere to hide this stuff," Jerome said through his beautiful teeth. "We'll have to try and take them. Take your gun back—"

"Don't be a jerk," Jennifer snapped, opening her pouch. "In here, all of it. Yours too. *Hurry*."

"Are you crazy?—what if they—"

"*Have you got a better idea?*"

The cop had left the sidewalk, was approaching with

routinely drawn gun; in a few more seconds he would be able to see the hardware. Smiling more winningly than ever, Jerome piled it into her pouch. "Damn it—"

"Shut up and listen. You're my uncle, get it? Mom's brother. I'm your favourite niece, down for a visit from Canada, and you're taking me back to the Museum because I think I lost an earring near there this afternoon."

The cop was conferring with the driver, his gun and eyes on the passengers. "I am sorry I mistook you for a child," Jerome said. "You are eight hundred years old." The doors unlocked and the cop motioned them out with his gun. "Yes, officer? What is the trouble?"

"Step outa the car, please. All of you." Jennifer liked that response. If it wasn't "Shut up, nigger" yet, there was hope. All three got out. A second officer trotted up and joined the party, a black man with an Afro under his uniform cap. The burly Irish cop had the two males assume the position, then took Jennifer aside while his partner checked their ID.

"Awright. Number one: are you with these guys of your own free will?"

She blinked and smiled. "Of course, Constable."

He sighed. "You a working girl?"

She gave him the little frown of puzzlement that made her look eight. "I'm still in school."

"That ain't an answer, Missy."

"Constable, I'm from Halifax. The capitol of Nova Scotia." She started to open her pouch.

"Hold it!"

She froze. "I was getting out my wallet," she said indignantly.

"Never mind that. What are you doing with *those* two at this time of night?"

"The black man is my Uncle Jerry. My stepmother is black, we're not silly about that like you Americans. José is my bodyguard. My father hired him."

"Huh," he said. "The nig—the black guy *doesn't* look like a skell at that." Jennifer rejoiced. This was going to work.

He got her name and her parents' names and address. The other cop was questioning Jerome and José just out of earshot. "All right, get over there with them." The two cops conferred in prison-yard murmurs. "You lost a gold earring?" the big cop called to her.

"Yes, a tau cross." It was the first thing that came into her head, she actually owned such a pair, but as the words left her mouth she knew they were a mistake. *Never embellish a lie, dummy.*

"Uncle Jerry over there says it was a diamond chip."

"I *told* you it was the gold tau, Uncle Jerry," she tried. "I wouldn't have worn the diamonds with this dress."

"How come you waited until now to come looking?"

"I just noticed it was gone a little while ago."

"What are you doing up this late?"

She was ready for this one. "I went to see the Juice tonight at Madison Square. It was great, I was too excited to sleep after." But again as the words passed her lips she knew she was stepping in shit. Jerome knew nothing of the concert, would have given some other answer to that question. "Look, constable," she said, moving forward, "I have the other earring here, see?" She contrived to look like she was lifting it out from under her hair for inspection while actually keeping her ear covered—she was not wearing earrings—as she covered the distance between them. The big cop watched her, gun at his side; his partner was well trained and kept his eyes and gun on the two males, so that after she kicked the big cop smack in the balls, she had time to shrug the pouch strap off her shoulder, catch it in her hand, and whip the heavily-weighted pouch around in a vicious overhand circle. She hit the wrist true and the second cop lost his gun. She meant to get his head with the next swing, but instinctively he leaped away from her and rolled, and José came off the side of the cab like a cannonball and intercepted him with an exquisite karate spin-kick that broke his jaw. José leapt over him, spun Jennifer around, pushed her square in the ass as hard as he could so that she ran instead of falling, and yelled "Run!" He came after her and in a few steps had her by the hand.

She glanced over her shoulder as she ran. "Wait!" They slowed and turned. The cabbie had grabbed Jerome's arm through the window, a good two handed grip, and Jerome was trying unsuccessfully to get free. The cop Jennifer had kicked, though on his knees and clearly still disabled, was trying to lift his revolver. He could not quite manage it; it went off and slug *spanged* off the pavement. Jerome broke the cabbie's thumb and vaulted in a single fluid movement over the cab, putting it between him and the gun. He yelled something to Jennifer and José and ran in the opposite direction.

José yanked her hand and they ran again. "What'd he say?" she yelled as they ran.

"I think he said to meet at the Museum."

Half way down the block she glanced back again. Cab and cops were out of sight around the corner and there was no pursuit. At the end of the block there was still no one visible, so they slowed to a walk, turned downtown, and entered the subway as soon as they had their breath back.

CHAPTER SEVEN

"Available records show that no fewer than 55 slave revolts occurred at sea between 1700 and 1845. During the height of the slave period, the 200 years from 1664 to 1864, there are recorded accounts of at least 109 slave insurrections which occurred within the continental U.S. Since it was customary to suppress all news and information concerning revolts lest they become infectious, it is reasonable to assume that the reported cases were of some magnitude, that very many cases were not reported, and that some cases which were reported have not yet been made available to research . . . the rate of infanticide was high. Suicide became a problem of such magnitude as to require the slave owners to devise 'the strongest arguments possible' (supported by religious and social taboos) to reduce the rate of self-destruction. Sabotage of livestock, machinery and agricultural produce was not unknown . . . Running away was a form of protest so common as to have been considered a disease. Southern physicians described its symptoms in the journals of the period and gave it the name 'monomania.' . . ."

—C. Eric Lincoln,
The Black Muslims in America

"The revolutionary despises and hates present-day social morality in all its forms . . . all soft and enervating feelings of friendship, love, gratitude, even honour, must be stifled in him by an icy passion for the revolutionary cause . . . day and night, he must have only one thought, one aim: merciless destruction."

—Nechayev, *The Revolutionary Catechism*

(Nechayev achieved little or no success himself; his only documented murder was of one of his own recruits; he died in prison . . .)

*   *   *

Russell decided that it was the finest limo money could buy. Its passenger compartment was large enough to accomodate all five of them in superb comfort. Thus laden, and with driver and shotgun up front, its suspension handled Manhattan pavement well enough to create the sensation that they were floating through the night. It was climate controlled, colour coordinated, softly lit, outfitted with the very latest and best gadgetry, and (he discovered at Michael's invitation) it made a genuinely excellent cup of coffee. The windows were one-way and bulletproof. From the sound the doors had made in closing Russell guessed the car would withstand rockets.

Physically he felt awful. A man who has drunk his way up to Level Three ought to sleep soon afterward, and Russell was not a kid any more. Psychically he should have felt just as bad; the day had been traumatic enough for anyone. But he was fiercely proud that he had succeeded in discharging his obligation to Michael, had won a measure of respect from Jerome in the process. Now he was committed to God knew what for God knew how long. It was exciting, and it struck him that for several years now, the only exciting things in his life had been his wife's performances and his daughter's report cards.

The man called Tom had been formally introduced to him as "General Thomas Worthing." He was in his late fifties, lean and trim, with distinctly negroid features and the air of a man who was used to command. But he deferred to Michael. Motormouth was a cartoon giant; his skin was even darker than Michael's, and he looked like a man who could punt a fire hydrant up through a second story window if the need arose. Clearly he was a devoted bodyguard, and Russell suspected he was quicker than he looked. He had not yet uttered a word.

There was no conversation on the way downtown. Mi-

chael faced forward with his eyes closed, his face peaceful
and relaxed. Russell sat facing him with coffee in one
hand and Dena's hand in the other. General Worthing was
tense, stared out the window and chainsmoked nonfilter
cigarettes. Twice he used a phone with an excellent hush
attachment to conduct lengthy conversations unheard.
Motormouth seemed both relaxed and alert; his eyes
watched everything and everyone but Michael. There was
a sense of history in the car; the image that leaped into
Russell's mind was, *like being on the train with Lenin,
approaching Moscow.* He remained silent partly from a
feeling that anything he might say would be inane in this
context, from a reluctance to interrupt Michael's thoughts
or absence of them at this time. Most people are the stars
of their own personal movie, but somehow Russell knew
that he was only a minor supporting character here.

And what was he supporting?

They took Lenox Avenue down past the Martin Luther
King, Jr. Towers, entered Central Park by the Harlem
Lake and followed the East Drive down through the park.
Just as they passed over the second transverse road, the
limo pulled over and stopped. There was no other traffic.
There were no functional lights nearby. Driver and shotgun got out first and made sure the area was secure before
tapping on the rear window. Motormouth opened the door
and got out, seemed to sniff the air before stepping aside
to let the others emerge. The driver got back in and pulled
silently away.

They stepped over a small stone wall and went down a
short steep slope, General Worthing in the lead. The great
bulk of the Metropolitan Museum of Art was visible through
a stand of trees ahead and to their left, a few hundred
meters distant. Between it and them stood a one-story
shed the size of a two car garage, surrounded by a high
strong electrified fence. There was a sign Russell could
not read in the dark, but he made out the trefoil radiation
warning. He guessed it was phony, there to discourage
prowlers and winos. Motormouth disarmed and unlocked
the fence and let them all in, then locked and charged it
again. There was enough moonlight to show a heavy
padlock, and an oddity that caught Russell's attention.

There were three tiny round windows in the door, side by side at head height, each the size of a half dollar. The outer two could have been lookout ports, but what was the middle one for?

Ignoring the padlock, Motormouth stepped up to the door and placed his eyes against the two outer ports. As he did so all three glowed soft red, giving the edges of his shaven head a rosy highlighting. There was an almost inaudible click, a sigh of pressurized air escaping, and the door slid aside, padlock and all.

Now Russell understood. The outer ports checked retina prints; the middle one was the business end of a laser.

Inside was a room, empty and quite featureless except for a door in the far wall, large enough to admit a one-ton truck. Perhaps twenty people could have stood in here without rubbing elbows. They filed in one at a time, Motormouth last. Russell expected total darkness when the door slid shut, but got the exact opposite: the room suddenly lit up brightly. "This is an elevator," Michael warned them. He touched a part of the wall that seemed indistinguishable from any other, did something with his fingers too quickly for Russell to follow. "Here goes." The floor dropped slowly.

Russell estimated the descent at over sixteen meters. They stepped out of the car and into a much larger room, were met by two armed guards who saluted General Worthing and nodded to Michael. The general returned the salute and Michael bowed to both guards and greeted them by name. "These are Russell and Dena Grant. They are my friends, but they are not to leave here until everyone else does or I say so. And if Mustapha Khan asks when he arrives, no white man has come out of this elevator all night. Catch?"

"Yes, Michael." Neither seemed to find anything odd about Michael having a secret white visitor tonight.

Russell's designer's eye took in a number of unobtrusive details and put them together. In all well constructed sword and sorcery tales, there is, between the passage from the outside world and the treasure chamber, a room whose sole purpose is to assassinate anyone who attempts to pass through it. This was the high-tech version of that

room. There were inconspicuous laser apertures at knee
and chest height, gas dispersion grilles along the base-
boards—glancing up Russell saw that the whole ceiling
could be brought down in chunks. He assumed there were
other, completely indetectible systems.

They passed through another door on the far side of the
room, found themselves in a huge airlock. No pressure
cycling was necessary; from the way the air behaved when
the inner door was opened Russell deduced that the space
they were about to enter was very slightly overpressured,
like a computer room.

Indeed, the chamber they entered looked like a cross
between a big computer room, a television control room,
and the fire control room of a Leviathan-class nuclear
sub. It had started as a vast cylinder lying on its side. The
cylinder was enormous, as big in diameter as the Lincoln
Tunnel and much longer than it was wide. A hardwood
floor had been laid down, and the resulting space filled to
capacity with a great deal of equipment and more than
three dozen people, all shaved bald. Each wore an armband
whose edges were scalloped in a curious pattern; the
armbands came in several colors. There were two very big
mainframe computers, state of the art; a sophisticated
telephone switchboard with ten operators; banks of dozens of VDT screens, some lit and some dark; console after
console of equipment whose purpose Russell did not
comprehend. Nearly all the busy workers stopped what
they were doing when Michael entered, and he bowed to
them all. Not one of them returned the bow.

"Good evening, brothers and sisters," he said, his voice
filling the great room without straining. "The Night of
Power is at hand. We fight now for our people. For our
honour. For our ancestors, and for our children. Bless you
all." It was not a speech, just a statement.

The cheer was loud and happy and filled even that large
room. Michael passed among them, contriving to touch
each of them and make brief eye contact as he went,
without stopping. Russell noted that his own white skin
drew only one or two angry stares: Michael's people trusted
his judgment.

A gasketed door led to a long corridor whose ceiling was

as high as that of the room they had just left. This was storage space, lockers and cabinets and shelves and bins of God knew what. There were also several restrooms; through an open curtain Russell saw a waterless Clivis toilet like the one in his country cabin in Nova Scotia. Through another door was another large cylindrical room, this one laid out as a TV studio with a rostrum, three robot cameras, and few dozen seats for spectators. By now Russell had figured out that they were in some kind of giant underground tunnel, but he was having difficulty believing it. It seemed impossible that a revolutionary militant group could have the funds to construct a tunnel of this size, let alone have managed to do so in secret. Moreover, subtle subconscious cues told him that it was *old*, decades old at least, no matter how ultramodern the furnishings. The air, though cooled and circulated, did not taste canned, which meant air exchange with the city above—no, there was simply no way it could have been built in secret. And where did Con Ed send the power bill for the TV studio, or for that matter for that giant War Room they had passed through? Either of those two IBM mainframes would have been adequate to handle NORAD's traffic load; they were top of the line.

In college Russell had been on reasonably friendly terms with three or four black militants. Only once had one of them displayed property of any real value to him: a Kalashnikov AK-47 with sniperscope. Russell could remember a Black Panther fundraiser, an afternoon of food and entertainment that had netted perhaps two hundred dollars.

This organization had money to burn, it seemed. Ever since he had left Garvey Park and seen the limo pull up to the curb, Russell had been feeling his preconceptions twisted like taffy. Now he had reached the point at which he was considering doubting his senses.

I am in Halifax, lying back in a hot tub and dreaming of what the upcoming trip to New York will be like. And I have a sick imagination.

As he bent his head to step through another gasketed, gas-tight door, Russell caught sight of the dried blood on his pants, and the feeling of unreality vanished.

They passed successively through a dining hall, a kitchen/commissary, a short washroom corridor, sleeping quarters for sixty which reminded Russell powerfully of a submarine he had once spent time in, an infirmary, and another storage area, emerging at last into a large room laid out as an executive lounge: the only furnishing not designed to provide physical comfort was a large video screen hanging on the right hand wall, with attendant control console. Ignoring all the powered and unpowered chairs, four women were standing at parade rest as Michael's party entered. Their armbands were all white. They snapped crisply to attention.

Between them, sprawled across a couch, was a naked man in great distress. His wrists and ankles were cuffed and a plastic sheet had been thoughtfully placed under him so that he would not stain the couch. His inhalations were long shuddering whispers, his exhalations were short explosive grunts. The one good eye rolled without tracking anything. Dena gasped.

Three of the women were carrying automatic weapons; the fourth had only a holstered sidearm. She was in her forties, shaven-headed like everyone else in this tunnel, and projected authority and competence. She wore a single earplug, louvered to let ambient sound through, and a nickel-sized throat mike. She stepped forward and spoke crisply to General Worthing.

"We got him, General. Lieutenant Jonas Robinson. Just as you ordered, we traced the outgoing and it led to his line. We took him cleanly—I don't believe anyone else in the War Room noticed—and he did not get off a second call."

"Well done, Colonel Moore. Could he have any confederates in this command?"

"No, sir." She glanced down at the traitor. "I could be wrong, but I'm positive. Mustapha Khan is due to arrive in twelve minutes, and is reported on schedule so far."

"Good."

Michael spoke. "Was all that hurting really necessary, Trezessa?"

She did not flinch. "Yes, Michael. The drugs don't work

on him. We stopped the moment he cracked. He was tough. Religious fanatic.''

"I see.'' Michael's face looked no sadder than it always did.

"Kill him painlessly, Colonel,'' Worthing told her, "and then wrap him up and put him in the disposal area.''

"Yes, sir.'' She produced a syrette, bent, and injected the man on the upper arm, and he died instantly and unspectacularly. The other three helped her roll up and carry him out.

"You know, Tom,'' Michael said mournfully, "I think that's where we misjudged Mustapha, right there. I think *he's* a religious fanatic.''

"Come on, Michael. He believes in Allah like I believe in Jupiter—that stuff is just to fool the sheep.''

"No, I think Mustapha is that rare thing: a powerful religious leader who *isn't* a hypocritical opportunist. It explains a lot. We've been assuming that reason, rational self interest, would guide his actions. We never allowed for orders from Allah. Why else would he take such a stupid risk, *now?*''

"Mmmm. Maybe you're right. I'll bear it in mind.''

"The question is: will he really still come?''

"Let's wear his sandals,'' Worthing said. "Mustapha gets a message from Robinson that a white man who knows about the Night of Power has a dying message from Willie Ray Brown that he wants to give you face to face. Mustapha knows what the message has to be, so he tries to have Grant hit. But nothing comes back from the hit, no killers, no car, no news—the gunfire takes out the central processor and that arcade goes silent, even Robinson can't tell him what happened. The TV and radio news say a white man died in that firefight, but he knows that we have brothers and sisters in the media, and anyway it might not have been the *right* white man. Sooner or later someone should make it to another arcade or other terminal and report back up the line, and Robinson can intercept that and pass the word. But Robinson is late calling. Mustapha's in the dark.''

"So maybe we know he's a traitor,'' Michael said. "Why take the risk of coming as planned?''

"If we do know, his only possible move is to drop everything and flee Manhattan tonight, Allah or no Allah. It's even too late to betray us to The Man, and there's no way he can stay on this island and live past tomorrow sundown. But if he leaves, he leaves *everything*. However the Night of Power turns out, he loses all he has. He *can't* do that when he doesn't even know for sure it's necessary."

"But if we *don't* know—"

"If we don't know, he has two options. Abort the hit and cooperate with us as he has pledged—or carry out the hit. Which one would depend on how suspicious of him we seem. Or what Allah tells him, I suppose."

Colonel Moore was back. "You understand that, Trezessa?" Michael said to her. "When Mustapha arrives, what he wants most is to find that he is an honoured guest, welcomed with joy and shared anticipation. Don't lay it on too thick, he'll be hyperalert for that."

"I understand, Michael."

"I'll greet him here, we'll peel his guards off him, and Tom and I'll take him and his shadow Bismillah into Tom's room for tea. Not less than ten and not more than twenty minutes later, Mustapha and Bismillah will die. If you hear them cry out or me call for you, take out his guards at once."

"It will be done, Michael." She looked savage. "They soil the Night."

"Don't expose yourself unnecessarily, Trezessa. I need you this night."

"Yes, Michael."

Russell and Dena had watched and heard all this in silence. Now Michael turned to them.

"Children," he said, "I have to get you out of the way. The next passage uptunnel contains living quarters for four. We will be using the near left room, so I'm going to put you in the far right. That's my room. I'm afraid it will be quite dull, there's nothing much in there. But it'll only be for a short while, and you should be safe there whatever happens."

"Whatever you say, Michael," Russell told him, and Dena nodded.

"I still say we should nail him as soon as he gets off the

elevator," Worthing said to Michael. "It's insane to let him have a chance at you."

"No, Tom. I have to face him. For one thing I need to know how far the rot spreads. We need the Muslims behind us; there has to be a smooth transfer of power tonight. I want to know how many layers down we have to go to find someone we can trust."

Worthing looked frustrated. "You're right—but I don't have to like it. You watch that bastard, he's tricky."

"Tom, better this war go forward without me than go forward headed by Mustapha. He just can't put it over. He thinks he's got God as a backstop. Russell, Dena, this way."

They followed Michael, accompanied by the everpresent Motormouth, into a short corridor with two doorways on either side. They went straight to the far right door. A little further on, the corridor opened out into a small area of full tunnel-width, which ended in a heavy armour wall. Russell could see that the great door set in it was another airlock. Beyond it somewhere must lay the corpse of Jonas Robinson. This was the end of the inhabited section, but the immense tunnel itself went on further, beyond that bulkhead. . . .

Several things clicked together in his mind. "Michael?"

"Yes, son?"

"This is Tunnel Three, isn't it?"

Michael looked surprised, then respectful. He smiled. "How do you know about that?"

"I was invited to work on it. I'm a designer, and they wanted an inexpensive self-cleaning system. I sniffed around, decided the whole project was doomed, and declined the job—but I did hear they got a good chunk of work done before the money ran out. Fifty years and more they've spent on this hole in the ground."

Michael nodded. "One of the great boondoggles of our time. Goes up a ways past the Harlem River and just stops. It wasn't being used, so I decided to borrow it."

"You'll give it back when you're done with it," Russell said ironically.

"Oh, no. There won't be any way to do that. I'm afraid I must lock you people in, now, until my meeting with

Mustapha Khan has ended. I don't mean to confine you, but to make sure Mustapha doesn't stumble across you. He must not know that a white man has spoken with me tonight. The room is soundproof. Someone will let you out within twenty minutes, however the interview goes down. All right?"

"You're asking me if it's all right with me?"

"That's right."

"Sure, Michael." Russell hesitated. "Good luck."

"Good luck, Michael," Dena said, speaking for the first time since they had left the park.

He smiled sadly at them. "Thank you both. We'll talk later."

He opened the door and ushered them inside, locked it behind them.

Russell cleared his throat.

Dena looked at him. His Dena, bald like all these strangers. There was time to talk at last. There was too much to say, nowhere to begin. He glanced around for distraction.

There was not much to work with. Except for a tatami, a small sculpture, and two books, Michael's personal room was utterly bare. Nonetheless it somehow felt lived in—scent, perhaps? Some subliminal clue. The sculpture was a miniature replica of Rodin's "Caryatid Who Has Fallen Under Her Stone." The two books were Clavell's translation of Sun Tzu's *Art of War*, and a November 1980 edition of the Marine Corps manual on "Military Operations on Urbanized Terrain (MOUT)." Both looked well thumbed.

He turned back to Dena. His instinct was to break the tension with a wisecrack, but he couldn't think of one. From her face he knew that she too was looking for words. Neither could find any that were adequate.

And then somehow, to Russell's astonishment she was in his arms and they were on the floor making love.

If he had considered the idea rationally, he might have decided to go ahead with it—surely it must take Michael and his friends at least ten minutes to kill several men and return—or perhaps the very cold bloodedness of that thought might have turned him off. But he never considered it rationally. He had seen death four times in the last twenty-four hours, and the third time he and Dena had nearly died themselves, and few things make a person hornier than a close brush with death. It simply happened, without their having to think about it; the strategic parts of their clothing melted out of the way as if by television.

And there the resemblance to television ended. For in a TV play it would have been the best sex either of them had ever had, magically healing all wounds and solving all problems, a mindless celebration of their survival and reaffirmation of their love. But once the physical joining of their loins had been effortlessly accomplished, their minds woke up and it stopped being effortless.

Part of it, of course, was simply that they had had sex only a few hundred years—God, only a few hours!—ago. There was always a chance that someone might come in. They were both of them both physically and mentally tired, and both were subconsciously concerned for their daughter.

Over all these things they might have triumphed. But there was unfinished business between them, and it intruded. Dena came as quickly as ever, perhaps quicker, but less forcefully, and as she did so he felt his erection flag. Suddenly uncertain that he could make it, but feeling somehow that it was essential he do so, he reached for a fantasy image. What surfaced were a few scenes from the magazine Dena had thrown in his face earlier that evening. They worked, after a fashion. He achieved a dry sneeze of an orgasm, and even managed to time it with her second, but it left him frustrated, wishing vaguely that he had let his erection wilt and tried again at a later time, or faked a climax. He hugged her fiercely tight, even after he had rolled his weight off her.

After a time it came to him that outside this room, perhaps at this moment, men he had never met were dying, because of a message that he had delivered. It was a sobering thought. Obligations yet undischarged . . .

"Dena, I'm so—"

"Shhh."

"But I should never have—"

"Hush. Neither should I."

"But you don't—"

"I've had a lot of time to think it over. Tell me if I miss anything. I should have realized you didn't have a chance to look through that magazine—you must have been hard-pressed to buy it at all. You shouldn't have mentioned it until you did have a chance to look it over. I should have told you before shaving my head, or at least have sprung it on you better; you should have handled it better. You shouldn't have picked a fight over that knifing you saw; I shouldn't have let you. I shouldn't have let Jerome into the apartment; you should have known I wouldn't do so without a good reason. You're unreasonably threatened by Jerome; I've been stupid in not realizing that before. Did I leave anything out?"

"Not that I can think of right now. Do we forgive us?"

"Might as well. We're going to be together the rest of our lives. We might as well be on friendly terms."

"I agree." He hesitated, undecided whether to speak. "But first I want to tell you why I am unreasonably threatened by Jerome."

"Russell, you don't have—"

"If we're going to forgive us, we have to know the whole story. I am *threatened* by Jerome because he's a former lover of yours, because he was a significant one, because he got under your skin, because he left you before you were ready and so is filed under 'Unfinished Business' in your heart. I am *very* threatened by Jerome because you are physically close to him in a sweaty state of seminudity every day. These things I should be able to handle; I've handled similar situations with you before. I am *unreasonably* threatened by Jerome because he is black."

"Oh, Russell—"

"Apparently my subconscious mind bought a piece of the ancient shibboleth that black men are sexier, more sensual and primitive and powerful than white men. I'm being as honest as I can. I think I could handle his being younger, better looking, a dancer—but he's black, and that throws me."

She averted her eyes. "What about black *women?*" she asked. "Am I sexier than the white women you've known?"

"*Yes.*"

"And is that because I'm black?"

He closed his eyes. "Dena, I don't have enough data points. I've only had one other dark skinned lover, Indian rather than African, and she was, well, average. I don't *know* how much of your sensuality and energy are genetic, and how much is uniquely you." He hesitated. "But I do know that from time to time people we meet give me a look that says, 'He must be one hell of a man to hold onto a black woman.' I didn't think I believed that. But I see now that I have been allowing myself to feel pride when I saw that look, and so I've bought a piece of the theory. Somewhere in the slimier recesses of my head, I think I've been wearing, quietly and happily, a little sign saying, 'Honorary Black Man,' and walking just a little taller because of it. And of course the flip side of that coin is the fear that one day a *real* black man will come along and steal you away."

"Russell," she said after a small silence, "how do your first wife and I compare in bed? On a scale of ten?" She met his eyes.

"I can't answer that," he said without hesitation. "I'm not trying to weasel out, Dena, but the question can't be answered. Janice was receptive more often, she didn't have a dance career to run so sex was a more important component of her life. But she could never have matched your inventiveness or enthusiasm, or your limberness. She had bigger tits, you have a . . . what I'm trying to say is, you're both tens—on different scales." He tucked his penis back into his pants and zipped them.

Dena dried herself with a single tissue. "Okay. Now suppose it turned out that she was living in the apartment above ours. She didn't really die in that plane crash, just used the opportunity to disappear and take a new identity. So she represents unfinished business to you. And she's a ten, and she's right upstairs while I'm off at work. Are you going to leave me and go back to her—assuming she wants you to? I know how much she meant to you, how good a marriage you two had. Would you leave me for her if that were a possibility?"

"No," he said at once.

"Why not?"

"On one level, because I owe you loyalty. But on a purely selfish level, I've invested too much time and sweet effort in our marriage to risk losing it, even for something else as good. It'd take something *twice* as good to seriously tempt me, and as far as I know there is no such thing."

"All right. Now, do you credit me with the same amount of morals on the one level, and intelligence on the other?"

He hesitated, and she started to cloud up. "Yes, Dena, yes of course, that's not why I'm hesitating."

"Spit it out."

"No, I would not leave you for Janice. But . . ."

"Speak."

"But I could plausibly imagine a combination of circumstances—innocent, understandable, forgivable circumstances—that could put us together in bed. Once. Or more. Just to see what the years had done. At least, I think you'd be nuts not to be worried about the possibility. And . . ." He looked down at his lap. "And besides, your analogy assumes that Jerome *isn't* twice as good a lover as I am."

She pulled away, sat up, and pulled her jeans back on. "Listen, dumb bastard, dumb bastard that I love, listen good because I am only going to go through this once with you and then I don't ever want to hear about it again. I am annoyed enough to answer your implied questions honestly, and it's up to you to live with it. I don't have enough data points for a racial analysis either. I've only had two black lovers, and one was *terrible*. As for you, on a scale of ten, with ruthless honesty, I rate you a nine and a half. You're always *thinking*, and it costs you points. But you are the most considerate and skillful and understanding sex partner I have ever had. Jerome, on the other hand—"

Russell held his breath.

"—back when we were fucking, clocked in at about— pause for suspense—about a six. Get that smile off your face, I'm not finished yet. As far as energy and gusto and—I don't know, *style*, he was a clear ten—he didn't have your technique or staying power, he didn't need them. But his problem was, he was totally self involved. Oh, he never left me high and dry, you know I'm quick, but he wouldn't have minded a whole lot if he had. That

brought him back to a six in my book. A touch of that
male arrogance can be appealing to a woman, for a time,
in just that primitive way you spoke of earlier—because
it's a challenge. The reason Jerome left a piece of himself
under my skin is that he walked out on me before I ever
got him to confront me as a person. I had it in my mind
that if he ever did, I might get him up from a six to a nine
or ten. But he got away clean.

"Now I've met him again, years later, and he is no
longer totally self-involved. At first I thought he was, I
thought all this revolutionary shit was just another hat for
him to wear so people could admire how handsome he
looked in it. But it isn't. He obviously has committed his
life to it. I have no use for religion, but I used to almost
wish he would believe in a god of some kind, something
outside of himself. He does now, he believes in Michael. It
makes him more of a man, do you see? He confronted me
as a person tonight, risked something very important to
him to warn me of danger—why, he's even confronted *you*
as a person.

"Over the last week or so the awareness has been growing on me, unconsciously, that he is a new and better
Jerome. And yes, that has elicited the unconscious question,
I wonder how high he and I would rate now, the suspicion
that we'd go at least nine and a half, maybe higher. He
has made no secret of wanting me, and I've made it clear
that it was never ever going to happen . . . but I haven't
kept him at arm's length the way I should have. I think I
just wanted him to know, to understand what he threw
away when he split on me. I think I wanted to let him *just*
begin to get his hopes up . . . and then cut him off at the
knees. A stupid and dangerous game, and unfair to you."
She grabbed his upper arm, hard enough to make him
wince. "Here comes the important part, baby. Watch my
lips. It. Is. Never. Ever. Going to happen. Never in hell. I
am going to keep him at arm's length from now on. I
won't risk hurting or losing you. Partly because a marriage is so *much* more than just sex, and you give me
many many things Jerome never could. And partly because no matter how much smarter he's gotten, the high-
est I'd ever get him is nine point nine. Whereas if you can

ever learn to stop *observing* yourself all the time, you and I are going to hit fifteen some day. Have I answered you?"

Russell found that his shoulders were knotted up to the point of pain, and forced them to relax. They would only relax so far, as though someone had taken up the tension in an invisible set-screw.

"Thank you for your honesty," he said, his voice croaking on the first two syllables. "I know it must be truth because it stings like a burning bastard." She smiled, and he smiled back. Lord God, his wife did have a beautiful smile. "Yes, you've answered me."

"One small revision. Only in bed should you learn to stop observing yourself. The way you keep yourself under careful observation the rest of the time is one of the things that keeps you lovable."

"Okay."

"What is Tunnel Three?"

It took him a moment to shift gears. "Excuse me, I don't think our retros fired at the same time. Uh—Tunnel Three is what we are in. Manhattan gets all of its water through two enormous tunnels from upstate. One is ancient, the other is twice as old. Both have chronically and desperately needed overhauling for decades—but there was no way they could possibly shut down half of New York's water for long enough to work on them. The obvious solution was to build a third tunnel—but as the Hard Times began, it looked easier and easier to just let the next administration worry about it. Tunnel Three has been in progress for fifty years, and the last work done on it was over ten years ago. You've noticed that the water in this town tastes even worse than Halifax water?"

"God, Michael's plan is bigger than I thought."

At those words Russell was thunderstruck. It burst over him that there was a conversation he and Dena ought to have had *before* they mended the tear in their marriage, before making love. A subject whose urgency transcended their own personal concerns, beside which even agony was a side issue. At any moment the door was going to open and the chance would be gone—possibly forever— but he suddenly wished with all his heart that instead of shoring up their relationship he and Dena had discussed how they felt about Michael's Night of Power.

He was by no means sure how he felt himself—how could he hope to guess how Dena felt? "Dena, listen—"

And yes, the chance was gone, for there came a gentle knock.

He cursed himself for a fool. By happy accident he had been vouchsafed twenty whole minutes in which to think things through and talk them over with his partner—and he had spent them on fucking and soap opera. In Dena's eyes he read dismay matching his own.

Too late. "Yes, Michael."

The door slid back. Michael had changed into a new robe, also red but cut differently, and there was a small cut visible at the side of his neck which had been very skillfully doctored. Otherwise he seemed unchanged. His movements were unhurried, his breathing slow and regular. It was hard to believe he had killed within the last few minutes. Was he indifferent to killing? Or worse, had he been unable to do it?

Russell found either idea upsetting. It came to him that he wanted them not to be true. He wanted, on an emotional level, to like Michael, to believe in him. Was that something to watch for and guard against? Was Russell being manipulated by charisma? Or should he trust his instincts?

"Thanks for your patience, friends. Coffee and sandwiches will be arriving in the Lounge in a few minutes. Russell, I'm having clothes fetched that I believe will fit you. It's late and you've both been through a lot, but we need to talk. I've got some time clear now, and I won't have again for several days. Are you up to it?"

Russell was tempted to plead exhaustion, so he and Dena could talk privately first. But he dared not throw away this opportunity. He needed more data. If he could just avoid committing himself—say he needed to sleep on it—

"Up to it and for it," he said, and Dena agreed.

A guard came past the doorway carrying a green body bag. Trezessa Moore brought up the rear; she called a halt, set down her end, and gave Russell the T-shirt and cords she had in her free hand.

He saw Michael's face as he saw the body bag. The overall expression did not change, but something subtle happened at the corners of the mouth and eyes. As a child, Russell had gone one summer afternoon to the home of Mr. Raffalli, an elderly teacher he loved. Mr. Raffalli had received him with his customary elaborate courtesy, had been a gracious host, had seemed in all ways normal save that he had the same strange thing happening at the corners of his mouth and eyes. A week later Russell had learned that on that morning Mr. Raffalli's beloved cat Rainy Midnight had been hit by a van, and he had been forced to kill it himself.

"It's all set, Michael," Trezessa reported. "Selim Khan will be here by dawn."

"Good. Thanks. How's Anne?"

"Fine. Doc says it's greenstick. Uh—" She hesitated. "She says she wants to stay on duty. She says she's entitled."

"What do you think?"

"She really is in good shape. She shoots better left-handed than I do right handed. I don't like being short-handed tonight."

"Okay, that's settled. Any bad news from outside yet?"

Russell was amazed at how beautiful Trezessa was when she smiled. "Not a discouraging word, Michael."

His answering smile was much less exuberant. "Thank you, dear. Carry on." She and her companion hoisted the bag again and left. Russell stripped off his bloodstained clothes and dressed quickly.

"Has there been any word on our daughter?" Dena asked.

"Not yet," Michael said. "It's early yet."

It was necessary to make cuffs on the cords. Russell folded up the soiled clothes and tucked them under his elbow. "Let's go."

Motormouth was just finishing a mopping of the Lounge floor. Russell recognized the colour of the water in the bucket; a long time ago he had worked as a janitor in a hospital. There were four powered armchairs; Michael turned three of them to face each other and pulled over a wheeled coffee table. He patted Motormouth's massive shoulder, and the giant smiled wordlessly and left with mop, bucket, and Russell's old clothes.

"Michael?" Dena asked as they sat, "Is Motormouth mute?"

"Not exactly. He is totally aphasic. When he was a twenty-year-old Marine, something happened to him in Lebanon. I don't suppose anyone will ever know what. He has fascinated a lot of psychologists. His intelligence is high, his reason is sharp. But he cannot understand speech, and he cannot articulate ideas in any form. He can understand simple *written* sentences, as long as they contain only lower-case letters. If there's a capital anywhere in the sentence, he can't read it. No one even has a theory about that. He has been my friend and bodyguard for more than ten years. He can 'read' an astonishing amount from tones of voice and body language, much more than ordinary people. A lot of people take him for mute, but nobody ever takes him for deaf or retarded."

Under any other circumstances, Russell would have been fascinated. "Michael," he said, "I'm bursting with questions, but I'm afraid to ask any."

"I know, son," Michael said at once. "This afternoon you were a law-abiding visitor from a friendly foreign country. Now you're inextricably involved in murder and high treason, and with every answer I give you, you'll get in a little deeper. The more you know, the more trouble you're in."

"And the longer it will be before you can afford to let us go free."

"Not true. Within a week, two at the outside, I'll have no more secrets at all."

"What I really don't understand is why, on this night, you have time to talk with us."

"Russell, I've been planning this night, with the assistance of a few hundred very good brains, for over twenty-five years. I did budget time for last minute disasters, but Mustapha Khan was the only one that's come up. And I find that I feel like talking. To both of you. You are a black and a white who have learned to live together without hate. You're both Canadians—though you were raised in this country, weren't you, Russell? You both have a personal interest in what is going on tonight, but you're both in a sense disinterested parties. And you are enough of a technical man to appreciate some of the fine points."

Russell was impressed. Michael could not have known he was a technical man without having him very efficiently checked out—in a short time, after office hours, across a border.

"Do you mind telling me what your politics are, Russell?"

He suppressed the temptation to give the answer Rick gave Major Strasser in *Casablanca*. "I'm a rational anarchist," he said, "if that conveys anything to you."

To his surprise Michael smiled and nodded. "Yes, I know that book. As a matter of fact, I've borrowed from it heavily. I stole his cell system, for one thing—the first breakthrough in revolutionary theory in centuries."

Russell raised an eyebrow. "Have you told the old man? I'll bet he'd be horrified. You did say you're engaged in treason?"

"High treason, yes."

"What's a rational anarchist?" Dena asked. "I didn't think you had *any* politics, honey." Motormouth came back with coffee and a tray of sandwiches. Russell noted that Motormouth was not paying any special attention to him or Dena. The big man had classed them as nondangerous. In his secret heart, Russell had not yet ruled out the possibility of assassinating Michael. Was Motormouth that bad at his job?

Michael talked while he ate. "A rational anarchist—correct me, Russell—believes that he is solely responsible for his own actions, and admits of no authority higher than his own reason. He believes that governments and corporations and institutions do not exist—only self-responsible *individuals*."

"He follows only the rules he's made for himself," Russell agreed, "and pays just enough attention to other people's laws to stay out of jail."

"How about you, Dena?"

"I have no politics, Michael. I've never voted in my life because I was never offered anything to vote *for* and I couldn't decide which of those packs of idiots to vote *against*. But I guess I'd go along with what Russell says. Talking politics is slippery. It's like talking religion—you're never really sure whether you're agreeing or disagreeing, because the important words aren't defined. Do you really define a race riot as 'treason'?"

"Not necessarily. But I have no part in any race riot. I've been associated with a few in the past. I stopped two, and allowed others to happen, but I've never encouraged one in any way. But what I'm doing tonight is high treason. I am at war with the United States of America, and have been since 1969."

"Sixty-nine?" Dena said. "Were you a Black Panther?"

"Lord, no. The Panthers were zealous and brave, and doomed. Bravery is no substitute for brains. What kind of revolutionary wears a uniform? And seeks out public armed confrontations with superior forces? The Panthers went a long way toward convincing America that blacks were dangerous idiots." He took a long sip of coffee. "Huey chose the Panther name because, he said, 'The panther never strikes first, but when he is backed into a corner, he will strike back viciously.' When you think about it, that's a stupid way to fight a war. I was being educated in the art of fighting a war at that time, in Viet Nam. There were really two wars going on there. Did you hear much about the black-white race riots in Nam? At the end of '69 as I was mustering out, they took a poll of black soldiers, asked if they planned to join a militant group like the Panthers or SDS when they got home. Thirty-six percent of the combat troops said yes. Six percent of the *officers* said yes. A few months later there was a Harris Poll: thirty percent of American blacks felt they would '*probably* have to resort to violence to win their rights,' and another ten percent described themselves as 'revolutionaries.'

"It was obvious to me that one day there was going to be open war between blacks and whites in this country. I never understood why it wasn't obvious to everybody.

"If the war was allowed to happen naturally, it would be a long and bloody and uniquely horrible one. And I didn't see how there could be many black people left alive in America when it was over. The record of history seems clear: there isn't anything on earth as dangerous as a frightened white man. I foresaw a Holocaust, a national pogrom.

"So did many people, I guess. But they seemed able to forget it somehow, or wish it away, and those gifts I never had. Long into the night though I prayed for them.

"Like you, Russell, I knew that I was a self-responsible individual, a human being. So it was up to *me* to do something about it. Since the day I finally got that through my head, I've done nothing else with my life. I just couldn't see any chance at all to avert the war, and my people could not bear to lose it. So it was necessary to win it.

"For twenty-five years I've been prosecuting the war. Following the precepts of Sun Tzu, I looked for a way to win it before the world knew it had started. A way to win it with minimal bloodshed. A way to win it that'd still allow for blacks and whites to live in peace when it was over."

What Russell wanted to say was, you are dreaming. What he said was, "You set your design parameters high."

Michael shook his head. "No. That was the absolute least I could settle for. Anything less would just be postponing the Holocaust. And I think it can be done. You do agree that open racial warfare is not far away?"

Russell nodded. He had finished an excellent sandwich and the coffee was first rate and he was feeling new strength in himself. "It's been coming for a long time. The U.S. has been in a steady decline since the '60's, and hard times aggravate racism on both sides. It's one of those things everybody knows, but you don't think about it much because you don't see anything to be done about it, so it just hurts to think about. Like the U.S.-Soviet arms race, or the fact that you're going to die."

"Just like dying," Michael said, "it's something you've *got* to think about if you're going to get it right. And you only get the one chance."

"All right," Russell said impatiently. "Enough philosophy. You've got a plan. I don't see how you could possibly have a plan. I never heard of your organization before today. How can you even dream of taking on the United States and winning?"

"A grain of sand can bring down an IBM mainframe—if it's in the right place at the right time."

Dena spoke up. "Then what are you doing tonight?"

"I'm taking Manhattan Island."

Russell was stunned speechless. His mind flooded with more questions than he could sort, let alone priorize, and he owned no expostulation equal to his need. His coffee mug fell unheeded to the floor. He squeezed his eyes shut.

Michael gave him time. Shortly the world steadied. He opened his eyes again. "My God, Michael," he said slowly, "I don't see how you can pull that off. How big an army could you recruit without coming to the attention of the F.B.I.?"

"There are a little under twenty thousand soldiers in my army. Of those, about twelve thousand are combat troops—most of them experienced and all of them trained. The rest are *very* strategically placed, and highly skilled in their professions. For twenty-five years people have asked my advice on career-choice—I've been farming Harlem, and infiltrating the rest of the city."

Russell shook his head. "Hard to believe you could keep that big a force a secret."

"Russell, what color is the Assistant Director of the F.B.I.?"

"Jesus Christ on whole wheat toast." He shook his head again. "What do the eight thousand noncombatants do?"

"Some of them have been working ten years and more already, helping me set this up, helping me steal the money to finance it. Most of the rest are going to help me keep the city running once I own it."

"Stealing how?" Dena asked.

Michael nodded at the question. "You know how important the German scientists who fled from Hitler were for America? The trouble they went to get to Von Braun and the others after the war? Long ago I acquired some brains of that level of talent in computer larceny. Some of the biggest banks in the world are underwriting my war. They just don't know it. And there are a few dozen other ways we get money, including voluntary dues from each soldier."

Russell was frowning. "Twelve thousand doesn't seem like enough by an order of magnitude. Make me believe it."

"Manhattan is fifty percent black by day and over sixty-five percent black by night. Whites—and Chinese, and lately even hispanics—have been hemorrhaging out of the city for years."

"Sure, but—"

"Let me talk a bit. Here is how it should go down, if I have planned rightly and luck is with us. At three AM, Manhattan will be physically isolated from the rest of the United States. Every bridge and tunnel will be destroyed or interdicted simultaneously. All TV transmission will cease, all radio and microwave communication will be jammed, newspaper presses will stop rolling. At the same time assault forces will take both major armories and assorted smaller ones—that part will be a boat race. They're loaded with ordnance for the African war, but by a coincidence that took a lot of arranging there are not a lot of white *troops* presently on Manhattan—a big wave left for Africa last week. Substantial fractions of Army, National Guard, and police personnel are black; I have men in key positions. Almost no white raise or military live in Manhattan, they commute—so once the bridges and tunnels are gone, we have only one shift to deal with, at their sleepiest and most disorganized. By dawn there's going to be a large pile of red stones where Police Headquarters used to be, right by the ruins of the Brooklyn Bridge, and I will control all key points in Manhattan."

Russell still could not sort out his objections; Dena spoke. "Michael, you say that nobody knows about your army that isn't in it? And you expect the black population of Manhattan to unite behind you tomorrow? Solidly?"

"I believe they will. Not unanimously, but overwhelmingly."

"Michael, this is nuts," Russell said. "Even if you could take Manhattan, how long could you hold it? And what would you *do* with it once you had it?"

"You met Tom Worthing. He is the second black general the Marines ever had, and he resigned his commission covered with honours. He assured me ten years ago that with two good divisions he can take Manhattan and hold it indefinitely."

"But—"

"Okay, you're the general assigned to retake Manhattan. How will you go about it? By the way, the Coast Guard base on Gouvernor's Island and the naval base in Brooklyn are ours too."

Russell thought hard. You could not drop paratroops onto the Manhattan skyline. The open parts of Central Park were all surrounded by high firing platforms—the skyscrapers—and what if, say, there were a million white hostages huddled there together in the summer sun? With several armouries full of sophisticated hardware, wire-guided this and heat-seeking that and robot drones and pulse disruptors, Michael's army could annihilate a helicopter assault. Russell was not intimately familiar with Manhattan's shorelines, but he did not see how any amphibious assault could be practical, even without Navy and Coast Guard resources opposing it. And what would you use for a staging area? Come east through heavily-black New Jersey? South through Westchester and the Bronx? West from Brooklyn and Queens? Black strongholds all.

Considering the people and artifacts and information and other assets held hostage, would you dare any assault at all? More than a million hostages, many of them world class VIPs . . .

Jesus Christ! *Who was going to do the assaulting?* How many all-white combat units did the United States of America have? With all-white support and logistics?

The magnitude and audacity of Michael's plan was slowly beginning to come home to Russell. Manhattan contained the World Financial Center. The World Trade Center. Wall Street. The Federal Reserve, in which sat a substantial fraction of the gold in America. The Diamond District. Jesus wept and died for our sins, the United Nations! Embassies of every major nation on Earth. The headquarters of many of the world's largest corporations. The garment center. Some of the finest museums and theatres in the world. The publishing industry. The true power center of the movie industry. The TV networks, the—

"Fuck!" Russell exclaimed. He looked at Michael with awe and horror. "*STI!* NAMSAT East!"

Dena was frightened by his voice. "Russell, what is it?"

"STI! Satellite Telecommunications International . . ."

"What? I don't understand."

"About ten years ago, a bunch of bright boys and girls quit Bell Research Labs and formed their own company. They had invented a major breakthrough called maxiplexing. I couldn't explain it to you in a week, but it lets a single satellite handle hundreds of thousands of signals simultaneously, *much* cheaper than any preexisting method. Cheaper by orders of magnitude. More important, they were as smart in *handling* it as Bell and IBM were in their day, maybe smarter. The story of the early years of STI will be studied for centuries. The point is, right now they have a virtual monopoly on satellite communications in the free world. *And their central headquarters is in Manhattan.*"

"I still don't see what's—"

The words were tripping over themselves. "Look, there are two STI satellites over North America, in geostationary orbit. Between them they cover the continent. There used to be a *lot* of satellites, a lot of satellite companies, but none of them could compete economically with maxiplexing. STI crushed or ate them all, the way Bell ate all the phone companies in my father's day, and their satellites are junk now, orbiting garbage—there's talk of using them as scrap to build the Space Station with."

"What do the satellites do?"

"If you make a long distance phone call to California, an uplink here in New York squirts your call up to NAMSAT East. The satellite relays it to its twin brother, NAMSAT West, which beams it down to your party in L.A. The same with television—there aren't half a dozen broadcast stations left in the country. That's why you can get the same 500 channels wherever you go. STI's NAMSAT net is *much* cheaper than broadcasting."

"I already own the STI Building," Michael said quietly. "You heard the news the same time I did; it fell while we were talking in Garvey Park. The east coast control uplink belongs to me."

Russell shivered. "Great blithering mother of shit. You control television, long distance phone, and commercial data routes for North America."

"That's right."

He jumped up from his chair and began to pace. "But—but—why, you could—" He shut up and paced, frowning furiously.

"Data routes?" Dena said. "You mean all the—"

"—computer information flow for this country," Russell said, "and more. The international banking community depends on the SWIFT systems of satellite information transfer. Michael could make every credit card in North America a worthless piece of plastic just by blowing up that uplink. Or no, he wouldn't even have to—just feed the satellites bad course corrections and cause their orbits to decay. The national, the continental economy would grind to a halt overnight, and the world economy wouldn't be far behind. If you graphed the dislocation, something as small as the Great Depression would disappear in the noise. Dena, Michael has the planet by the balls."

"I wouldn't want to destroy sophisticated technology like that," Michael said. "I don't even intend to interrupt data flow if I can avoid it—that would bring suffering and hardship to hundreds of millions, and I plan to hurt as few people as possible. But it all passes through STI's computers for encoding and maxiplexing. Suppose I changed the parity bit, or just injected spurious bits at random, at unpredictable intervals? Suppose I just *threatened* to?"

Russell was aghast. "I think they might very well nuke Manhattan. No, of course they wouldn't, they couldn't risk even a neutron job; they'd never get the satellite back, you'd have instructed it to ignore any uplink that wasn't coded your way and they'd never find the code. But Jesus, Michael, just the *threat* would make the whole system useless. They couldn't trust it, so they wouldn't dare use it."

"Exactly."

"I don't follow you," Dena said.

Russell was too upset to speak; Michael had to take it. "Dena, let's say you walk into Chase Manhattan tomorrow and utter a cheque for five hundred dollars. You do your banking with Halifax Metro Credit Union?"

She raised her eyebrows. "How do you know so much about us?"

He smiled that warm sad smile. "Child, all I know about you are the experiences we've shared—and everything about you that ever went into a computer."

"So I write a cheque for five hundred."

"What does Chase do? It asks your Credit Union if you have funds on deposit to cover the cheque. The clerk punches the question into a computer—which sends it to STI, which bounces it off NAMSAT East to Halifax. The Credit Union computer agrees that you're good for the money, and bounces that reply back to New York. The clerk accepts your cheque, counts out cash, and tells his computer to get the money from the one up north. Again, both steps go through NAMSAT. And, since your cheque is for Canadian dollars, both sides have to go through NAMSAT again to get the precise exchange rate for that moment. Six messages ricocheted off that satellite, and they all go through the STI master computer. Billions of dollars a day go through that very process. Most of the money on the planet is just bits in the computer net.

"Now suppose a playful old darkie in New York, with a nasty sense of humour and a bad attitude, has been amusing himself with the master protocols of that computer. Suppose, just for fun, it's been told that any time a transfer sequence comes through for any person whose first name ends in 'A,' it is to record the funds as transferred, without actually taking them from the bank of origin. Your money is credited as received by Chase, but it isn't debited back home. You just made five hundred dollars out of thin air, and the international banking system is none the wiser. Oh, one day *you'll* figure it out, probably the next time you get a statement from the Credit Union. But will you report it? If you do, how many reports will they need to figure out that the final 'A' in your first name was the operative factor?

"Or suppose the computer has been told to ignore the correct dollar exchange rate, and substitute one that var-

ies with the number of "M.A.S.H." reruns that are being
sent over the same satellite at that hour?

"You see the problem now? If the international banking
community can't trust the system, they can't use it. And if
they can't use it, they can't function. They committed
themselves irretreivably to computers all the way back in
the '70's, and it's too late to switch back. The same situation applies for the stock and commodities exchanges, for
most of the federal government and all major corporations.
The IRS, the Social Security system, the Federal Reserve—
Dena, any system bigger than a city that has to communicate with itself or the world funnels through STI, and a
lot of them use NAMSAT East on a daily basis. I could
wreck them all. Or I could just hurt them all very badly.
But if I just *say* that I'm doing anything *at all* to the
system—even if in fact I'm not—they all have to stop
using it at once. *Have to.* And they may not even be able to
fall back on transferring information verbally, by phone—
because long distance phone goes through the same system.

"So I have to be very careful not even to *threaten* to
monkey with the system."

"But how did such a stupid system ever get set up in
the first place?" Dena cried. "How could they put all their
eggs in one basket that way?"

"Any question that begins, 'Why do they—?', the answer
is 'Money.' Because it was irresistibly cheap. Because it
brought the cost of information transfer very near to zero.
I'll tell you this: the force that took that building is *much*
bigger, and took more planning, than the one that's going
to take the big armoury in a while."

Russell had his voice back by now. "The three people
who founded STI were very cagey, hon. They never pat-
ented maxiplexing. So nobody else knows how to do it. To
recreate their work, you'd have to do what they did: plunder
the resources of an outfit the size and quality of Bell
Research Labs for a decade, and be three geniuses with a
lot of luck. Cleverly, they made it *much* cheaper to simply
do business with them. The only major holdouts were the
military, who maintain their own satellites and uplinks.
They do *not* have channels to spare for commercial and
nonmilitary interests. It's really no stupider than having

all the electric power for the East Coast interconnected in a system that can be brought down by three lightning strokes in one hour. That's happened three times already, and they're still using the same system. Michael, that reminds me—what will you do when they cut your power and water?"

Michael frowned. "As to water, I sincerely hope they will not interrupt service. For one thing there would be a lot of thirsty white hostages. For another, since there are always fires, even in the most peaceful of times, it wouldn't be long before much of Manhattan was embers. As to power, by five this morning we'll be cut out of the power grid. There are twenty-four power stations on Manhattan, nineteen in Queens that are being seized as we speak, eleven in Brooklyn the same, more on Staten Island. Most of them can be taken simply by rattling enough garbage cans to wake up the guards—though you might still need machine guns for the rats, in Brooklyn and Queens. The combined capacity of all those plants—true summer capability, not nameplate rating—is just short of 10,000 megawatts. In a pinch we could get by with the ones here on Manhattan plus 'Big ALLIS' over in Ravenswood. We've got power as long as the coal holds out, and we've got plenty."

"So the limiting factor is food."

"Yes."

"I heard once there's only three days worth of food on Manhattan at any given time."

"An exaggerated figure. And if the Navy *does* blockade New York Harbour to prevent any food from being shipped in by sympathetic groups, it'll soon become impossible to feed white hostages. Soon after that some of my people would begin to feed *on* them. But it'd be a good week or two before things actually reached that pass, and long before that I hope to have the war won. Bear in mind that a lot of that so-called three days' worth of food is intended for commuters who won't be around to eat it—one of many reasons why we're striking in the dead of night."

"I'm lost again," Dena said plaintively. "How can they even try to starve you out if you can screw up their data routes on short notice?"

"Ah," Michael said, "that's what I started to say before. I have to be extremely careful *never* to threaten such a thing. If I do, the damage is done. A compromised system is useless. If I play this right, they'll all end up *wanting* to believe that I'm too dumb to have thought of it, or too unsophisticated to pull it off, that I've only taken over the uplink to monopolize TV transmission and control the phone system. The first thing any intelligent revolutionary does is seize control of communications.

"But they'll *never be sure*, and it'll give me a strong psychological edge when I start to negotiate."

Russell shivered; the wicked elegance of the scheme was breathtaking. "If the military ever realizes how sophisticated you really are, they'll nuke you on the spot and to *hell* with the world banking system. Why, you could use NAMSAT to feed false data into *their* satellites—no, I don't want to think about that. I don't want anyone anywhere ever to think about that."

"I'm not thinking about it, son. Not for a second, not even in extremis, not even if we fail. Take it off your mind."

"Tell me about this negotiating, instead. You've got Manhattan held for ransom, and you've got the U.S.—and for that matter Canada and Mexico—by the throat. Okay. *What's your price?* What ransom can you ask? That they can possibly give?"

Michael started to answer, then checked himself. "What would you ask for in my place, Russell? Dena?"

He shut his mouth firmly and thought.

"God," Dena murmured after a minute, "how much money would it take to make up for what America has done to its black people? More than they've got, for sure. More than there is."

"You miss the point," Michael said forcefully, and Russell and Dena both started. They had not heard that much steel in Michael's voice since the day he had discussed the treatment of pushers with two black cops in Harlem. "*Nothing* can 'make up for' what whites have done to blacks in this country. Nothing can 'make up for' what blacks have done to whites in this country! What has kept this racewar inevitable for so long is that *both* sides have legitimate grievances, both sides have done unforgivable things to each other. Which side did *the most* unforgivable thing *first*, or *most recently*, is absolutely irrelevant! The whole point is that all the unforgivable things on *both* sides must be forgiven, and if they can't be forgiven then they must at least be forgotten. We *have* to wipe the slate clean and start over, or else kill each other now and have done with it."

There was a short silence.

" 'Wipe the slate clean—', you say," Dena said.

All at once Russell got it. The idea was like an explosion of flashpowder at arm's length. It was so simple, so obvious, so necessary—and so enormous that an hour ago he would have, if he could have entertained the idea at all, dismissed it as an unattainable fantasy.

"Of course," he breathed. "A black homeland . . ."

Dena gasped and Michael smiled his melancholy smile. A portion of Russell's spinning mind noted that Michael's sadness was a large part of his charisma. Your heart instinctively went out to anyone who sorrowed that deeply, and could still smile, still function. It helped you to forgive him for being such a perceptive judge of character. "An Israel," Michael said. "A Zimbabwe. A Quebec. Hopefully more successful than any of those. Later today we'll announce the formation of a new nation, and petition the United Nations for recognition. If luck is with us, I hope to have it within two weeks."

"A black homeland," Dena repeated wonderingly.

"There's background for the petition. Black Americans have been petitioning the United Nations for half a century. Back in 1983 the Minnesota chapter of the Black American Law Student Association petitioned the UN Subcommission on Human Rights in Geneva, on behalf of all black citizens of this country, asking for relief from a 'nationwide police campaign of terror.' It's been done five times since—to no effect, of course, but it's there on the books. We've got a solid legitimate case going back two hundred years. I have a fairly stable interim government lined up and ready to go, a constitution I think I can get ratified in a week, and general elections due in a matter of weeks."

"Where?" Russell asked with a voice gone rusty. "What do you have in mind for your Quebec?"

"Well," Michael said. "I intend to go in asking for what we deserve. We are one tenth of the population; we deserve ten percent of the real estate and assets. But that's just a bargaining position. I'm willing to settle for only two states out of fifty-one. New York and Pennsylvania."

As a designer, Russell was accustomed to thinking in the largest terms in brainstorming sessions, but this tripped his circuit breakers. "Why not throw in Jersey?" he asked ironically. "Heavy industry, farmland, good highway system—"

"It's not Uncle Sam's to give," Michael answered with equal irony. "It belongs to the Mafia. Besides, that would give us a whole thirty-fifth of the land surface area of the U.S. On behalf of a tenth of the population, I'm willing to settle for a thirty-seventh, less than a hundred thousand square miles. For one thing, many black people just won't move—perhaps as many as half of them, though I hope not. I need to house from twelve to twenty-five million people—and New York and Pennsylvania together currently hold thirty-two million. Yes, we'll need more *lebensraum* some day. Maybe we'll end up invading Jersey. *I* hope we'll *buy* it one day. Meanwhile we can be self-sufficient for water, power, and most of our food, and I think we can build a solvent economy. Put it this way: I have a secret commitment from the International Monetary Fund. If we can get UN recognition, the IMF will bankroll us. Excuse me—"

Trezessa had knocked and entered the room. At Michael's nod she approached, bent low and whispered in his ear. Russell paid no attention—he was busy rearranging the map of North America in his head. He had long since stopped doubting that Michael could do what he said he could do. But what to label the new anomaly? What name had Michael selected for his new nation? Trezessa finished her conversation and Russell started to ask—but at the sight of Michael's face he forgot his question. There was now so much sorrow there that somehow Russell knew some of it was about to spill onto him.

"Russell, Dena, I'm very sorry," Michael said. "That was a report from Jerome Turner. They ran into trouble on the way here, and they got separated. He can't locate your daughter and her bodyguard."

Dena screamed, "Oh God, *no!*" and tried to rise. Russell barely managed to catch her before she hit the floor. On his knees, cradling her in his arms, he threw back his head and howled Jennifer's name.

CHAPTER EIGHT

"The conduct of military operations on the various types of urban terrain challenges the resourcefulness and ingenuity of commanders. Heavily structured, multilevel buildings provide fortified positions, as well as cover and concealment, for all combatants—the defender receiving the greatest advantage. These structures limit fields of observation and are obstacles to the movement of military forces. During combat operations the rubble that results from the destruction of buildings further impedes movement. The large number of civilians in urbanized terrain also creates special situations and attendant problems. . . . A skilled, well-trained defender has significant tactical advantage over an attacker. He occupies well-fortified positions which offer cover and concealment, whereas the attacker must maneuver over terrain which is channelized and compartmented—thus exposing himself in order to advance."

> —United States Marine Corps
> Operational Handbook (8-7),
> *Military Operations on Urbanized Terrain (MOUT)*,
> November 1980 edition

"Only a fool will attempt to take a city."

> —Sun Tzu,
> *The Art of War*

"It wouldn't be so bad to have blacks in government [in South Africa], Mr. Breedt allowed, so long as whites kept control, but once whites lost control, nothing would stop

213

'Communism.' When I asked why, his son Frikkie, a teacher, answered: 'It's because they don't believe in God. Because they don't have strong characters and because they're not educated and can't think for themselves.'

"His father nodded ruefully. 'I think we've stayed too long,' he repeated."

—Joseph Lelyveld, "Inside Namibia,"
New York Times Magazine, August 1, 1982

* * *

"Dena, honey, wake up." His voice was soft and calm.

She sat bolt upright in Michael's bed. *"Jennifer?"*

"No, darling," Russell said at once. "They haven't turned up yet."

"Then why did you wake me up?" She was still essentially asleep.

"Because it's time now," he said, still calm. "You have to get up and come with me."

She began to return to true consciousness. "How long have I been out?" Oh God, my little girl.

"Almost four hours. You went from a dead faint to a deep sleep. Your body is wise."

She could see that he had not slept. "Stop a minute. Fill me in on what's happened. Then tell me where we're going." She leaned back on one arm and thumbed her eyes.

Russell glanced at his watch. "We've got maybe five minutes. Apparently Jerome and José and Jen were on their way here in a cab, and got pulled over by the police. There was a flurry. Jennifer and José went west, Jerome was forced east."

Her heart turned over. "Had he already taken their weapons? Are they unarmed?"

He almost smiled. "Brace yourself. They have *all* the weapons, Jerome's too. Jen hid them in her purse while the cops searched the men. *She* took out one of the cops."

Dena gasped. "Between the two of them, they may just come through this. Now: as they were splitting up, Jerome yelled to them not to go to the Museum, so that they couldn't accidentally lead the cops here. He went back to the apartment and waited for them for almost an hour

before he called in. Michael had people up on the ground
by the Museum search for her, but she hasn't turned up."

"Is Jerome still at the apartment?"

"No."

"Why not?"

"Honey, listen to me. Ten minutes after Jerome called
in, the clock struck three and the war began. The first
battle is already over. Probably sixty percent of the people
in Manhattan don't know it yet, but Michael holds New
York. Bridges have fallen. Soldiers and cops are under
attack or dead or surrendered or on the dodge all over
town. The armories fell at once; there are tanks and half-
tracks and artillery rolling on the streets. Every radio in
town is jammed useless, on all frequencies. Every television set in America is showing, on every channel, a card
saying 'please stand by.' The Mayor is a prisoner."

"What about Jerome?"

"He couldn't get into our apartment without a key. He
couldn't risk hanging around on the street in a white
neighbourhood once the war started, especially unarmed.
There's a National Guard post right up on 33rd, First
Batallion, 71st Infantry. He wanted to stay, but General
Worthing ordered him to go reinforce the garrison at
Bellevue and Michael backed him up."

"Then what if—"

"Dena, let me tell it. The idea was that I would call the
apartment at fifteen minute intervals to catch them if
they came back there."

"And they *still haven't answered?*"

He took her by the shoulders. His voice was still gentle.
"Listen. I can't get through to them. Michael's people
blew the Long Island Rairoad tunnel to Queens—not
underwater, they didn't want to flood Penn Station—but
it runs underneath 32nd and 33rd Streets, and when they
blew it they unintentionally took out four blocks worth of
phones. Including ours."

"We've got to go and look for them!" She tried to rise,
and he restrained her, so forcefully that she was startled.

"Sit still a minute and take deep breaths."

"Russell, God damn it—"

He shook her, hard enough to shock her. For the first

time his voice had an edge. "You *must not* go to pieces. I am fresh out of glue. Breathe slow, damn you, I need you with a working brain. Do it!"

She could not remember the last time her husband had laid violent hands on her. She did as she was told, and when her breath began to regularize she felt the panic rinsing out of her mind. Russell held her with his eyes, and the grip of his hands on her shoulders now was softer. At last she nodded, and he released her and sat back on his heels.

"Michael can't let us go," she said. "We know the location of his command headquarters."

"Among other things," he agreed, his voice soft again. "Even if he were absolutely certain that both of us are solidly on his side, he couldn't chance it. Everyone in the world who knows that this is Michael's headquarters is down here now, and no one is going to leave until the United States surrenders. Best guess seems to be ten days, but they're prepared for a month if necessary."

"But Michael will let Jennifer and José in if we can locate them?"

"Yes. It's been promised."

"Then we have to locate them."

"I'm open to suggestions."

"Michael has ten thousand people on the street!"

"Sweetheart, Michael is very grateful to us. By extension so are Tom Worthing and all of Michael's people. But if you think ten thousand troops in the process of making war on America are going to be told to keep an eye peeled for a little white girl with a Puerto Rican, you need a cup of coffee very badly."

She sat very straight and breathed deeply: she had been on the verge of crying out, *"Then what do we do, Russell?"* But the edge had crept back into her husband's voice on his last sentence, and it reminded her that he was just as worried as she, and had had hours less sleep. Russell was one of those rare people who, though bright and sensitive, had so secure and confident a personality that he tended not to panic in a crisis—and Dena liked to believe that she had been learning from him for the five years of their marriage. She remembered a time when she had been

driving the two of them in a rental car to somewhere on a
four lane highway, next to no traffic, holding it steady at 110
kph. Around a blind curve and just over a crest, a farmer had
decided to change a flat tire in the left lane. Sixteen-
wheelers were pacing her in the right lane; when she saw
the red pickup she knew she was dead. The monstrous
unfairness of the farmer's stupidity paralyzed her mind:
instinct made her stand up on the brake, but even as the
wheels locked she *knew* she was going to hit him. The
pickup grew larger and larger for what seemed like an
hour, and then Russell was doing things to her and the
car too fast for her to follow, and a horrible roaring grind-
ing filled the world, and their front bumper *kissed* the
tailboard of the pickup as gently as one of the "shadow
kisses" Jennifer gave her every night. Afterwards she re-
constructed the sequence: Russell had yanked her shin
sideways so that her foot slipped off the brake and onto
the accelerator, then thrown the automatic transmission
into reverse, then leaned hard on her knee. The maneuver
demolished the transmission, totalled the car, and saved
their lives. "Darling," he had told her—*after* he had hus-
tled her out of the car and set flares back up over the hill
and broken the farmer's jaw—"when the lion has you half
swallowed, probe with your feet for a vital spot; maybe
you can kick him to death from inside."

Dena got hold of herself now and thought things through.

Assume they're alive. At three o'clock, they heard explosions in the distance, wherever they were then. Distant
gunfire. They headed back to the apartment and José got
them there safely. That place is a fortress. As soon as the
situation clarifies and he can spare the time and manpower,
Michael will send people there, and they'll bring Jennifer
here. Is there anything I can do to ensure that, or hurry it
along? Not a damn thing. What do I do, then? Put it out of
my mind and take up the next responsibility: helping my
mate to keep it together.

When she spoke her voice was, for the first time, as
calm and measured as his. "So where are we going?"

He studied her closely for a moment, nodded, got up
and went to the light switch, dialing it higher. "Better
start adjusting your eyes, it's bright out there. History is

about to be made, and we're invited to be present." He looked at his watch. "And we have maybe two or three minutes to get there. Michael is going on TV to announce the news. The rest of the country is getting a tape he cut weeks ago, but he's going live to the New York area. I knew you wouldn't want to sleep through it."

"Thanks. Russell?"

"Come on, we've got to go."

"Something you said a minute ago—"

She felt that he knew what she was going to say. "If we're late they won't let us in—"

"Russell, stand still and listen. What you said was, 'even if Michael were absolutely certain that both of us were solidly on his side . . .' Tell me: where do you stand? Are you for this war, or against it, or neutral?"

"Dammit, there's no time—"

She stood up. "This is the only room in this tunnel that probably isn't bugged—and we're bunking elsewhere from now on. This may be our last chance to talk privately for a long while. Take two seconds and then we'll run there together. For, against, or neutral?"

"I can't answer yet," he said desperately. "I've been thinking about it for hours and I just don't know. All my instincts tell me to beware of anyone with that much charisma who wants to change the world with bombs and guns. But I just don't know . . . how about you?"

"I trust Michael, as a human being, with all my heart. There is no evil in him anywhere, I'm *sure*. But whether his war is going to save black people or get them all killed . . . I haven't got an intuition yet. One thing I know: if we haven't made contact with Jennifer by nightfall I am going to bust out of this sewer some way and go find her—and if the FBI gets me and drugs Michael's secrets out of me, that'll be tough shit."

Russell grinned. "Attagirl. I'm with you there. Just be careful, and try not to leave without me if you can help it. Come on."

A guard, a woman she had not seen before, waited impassively in the corridor.

The video studio held two or three dozen people. Dena still did not understand the armband insignia system, but she gathered that most of these people were of high rank in Michael's army. The atmosphere was of quiet excitement, of restrained joy—the war was obviously going well so far. History was being made here.

Dena was surprised by one thing: though many people looked up when she and Russell entered the room, and some of those studied Russell carefully, not one displayed any visible animosity or distrust. It seemed to be common knowledge that Russell had risked his life to save Michael's; even so she would have been prepared to bet cash that a white man—*any* white man—would be as welcome in this place at this time as a leper on fire. She and Russell found seats together on a couch, all eyes left them, and Motor-mouth offered them coffee. A smile was playing at the corners of his mouth. Dena found herself liking him a great deal.

Michael sat alone against the far wall, looking toward his audience and into the three robot cameras. He wore the same red robe he had been wearing when she last saw him, a lavaliere mike pinned to it, and he was beautiful. The TV lights were not harsh enough to make him squint, but they made his skin glisten with highlights and soft-ened the lines on his forehead and round his eyes and mouth. There was an inconspicuous earplug in his right ear. His face was serene, patient. He could have been waiting to face a firing squad or to enter into Heaven. He was staring straight into the middle camera, as though something important lived inside it, but as she watched his gaze slowly tracked around until she was looking di-rectly into his eyes. Something she did not understand happened in her head. It was like a plank being snapped across, and it was like a basket of tumbling kittens, and it was like a cool hand on a fevered forehead. Michael's expression never changed, but she knew that she and Jennifer were in his mind, even now.

She smiled at him, and in a moment he turned his gaze back to the camera.

There were several monitors on the walls; each showed a card urging viewers to stand by for an important announcement. The director, camera operators, and mix board were in some other room—or possibly, for all Dena knew, at STI Headquarters in the old NBC building downtown.

She got three good slugs of coffee down, felt her alertness increase. Then, although there was no conversation anywhere, Trezessa Moore said, "Quiet, please; stand by," and the room rustled for a moment and was still.

The title on all the monitor screens began to roll upward. The prerecorded voice of Michael read the text aloud. Dena was prepared to bet that this program was closed-captioned for the deaf as well.

"People of New York, good morning. The announcement you have been waiting for will come to you live in ninety seconds. Meanwhile, do two things. Satisfy yourself that this message is coming to you on all TV and radio channels. Then wake up every friend and loved one you can reach and have them tune in at once. Don't worry if there's someone you can't reach right away; the announcement will be taped and rebroadcast all morning. But I must reach *all* of you as soon as possible. Significant changes took place in the night, and ignorance of them could easily get you killed. Don't worry about being late for work. Hardly any of you will be going to work today.

"You should be in no immediate danger if you stay indoors, and there is no cause for undue alarm. Transmission begins in forty-five seconds."

The announcement repeated. Colonel Moore went around the room, turning down the volume on all the monitors. Michael stood.

The title crawl reached ". . . undue alarm" and went to black. After a few seconds the red light glowed on the middle camera and Michael's face appeared in medium closeup on all the monitors. Without preamble or throat clearing or haste, he spoke:

"If you are black or brown, you know me. If you are white you may know *of* me. I am called Michael. I've used no other name for twenty-five years, but I was born Michael Hall in Harlem. Today I speak to you as Director Pro Tem of the nation of Equity.

"Equity is a new nation comprised of former black Americans who have renounced their allegiance to the

United States. Any human who can lay claim to Negro blood is eligible to become an Equitan citizen, and any non-Caucasian may become a Landed Immigrant.

"Early this morning at 2:55 Eastern time, a formal declaration of war was hand delivered to the President of the United States, by the former Assistant Director of the FBI, Raymond Tolliver, who had resigned earlier that day. Someone else can decide whether it should be called the Second American Revolution or Civil War II or just The Racewar. The simple fact is that the nation of Equity has declared war on the United States of America.

"Five minutes after Raymond Tolliver became a prisoner of war, forces of the Equitan Army launched an attack on and around New York City. As I speak to you at 7:01, we have seized complete control of Manhattan Island and outlying areas. We can hold it forever if we have to."

Atop the camera nearest Michael, a small blue light flashed once, twice. On the third beat the red light lit and the red light on the first camera died; Michael's face now filled all the screens in extreme closeup. Dena was struck by the professionally perfect timing with which Michael's eyes switched from one camera to the next. There was never a moment when he was not looking directly into your eyes, and she had had enough media exposure to know how hard that simple trick was to bring off.

"Listen to me. Manhattan is no longer a part of the United States. It is almost totally sealed off. The very few bridges and tunnels still in existence are presently impassable and exist at my pleasure. No one can enter or leave Manhattan without my approval. There will be no commuters today. We have taken both major armories and several lesser ones. We have destroyed Police Plaza utterly. Most of the police and National Guard and armed forces still alive are with us; most of the rest have already surrendered. We have taken prisoner Mayor Winch, Police Commissioner Sullivan, and over a hundred other officers and officials; most of them are unharmed and none will be mistreated. We control power, water, food, and phone service. We control the MTA's subway center at 45th and

Seventh, and we control the streets. The nation of Equity has physical existence; you are in it; listen to me now—"

Medium closeup again. Dena had stopped watching the live Michael, but his voice drew her eyes to him now. That voice was a magnificent instrument, compelling attention. Russell's hand clutched hers tightly.

"If you are white, don't be afraid. It is not the policy of the nation of Equity to mistreat interned aliens. You'll get a better deal from us than our ancestors got from you. You will not be harmed unless you bring it on yourself. There will be no rioting, no needless killing, no looting by any Equitan forces. If you see any civilians doing these things, dial 999 and call it in and we will despatch troops to protect you, whether you are black, white, or green.

"I am officially declaring a state of martial law in the nation of Equity. Effective within one half hour of this announcement, all whites are under curfew until noon tomorrow. You may not leave your homes at any time after 8:05 AM, under pain of death. I'll repeat that: any white person on the streets of New York after 8:05 AM will be shot on sight. If you are trapped away from home, dial 888 and we'll see that you get escorted to shelter. If you have a genuine emergency need to leave your building during the next twenty-four hours—labour pains, appendicitis—call 777 and we'll work it out. But if you're out of cigarettes, you'd better hope a neighbour will lend you some or you're going cold turkey. If your wife is at her mother's, you're sleeping apart tonight. There will be no exceptions, and no appeal against summary execution. You're safe in your home, but if you leave it without an escort you *will* die.

"I speak now to the black people in the nation of Equity."

Full closeup again. Dena returned her gaze again to the nearest screen. Michael was talking to her, personally.

"Parents and children, brothers and sisters, hear me out before you take any action. The fate of all black people in North America is in your hands. I have forced a choice on you, the most important choice you will ever make. I beg you to think it over very carefully before you do *anything*, and to hear me out *before* you start thinking. Listen now . . .

"What I'm doing is simple. Fancier language is being used on the tape that the rest of the country is seeing right now, but I'll give it to you in plain language. I've taken Manhattan, and I plan to hold it for ransom. I hold the World Financial Center and Trade Center, the Federal Reserve—forty percent of the gold in the country—a whole lot of corporate and fiscal data bases, the machine that controls national TV, radio, and long distance phone, the finest museums in the country, and almost a million hostages including some of the richest and most powerful people in the world.

"I hold all these things on behalf of you, on behalf of all black people. What I want from the United States in return for all of these things is a black homeland. I want the states of New York and Pennsylvania evacuated and turned over to us. Two out of fifty-one states. Industry, farmland, seaport, resources—everything needed to house and feed every black person now living in America, with room to grow in for decades to come.

"I want to found a new nation on that land, of and for black people, and call it Equity."

The third camera came on for the first time, a long shot of Michael's whole body. He spread his hands.

"You all know me. You know I'm not a radical. I'm not a politician. I'm not even a preacher. None of you can name a time I've taken a collection or accepted a fee, you know I have no money. I have no address, no car, no family left in the world, no property. I've talked to most of you, helped a lot of you, some of you I've come down hard on. For twenty-five years, I've only been doing two things with my time. Planning this war—and trying to become the kind of man you would trust to lead it for you.

"I promise you now that if I win this war, I will immediately call a convention to form a government of your choice, and once its Constitution is signed, I will abdicate all authority and go back to being a private citizen. A citizen of Equity. That's all I want to be, all I've ever wanted to be all my life.

"I think all of you know why I have done what I've done. A marriage cannot endure without trust. To sleep beside someone, you have to trust them not to cut your throat during the night. Otherwise you lose sleep—and one day you start to wonder if you shouldn't cut *their* throat as a simple precautionary measure. Black America and white America do not have that basic trust. We haven't lost it: we never had it. We've been free now for almost as long as we were slaves here—call it a hundred and thirty years—and still neither side trusts the other. They perceive us as lazy and violent and racist; we perceive them as hypocritical and violent and racist. Try as we will, we cannot learn to live together in trust. So we must kill each other—or divorce.

"The white man will never get over his shame at having enslaved us, or his fear that we will seek revenge. We will never get over our shame at having allowed ourselves to be enslaved, or our fear of the policeman's gun and the Klansman's rope. Both sides are right to be ashamed and afraid, and neither side wants to admit that they are. That means we can't live together."

Medium shot again.

"For just a while, back in the '60's, I hoped we might be able to do it. But promises turned out to be lies, and we got mad. Then the economy started to go to hell, and by the '80's it was pretty evil out. The Third Wave came along, the silicon revolution, and took away all the jobs that didn't require an expensive education. I don't have to tell you the shape we're in today.

"I *do* have to tell you that in the course of prosecuting this war I took a walk through the Defense Department's computers. There are a lot of black people in the Pentagon. And in there I found proof that we can't continue to live in the United States. We're ten percent of the population, and the government admits that we supply nearly twenty-six percent of the draftees. Ten percent *more* than we did in Viet Nam. Well, they say, there seem to be fewer young black men in college, somehow or other. My friends, they lie. Their own classified records show that *forty-four percent* of draftees for the African conflict are black! And when the judge says, 'Enlist or do hard time,' the odds are five to one he's talking to a black man. The true casualty rate for black soldiers in Africa is three times as high as for whites. They seem to use us up faster."

Dena was shocked; dimly she was aware that Russell was too. If those figures could be documented . . .

"Their logic is impeccable. It's clearly to their advantage to eliminate as many of our strong young men as they can. Whether they realize it or not, they already know in their hearts that a racewar is coming.

"I confess to you now that I had these figures a year ago, and I kept them just as secret as the Defense Department. For exactly the same reason: to prevent riots. I knew this information would make you angry, and I wanted to wait until I could offer you an alternative response, an intelligent response, something better to do with your anger than riot. That day has come.

"When I was a boy, bullying husbands told their wives, 'If you don't like it here, you can leave,' because the truth was that there was no way for a single woman with kids to make it then. That got so bad that the rules got changed, and nowadays as often as not the woman will throw *him* out. When I was a boy, bullying parents told their children, 'If you don't like it here, you can leave,' because the truth was that the only jobs a child could get were prostitute and dope runner. That got so bad the rules got changed, and nowadays you find children collecting heavy alimony—I've heard of a few that employ grownups to carry out the garbage and mow the lawn.

"When I was a boy, bullying whites told their Negroes, 'If you don't like it here, why don't you go back to Africa?' My Lord, but black Americans have emigrated to many places looking for a home. British Columbia, Nova Scotia, Sierra Leone, Trinidad, Bermuda, Liberia, the only thing all the migrations had in common is that none of them worked. American blacks have gone many places in search of a home, without ever finding one."

Closeup. Michael's eyes shone.

"Home is here.

"Home is where we were born and the culture we grew up in. The North American culture. We share a common language and tradition, similar to that of white America but uniquely our own. All we have ever needed was a homeland, a place where we made the rules. An Israel, a

Zimbabwe. And I think that with your help I can get it for us now."

Medium shot.

"Let me report progress so far. At five o'clock this morning I spoke with the President of the United States by videophone. We spoke for almost an hour. I told him, in essence, that I will turn over the gold, the diamonds, the museum treasures, a million hostages, and—most important of all—the data bases and the STI satellite uplink, if he will give us New York and Pennsylvania. How he compensates the present white residents of those states is his problem; so is moving and relocating them. In the meantime, I have asked for white-flag food shipments, and a promise that the food supplies which are presently being shipped by friendly regions and nations will not be embargoed. He told me, in essence, that we are to consider ourselves under siege—but he'll allow food to come in as long as white hostages receive a fair share and are not mistreated. We're working out ways to verify all that.

"As of seven this morning, the nation of Equity has been granted diplomatic recognition by fourteen countries, including Switzerland, Israel, Quebec, Zimbabwe, Rhodesia, Beninia, and West Germany. That figure will be updated each time this tape is rebroadcast. At 4 AM we began evacuation of United Nations personnel and their families to the UN Building, which has twenty acres of floor space they can sleep on. We've petitioned the UN for admission, and the General Assembly has been in emergency session since six. I do not expect a decision soon, but I'm confident of the ultimate outcome. Regrettably the escape tunnel which runs from under the UN parking building west to New Jersey was damaged by an explosion on the street above, but I've assured the Secretary General that the nation of Equity guarantees the safety of all UN diplomats on its soil—until such time as the siege is lifted and they can leave safely.

"Brothers and sisters, parents and children, this thing is done. The nation of Equity is committed. I will not compel anyone to join it. You're welcome to leave it along with the white refugees when the time comes, or sooner if you can figure a way off the island.

"But I do ask you not to screw it up.

"We need the weight of world opinion on our side if we are to be accepted as a genuine nation. So long as I'm directing Equity, all non-Caucasians retain the right to freedom of speech and freedom of assembly—within forty-eight hours I hope to lift communication censorship and make ten channels available for community access so we can thrash this out together. But in the meantime there must be no rioting, no looting, no wanton killing, and no destruction. Only barbarians torture their prisoners, and any real estate you harm is your own property."

Closeup.

"I know this will be very hard. Some of you have *nothing*, and how it seems that there is so much around you for the taking. If enough of you yield to temptation, the black homeland will be destroyed in the moment of its birthing. You know I speak the truth. But if you will be strong and measured, I promise you that you will not be sorry."

Medium shot again.

"Now: I expect scattered fighting here and there for several hours. So I urge all of you who are not in essential jobs to stay in your homes until twelve noon. Those of you who *are* essential—medical personnel, fire department, and such—are urged to report for work and try to cover for missing white co-workers. If you have trouble, call 666 and we'll try to bring you any whites you absolutely need, or replacements.

"The only other people who should leave your homes *at once* are those of you who live in predominantly white neighbourhoods and fear reprisals. Call 555 at once, and we'll try and get you uptown as quickly and safely as possible.

"When noon strikes, the nation of Equity will begin accepting job applicants.

"We have literally hundreds of thousands of jobs available *immediately*, and we'll pay generously in U.S. dollars. When those run out, we have an awful lot of gold, and eventually the government you choose will doubtless issue its own currency—but in the meantime any black, brown, red, or yellow person who wants to work can earn good dollars, cash on the barrel at the end of each shift. If you are handicapped or invalid, call 444; we have work that you can do, at home if necessary.

"Able bodied men and women who wish to enlist in the Equitan Army are invited to go at noon to their local police precinct house. Please do *not* try to enlist unless you have fighting experience of some kind *and* you are prepared to follow orders. The Equitan Army maintains discipline comparable to the U.S. Marines, and irregulars will be expected to match it. Remember that this is wartime: a court martial can take thirty seconds or less. If you don't want to be a soldier, we still have a job for *you*, in any area or level of skill from executive to dishwasher; simply go to the nearest video arcade that features programmable games and you'll find an employment team with access to our computers. I urge you all to do so; there will be no more welfare or unemployment cheques coming in from Albany, no more social security from Washington. Equity has jobs for all citizens, from ten to a hundred and ten, and if we can't find a job that you can handle we will support you. If you don't want or need a job, you don't have to take one. If I have my way, no citizen of Equity is ever going to be drafted to do *anything*.

"What it all comes down to is how much you want Equity to live. You, personally. I already have the official endorsement of the Black Muslims, the Rastafarian community, the Afro-American Coalition, the Guardian Angels, a number of black Christian churches, and the warlords of all the major black and hispanic and oriental street gangs in this city. But your leaders and ministers and warlords can't speak for you, and anyway speaking isn't enough. Right now I have enough manpower to take this city and to hold it indefinitely and to keep order in it. But I haven't got a fraction of the manpower to *run* it, to keep it alive and growing."

Cut back to a long shot. Michael held out his hands in supplication.

"I caution you once more against taking any reprisals against whites. If there's any needless killing, the UN is going to bolt and the nations that have already recognized us will repudiate us and the United States just might neutron bomb us. I want no old scores settled today.

There are still raise on the set—but their uniform is a shaved head and red shades and a white armband, and they work for *me*." Michael lifted his right sleeve to his shoulder. "Each will wear an armband just like this, except that theirs'll be white. Look at it closely: it's almost impossible to counterfeit this scalloped edge in a hurry. Don't believe anyone who doesn't have an armband just like this; I have plenty for everyone who enlists.

"One last note: any whites who are married to a black person, and any children of such a union, are to be considered honourary black people, and are invited to become Equitan citizens. They can nominate other family members if they wish. Such people should call 333. José Johnson in particular is requested to call at once; Jennifer Grant's parents are worried."

Dena's heart leaped. She gave a small cry in spite of herself, felt Russell's hand crushing hers. She looked at him, and his expression was that of a man who has been unexpectedly slapped. They broke into broad grins together. Over the roaring in her ears, she heard Michael finishing; turned back to see him once more in full closeup.

"Brothers and sisters, parents and children, friends and enemies, we have now what we always said we wanted. Freedom. Pride. A safe home. A fair chance. An even break. After all the centuries of bondage we're truly free: like free men and women everywhere we can root, hog, or die. If you—all of you—don't turn out today, and turn to, and work to build up your Equity ... it's going to just melt away." He grinned suddenly. "And then a whole lot of happy racists all over the world will say, 'You see? I knew those niggers could never cut it.' I would truly hate to see them get that chance.

"It's up to you. Come out at noon and show your heart to the world."

Michael finished speaking, and gazed into the camera. It went dark, and a crawl informed viewers that the tape would repeat continuously until noon.

The silent stillness seemed to last forever. Michael did not move, kept looking at the dead camera with that magnificent sorrow in his eyes. No one moved or spoke.

An air-conditioner sighed back into life, and even that did
not break the spell.

And then, on all the silenced monitors, Michael's face
reappeared, began repeating his message, and suddenly
the room rang with applause and cheers. Dena found that
she was shouting along with the others, that she was
being hugged by strangers, that *Russell* was being hugged
by strangers, that Russell was hugging her and smiling
and weeping and frowning all at the same time.

Hugging him back, she looked over his shoulder . . . and
tapped his shoulder so that he released her. Motormouth
stood alone, smiling and weeping like everyone else but
alone, his eyes sweeping the room even in this moment for
possible assassins. Russell saw her intention and nodded.
She went to Motormouth, stood before him, smiled at him
and put her arms around him. The big bodyguard did not
draw away but stood inert, his eyes seeking out Russell.
Her husband approached and smiled. Motormouth opened
his great arms then and gathered them both in. Past him,
Dena could see Michael. He was looking at the three of
them now, and smiling.

Perhaps it was a trick of the light, but his face did not
look sorrowful now at all.

Dena got them permission to return to Michael's room;
Russell was visibly suffering from lack of sleep. Tunnel
personnel would not begin their sleep shifts for several
hours yet, and so the bunkroom to which she and Russell
had been assigned was presently too noisy and traveled to
sleep in. As before, a guard unobtrusively tagged along.
This one was young and friendly and had the body language of a happy puppy. He gave his name as Homemade,
and asked if she were Dena St. Claire the dancer from
Canada? It turned out that he was a friend of Jerome's
and knew of her through him. She was surprised to learn
that Homemade *had not known* Jerome was a member of
Michael's army until she told him so. The young man
made a special effort to be respectful to Russell. "I understand that you saved Michael's life somehow," he said.
"Thank you for that." Russell told him gravely that he
was welcome. Before they left him in the corridor, Dena

gave him her Number Three lecture on posture and corrected his spinal alignment for him. He thanked her.

Once the door had sealed behind them, Russell said, "He wants you."

She smiled slightly and nodded. "I felt it when I put my hands on him. I wonder what Jerome told him."

"Whatever it was, I hope he's thinking about it now. Dena, if you walk out that door naked, he is going to turn to stone for that fatal second, and I'll have the drop on him."

"*What?*"

"I won't hurt him—but we need him quickly and quietly unconscious, and I want his sidearm. Darling, *it's time to go.*"

"Go *where?* Why?"

He took her hands. "This is a war zone. I plan to get my family out of it as fast as possible."

He was serious. "What about Jennifer? We can't leave until she calls in."

"Michael's tape is on its third or fourth repeat by now, and she hasn't called in yet. They're back at the apartment, they *have* to be, but they're not watching TV. Maybe they're asleep, or the TV's busted, but they have to be there by now, and this is the very last chance you and I are ever going to have to bust out of here and get them."

"What chance? Which way to the egress?"

"The inhabited section of tunnel ends just outside that door. Beyond the bulkhead is big empty tunnel, all the way up to the Bronx."

"Won't it be mined?"

"Of course, but not right up to the bulkhead. The nearest mine will be far enough away that it won't wreck this section of tunnel if it does blow—and somewhere between there and here we are going to find an exit, believe me. A bolt hole—there *has* to be one. I wish I'd been able to swipe a flashlight, but at least I've got my lighter. Once we're on the street we swipe a car—you drive and I stay down on the floor. When we've got Jen and José we head uptown. I've got a scheme to get us across the East River, it's so crackbrained it'll probably work—"

"Russell, *this* is crackbrained. You don't know that there's an exit. You don't know that we can use it—maybe you need a key, or maybe it's like the door at the other end, retina prints and laser—"

"—it'll be designed to keep people out, not in—"

"—you don't even know that we can take that boy out in the hall. Most important, you don't *know* that Jennifer is at the apartment."

"If José hasn't been able to get them back there and holed up by now, I have to assume they're dead."

"Maybe they were arrested by the police before the war started. They could be in a holding cell right now—"

"No. I spoke with Michael about that while you were sleeping. He *owns* all the precinct houses in town, and she's not at any of them. Neither she nor José has been admitted to any hospital, and especially not to Bellevue, which is the nearest one to our place. Dena, maybe we can't pull this off. Maybe we get home and she's not there and we have to think again—and maybe we end up coming back here and asking nicely to be let back in. But this is the last chance I'm going to get to get my family off this island, away from this war."

"*Why?*" she cried.

"Because right now there is maximal confusion and minimal congestion up there on the streets, and at noon they're going to fill up with crazy black people; because right now there is a celebratory mood down here and they're off their guard; and most important, because this is the last time we're ever liable to be up at this end of the tunnel with only a single guard to deal with."

She shook her head. "You answered the wrong question. Not, 'Why does it have to be now?' The question is, 'Why does it have to be?' "

"I don't follow."

"If Jennifer is *not* at home, there's nothing we can do to help her, and we can't leave town until we know where she is. So we may as well wait. If she *is* at home, sooner or later she'll turn on the TV or get Michael's message some way, and call in, and he'll send a car and we'll all have lunch together. The safest thing we can do is wait."

Throughout this conversation she and Russell were in motion—pacing back and forth, circling round each other,

approaching and retreating, gesturing and gesticulating—
and all at once she saw them as dancing, as dancers of a
dance choreographed millennia ago by evolution. Mates
at a crisis arguing about what to do. They both knew the
steps because the steps had been memorized by their
DNA. Once she saw it in those terms, her dancer's mind
was able to extrapolate the dance, to sense where it was
leading and how it would be shaped, much faster than her
conscious mind could have processed its way through the
surface logic of their words. She saw that what had been
danced so far was only warmup, prologue—the theme of
the piece had not yet been explicitly stated.

Sure enough, here it came. Russell squared his feet,
leaned forward slightly, clenched his fists and his teeth,
and spoke in the strangled tones of a man who would be
shouting at the top of his lungs if he dared raise his voice:
"We have to get out of here while we still can!"

She took her position, waited for the count—odd, her
lower back hadn't hurt since she'd left her apartment—
and responded with matching force: *"Why?"*

He trembled as if about to explode into a series of leaps,
then fell out of his contraction, took a deep breath and
spun away from her. She started to react in counterpoint,
got a grip on herself and held still.

Damn it, girl, this is important! Get your stupid wander-
ing mind off choreographing this—

Choreographing? Me?

"Dena, listen to me." His voice was dangerously low
and quiet. "We are Canadian citizens. This is not our war.
I don't plan to die in it if I can help it. I want out—of this
city and this country, as quickly as possible. Back home to
Halifax, where all I have to worry about is Soviets lob-
bing neutron bombs into the Harbour. In fact, it occurs to
me that now would be an excellent time for them to lob a
few at the U.S., while it's distracted—half of its forces tied
up in Africa and the rest mutinying all across the country.
In any case, America is no longer a safe place for an
interracial couple. If it ever was."

"We're not *in* America."

"No," he snapped, exasperation showing through. "We're
in Equity, right in the fucking heart of the danger."

"The eye of a storm is a good place to be. What do you think of Michael's war?"

He shrugged his shoulders and words burst out of him. "Dammit, I don't know, the problem is so big I can't seem to get my mind around it. The most astonishing part is already over. I was in the War Room while you were sleeping, I heard the reports coming in. Michael really does own Manhattan. His troops *are* as good as Marines, and much luckier. There was not one major fuckup—oh, there's still fighting going on, but just about every major objective has been secured. Now, if all Michael had was the island of Manhattan, I mean, if the STI uplink was somewhere else and he had everything but that, I'd give him about one chance in ten of victory—damned good odds for any revolution! But with the uplink in his control, he *has* to win. Picture the U.S. and Russia as two giants locked in an arm-wrestle, over there in Africa, and other places too. The U.S. *cannot* afford to suffer a stroke and have half of its body blind and paralyzed—the side toward Africa at that, the side with Washington on it.

"But don't you see the antinomy? They *have* to pay the ransom, and the ransom is not excessive, but it may simply be *beyond their power to give*. It may not be politically or humanly possible to do this thing. For one thing it physically divides the United States, separates New England from the rest. They'd have to change the name of the fucking country.

"As I see it, the government of the U.S. has an insoluble dilemma. It may go catatonic, and it may go berserk. They could neutron bomb this city and take the uplink back the next day when it cooled off. More likely they'll stall, try to starve us out, hostages and all. *I* don't the hell know, I know nothing about current U.S. politics and less about how the minds of the *real* people-in-power work in crisis. For all I know, Michael might just pull this off."

He was pacing again, and she was holding herself still with an effort. This was his solo.

"But I want to read about the outcome in the papers, back home in front of my fireplace. Dena, four hours is our escape-window, and I need one or two of them to get us ready to leave the island. We have to get Jennifer *now*,

right away. Then once we reach Brooklyn, we strike for
my dad's, pick up the car, take the ferry to Connecticut
and drive like a bastard for the border—"

Her cue. "Russell?"

"—we could be there by—what?"

"I'm not going."

He spun on his heel and faced her. The blood was
draining from his head. "What did you say?"

"Ah, you heard me that time. First thing you've heard
right since you came in this room. You just answered the
wrong question again, at great length. I asked you what
you thought about Michael's war. You told me what you
think of his chances of winning it. That's interesting stuff,
but it's not what I want to know. What do you *think* about
his war? What do you think of the idea of a black
homeland? Supposing it can be done, are you for it or
against it?"

He shook his head violently, shook invisible water drops
from his fingers. "I can't answer that question. I don't
know what that question means."

"Are you rooting for Michael, or not?" she said patiently.
"If he wins, do you think Equity will be a good thing or
bad?"

"For who?"

"You're dodging. I want to know if Equity is a place you
can imagine yourself living in. A place you can imagine
dying for."

His eyes widened in horror. "God, no. Don't say it. Lord
desperate Jesus, you're not serious."

"Why not?"

"Tell me you haven't become a Michael-worshipper like
the rest of these morons!"

"I don't worship him, Russell. He's a man. I admire
him. There is no evil in him, that I'm sure."

"There's no evil in a tiger, Dena, listen to me for Christ's
sake. Michael is a *saint*."

"I'd go that far."

"Honey, 'saint' is just another word for 'psychotic.' People *die* around saints. There are many things about Michael that I admire, but he's fucking insane, he's a

dangerous lunatic, and this whole Equity idea is a doomed fiasco."

"Why?"

"God dammit, you know as much history as I do. He's a monomaniac. He has Good Intentions. He Means Well. Sometimes people like that lead successful revolutions, but they never keep control of them. Power always ends up in the hands of the ruthless ones. A power struggle will topple Michael within a week, if he lives that long—and even if it doesn't, his new nation will be a disaster."

"Why does it have to be a disaster?"

"Oh Christ, Dena, use your head. Don't make me say it."

She frowned. "Say it."

"Never mind, if you can't—"

She overrode him firmly. "Russell Grant, in five years we have never had a really serious conversation about race. I've been assuming I knew where you stood. Now you are going to have to tell me." He looked away. "Tell me, dammit!" she shouted.

He looked up suddenly and his expression was pleading. "Dena, you've lived in this city with me for almost two weeks now. You must agree that a certain portion of its inhabitants are . . . are human garbage. No, subhuman. Animals, held in check only by a vicious, aggressive police force, by security systems and iron bars and an armed citizenry. You've walked the streets; you know what you've been afraid of. I would put the ratio of undomesticable animals to human beings in this city at about one to four. Now, some of these animals are white, and some are hispanic, some are Chinese, and some are fucking Cherokee Indians for all I know, but I put it to you that the overwhelming majority of them are black.

"Listen to me now, God damn it—I gave up talking about race to black people because I never found one that would hear me out, but you are my wife and you insisted I say this and I fucking *command* you to hear me out. I am *not* going to get into the circle-jerk argument about whether such people are genetically defective, or societally damaged, or some combination of the two—I don't care who victimized them or how. I am *not* saying that a black skin predisposes one to savagery: I am *observing*—and I don't believe you can honestly deny—that most of the savages in this city seem to have dark skin."

"Define 'savage'," Dena interrupted. "If you mean, like, rapacious, dishonest, wicked, it seems to me you could put Harlem on one side of the scale and the Financial District on the other and it would just about balance out."

"Shit, don't play word games with me; you know perfectly well what I mean. Savages. Killers. Rapists. Junkies."

"Then your figures are off. One to four is much too high a ratio. Much less than a tenth of the people in New York are that crazy."

"You *know* what I'm talking about. To the animals add the ignorant, the illiterate, the incompetent, all the fucking *losers*. Right now things are relatively quiet up there on the street. Guns are going off, but most people are indoors thinking hard, trying to fortify their apartments. In a few hours, a million black people are going to step into the noonday sun and look around. They will see many entrancing things. Unguarded stores. Banks, jewelry stores, food stores, *liquor stores*. Thousands of unprotected women. They will stare, and blink at each other for a silent moment—and then a voice will be heard on 125th Street and Lenox Avenue, a lone shout that echoes the island 'round, crying: 'Paaarr-*ty!*' Michael can't maintain order with only ten thousand effectives. By this time tomorrow every bottle in Manhattan will be empty, and every hospital will be full. When it gets bad enough, the whites will get mad enough and scared enough to come out and band together and fight. And you can bet there'll be white and Puerto Rican and Cuban and Chinese savages, looters and killers who figure that the racewar gives them cover. They're probably oiling up their machine guns down on Mulberry Street right now. We'll be lucky if the whole city doesn't go up in flames. But one thing I guarantee you: by this afternoon it's going to be a zoo up there. If we stay here this marvelous underground hideaway will be our prison and eventually our tomb. *We've got to find Jennifer and get her out of this.*"

He ran out of words and waited. Dena felt paralyzed, numb, confused; she did not know what the next steps were.

This was where her attempts at choreography always got stuck. She closed her eyes and bit the tip of her tongue and in her mind she hollered a question which was not formed into words but which was somewhere between "What is the next step?" and "Who am I?" and "Do I have to?" She could not have said who or what the question was directed to, for she did not believe in a personal god, but an answer came back nonetheless and she did not question it. She opened her eyes and took her stage.

"Russell, if you feel you have to go, I'll strip down and help you fake out Homemade. I'll resent you for dividing my loyalties, but I'll do it." He started to register great relief; she continued firmly: "But I will *not* go with you."

He gaped. "I can't do it without you, Dena." His face twisted. "I need you to drive the car—*I haven't got any burnt cork.*"

"I'm sorry. I'm staying put."

"Damn you to hell," he cried, raising his voice for the first time, "if my daughter dies because I wasn't there—"

She raised her volume to match, and drowned him out. "I think you'll be making a very big mistake if you go—I think if you do find Jennifer you'll only bring her into more danger than she's in now or would be here, and *she's my daughter too.* But I can't stop you. Personally I'm pretty sure you'll get yourself killed before you ever get to 31st Street—because you've got a racist attitude."

"A *what?*"

"I think you're like most white people—you get your ideas about black people from TV and movies, and from your own secret fears. We're all pimps and whores and lushes and junkies, or anyway half of us. Uncontrollable savages."

"Dena, for chrissake what is this 'us'? I'm talking about *New York City* black people—"

"So am I, I know 'em better than you do. We drove down here through Harlem. How many black people do you suppose we drove past? Fifty thousand? More? How many tried to terrorize us? *Knowing* that the Harlem raise were all black and probably wouldn't stop them? I counted three." She raised her volume a fraction. "And Michael talked them out of it."

Russell had opened his mouth to reply; as her last sentence struck home he closed it.

"So I am going to sit tight and pray that Jennifer turns on the fucking TV set and gets to a phone. And meanwhile, when the Equity Employment Office opens at noon, I plan to be one of the first applicants on line. I wish you'd be next to me."

He sputtered. "But—I—you—"

Suddenly she saw the ending of the piece, a bare step away. She understood the weak spot in his armour, realized she had known it all along but had never expected to need to use it. She had a key to him:

"What else were you doing with your life that's more important?"

CHAPTER NINE

"Pamutunhu ukaite jee, pano sara pachi mire nhunghu mira."

—Shona saying:

"If you do not climb while the way is still open to you, weeds will spring up before you—or you might get through but the weeds will close after you and those behind will not be able to get through."

"When the Mandinka tribe has the enemy surrounded on three sides, what should they do?"
"Close the gap and surround the enemy."
"No. The goal of war is not to kill. The goal of war is to win."
"Should you not kill your enemy?"
"It is impossible to kill an enemy. If you kill a man, his sons are now your enemies. A warrior respects his enemy. He kills only to feed his family, or to prevent becoming a slave."

—Mandinka manhood ritual, quoted
in *Roots* by Alex Haley

"The rich man and the policeman are regarded by the people with equal suspicion. The outlaw, on the other hand, is regarded with sympathy, as he must have had an excellent reason for becoming an outlaw."

—Liang Shan Po

* * *

The trees rustled in the wind, or perhaps it was the other way round. Otherwise, Fifth Avenue was quiet. Traffic was infrequent, pedestrians rare.

"I think we blew it, José."

"Maybe. Let's give it another couple of minutes."

"Okay. But he's not going to show."

"You said you heard him say 'museum,' right?"

"Yeah, he yelled something with 'museum' in it—but it could have been, 'Stay away from the Museum!' for all I know."

"I don't know, Jennifer. Why wouldn't he want us to come here?"

"So we wouldn't lead the cops here."

"To *what?* I could see it if this was some kind of secret headquarters or something—but we been here over half an hour and there ain't shit going on. You can't tell me no revolutionaries got offices in the Museum of Art. This is just where somebody was gonna meet us and take us to your folks—and they might show up yet."

"Not without Jerome with us, they won't. *I* wouldn't."

"So where do you figure Jerome is?"

"Back at the apartment, of course. What other rendezvous do we all know?"

"Then why didn't he yell, 'Back to the apartment'?"

"Because he probably thought I'd given that cop my address; I didn't, but Jerome couldn't have known that."

"So right now he's hanging around outside your spot, figurin' out that we must have heard him wrong, and sooner or later he comes back here lookin' for us, and we pass each other on the way. We could keep that up all night."

"Think about this: maybe he didn't get away clean, maybe the cops picked him up. In that case our best move is to get home and hole up there. Jerome is smart and he knows I'm smart. Here we're exposed and we have no information. At home we're safe and we can be reached by phone. If he is still loose and we *do* miss him, at the least he'll be smart enough to have left some kind of message for us there."

"Yeah, that's all very logical. Now *you* think about *this:*

your parents didn't want you in that apartment, 'cause some kind of bad news is gonna happen in that part of town tonight. We don't know that anything's gonna happen here. I can't picture a guy like Michael havin' somebody blow up the Museum of Art, for Chrissake."

"José, that is Central Park over there across the street. Maybe that doesn't bother you; I'm from Halifax and it scares the shit out of me. I'm tired of standing here scared with insufficient data waiting for something to happen. *I want to go home.*"

He turned away, walked a circle of ten steps' circumference and stopped. "Yeah, let's go back home. It's a hot night. I don't know whether Jerome is jugged, mugged, plugged, or bein' hugged, but standin' here waitin' for him is bullshit. Fuckin' A, let's go."

"Let me leave a note for Jerome. No, really, I'll leave it on the lamppost over there. We're right across from the Museum; maybe he'll see it."

"How are we gonna stick it up? Chewing gum?"

She got out pen and paper and began writing. "I've got some cyanoacrylate adhesive in my pouch."

"Some who?"

"Wonderglue."

"Hey, be careful, that stuff bonds skin instantly—"

She gave him her very best withering glare, and he dropped his eyes. "I've been allowed to cut my own vegetables for weeks now. Next year they're going to let me cross the street by myself."

"I'm sorry."

"Dammit, I've been using power tools since I was ten."

"I said I was sorry. Fuckin' A."

"So you did. What time is it?"

He thumbed his watch alight. "Twenty to three."

She added the time to the note. It read:

> *"Jerome: gone back where we met. Will wait there.*
> *—J. & J. [2:40]*

"J. and J.," she repeated aloud.

"All the way," he said soberly, and she glanced up at him. His expression was unreadable in shadow.

"Fuckin' A," she said, and got the laugh, but she moved at once to place her own face in shadow because she had the horrid feeling that she was blushing. She posted the note with care, but without rubbing his nose in it, and returned the tube of adhesive to her pouch. "There."

"Let's crank."

They had gone half a block east on 82nd when a bald black man emerged from behind the north end of the Metropolitan Museum of Art. He was not wearing his red shades and had not yet put on his armband; his automatic rifle was in a place of concealment. He sauntered casually out into Fifth Avenue and glanced up and downtown, checking both sides of the street. He saw no hispanic, no shade teeny, and when he had returned to his post he reported this to his sergeant, who relayed it to HQ.

The 86th Street subway station had doubtless seen better days, but they did not seem to have left any mark. About twenty people waited for trains, or for a transit cop to roust them; this neighborhood had not yet deteriorated enough for sleepers to be allowed in the subway. Everyone except Jennifer and José was drunk or crazy, none charmingly so. She was glad that his menacing glower kept them all at a distance. One scabby old starer in particular made her flesh crawl. "I wish we didn't have to take the subway."

"Me too, but the fuckin' buses stopped runnin' hours ago and we can't take a cab. That cabbie Jerome busted up must have put our descriptions out on the radio; they'd bring us right to the raise. Them cabbies take care of each other."

"I wish the damned thing would come, at least. We've been here half an hour."

"They run slow this time of night. When they run at all. You're doing okay."

"What do you mean, I'm doing okay?"

"I mean, you're handling all this crazy shit pretty good, for a girl from Halifax. You been through a lot so far, and you still got it together. The way you took that cop was like a work of art. I gotta keep like remindin' myself that you're thirteen, you know?"

"I haven't been that old since I was seven. Father believes adolescence is a stupid invention. He's determined to get me from childhood to adulthood in one step. He's always talking about how in most of the world women are having their first baby by age thirteen. Which, he always adds, is why the world is so overcrowded so he doesn't recommend it; he just means I should be ready to make adult choices by the time Nature forces them on me and not years later."

"He's right, man. I grew up in the barrio. When I was nine there was this girl a year older than me had a baby, and it lived. She made a good mother, you know? She was an adult."

"José? Am I an adult now? Because I started bleeding tonight?"

He must have heard the bleakness in her voice; he became flustered. "Hey, I don't know, fuckin' A. How would I know? Uh—" He thought. "I always had it worked out that the day you become an adult is the day you get it through your head that some day you're gonna die. That you can die, and that you will."

She smiled. "Then I'm not an adult, yet, and I refuse to be one. I'm going to live forever and have a wonderful time. That ten-year-old . . . were you the father?"

He became even more flustered, and strove to hide it. "I don't think so. I coulda been, but I don't think so. I figure at nine I hadda be shootin' blanks."

"So? Did the baby look like you?"

"I wish that fuckin' train would get here."

A Guardian Angel was making her way along the platform in their direction, speaking to each person she came to, telling them something that displeased them. "Ah, *shit*," José said. "Wouldn't you fuckin' know?"

The Angel, a young hispanic woman whose beret was too large for her newly-shaven head, approached them. "Sorry, no more trains tonight. You might as well go home or get a cab."

"Fuckin' A. Power failure or what?"

She shrugged. "The word came down there won't be no more trains tonight, uptown or down. That's all I know."

"All right. Look, thanks, sister."

"No problem."

There was a distant rumbling from uptown. The three exchanged glances. Obviously a train was coming. The Angel shrugged again.

They waited. The sound grew louder and louder, and then a train came into view.

"What number do we want?" Jennifer asked.

"Number six, but I don't think it—"

The train roared by at top speed without ever slowing. It was followed by another, then a third. All three were packed, from end to end, with bald black men who wore white armbands and carried automatic weapons.

When the last car had disappeared downtown, there was a pause. The Angel shrugged her shoulders a third time and said, softly and not unkindly, "Why don't you folks do yourself a favour and get the fuck out of here?"

José pursed his lips. "I can't think of a reason in the world why not." Jennifer had nothing to add.

As they reached the stairs up to the street, something caught Jennifer's eye. She knew it was the wrong time and place, but she couldn't help herself: she roared with laughter.

He tried to shush her. "What the hell is wrong with you?"

She couldn't stop giggling. "The only thing good about the U.S. government is that it *almost* makes the Canadian government look intelligent."

"What—"

She gestured. "Your tax dollars at work."

José looked where she pointed, squinted a moment—then barked with involuntary laughter himself.

On the station wall was a Department of Education poster. It read:

"ILLITERATE?
WRITE FOR HELP!"

and gave a box number to which one could write for a free brochure.

Jennifer could *not* stop giggling. "It's a joke. It can't be serious."

The Guardian Angel had come up behind them to find out what was going on. "It is one hundred percent dead serious," she said, "and I do not see a single fucking thing funny about it."

They sobered instantly and left.

They heard distant gunfire even before they reached the top of the stairs. "Fuckin' A," José said softly. He transferred his little .22 automatic from his boot to his pants pocket, hitched at one of his knives, and flexed the fingers of his left hand. He made her wait while he stuck his head out at knee height and checked the street, then waved her up.

The street looked perfectly ordinary. Sparse traffic proceeding normally, a few pedestrians walking, no signs of any unrest. "What do we do?" she asked. "Try to bribe a cabdriver?"

There came faintly the sound of a huge explosion many blocks distant, followed by the sound of a much bigger one much further away.

At each sound, the New Yorkers on the street froze momentarily in their tracks, without looking at each other—then resumed walking, only a little faster, as if nothing of importance had happened.

"Fuckin' B," José breathed. "Come on."

"Where?"

"Just *come on*, god dammit."

They walked west, back toward Fifth Avenue and the Park. The faraway gunfire now included machine guns. José carefully examined each car they passed without being obvious about it. It was Jennifer who first saw the trouble ahead. "The raise, José!"

"Fuckin' C." About ten cars ahead, on their side of the street, a blue and white was parked facing away toward Fifth Avenue. "Keep walkin'—they can see us in the rearview." At least the guns mounted on the fenders were not aimed their way.

"They're arguing about something—hear them shouting?"

"Probably arguing over whether to bust us. If we can't talk our way out of it, don't you try nothin', you hear me? A nice safe jail cell sounds pretty good right now. Here we go."

They were almost up to the police car, and its occupants were indeed arguing loudly. The driver shouted some final phrase, opened his door and began to get out; his partner shot him three times in rapid succession. He danced past them in three big steps, ran his head into a brick wall and rebounded to land just in front of them, on his side, blood fountaining from his belly and back. He was red-haired, in his thirties, built heavily and gone to fat. He looked up at them appealingly, eyes wide, and gestured with a wet hand that lacked two fingers. "Partners fifteen years," he said. "I love the cocksucker." Then his mouth overflowed with thick rich blood, and he jack-knifed and died.

Jennifer stood frozen, vaguely aware that she was getting blood on her sneakers. She turned to look into the police car. The other policeman was black, his Afro trimmed to conform to Department regulations. He was looking at his dead partner and did not see her or José at all. His weapon, a non-regulation .44 Magnum, was shaking in his hand. Suddenly he registered their existence. She was too scared to move, and waited to be shot.

"Excuse me, officer," José said in perfectly normal conversational tones, "My friend and I was thinking of clouting a car and getting the fuck out of here. Are there any vehicles in the neighborhood you would especially recommend?"

There was a long pause. For Jennifer it was hours. She had time to think *well, it probably won't work but I can't think of anything better he could have tried,* and *the damned minipads chafe,* and *this is all my fault, Jerome's probably reading our note right now,* and *I've been using Wonderglue since I was seven,* and *goodbye Daddy and Mom,* and *I'm sorry José,* and to briefly review the plans and hopes that would now never be fulfilled. Then the cop lowered his gun.

"There's a Chrysler minilimo a block up," he said. "It'll stop small arms fire."

"Hey, thanks a lot," José said, and slowly turned to walk away.

"Do you need any tools, brother?" the cop asked softly.

"Uh . . . well, maybe a screwdriver?"

"Flathead or Phillips? No, wait, for a Chrysler you'll

need a Robertson Number Two." He rummaged in the glove box. "Here." He tossed it to José.

To Jennifer's amazement, José almost dropped it.

"Thanks a lot, brother. Goodnight. Come on, Jennifer."

Still not quite believing, she followed him, half expecting a bullet in the back. After a few steps José stopped and turned and she almost screamed at him to keep going. "Brother?" he called back to the blue-and-white. The cop looked up. "Uh—I'm sorry. You know?"

The cop nodded, and dismissed them from his mind. They walked on, and when Jennifer had counted twenty steps she remembered to start breathing again. José caught her as she fell and held her up while she shook and trembled. The moment her trembling stopped he made her start walking again. Just before they reached Fifth Avenue they came to the minilimo. She leaned against it, the metal cool against her cheek, while he broke in and shorted the ignition.

As she fastened her seat belt she became aware that he was speaking to her. "Jennifer, listen, God dammit. Do that breathing thing you do or somethin' but snap out of it! It's fifty blocks home and I need you alert, you understand?"

"Yes, José." She did as he told her, and felt herself coming fully awake again. "Sorry. Long night."

He put the Chrysler in gear. "Just getting started. See what you can get on the radio—try 1010, it's all news—"

She got an ancient Stevie Wonder song she didn't know. She punched for another frequency, and nothing happened: the song kept playing. She punched random search and the song kept playing. The readout said she was changing frequency but she could not lose the song. It seemed to be called, "You Haven't Done Nothin'."

"This thing is screwed up somehow," she said.

"You sure you don't got it on 'tape' position?"

"Fuck you," she said, then: "I'm sorry. Yes, I'm sure. Wait a minute." She tried the whole FM band, AM, shortwave and several other bands. They were all carrying the same song. While she searched, the song ended in a fadeout doo-wop chorus and was succeeded by another song, a live recording. She and José exchanged a glance as they recognized it: they had been present at the taping, only a million years ago. The Juice. "Night of Power."

The car lurched sickeningly. "Fuck you, pothole," José yelled and fought the wheel; he reduced speed to something in the forties. Grand Army Plaza came up on the right, the southern end of Central Park. "That radio is blown; what kind of a stupid rich bastid has a eighty-thousand-dollar car with a radio that don't *THANK YOU, POTHOLE!*"

His gratitude was well-placed; they would surely have hit it if the pothole had not made him reduce speed. Crossing Fifth Avenue eastbound against the light at sixty kph, directly in their path: a tank . . .

Jennifer didn't have time to scream. Brakes locked, they careened past the tank, missing its rear end by perhaps a meter. They were clear of the Park now; as they sailed through the intersection sideways Jennifer was looking west down 59th, saw armed men firing into the lobbies of the Plaza and Park Lane Hotels. Then José regained control, got the nose pointing south and gave it the gun. He was swearing steadily in English and Spanish. She turned the volume down but left the radio on.

He approached the next intersection cautiously, and sure enough a pair of army trucks went by going east, one of them towing a howitzer, both loaded with armed blacks.

Jennifer stared around her in wonder as they kept going south. They went by Bergdorf Goodman, Van Cleef & Arpels, Tiffany, Bonwit Teller, Gucci, Fortunoff's, and all these bastions of wealth were intact, unlooted—some actually appeared to be *guarded* by bald black men with white armbands and riot guns. "What the hell kind of riot *is* this?"

"It ain't a riot," he said. "Jerome told us it wasn't."

"What *is* it, then?"

"I don't know. It feels like a war."

They drew small arms fire as they went by Cartier. The limo handled it, but it terrified Jennifer nonetheless. Then a block later they hit real trouble. Apparently a mixed group of white cops and G.I.s were making their last stand at St. Patrick's Cathedral, besieged by several dozen blacks with better organization and better weapons. Bullets flew in all directions, a grenade blew a massive stained glass window into glittering ruin, and José spun the wheel to the right and accelerated. They screamed round the corner in a perfectly controlled skid, José roared, "Mother-*fucker*," they just missed a stationary tank, the skid went uncontrolled, they were on the sidewalk, knocking over one of the ubiquitous bald black men, they were back in the street and 51st Street appeared to be full of troops and half-tracks. José took a hard left; they glanced off the face of the Associated Press Building and ricocheted back out into the street, bullets *whing*ing off the windows. There were two more tanks dead ahead, at either end of the Satellite Telecommunications International Center, the former NBC Building. The nearest one was facing them; they had appeared too swiftly for the cannoneer to track them but the machine gun opened up and their bullet-proof windshield began to show cracks at the perimeter. "*Father*fucker," José screamed and brought the limo to a careening halt in front of the STI Building, directly be-tween the two tanks. Jennifer glanced to her right; her eye was caught by a huge sculpted facade over the main entrance, left over from the days when the building had been NBC Headquarters: under a marble Jove hurling thunderbolts were the words, **"Knowledge and Wisdom shall be the Stability of thy Times."** A bullet *spang*ed off the roof from the other direction; she looked that way in time to see a sniper opening up from the roof of the Nikon Building, past the Rockefeller Plaza skating rink. On the building's facing wall, in huge letters, was the slogan, **"New York—it's yours for the taking!"** She wanted to laugh but could not remember how. José waited until the tank ahead cracked its hatch, murmured, "*Pig*fucker," and stepped on the gas. Both machine gunners opened up for just long enough to scare the shit out of each other, then shut down. José aimed straight for the tank ahead, was doing 80 kph by the time he reached it, jogged the wheel and was around it. The shortest distance out of line-of-sight was straight ahead; he put it to the wood and was screaming right onto 48th Street before the tank's turret could swivel around to track him.

He did not turn south again until he had reached the

theater district. All the lights were out on The Great White Way. Things were relatively quiet for half a dozen blocks, then, until they reached Times Square, where a full-scale riot was in progress. Broadway was blocked with jammed-together burning cars, so José turned left and rocketed up 42nd Street, dodging dead cars and dead people at high speed. Within a few blocks he had hit more than half a dozen people and lost his left headlight. On either side of the street Jennifer saw a parade of clubbings, knifings, shootings. She saw something that had once been a white policeman; she saw a bag lady murder a child her age, only to have her own throat cut by a weeping priest; she saw a white woman in full dominatrix gear running from a pack of black boys, trying to clear her path with her whip. Jennifer put her face in her hands and closed her eyes.

José warned her before turning right. They were back on Fifth Avenue, and all at once the trouble was, incredibly, behind them. They saw absolutely nothing out of the ordinary all the way down to 33rd Street. There were calmly strolling pedestrians and singing drunks, necking couples and break-dancing kids.

At 33rd they saw a truckload of National Guardsmen of the 71st Infantry, attempting to flee their captured post, overtaken and machine-gunned by U.S. Army jeeps; the truck crashed and burned half a block east of them. José slammed down 32nd Street, right on Second Avenue, brought the car to a shuddering halt in the supermarket shoppers' drive-through immediately around the corner from Jennifer's apartment. They made it to the building at a dead run, each openly brandishing a gun, and did not relax until the inner door had closed behind them and they were safe in the hallway.

She put Jerome's gun back in her pouch, and José put his in his belt. They leaned back against the wall, and looked at each other, and suddenly they were laughing helplessly together, holding each other and shaking with laughter. Somewhere in there his cheek brushed hers. He badly needed a shave, but the contact produced a stronger reaction than that could account for. She flinched, felt an indescribable rush of sensation somewhere between navel

and knees; her head felt too heavy for her neck to support.
This was like what she had felt twice at the Juice concert,
but different somehow. Much milder. Was it something to
do with menstruating? It scared her. Still laughing, she
backed away from him, and he let go of her at once.

"What is going *on?*" she said through her diminishing
laughter, adding almost immediately, "—out there?"

He shook his head, his own laughter drying up. "I told
you: a war. Only thing it can be. A racewar. The black
people finally had enough of this town, they're gonna
plough the motherfucker under."

"I can't believe Michael is involved in this."

"Maybe he's tryin' to stop it; maybe your folks too."

"They're not doing so good, if that's true."

"So let's go in and wait for them to call us."

She got out her keys, beginning to think about her and
José alone in the apartment and what could happen, opened
all three locks and opened the door wide and opened her
eyes wide. "Mr. Shaw! What are you doing here?"

He smiled pleasantly. "Waiting for you, my dear—hello,
José—and for your parents. Are they with you?"

"No." Confused, she was vaguely aware that Shaw was
not alone, that a large redfaced man was also present,
but it was not until José, behind her, sucked air through
his teeth that she registered the fact that both men were
holding guns.

The redfaced man addressed José. "You. In." He pointed
his pistol at José's face and cocked it. "Hands in the air.
You too, sugarlips," he said to Jennifer.

She looked helplessly to José. He tried to smile re-
assuringly, very nearly made it. "Do what he says, Jenniflower. Everything's cool." He raised his hands high. She
looked at him for a long moment, then raised her own
hands and entered the apartment.

"Before I forget, dear," Shaw told her, "there was a
note on the door from someone named Jerome. He couldn't
wait any more, and you're to wait for a phonecall. Of
course, the phones don't work any more than the TV or
radio. I think your black friends have betrayed you."

"Cover 'em, Uncle George," the big redfaced man said.

He approached Jennifer, keeping out of Shaw's line of fire and keeping his own gun on José. He took the pouch from her shoulder, stepped back a few paces, put it down on the circular kitchen table and peered into it. "Oh ho." He rummaged, and lifted Jerome's revolver out by a pen thrust down its barrel. "Nice toys you play with, girlie." He found no other weapons. He brought the pouch back, replaced it on her shoulder and touched her cheek caressingly. "We're gonna get along just fine."

She was numb. José would get her out of this. The cavalry would come. At the other end of the room the TV was on; it said "Please stand by," and she felt that to be good advice.

"Back against the door, sweetheart. You: assume the position." They did as they were told. The beefy man removed José's gun from his belt, patted him down for other weapons. He found a knife in José's boot. "Well done, Thomas," Shaw said. "Let's—"

"Wait a minute. Spic *priests* carry one knife. A skell like this'll have another one someplace." He kept searching, found a second knife strapped under José's shirt with its hilt just hidden by his collar. "Thought so."

Ah, Jennifer thought. Now this script is back on the rails. He missed the third knife; José will save us.

"Wait a minute! Look at this—another one on the other shoulder blade! Cocksucker must be ambidextrous." Thomas dumped all the hardware on the kitchen table and herded them both to the other end of the room. "Cover 'em good, now, Uncle George." He took out a pair of handcuffs, opened the door out into the garden, and tested the strength of the security gate. "Over here, skell." He cuffed José's wrists to the grille behind him.

"Stay clear of him, Thomas," Shaw advised. "He's quite adept at that kicking business."

"No problem." He produced a second set of cuffs, went down on one knee and cuffed José's ankles to the grille.

"Shouldn't you save a pair of bracelets for the young lady?"

Thomas grinned at her. "I don't think I'll need 'em."

José was disarmed and immobilized. He was *not* going to save her. Wake up, Jennifer, it's up to you!

"All right, cutie, where are your parents?"

"Aren't you supposed to read them their rights first?" Shaw interjected. She could tell he was high on alcohol. He sat down by the TV and began idly flipping channels; each showed the same standby card, just as all the radio stations had been playing the same song.

"Shut up, Uncle George. I'm a cop, sweetie. Where are your parents?"

The best way to lie is to tell the truth, but not the whole truth. "I don't know."

He smacked her hard across the face, then, as José strained at his bonds, spun and punched him with closed fist. José's head banged off the metal gate. Thomas whirled back to her. "I said, 'Where are they?'"

"I don't—don't *hit* me, I don't know!"

"Listen to me, listen good: there's a race riot going on out there, and your fucking parents are Commie agitators sent here to help start it, and if you don't start coming up with some information I'm gonna break every bone in your little body, you get me?"

"You're crazy. My parents aren't—what you said. My mother is a *dancer*. My father is a retired designer, a famous—"

"Yeah, yeah, Uncle George told me the whole cover. Your 'mother' is a nigger and your father is a renegade American and you all just happened to come down here from a socialist country two weeks before the riot starts. We looked around. Black Muslim literature, some really disgusting pornography. Most of them artsy-fartsy bastards are commies anyway—and your fucking father probably told 'em how to screw up the radio and TV, niggers never could have figured that out for themselves. You listen to me: I seen three of my friends get whacked tonight, one of 'em a thirty-year man, I hadda hide at Uncle George's or they'd have whacked me too, there's niggers in fucking *tanks* out there in the street, if you don't tell me where your fucking parents are I'm gonna break your fucking skull!"

"Thomas, it's possible she knows nothing of their activities. Why would they—"

"Sure. And her and the spic just came in from a late

movie, right? She got that fucking piece on the table for a door prize." He glanced at José. "What do you know about this, asshole?"

José looked straight ahead, blood trickling from the center of his upper lip. "I know a scumbag when I see one."

The big cop blinked at him, then slowly smiled. The smile became a giggle. "Used to collect used ones for your mother?" he asked, and laid José's cheek open with his gun barrel.

"No," Jennifer cried, and sprang at him. It was a mistake; he grabbed her with a big hand that *hurt*. "Oh ho! He means something to you, huh? Jesus Christ, your parents let you fuck a spic?" He shook his head. "Yeah, they probably do." His expression changed. "Uncle George, I'm gonna take Little Miss Muffet here into the next room and interrogate her a little. You wait here; maybe the spic'll have something he wants to talk about while I'm gone. If it's interesting enough, you could try to interrupt me."

Shaw giggled, a ghastly sound. "Perhaps that's wise, nephew." He glanced at José. "Besides, I'm *certain* José and I have many things to talk about. There's an attache case I'd like to discuss . . . you go on." He looked Jennifer up and down and licked his lips. "Perhaps we could trade places in a while."

Thomas frogmarched her into her parents' bedroom, her left arm twisted up behind her. The pain was shocking. She had not known there was that much pain. He flung her onto the bed, uncocked his gun, set the safety, and tossed it out onto the living room floor behind him. "Take care of my piece, will you, Uncle George? That way I don't have to keep track of it." Shaw giggled again, collected the gun, and Thomas shut the door. Now the room was pitch dark.

At the sound of the door latch clicking shut, something clicked in Jennifer's mind. No one was going to help her. She was on her own. All at once she remembered for the first time in hours that she still had a knife between her legs. She strove to measure her breaths, to regain control. "Don't hurt me," she said submissively. "I know what's

going to happen but you don't have to hurt me. I'll make
it good for you."

His chuckle came out of the darkness. "You don't
understand. When I hurt you: that's when it's good for
me. Open the shade."

She did as she was told. Faint light came in through the
bars. She made out his bulk by the door. Did bars make
him feel more at home?

"That's better. Stand up."

She stood beside the bed.

"Drop that purse on the floor and take off your dress.
Don't hurry."

She obeyed, in a manner that she hoped was subtly
provocative.

He whistled through his teeth. "Nice. Jesus, look at the
little set of jugs on you. If you were my brat I'd make you
wear a bra."

"You have a daughter my age?"

"I used to. Little bitch. I threw her out last year."
(Jennifer interpreted: his daughter had divorced him just
as soon as she legally could.) "Get them pants off, I'm
gonna give you what I shoulda given her."

She removed them quite carefully. He came closer as
she did so, and she tried to let the hand holding the
panties drop unnoticed to her side.

"Jesus. Just like peach fuzz." He reached out and pinched
her left nipple, hard enough to make her yelp. "All right,
let go of them drawers and start taking *my* clothes off."

She could *not* get the damned pads separated with one
hand; she could touch the knife with two fingertips but
could not get a grip. "Just let me throw away this minipad,"
she said, turning toward the wastebasket.

He was quick, snatched the panties from her hands
before she knew he was going to. "I don't believe it, you
ain't old enough to bleed." He squinted into the panties.
"*Jesus!*" He flung them from him as if they were something disgusting, wiped his hand on his pants. The panties
went all the way across the room and landed in the open
closet. "I guess you are. Well, it was gonna bleed anyway,
one way or another. We're gonna have a *good* time. Now

get my clothes off." When she hesitated he hurt her
dreadfully.

All the time she was undressing him she tried to think
of a way out. None presented itself. The knife—and the
hatpin in her dress—were hopelessly out of reach. She
knelt to take off his shoes and help him step out of the
pants. She tugged the dirty boxer shorts down, flinched
away as his penis sprang free. He guffawed. She could see
veins pulsing along its length; god, it was enormous. He
thrust his pelvis forward, laughed as she jerked away.

She met his eyes.

"Let's see, now," he said jovially, "how are we gonna
stick it up?"

She knelt at his feet and stared up at him, and distantly
heard José crying out in pain in the next room. She guessed
how much it would take to make José cry out; even the
earlier pistol-whipping he had suffered silently. José, she
thought, guess what? I'm an adult now. Just in time.

And somehow her mind made an association between
José and Thomas's last words. Sometime earlier in the
evening, geological epochs ago, José had used the exact
same words, in a different context.

"Please," she said, total surrender in her voice, "let me
grease it up first. I've got some of that love gel stuff in my
bag."

He was surprised and pleased. "Boy, can I pick 'em or
what? Yeah, sure, no sense scrapin' *my* skin off. Make it
snappy."

She kneewalked over to her pouch, rummaged carefully
inside. As her hand came out he was on her, grabbing her
wrist. But he relaxed when he saw the tube in her hand.
"For a second I thought you were up to something. All
right, come on, slick it up and then get up on the bed."

She unscrewed the tube with one hand, awkwardly
stroked his erection with the other. Her fingers just met
around it. It felt odd, somehow: for all its hardness, it
seemed bouncy, loosely attached. Curious.

She looked him in the eyes. Big jolly detective, having
the time of his life. "I'll squeeze a big glob on," she said,
her voice trembling, "and you rub it all up and down with
both hands while I put some up me."

"You bet, sweetie."

She squeezed the tube with both hands. He mock-shivered as the cool liquid contacted his skin, and giggled. He took the shaft in his right hand, cupped the glans with his left, began to rub, and grunted in surprise. "What the—Jesus!" Shriller: "*Jesus!*"

By then she was standing, stuffing the tube against his mouth and squeezing carefully. At this point he was startled, confused, afraid, and angry, but he had not yet worked out what was happening to him and so he was not yet terrified. Instinctively he tried to spit out the cool runny stuff spilling over his teeth, and this was a grave mistake, for when he pursed his lips they stuck together, and his tongue stuck to their insides. He still did not understand, but he was terrified now nonetheless. He began to grunt loudly and rhythmically through his nose; snot sprayed down his upper lip. He wanted to pry his lips apart, but his hands were elsewhere engaged. His eyes rolled wildly. He was beginning to get it.

Jennifer remembered a takedown that José had taught her. She tried it and it worked perfectly. He landed on the bed, thrashing violently, kicking his legs up and down as he tried to let go of his by now fully flexible penis, still grunting his muffled grunt. She managed to trap his legs with one arm, used the Wonderglue to seal them together—for a frightened instant she thought his struggles had gotten some on her. She rubbed excess glue from the tube off on his shin, held the tube high and backed away. He tried to sit up and throw his legs over the side of the bed. She chuckled and moved the tube toward his eyes. He lay back at once, his cheeks puffing with the shouts he could not get out, arms straining. She held his head down against the pillow by his hair. She put her face close to his.

"I'm sorry I don't have more time," she whispered savagely. "Take a deep breath."

His eyes widened even more. Now he got it. He thrashed so violently that the hair in her hand tore loose. She got a better grip and repeated, "Take a deep breath. It'll last longer."

He must have realized she was right, for he emptied his lungs and held his breath. She smiled broadly and waited.

Finally he gave up and inhaled, and as he finished inhaling she squirted glue up both nostrils. "Goodbye, you bastard," she said, and pinched them shut. Her smile was gone now. She watched with solemn interest. His feet banged up and down together on the bed as he tried to drum his heels and arch his back. The whole bed shook and bounced loudly and rhythmically. She heard Shaw giggle in the other room, and that made her smile again briefly. For realism's sake she made a few appropriate moans of her own. Urine fountained from between his fists, spattered his chest; an instant later his bowels let go. She wrinkled her nose and kept watching. His struggles grew weaker, and she timed her groans so that the sound of her mock-climax was the last thing he ever heard. When she was certain he was dead she took a moment to look him over. His eyes bulged out, his skin looked as dark as Mom's, and damned if he didn't have an erection again. That gooey stuff on his belly—that must be semen. Dying body's last attempt to reproduce. It *did* look like creme rinse. Interesting. She tried to close his eyelids, and they would not stay closed, so she used the last of the Wonderglue with great care. Then she went to the closet, retrieved her underpants, got the little knife. She held it flat against her thigh, hidden by her palm, and went into the living room.

José's shirt had been cut off; there were four long cuts on his chest, bleeding freely. Shaw stood in front of him, a carving knife in his hand; he had set his guns down on the TV. He gaped in happy shock at the sight of her. "Oh, *my*," he breathed.

She jerked a thumb over her shoulder. "You're next. He says he wants to watch, and do things while you're doing it."

"Splendid," he said, blinking furiously. "That will be quite satisfactory. Don't go away, José—I *still* think you know where the Grants are." He came toward Jennifer, smiling.

"He says to kiss you first. Out here where José can see."

"Splendid," Shaw repeated, smiling even more broadly and blinking a mile a minute. He reached out and bent toward her and she cut his throat from ear to ear. He straightened, blinked some more, felt his throat. He tried to speak and achieved only a fluttering, kazoo-like sound. He examined the blood on his hand, rolled up his eyes and died. His corpse fell to the floor, carving knife clattering.

Jennifer looked at José, said, "Do I have to do *everything* around here?" and burst into tears.

"Just the one more thing," José said gently after a time. "Get the keys to these cuffs out of the bastid's pants. Then I'll finish up the rest.'

She did so at once, not stopping to look at the thing on the bed. When José was free she flung herself into his arms, still weeping furiously. Everything went away. An indeterminate time later she identified a warm feeling on her skin. She yelped and pushed him away. "Oh, José, I'm sorry! You're bleeding, your cheek, your poor chest—"

"*De nada*," he said. "That little cocksucker didn't have the *cojones* to cut deep. He was workin' up to it, though."

"Let me get antiseptic and bandages—"

"Later. We gotta get rid of the meat."

"Right now?" She snuffled and wiped her nose.

"Did you ever wake up in the same house with a stiff? Bandage me later; I'd just start bleedin' again. Jeez, this rug is shot. How about the other bastid? He bleed like this when you cut him?"

"Uh . . . I didn't cut him. He threw the knife where I couldn't get it."

He gave her a puzzled frown. "How'd you take him, then?"

"Well . . . you remember how I put that message for Jerome up on the lamppost, by the Museum?"

"Yah."

"I told him it was love gel."

His eyes widened. His mouth hung open. Silently he walked to the bedroom door, leaned in, and put on the light. She waited, suddenly afraid. He would be horrified, would hate her . . .

He whooped with laughter. He laughed louder and harder than she had ever heard anyone laugh before, much louder than he had when they'd first come home. He whirled and looked at her with bright merry eyes, with amazement and approval and respect and congratulations in those bright merry eyes, and shook with his laughter.

And she thought of what Officer Thomas must look like in bright light, and she lost it too. They reeled like drunks, howling and helplessly waving each other away as though, if they were to touch, their combined mirth might exceed some kind of critical value and destroy them both. They knocked things over and fell down.

It was so powerful a physical experience that it reminded her again of the Juice concert, reminded her that she had been awake an ungodly long time and had expended emergency reserve energy, reminded her that she must be exhausted. But as the laughter ended, she realized that she was wide awake and alert. She felt as though she could run to Halifax and back.

"Come on," José said, still grinning. "Get up and help me with these chumps."

"Get up yourself. Where the hell do we put them? In the garden?"

"Liable to get us talked about. The basement door is right across the hall. I got my keys. We can just kick 'em down the stairs and figure something else later."

They wrapped Thomas in the blanket he had died on, Shaw in the damp stained sheet under that. José needed her help with the carrying; his strength was equal to the weight but both bodies traveled awkwardly. Somewhere during the process Jennifer remembered for the first time that she was naked, but put it out of her mind. The work was too messy for clothes, and she and José had been through too much together to waste attention on trivial, utterly junior things like body modesty. A little while later she noticed that José was half naked; she found that harder to put from her mind.

At last he clicked the last of the apartment locks shut and slumped against the door. "Okay. Time to get you to bed. We'll clean up in the morning."

"José. Go to my bedroom. Lie down. I'll be in in a second with bandages." He began to protest. "My parents aren't coming home tonight, we both know that. So I'm your boss. You're still bleeding. *Go lie down.*"

He gave up.

She sponged herself quickly in the bathroom. As she was leaving she saw the box of sanitary pads, remembered that José was not the only one bleeding. But when she checked, nothing was dripping. The first heavy flow was over, she must be in the stage called "spotting." She went to her bedroom. On her way through her parents' bedroom she slipped on one of her mother's robes and located her father's Irish whiskey. José thanked her and took several pulls from the bottle while she dressed his wounds, kneeling on her heels beside him. As he'd said, the wounds were grisly-looking but not deep.

"José?"

"Yah." His voice sounded sleepy. The only light was the bedside lamp.

"Something you said before. You become an adult the day you understand you can die. I'm an adult now."

His face became somber. "I know, *chiquita*. I'm sorry. It wasn't supposed to happen for years yet."

"Don't be sorry. If it had come two minutes later . . ." She finished the last bandage, left her hands on his chest. "José?"

"Yah."

"Shaw was going to kill you, wasn't he?"

"I don't think so. The one time I pretended it really hurt and yelled he almost shit his pants. But he was calmin' down. Maybe. I figured he was gonna hurt me, but the other bastid was gonna kill me, the fucking nephew."

"So I did save your life?"

He met her eyes. "That's fuckin' A."

She slid one hand down to his belt buckle. "God damn it, do I have to do everything around here?" The robe slipped off one shoulder.

He grabbed her wrist. Quickly:

"Jennifer, I can't—"

"—the hell you can't, you've had a hard-on since we dumped Shaw—"

"—your parents—"

"—if I'm an adult it's none of their god-damned business, is it—"

"—dammit, you said you wasn't gonna do this no more—"

She raised up onto her knees, pulled his hand up between her legs and clamped it there. "I said no more teasing."

He closed his eyes. "Fuckin' A."

She released his hand, unbelted the robe, and shucked it off. "Look."

He looked. Then he sighed and unbuckled his belt. She lay down at once and waited impatiently while he undressed and rolled onto her. Nonetheless his entrance came as a vast, astonishing surprise. She had been expecting pain.

Her last semiconscious thought was a vague, distant relief. She was enjoying it more than she had enjoyed the killing. Then the universe exploded.

When she woke the room was in daylight. The garden outside was in direct sunshine, it must be near noon. She was stiff and sore in many places—her legs, feet, her shoulder where Shaw's nephew had grabbed her. To take her mind off her hurts she studied José. In her limited experience, sleeping people looked like hell, but she could find no flaw in him. Even his snoring was melodious. She marveled at the cleverness with which his body had been made. Four of the five bandages had survived their lovemaking; the fifth and least serious wound was angry red around the edges. There was an old scar on his belly that did not look surgical. His body was flat and hard and relatively hairless. His pubic curls were miniature replicas of those on his head. His penis was erect. It didn't look like the pictures she had seen, or like the fat cop's or Bobby Amatullo's. The shaft tapered from the base, then flared out sharply at the plum-shaped glans. It curved gently to the right, and the glans looked as if someone had given it an eighth-turn counterclockwise.

Soon reality would return, life would restart itself, she would have to think about her preposterous situation and make plans and, very likely, get killed somehow. Here was a distraction, a postponement. Trying not to wake him yet, she reached out and touched him.

His eyelids opened at once, pupils already swiveled toward her.

The effect was comical; she chuckled. "Good morning."

"Uh . . . *oh*. Good morning, Jenniflower."

"You called me that last night. I like it."

"What time is it?"

Her hand moved. "About five minutes to orgasm."

He closed his eyes again. "Fuckin' A."

"B, actually. A was last night. Oh shit, I'm lying in a puddle." Virgin's blood if any must have dried long since; her period must have resumed heavy flow. She grabbed tissues and dabbed at herself, suddenly apprehensive. This was messy, yucky, it would turn him off—

"No problem. Come over here on my side." He made room.

She disposed of the tissues and snuggled gratefully into him. His hands began to move on her, and she caught her breath. "José?"

"Yah."

"I was horny for you the first time I ever saw you. I just didn't know that was what it was."

"Huh. Me too, now I come to think about it. Spread your legs, Jenniflower."

This time there was some soreness, but she did not care. His breath and hers were both foul, but she did not care. As she had been the night before, she was astonished— not, this time, by the magnitude of the explosion, but by its duration. She beat him to completion by a full ten seconds, but the last aftershock did not fade until long after his breathing had returned to normal.

She wanted to lie there unthinking forever. But her bladder was full and he was lying on it. "I have to pee."

"Me too," he said without moving. "Who's first?"

She moved to expel him, and he grunted. "You're a man. Use the sink." She pushed him off her, onto the wet spot, giggled and raced for the bathroom.

She yearned inexpressibly for a very long very hot bath. She settled for a quick shower and decided not to wash her hair. As the water sluiced off the grime of the night past—surely the strangest assortment of things ever washed from her body—reality restarted. Time-out was over; normal life began again, slowly but with increasing acceleration until all at once she was back in the world again and considering the events of the last twelve hours. Just as her head began to throb José got into the shower with her and wanted to touch and hug. Her own reaction surprised her. Not fifteen minutes ago she had been urgently attempting to weld their bodies together irrevocably and forever (and yes, she had thought then of Wonderglue)—and now she wished José would leave her alone to get some thinking done. But his libido did not seem to be capable of such instant 180° course corrections. Men were just what Dena had told her they were: damned romantics.

For once, she was glad when the hot water gave out.

"You make breakfast," she said as they toweled off. "I've got things to do."

"Like what?" He was feeling argumentative now.

"Oh, nothing special. Watch TV, listen to the radio, play with the computer, make a few phone calls—"

"*You* make breakfast."

She yanked the towel out of his hands, startling him into coverup reflex. She moved close, invaded his personal space. Now that he was not wearing two-inch bootheels, she did not have to tilt her head much at all to look him in the eye. "José, listen to me. We're in a war together, and we're a team. You are a terrific warrior, strong and skilled. I am neither. I am a lousy soldier; therefore it falls to me to be the general."

"Bull*shit* you're not a warrior, you iced two guys last night! One of 'em a fuckin' gold shield! While I stood around wondering how the mortician was gonna fuck me up."

"That wasn't being a warrior, that was being a sneaky bitch. If you'd been loose, you wouldn't have *needed* to be sneaky. Who got us home past all those tanks and soldiers? With only *one* hand tied behind your back, you'd have taken that fat slob without working up a sweat—that's why you're the soldier. *I'm* sneaky: that's why *I'm* the general." She remembered Mom telling her: treat them like insecure children, stroke their egos—but be firm.

"But you make better scrambled eggs than I do—"

"Listen to me. You are bigger than me, stronger than me, older than me, more streetwise than me, more sexually experienced than me: true or false?"

"True."

"That makes you the perfect top sergeant, according to the books I've read. Now—I am smarter than you: true or false?" Refusing him permission to look away: "True or false?"

"True."

"So I am the general, and the general is suffering from insufficient data and hunger, so you are going to cook while I try and get information, and at the next sign of mutiny I will stop fucking you, and I want mine scrambled with cheese and served on the toast so I can eat one-handed. Oh, and Sergeant?"

"Yes, General?"

"The next time there's a break in this damned war, remind me to have you tutor me in oral sex."

"Yes, General." He kissed her on the forehead. "Mind if I put on my pants first?"

"Mmm. Yes, but carry on."

She powered up the entertainment console and tried tuner mode first. As she had guessed, a program of old and new songs with racial themes or subtexts was being broadcast on all frequencies, burning everything else off the air just like the night before. She was forced to conclude that there was no more FCC in New York. This tuner had an unusually wide frequency spectrum—her father had built it—but even on military, police, and other out-of-the-way bands she got the same music. So the police and the U.S. military could communicate only by phone and data links. Or could they? She picked up the phone, heard no dial tone. There went phone and data links—no wait, that wasn't certain. She had no way of knowing whether the entire New York phone system was down—or whether her particular phone had picked this particular time to go out of service for the third time in a week and a half. She could hear no distant explosions or gunfire, and the window was open. Come to think of it—

She went to the window, suppressed the sound of José overcooking the eggs, and listened hard. She heard *nothing*. No voices, no blaring music, no traffic echoes, nothing. No, wait, there was music—the song she had just switched

off on the tuner was barely audible: something by Mingus.
There was an odd quality to the sound. She could not tell
if it was being played nearby at low volume, or far away
at high volume. It was just in the air. The tune was
frenetic, angry; she heard Mingus shouting something about
Mama's little baby not wanting any damn shortnin' bread.

Where are my Mama and my Daddy? she wondered.
They are with Michael. Where is Michael? Could there be
any truth in the nonsense Thomas was spouting last night?
Could Mom and Daddy have something to do with this
racewar, could that be why we came to New York? *Is that
why Michael saved us in Harlem?*

Impossible. I'd have figured it out long ago. *I* could fool
them about something this big, but the other way around?
Bogus program. But maybe they got just a *little* advance
warning about this thing—from Jerome, say—and appealed
to Michael for sanctuary. How did they contact Michael?
Through Jerome? Where *is* Jerome, that he hasn't gotten
back here by now? Is he with Michael? *Where is Michael?*

It was already warm in the apartment; the slight breeze
through the window was welcome. She checked the time:
it was 11:40 A.M. She started to turn away, barely heard
an odd sound, and paused. Somewhere outside and upstairs,
softly creaking metal. She heard a sudden grunt of effort,
and a man appeared outside the window, performed a
rapid plié. It took her a stunned second to work out that
he had dropped from the second-floor balcony. She vaguely
recognized him as the man who lived above them. He was
overweight and unshaven, wore baggy pants and a shabby
t-shirt, and carried a small and cheap-looking pistol.

She stood frozen. He saw her and smiled with one side
of his mouth. He came the few steps to the window,
pressed his face against the bars. He looked past her at
José, who must have had his back turned because the man
looked back to her and took the time to look her up and
down quickly. Her throat would not pass air in either
direction. He did something she had seen actors do on TV,
pointed the pistol skyward and then began to bring it
down to draw a dead bead on her face. He had time to get
it halfway down and to say "Nigger-lovin' bas—" before
his throat grew a carving knife. It bisected the hollow of

his throat almost perfectly. He made a gulping sound, weirdly similar to the one she made at the same instant. Fragments of cheese still clung to the knife; as blood welled over it she thought wildly of Italian cooking. Then he fell away from the window and began a high shrill gargling sound that was over soon.

She stood motionless for several seconds after the sound had stopped. At last she turned to José. "We're going to need a bigger cellar soon."

He shook his head. "This time maybe we leave him where he is. I know the people in this building. Maybe a few others feel the way he did, but there ain't another pair of balls like his around. If he don't come back, they might come find out what happened to him—but if they *know* what happened to him, they'll find something else interesting to do. When it gets dark maybe I'll go push him away from the window."

"José?"

"Yah."

"Thank you."

"It was my turn, that's all. Hey, these eggs are ready."

She started to say that she couldn't possibly eat scrambled eggs after what she had just seen—and discovered that she was ravenous.

The eggs were dry and overspiced, the toast burnt; overall the most satisfying meal she had ever eaten. She drank a full litre of orange juice—it was almost worth living in New York to have access to real orange juice in unlimited quantities. Rather, it *had been* almost worth it. By the time she was full her brain had come up to speed. She was still woefully short of adequate intelligence. No matter what question she formulated, the answer came up "Insufficient data." Had she neglected any sources of information?

Well, the TV. But that would just have the "Please stand by" legend that Shaw had gotten the night before on all channels . . .

Wait a minute! The black revolutionaries couldn't possibly control all the TV stations in North America, could they? Shaw must have been trying only local channels—

On the way to the console she realized her error. The

rebels hadn't bothered to take a few dozen individual TV stations, any more than they had bothered with individual radio stations. They must have simply taken over one of those two big satellite uplinks. God, what an audacious bunch they were! Jennifer did not yet see all the implications her father had grasped at once, but she understood that this was much more than a simple, garden-variety massive riot. Without any hope at all, merely to confirm what she had already figured out, she finished the act of switching on the TV—and yelped.

"—and show your heart to the world," Michael said.

"José, *come here!*"

The screen had reverted to the standby pattern. "What? What was that?"

"That was *Michael.*"

"No shit? You sure?"

"Hell, yes. I told you what happened—I ought to remember that voice. Wait, here he comes again." She switched in the recorder.

Together they watched the final replay of Michael's tape, and when it was over and they had most of the answers they wanted, it was twelve noon.

Outside, the streets of New York were filling with black people. . . .

CHAPTER TEN

"Anyone who has begun to think places some part of the world in jeopardy."

—John Dewey

"The machine gun on the corner is the symbol of the twentieth century."

—Richard Wright

*　*　*

Russell's head throbbed. He had gotten just enough sleep for his whole body to stiffen up and for the inside of his mouth to grow rank hair, and then his brain had woken him. He had come to consciousness to find his mind revving wildly at speeds close to overload. He sat now in the lounge with his wife, making no attempt to slow his thoughts.

He knew that he would be lucky to get even five minutes of Michael's attention today, and so he tried desperately to put his thoughts *in order*, to condense and compress and formulate and priorize the things he wanted to say and the questions he wanted to ask, if and when he got the chance. He was filled with an emotional turmoil so vast that it threatened to burst him, and he could conceive of nothing to do with it except spill it onto the man who had generated it. He had been assured that Michael was good at this. But he felt that it could take several hours to simply articulate his pain, and of the few minutes he was likely to get he wanted most of those to be occupied by *Michael* talking and him listening.

So he ignored his physical hurts and Dena and Homemade and the occasional flutter of furious activity that passed through the lounge, and tried to draft successively shorter versions of what he wanted to say. The first step was to just let it spill:

Michael, all my life I've tried to like black people, to get along with black people, to treat black people as I would want them to treat me. I was raised in the '50's and '60's, when all right-thinking northern liberal whites raised their children to believe that racism was a kind of deadly sickness, doubtless spread by a virus or germ but inexplicable in any case, and confined to the southern U.S. Then as I grew up, I learned about racism.

And I learned at least as much—and as thoroughly—from blacks as I did from whites. Because of the cocoon my parents tried to raise me in, the first racism I became aware of was directed *at me*, by black kids.

No, that's not true. Long before I got the shit kicked out of me that time, I heard my father tell nigger jokes to friends on the phone, and heard my school friends pass on the ones they'd heard *their* fathers tell. But then again there were Italian jokes, and Polack jokes, and even WASP jokes. . . .

Am I a racist, Michael? I have tried not to be, all my life, and I don't know if there *is* any way to be that is not racist. If you hate blacks and treat them badly, you're a racist. If you ignore their blackness, you're a racist because you are not addressing the issue of their continuing oppression. If you show compensatory favoritism, you're a reverse racist, held in contempt by *both* sides. But if you *don't* try to treat blacks just a little better than you do others, you run up against the unpleasant fact that *all* people treat each other a little shabbily at best, and many blacks interpret that as racism.

If you repudiate any guilt and shame for what your ancestors did to theirs, you are morally irresponsible, like a city that repudiates its long term bonds once the bridge is built. If you accept that guilt and shame, you're immediately recognized as a patsy and fastened upon by opportunistic blacks. Who are after all only behaving as they've been taught: exploit those who display any weakness. If you don't agree that the appallingly bad record of socialization of blacks into American society (compared to other despised immigrant groups) is *entirely* the fault of the white man, blacks call you racist. If you don't agree that it's *entirely* the fault of the black man (or woman), whites call you racist. If you suggest that it might be a mixture of the two (no matter what ratio you assign) both sides call you racist. If you even attempt to bring up the question, to examine any data, as Professor Sowell did, as Professor Shockley did, you're a racist. If you ignore the question, you're a racist by default.

Am I a racist, Michael? I think of my music collection, such an important part of my life. The majority of the music I own, and the overwhelming majority of the music I treasure, is the work of black artists. If you destroyed every disc, tape and chip I own by white artists—well, I'd really miss Zappa and The Beatles, but I guess I'd survive the loss. But how could I live without Betty Carter, Ray Charles, Miles, Bird, Lady Day, Mingus, Jon Hendricks, Carmen Lundy, the Duke? The best dancers in the world are blacks, from Bojangles right through Debbie Allen and Judith Jamison and Gene Ray to my own wife. The best athletes in the world are black, from Jack Johnson to Bikila to Willie Mays to Abdul Jabbar to Muhammad Ali to Bobby Friday. The best comedians, Pryor, Cosby, Murphy, Gardner. Am I a racist if I treasure these people, support them and black writers, actors, poets, playwrights? If I cherish Ntozake Shange and Fred Ward and Cicely Tyson and Alfre Woodard and Charlie Saunders and Samuel Delany? Do I thereby somehow "condemn" them to be "nothing more than" superb writers, artists, athletes, and entertainers, and thus somehow perpetuate their enslavement?

Leroi Jones once said: "All the hip white boys scream for Bird. And Bird saying, "Up your ass, feeble-minded ofay! Up your ass," And they sit there talking about the tortured genius of Charlie Parker. Bird would've played not a note of music if he just walked up to East 67th

Street and killed the first ten white people he saw. Is that true, Michael? (And does that mean that you have aborted the careers of several Charlie Parkers today?)

American black people excel in *all of the professions that are rooted in or built around pain:* is it immoral for me to take aesthetic pleasure from the results, however much I offer for the privilege in money, respect or acclaim?

Richard Matheson wrote a poem I've remembered all my life, about a white scientist who invented a machine that could translate a black sax-man's solos back into the pain that had produced them. The sax-man killed him and smashed the machine. The last lines were something like: "Take all the rest, white daddy/You will because you have/But don't come scufflin' for our souls." I've remembered that all these years, at least in part because a white man wrote it.

Michael, if a racist is anyone who does not fight against racism, then I guess I am a racist, because I am *damned* if I know how to fight racism. It's been years since I thought I had a clue as to where or how to fight so that it could accomplish anything more significant than expiation of my personal sense of guilt. I was too young for the first Freedom Marches, but I cheered them with my mother. In the '60's I marched, and as a matter of fact I marched more for blacks than I did to end the war—and not only did it accomplish nothing, I was victimized by many of the blacks I came in contact with.

College really began my education. The black students' quadrangle, through which *no* white student walked. The absurd demands to which the university acquiesced. My first-ever mugging, by a black man, on campus—he took my money and then cut my new jacket anyway. The three black rapists who worked the campus through the winter of 1969 with total impunity, because neither the administration nor the campus police nor indeed the white student community dared publicly acknowledge that the situation existed.

Then again, I remember the time SDS took over the Library, and "Easy Company," the campus's right-wing extremist group, announced their intention of going in there and kicking ass. I thought the SDS were custard-heads, but I *hated* Easy Company, born thugs whose idea of fun was to hospitalize long-hairs on sight. The campus cops all suddenly found someplace more pressing to be, and the Easy Company goons approached the Library entrance with their ball bats and pipes . . . and suddenly a phalanx of black students blocked their way, just as heavily armed, saying, "No you don't either." I admired the Black Students' Alliance that day. . . .

After I graduated, Michael, while I was still working for other people, my girlfriend's sister Susan finally made a serious enough attempt at suicide to get herself locked away in a hospital on Long Island. I used to visit her, design little toys and games she could make with available materials and so forth. She introduced me to Eartha from down the hall. Eartha was small and quiet and funny, and Michael, yours is the only smile I've ever seen sadder than hers. She'd been attempting suicide for five years, getting closer each time. Her inpatient status allowed her people on the outside to sign her out for a few hours every other week. One day I showed up to visit Susan, and she told me that Eartha's people had screwed up at the last minute for the third time running, and Eartha was really down about it, and why didn't I sign for her and take her for a drive?

I drove us around for hours. She'd been in that hospital a long time: it was a big deal for her to walk into a Burger King and order a Coke, with strangers and lights. I gave her the money so she could do it herself. She came back with the Coke so proud and scared and happy I wanted to cry. We drove, and she talked. She'd been part of a girl singing group on the rise, dating one of the Temptations, tasting fame just around the corner. One night she took a chance, left her two babies home alone for just an hour while she slipped out. The building must have started burning just as she turned the corner, for there was nothing left but smoking rubble when she got back.

Ah, Michael, we parked by the shore of Long Island Sound and we talked away the hours, and then she was telling me how grateful she was and all of a sudden she was all over me. She'd been locked up with other women for a long time, and she was as horny as a tabby in heat.

She was hurting and lonely and grateful. Perhaps I am an immortal fool. I had never had a black lover, and in retrospect it would have cost me nothing to give her what she asked. But I was young, and it had for me an inescapable flavor of shooting ducks in a barrel, of taking unfair advantage of vulnerability. God help me, I was not sure then, and do not know to this day, whether the prospect had been in my subconscious when I'd agreed to sign her out. As gently as I could I refused her, tried to keep her from taking it personally. I told her I already had a girlfriend, Susan's sister—but that once Eartha had been out of the hospital for a while and gotten her life back in balance, all she had to do was call and I'd come running, and meanwhile I wanted to be her very good friend. And I gave her my phone number and drove her back to the hospital.

Some months later, Michael, Eartha was released. A few weeks after that she called, gave me her address, asked me to come see her because she was terribly lonely. I broke a date with Susan's sister and drove over that night. She was living in a commune of blacks in Wyandanch, in a one-room flat in the garage of a house owned by a minister. She greeted me warmly, but when I started to close the door of her room behind me, she *leaped* up and stopped me. "It's your life if that door closes," she told me. Okay. We began to talk, she started telling me about how she was trying to rebuild her life, how many things there were to relearn about living in the world. Suddenly there were two large angry men in the doorway. "You *will* come with us. Now." Upstairs to the dining room. Eartha wasn't allowed to come. A dozen men, including the minister. No women.

First they talked and I listened. It was obvious and inarguable that I was here for only one possible purpose. For the thought alone I deserved to die, let alone the attempt. I was to leave this place, praising God for the chance, and if I ever attempted to return or to lure the sister to another place or to contact the sister in any manner I would die. The minister spoke the longest, describing the way in which I would die and estimating how long it would take me.

Then, to give them credit, they let me talk. I remember everything I said. To this day I believe I spoke eloquently and honestly and with unmistakable sincerity. I even acquired the courage somehow to point out that in this houseful of loyal protectors, sister Eartha said she was lonely. I might just as well have been speaking Mandarin. They didn't interrupt, but when I was done they nodded and repeated everything they'd said before. They showed me the door and I left, and I never tried to contact Eartha again and I never heard from her again.

But I heard *of* her. Two months later when she finally got it right. I happened to see the obit. Eartha was twenty-eight when she died. To this day I'm sorry I didn't have the guts to go to the funeral, and I wonder how many of her brothers did.

On the other hand, the people here in your tunnel have not shown *any* of that implacable, intransigent hatred of anything wrapped in pink skin. And they all *know* that I sleep with my ebony lady. . . . It occurs to me to wonder whether you had anything to do, behind the scenes, with the downfall of the fanatic Mau Mau Party, Michael. . . .

Am I a racist, Michael?

I know that I am a most self-centered man. I want most for the world to go away and leave me alone. I have few friends and none I would die for. I want me and my family to be well and safe and healthy, and while I'd prefer not to have to hurt anyone else to accomplish that, if it is necessary I will. My brain wants no part of your crusade, tells me that it is not my fight. But what of my heart?

You are fighting the United States of America. I beat the Viet Nam draft, but once I was in India, working on a hydraulic systems project in association with the UN, and I found myself increasingly involved with the CIA. I learned a lot about the way the world works, and the way America works, and the way a gun works. I learned things a lot of my contemporaries had learned in Nam. And then there was trouble and a good friend was murdered, and when I got back to the States I moved to Canada for good. It was the only way out of an irresolvable conflict, and it has worked out very well over the years. But I have never been able to completely lose that bone-deep love of the United States of America and everything it claims to stand for; I've never been able to stop myself from mildly defending it to my kneejerk anti-Yank neighbours. *No* nation ever has lived up to its ideals, but no nation in history has ever *had* such magnificent ideals as those of the United States. I don't want to live here—but I love the place. Will your racewar hasten, or forestall, the inevitable day when the country is torn apart and destroyed by its own racism, by the anger and shame of whites and blacks? I know that you have no use for the Soviet Union or for Marxism in any form, you've convinced me of that—but will the dislocation your racewar creates give the Soviets a crucial edge? Or is that question just a refried attempt to use the Commie Menace as an excuse to perpetuate repression at home?

And what are you fighting *for*, Michael?

You are fighting for Equity, for equity. What if you've miscalculated, what if America *cannot give* what you demand? The American black might be annihilated within the year. And what if you succeed, and you are assassinated, and your brave new nation falls into the hands of the radical and ruthless?

And what about the horrors that will surely ensue when masses of black Americans begin to try and cross the country to get here?

And if you pass all these hurdles and found your nation: what kind of nation will your crippled, hobbled, *damaged* people be able to build? I talked with General Worthing while he was eating, and he said you had been able to get tentative backing from the International Monetary Fund by promising them that the nation of Equity would make technological education and research its top priority, that you intend to make Equity the high-tech industrial center of this hemisphere. I applaud the idea and the strategy—but can you pull it off? What will you do with the muggers and junkies and drunks and rapists, and with the honest citizens who are just too old to learn, while you're raising up your new generation of streetsmart techies?

But then, is there any such thing as a person who is too old to learn—given enough motivation?

Am I, for instance, that old?

I know that I cannot fight *against* you, Michael. Oh, intellectually I can think of two or three lines of approach, but I know I'm not going to do anything about them. They all involve killing you, directly or indirectly, and I would not see a brain like yours destroyed for *any* reason. (Is it true, as Tom Worthing told me, that you were a brilliant young financial analyst before you went to Viet Nam?) Only a supernaturally good judge of character could have assembled an army in secret over twenty-five years, and I am developing the sneaking suspicion that it's *Motormouth* who's your secret litmus-test for character—and right from the moment we met he has *never* been wary of me for an instant. He knows I cannot intend you harm.

So my two choices are to work *for* you or to remain neutral. I have been neutral about everything under the sun for an uncommonly long time, and it just now comes to me that perhaps that, multiplied by most of the white population of North America, is how the world *got* this screwed up. In any case, I think I've finally had enough of being uninvolved, exempt, immune.

I know I could be of help to you. I've never taught anyone but Jennifer before, but I know I'd be good at it, and I'm certain an emerging nation with high-tech aspirations could use a designer as good as I am. I retired because I had all the money I needed for myself and my family, and could think of no other rationally defensible reason to work. People don't *want* you to make their lives easier, I learned that in India and here in the States a long time ago. Would it be any different in Equity?

One thing I know, Michael. If I decide not to join you, I lose my wife. She's determined to stay here. For one thing, it solves her problem of what to do with her life when she can't dance any more; for another it makes up for the free ride she got by being born into the middle class in Halifax. If I leave, sure as God made little green parking tickets she is going to stay, and likely she'll end up having Jerome's babies instead of mine.

But that's not a reason to join a revolution, Michael. At least, not one that I can accept. Neither is the rationalization that your way is the least of several evils. I agree that the U.S. has been poised for a long time on the verge of a nationwide firecracker-string of riots, rebellions, and insurrections leading ultimately to national pogrom. Your surgical intervention cannot hasten it by all that much, and may just head it off—but *what is that to me?* In my life, black people and white people have both treated me badly, robbed me, assaulted me, cheated me, threatened me, criticized me, mistrusted me, and rejected my friendship. A plague on both their houses. Why does the outcome of their dogfight concern me if I can get clear?

I've never tried to harm a man because of his race, and I've never allowed racism to go down in my presence without denouncing it—even in my father's home!—and I've never wavered in my conviction that mixing races combines the best features of both—I've never met or seen a mulatto or Eurasian or person of any mixed racial background who wasn't both beautiful and intelligent— and I know that I'll never understand the blackexperience but I've tried my very best. Teacher, I've written "I am not a racist" on the blackboard five thousand times, and now I feel I've done enough and I want to go home. Why do I have to stay?

Wait . . .

In the background I hear the radio, which has been playing songs by black artists all day, and it comes to my attention now because it's playing one of my favorite tracks in the world. Billie Holiday (born Eleanora Fagan, of mixed parentage) singing "You Don't Know What Love Is," from *Lady In Satin.* I've taken hours of pleasure from that album; I think it is one of her finest. It is also her last—recorded just before trying to live in the nonexistent country between black America and white America finally killed her. Her pipes are shot, her throat is raw—but her control is *perfect* and her heart is full and her technique is as good as it's ever going to get, and the results are something you hear with your spine. It's all in there, pain and anger and a wry awareness of futility—and simple persistence.

If I have taken aesthetic pleasure from what she did with all her pain, and have not devoted my life to doing something about it, am I a racist, Michael? Is that why Dena and I should stay here and raise our babies in a war zone?

Michael, I lost a wife once. Another designer killed her. He took a dive on a design for a nose gear assembly on an airliner, specified some substandard components he had a financial interest in. My first wife died in the first crash resultant. By the fourth, a year later, industry rumours reached me. I spent three months discreetly confirming the story. Then I spent four months in planning and preparation. Then I killed him with my hands and got away clean. I don't regret it even a little, but it was enormously less satisfying than I'd expected it to be. It didn't change anything. That was my last crusade, almost a decade ago, and I swore I'd never go on another. I decided I'd been a damned fool to risk Jennifer's future that way.

I still feel the same way, Michael. Why must I join *this* crusade, place my only child in jeopardy, my only reminder of Janice? If I stay here there's nowhere I can send her, no one in Halifax I could give her to. I won't send her to live with Regina no matter how far away she makes Dad move them. (Jesus, my father keeps all his money in a New York bank—I think he's broke!) Do I risk my daughter to keep my wife? In a few more years she'll be a woman; is this the time of her life to pitch her into a revolution?

And as Russell reached this point in his thoughts, he looked up and Michael was standing before him. He felt his lips start to open like floodgates, and before the first words could spill forth, Michael spoke first.

"Jennifer is on her way, Russell. She'll be here in fifteen minutes."

The words meant nothing. Sounds in some unfamiliar language. Beside him, Dena cried out, and he spun to her, thinking that she must have cut herself on something. Then it hit him. His ears roared so loudly that for a mad instant he thought the tunnel was flooding somehow. Dena's face disintegrated as his vision began to grey out. He was vaguely aware of Michael taking him by the shoulders.

For over fifteen hours, asleep and awake, he had been refusing to permit himself to feel the extent of his terror for his only child. The relief was like being struck under the heart with a baseball bat.

"She's alive," Michael was saying in his ear. "She claims to be unharmed. I've got armoured escort fetching her now, and I'll send Motormouth topside to get her."

Russell got his legs under him and threw himself into Dena's arms. Her head was almost as scratchy as his unshaven chin; the pain made them both smile.

"By the way," Michael said, "a call came through on the 333 line from out on Long Island. Your father has applied to claim Equitan citizenship, for himself and his wife."

Russell and Dena burst out laughing.

Over the last few minutes Russell anticipated the reunion. He would swing his little girl up in his arms and whirl her around and around in the ultimate Battle of the Kisses. He would apologize profusely for leaving her alone and promise never to do it again. He would thank José as best he knew how for protecting her, find out whatever it was the boy wanted most and try to get it for himself when he could. And he would find *some* way to break him and Jennifer out of this tubular coffin, and find *some* way off this fucking island, and get her back to a sane country, where people only killed each other over sensible things like what language they spoke.

Then Motormouth came out of the elevator followed by Jennifer and José, and at the first sight of them he knew, somehow, that he was going to have to think again. As he rushed forward for the sweeping and whirling and kissing, he stopped in his tracks, derailed. So did Dena.

This was a stranger patterned after his daughter. She seemed inches taller than he remembered. Surely her breasts had not been that big, her hips that rounded the last time he'd seen her. Surely her eyes had not been . . . it came to him that he must not have been *seeing* his daughter for some time, for she could not have grown so much older overnight. She was dirty and wild-haired and haggard. Her sweater was torn at the right shoulder. She was supporting at least half the weight of José, his arm around her shoulder, her arm around his waist. There was a ragged hole in the leg of his jeans, and his boot was overflowing with blood.

"Hello, Dad; hi, Mom. They said there'd be a doctor here."

"I know where the infirmary is," Russell said, starting forward. "I'll take you there, José."

Jennifer and José did not separate, did not move, and so when he got there all he could do was say, "This way," and turn around again. They followed him through the busy operations room and uptunnel to the infirmary, where a doctor was waiting. She helped José up onto the operating table, held his hand and stroked his hair while the doctor began cutting away his trouser leg. "Hello, Russell," the boy said thickly. "Hello, Dena. Quite a day, fuckin' A."

"Hello, José," Dena said softly. She came up behind Jennifer and began kneading her shoulders, working the kinks out. Jennifer accepted it gratefully but did not take her attention off José. The doctor finally looked up and said, "You were lucky. You'll be walking again in a week; the limp will be gone in a few months." Only then did Jennifer relax and start to talk. Even then she spoke slowly, quietly, in the measured tones of an adult. Russell was thunderstruck—where was his chatterbox little girl inside this somber stranger? He and Dena exchanged a glance, let her speak uninterrupted.

"We turned on the TV just before noon. We had to wait an hour or so for the streets to clear and the gunfire to stop. We needed sanctuary and a safe telephone, and the nearest place that might have both was Bellevue Hospital. We had this limo we stole uptown last night, it was bulletproof so we drove the few blocks up there. We told the guards in the Emergency Room that we were the people Michael mentioned on TV, and they brought Jerome to us. There were a lot of wounded there. We were going to call in, but just then the heavy shooting started. It was a three-way war. The Mafia and the Black Smack Pack from the Lower East Side were fighting each other and Michael's hospital garrison. Bellevue must be the last source of narcotics in the city. There were reinforcements supposed to be on the way, but we decided to split in the limo." She winced once or twice while speaking, but only when something hurt José. "Jerome called the UN garrison uptown and told them to look out for us. Then he got killed covering our escape. I saw a black boy about my age shoot him in the head." Dena's hands stopped working. Russell felt a surprising amount of sorrow; he learned that he had been looking forward to knowing Jerome better someday. "The same boy shot José, so I took Jerome's gun and killed him and got José in the car and figured out how to drive and the UN guys brought us here in an armoured truck. This is a really spacey hideout, is Michael here? Mom, do they have any minipads here? I didn't bring any spares and I got my period, uh, last night."

She was holding José's hands, now; before Russell or Dena could conceive of anything to say, José bucked on the table and their joined hands whitened. The doctor had located the slug. Neither José nor Jennifer uttered a sound; the rest kept silent in respect of José's courage until the slug was out. Then Russell and Dena and Homemade and Jennifer all sighed at once, and José began speaking hoarsely and rapidly:

"Russell, listen to me, I'm gettin' pretty sleepy, okay? A *lot* o' things happened last night, I take full responsibility, but your daughter ain't thirteen no more, you understand me? She's been in a war. She killed three guys, two white and one black; you know Shaw Nuff, she cut his fuckin' throat; she saved my life about six times; she got her period like she said. It was a long night. While I'm under you get her a shower and food and them minipads, and you get her some kind of contraception too, you dig?"

It was the doctor who spoke first, saying kindly, "We can supply all those things right away. You let that shot take—" And then his thoughts stepped outside of medicine for the first time and the implications struck him. He looked at Russell, at Dena, at Russell.

Russell felt everyone's eyes on him. He had time to think, she is only thirteen, and then to remember all the thirteen-year-old mothers he had seen in the war zone near East Pakistan. Looking him in the eye, Jennifer said to the doctor, "I think a one-year renewable implant would suit me best to start, if you can do that here."

The doctor hesitated. She looked at him and he said, "Yes, I can do that."

Well, Russell thought, *he* can see who wears the pants in this family. He unstuck his feet from the floor, approached José, saw Jennifer tense out of the corner of his eye, met the boy's anguished gaze. "Sleep now, son. We'll take care of her for you."

José's eyes closed and Dena was hugging Russell from behind and Jennifer was looking down at José with perfect serenity.

And from the doorway of the infirmary, Michael said softly, "I'm glad you're all right, Jennifer."

"Hi, Michael," she said just as softly.

"I see you've grown up."

"Yes."

"I hope it didn't hurt too bad."

"No. No, it wasn't too bad. Michael?"

"Yes, Jennifer."

"How did my parents get involved with you?"

He explained briefly. "You can all stay here, and you'll be safe even if they bomb Manhattan."

"Okay. I guess we were awful lucky the day we met you, Michael. I still don't get it. Ten days before you were going to start a war against white people, you went out of your way to help a few. Why? Because Mom was there too?"

Michael smiled. "Partly. I think highly of anyone with the guts to intermarry. But I didn't see your mother until I got close. What drew my attention were your Nova Scotia license plates."

"Why?"

"Some of my ancestors lived there, in a place called Horton Bluff."

"*Really?* I don't know that place."

" 'Michael Hall'—" Dena said. "Michael! Was *William Edward Hall* your ancestor?"

"That's right."

Russell was as startled as Dena. Everyone who knew anything about Canadian blacks or Canadian military history knew about William Edward Hall. Son of an escaped slave from the States, the first Canadian to be awarded the Victoria Cross! Yes, by God, Michael looked like pictures he had seen of Hall, without the beard. . . .

Even Jennifer got the reference. "Wow. You Halls fight pretty good."

"He took a city singlehanded. I needed a lot of help." He looked at all three Grants. "Jennifer—do you remember the last thing I told you, the day we met?"

"Yes. *Oh*." She seemed to come out of a trance. She gently disengaged the sleeping José's hands, came round the table and embraced both her parents.

Russell too remembered Michael's words: *"You three have a strong connection going. Don't let it go, no matter what. Don't let it go, and happen you'll be all right.* Don't you let it go!" He swam in that hug.

"I missed you at first, Daddy," she said, and "I missed you, Mom," and "I hope you weren't too scared," to both of them. Shortly all three were smiling and pouring tears, and Russell felt strength flowing into him. Through his happy tears he could see Michael watching them all with that slight, mournful smile, and all at once he felt that the long speech he had wanted to make to Michael could be edited down to no more than a few minutes, a few paragraphs. He caught Michael's eye, left Jennifer to Dena, and said in a low voice, "Can I talk with you, Michael?"

"Only for a minute, son. Come out in the hall."

All right, dammit, a few sentences then. "I—"

A beeper on Michael's wrist went off. "Sorry, son, wait a bit—" He stepped back into the infirmary and activated the vidphone on the wall. General Worthing's face swam into view. "Bad news from Bellevue, Tom?"

"No, that's under control now; this is worse. National Guard units coming across the Harlem River, Michael. Some local commander acting without orders. Maybe eight hundred men."

Michael's face fell. "The *fool*. Throwing away lives . . ." He closed his eyes.

"I hoped they'd be smarter than this," Worthing agreed. "There's no good reason for all those boys to die." His voice became slightly louder. "Your orders, sir?"

Michael reopened his eyes. "Repel invasion to plan, Thomas. Annihilate them. Damn it. I'll be there as soon as

I can, and I'll want lines open to the President and the Secretary General." He cut the connection, turned to Russell. "I'm sorry, son—you see how it is."

All right, then: *one* sentence.

"Michael—*can you use me?*"

Behind him Russell heard the sudden intakes of breath from his wife and daughter, felt the back of his neck grow hot. Michael paused in midstride. He looked at Russell for a long moment.

His smile flashed then. "I've been hoping you'd ask. Hell, *yes*—come on!"

Russell turned back to his family—but the two who were awake were waving him to go ahead, and Michael was already leaving.

As he cleared the door he heard the radio playing the Ray Charles/Cleo Laine *Porgy & Bess*. Brother Ray was singing: "There's a Boat That's Leavin' Soon for New York" . . .

STEVE PERRY

THE MAN WHO NEVER MISSED

Khadaji was ruled by the brutal forces of
the Galactic Confederation—until one day he had
a revelation...and walked away from the battlefield.
He was a new man, unknown, with a secret plan that
he shared with no other. Not his mentor.
Not even with the beautiful exotic whom he loved.
Now, no one can understand how the Shamba Freedom
Forces are bringing Confed to its knees.
No one sees them. No one knows who they are...until
Khadaji is ready for them to know.

_____ **The Man Who Never Missed**
by Steve Perry/0-441-51916-4/$2.95